Roses and Skulls

Roses and Skulls

Rebel Skulls MC Book Three

LM Terry

Dedication

To the uncles I wish I could have spent more time with. I'll never forget the rumble of bikes as you all pulled into grandma's driveway. Thank you for being my inspiration for this series. I love you more than you'll ever know.

The brave don't live forever... the cautious don't live at all. ~unknown.

Table of Contents

LM Terry

Preface

Billie Rose ~ Seventeen years old

"Thanks for picking us up." I slide in next to Grandpa Bill in his old Chevy pickup. He's picking my friend and I up from the homecoming dance. "I thought dad was coming for us?"

He chuckles and shakes his head as Lanie struggles to climb up in her three-inch heels. "He had some last-minute business."

That means club business, so I'm not even going to ask.

Lanie glances around distractedly, tucking her hair behind her ear.

"How was the dance?" he asks.

"Good," I tell him, reaching over her to pull the door closed since she hasn't done it. Not unusual, she's a bit of a scatter brain.

Grandpa pulls away from the curb and heads to Lanie's uncle's house. "How many boys did you dance with?"

"I lost count," I tease.

Lanie huffs. "Lost count?" She leans forward, scowling at me. She holds up her hand, forming an O with her fingers and thumb. "How can you lose count when the number is zero? A. Big. Fat. Zero."

My grandpa's eyes dart from her to the road, then back to me. "Sweetheart, why didn't you dance with anyone?"

Lanie answers for me. "She never does. The only person she dances with is me. Not that I'm chopped liver or anything but come on, gramps, we've got to get this girl some action."

His eyebrows raise a bit, eyes going wide at the thought of me getting any sort of action.

"Not that kind of action," I add quickly, bumping my knee into hers, hoping she'll shut up already.

"Why do you turn the boys down?" he asks.

Sighing loudly, I stare at the road ahead of us. "I don't turn them down, they don't even ask, okay? Now can we drop it? It's fine. I had a fun time and that's all that matters."

We pull up outside of Brody's house. "See you at school Monday," she says, struggling just as much getting out as she did to get in.

"Tell Brody hi for me," Grandpa yells to her as she wobbles down the broken sidewalk. She pauses a minute, staring back at us and then her shoulders drop, and she gives us a small wave.

We both chuckle as we watch her trip inside the house.

Lanie is one of the few people willing to be friends with me. Her uncle is a Skull, so she understands the life, more so than any other kid at my school. She stays with him during the week so she can go to school here. Her mom and step-asshole live over in Trap County. I hear it's not a good place, but I wouldn't know, my parents have never let me visit her there.

In fact, my parents don't let me go much of anywhere without a chaperone. They haven't even taught me how to drive yet. Yeah, pretty lame, huh? But grandpa has secretly been teaching me, so hopefully I'll have my license soon.

I notice we haven't moved. Grandpa Bill is looking at me all sad and shit. "What?"

He reaches over and tucks a runway curl behind my ear. "Want to stop by the bar and whip up some root beer floats?"

Giving him my best smile, I nod my head. "Do you even have to ask?" Ice cream is kind of our thing. He laughs, shifting into gear. The drive to the bar is just a couple of blocks away.

"I was just getting ready to head home when Dirk called. Perfect timing because now I get to enjoy some quality time with my favorite granddaughter." He flips the light on as I make my way to the back to get the ice cream out of the freezer.

"I'm your only granddaughter," I yell, hearing him chuckle.

When I come around the corner, he points to a stool where two frosty mugs await. I scoop generous amounts of the white creamy stuff into the glasses, then he tops them off with root beer and takes the seat beside me.

"I've missed this." He waves his spoon between the two of us. "You grew up too fast. Just like your mama."

"Grandpa, I'm always down to have ice cream with you, no matter how old I get."

"So, about this boy problem."

I groan, shoving my spoon in my float. "It's not a problem."

"Why don't boys ask you to dance? You're a very pretty girl."

My cheeks heat at his compliment. "That's not the problem."

"Oh, so there is a problem. Admitting it is the first step to finding a solution."

I stick my tongue out at him and he laughs, throwing his head back. "Really? You shouldn't have to ask why no one wants to dance with me."

He runs his fingers through his snowy white beard. "They're scared?"

"Uh, yeah," I answer. "Dad literally made Davie Johnson piss his pants when he asked him for permission to take me to winter ball in eighth grade. Nobody wants to risk that kind of humiliation."

Grandpa laughs again.

"I'm doomed to be a crazy cat lady." I roll my eyes up to stare at the ceiling. "Oh, wait, no, that will never happen because my parents won't even let me have a pet because it might die and then I would be sad, and we can't have that."

He grabs my knee and turns me so that we are facing each other. "Honey, I know your parents are a little overprotective, but they have good reason to be the way they are."

"Which is?" I know he isn't going to tell me. No one tells me anything.

Now, don't get me wrong. I love my family. But they are annoying when it comes to protecting me. I can't even sneeze around my mom, like literally, I can't do it. Because if I do, I'll find myself in the waiting room of Dr. Langley's office. She's crazy. Crazy, crazy.

Don't even get me started on my dad. Every day, it's like playing a game of twenty questions which will be the first thing on my agenda once we get back to the warehouse. I already have my answers down. No, no one touched me. No, I didn't drink anything. No, nothing, I swear. Yes, I stayed close to a teacher the whole time. Yes, I took Lanie to the bathroom with me every time. No, I didn't give my phone number to anyone. Yes, I'm going straight to bed. And on, and on, and on. You get the picture.

I shouldn't complain. My life is good… the best. I'm surrounded by people who love me. What more could a girl want? I'm so lucky in fact, I hate to even wish for anything more.

But I do. I just want one dance, with someone other than Lanie. Just one lousy dance. Before I graduate. It's never going to happen though. I'm sure of it.

I try to turn back to my root beer, but grandpa isn't done. "Someday, a boy is going to come into your life, and he isn't going to be afraid of your dad. Nothing will stop him from stealing your heart. Not even Dirk."

Now, it's my turn to laugh and shake my head. "Grandpa, you tell the best jokes."

"I do but I'm not joking here, sweetheart."

"I've never met anyone who wasn't intimidated by him… or mom." I shove a spoonful of ice cream into my mouth, pulling it out with an exaggerated pop.

"I'm not saying he isn't going to have his work cut out for him, but he'll find you and he won't let anything get in his way. He'll see you're special."

"Special enough to risk losing his nuts?"

Grandpa spits root beer all over the counter, slapping his palm down on the bar. "Oh, girl, I love you. So much like your mama."

I roll my eyes. "I'm nothing like her."

"Oh, you are. You just don't see it yet. You're the best of both of them."

Grandpa gets quiet, a faraway look appears in his eye. I finish my ice cream, watching as he mindlessly works on his. "You okay, grandpa?"

He blinks a few times before turning to me. "Just fine, honey. You ready to head home? Your mom and dad will send out a search party if we take much longer."

I nod, getting up and putting our glasses in the sink.

He grabs my hand as we walk back to the pickup. "Be patient with them. They love you more than anything… we all do."

6

"Yeah, yeah, the Skull's little MC princess," I tease, wrapping my arm around his and snuggling into his side. "Thanks for the pep talk and the ice cream."

"Anytime, baby girl." He kisses me on the forehead, then stops. "Wait, we can't end the night yet." He rushes around the truck and opens the door, turning the radio on full blast. When he comes back to the front of the pickup, he holds his hand out to me. "May I have this dance, m' lady?"

I giggle. "Of course, kind sir." I place my hand in his and let him twirl me around. Grandpa is a good dancer. When I was little, I used to stand on his feet as he led me around. I don't think he would appreciate me doing that now.

Both of us laugh and spin under the light of the moon. This reminds me of the days he played with me in the woods behind the warehouse. My dad and him built an entire fantasyland amongst the trees. Sometimes, we were dragons, other times, witches, explorers, our imaginations always ran wild. I think they just felt bad for me because I didn't have any other girls to play with.

"Thank you for the dance," I say as we get back into his truck.

He turns the keys in the ignition, his eyes running over my face. "You are a breath of fresh air, Billie Rose. Promise me you won't let anyone steal your spark. Okay?"

"Promise," I say, linking my pinky with his. He leans forward and presses his lips to my forehead.

On the way home, Grandpa watches the road as he listens to me chat away about all the shenanigans that happened at the dance. We're almost there, so I talk a mile a minute, trying to tell him everything before we get to the warehouse.

I turn to face him, laughing as I ramble on about the prank Lanie played on one of the teachers. It's then I notice a bright light out his window.

I scream.

The sound is horrific as metal crunches and glass shatters around us. I squeeze my eyes shut tight as we violently spin and tumble and roll.

And then it's quiet. So incredibly quiet.

"Grandpa," I rasp, my voice doesn't sound like my own. I blink as dust settles around us. He's slumped back against his seat. He moans. "Oh, grandpa!"

My hand roams down my side, searching for my seatbelt so I can release myself. I need to help him. It won't unbuckle. Tears cloud my vision as I struggle with the belt. Suddenly, a man appears at his window. He looks at my broken grandpa and smiles. I... I don't understand, then the man's eyes slide over to me. "Shit!" He pushes away from the truck, shoving his hands in his hair and I hear him yell at someone. "He's not alone!"

"What?" another man hollers back.

A second man rushes to the window, his flashlight blinding me. "Please, please help him," I whimper.

He presses his fingers to my grandfather's neck and then his attention turns back to me before he backs away. "Wait, please don't go." I'm not sure they heard me, my voice is choppy, and it hurts to talk.

The men continue to yell at each other outside the pickup. "Grandpa?" I reach out and shake his arm. He moans again, his eyes blinking open.

The second man appears at my window. "Please help my grandpa," I beg.

He flicks a piece of broken glass from the window and rests his arm on the mangled metal, studying me. "Grandpa, huh?" His eyes drop to my neck. My grandpa starts whispering something. It sounds like he is saying crow repeatedly. The man looks at him and laughs before turning his black eyes on me.

He takes my hand in his and presses it to my neck. I try to pull out of his grasp, but he tightens his grip around my fingers, causing me to cry out.

"Don't. Touch. Her," grandpa grates out between clenched teeth.

"Shut up, old man. Listen to me, honey, keep your hand pressed right here on your neck and just maybe you'll live."

When my fingers touch my neck, I let out a sob. My flesh is torn, wet and sticky. No wonder it hurts so much to talk.

"There, there, don't cry. It's up to the fates now." He keeps his hand over the top of mine as we stare at each other. My body trembles, pain beginning to register in my brain. I'm dying. I'm going to die and the last thing I'm going to see are this man's cold, heartless eyes.

My grandpa reaches for his gun which is strapped to his side. The man's eyes slide over to him. "I don't think you want to do that while I have your granddaughter's life in the palm of my hand."

Grandpa stills.

He returns his attention back to me. His eyes slide over my hair, my face, my breasts. I shiver and he smiles. "If you live, maybe we'll bump into each other down the road. I'll give you the answers no one else will." His hand leaves mine and comes up to cup my face. I try to pull away from him but there's nowhere to go. "Such a pretty, pretty little girl." His hand trails down my body as he lets go and backs away.

There's laughter, car doors slamming and then nothing.

I try to speak but it comes out garbled.

"Don't try to talk, baby girl. Help is coming. Help is coming," grandpa says quietly.

Tears stream down my cheeks as I turn my head slightly to look at him. He gives me a small smile. "Do you hear the wind chimes?" he asks.

I shake my head no.

"Wind chimes are whispers from Heaven." He smiles and closes his eyes.

I reach over and shake him. He blinks at me. "I can't hear them, grandpa," I say as carefully as I can, afraid of the sound of my own voice.

"I hear them, baby. They're calling me home."

"No," I cry.

He smiles again. "Don't be afraid. Your dad will be here soon. Don't be afraid. Don't be afraid." He takes my hand in his and squeezes as tight as he can. "I love you, baby girl."

"I love you too," I choke out.

"Shh, don't cry, sweetheart. Don't they sound beautiful?" He looks at me as if he can see right through me.

I watch his eyes drop closed. He doesn't speak to me again nor does he move. I pull my hand out of his and frantically try to get the seatbelt off me. I want out. I need out!

Black spots dance on the edge of my vision. I must fall asleep because I wake to the sound of roaring bikes and then a roar of a different sort. My dad. The sound he makes is unlike anything I've ever heard. It's the howl of a wounded animal, a haunting sound that could wake the dead.

He came, just like grandpa said he would. My head lulls to the side so I can see if Grandpa hears him too. Maybe I'm hallucinating like grandpa was with the chimes. He must be sleeping; his eyes are still closed.

I'm cold. So cold.

My dad appears, struggling to open my door with a crowbar. He tries with all his might to pull it open, but the metal is too mangled. My Uncle Dan urges him to stop. "Let the first responders do their job, Dirk. They'll get her out."

It's then they notice I'm awake. "Baby," my dad cries. He cradles my face in his hands. I close my eyes, drifting once again. Nothing hurts now, everything is going to be okay. I open my eyes to tell him that but red and blue lights flash over his face and I see how scared he is. My dad is never scared, never.

Men in big yellow coats come to his side and drag him away. No, don't go! *Dad, don't go*! I want to scream but I can't.

More men come. They tell me they are going to get me out of the vehicle. Help grandpa first I want to say. And they do. They pull him out and then a man slides in beside me and covers me with a blanket. He stays with me, keeping the blanket held up in front of my face to keep the flying glass and metal from hitting me as they slowly cut grandpa's pickup away from me.

When they slide me onto a board, I stare at the stars. They seem so close. My hand rises to reach out and touch them. Something is different. I can't place my finger on it but they're more beautiful, brighter maybe.

I drift to sleep again, so tired I just can't keep my eyes open. The next time I open them, we are moving. My dad is here now. He's holding my hand as strangers hook me up to all kind of scary things. He's crying. Which scares me more than anything. Why is he crying? I don't think I've ever seen him cry.

And then a nothingness swallows me.

When I regain consciousness, I notice something smells funny and my nose tickles. I blink awake slowly. My dad is sitting on the edge of my bed, his face buried in his hands. Mom is sleeping on a little couch in front of big windows and my cousin, Jackson, is asleep in a chair on the other side of me. His boots kicked up on the end of the bed.

What? Where are we? I try to scoot up, alerting my dad that I'm awake.

He turns to me, his eyes swollen and red. "Hey, baby, it's okay. Don't try to get up, you need to rest." He brushes my hair away from my face.

I open my mouth to speak but he stops me. "Shh, don't try to talk. You just had surgery on your throat. It's going to take some time." He offers me a forced smile.

That's right, I remember, grandpa and I were in an accident. My eyes lock on dad's, *grandpa, where is grandpa?*

"Oh, baby girl, all I've ever wanted to do is protect you from getting hurt. I didn't do a particularly good job, did I?" he says, his eyes roaming over the monitors beside me.

I hold my hand up and motion for something to write with. Reluctantly, he hands me a small pad and a pen. Two words. *Where's grandpa?*

He closes his eyes and when they open, he doesn't have to tell me. His gaze says it all. He's gone. Grandpa Bill is gone.

I shove the paper and pen back to him and close my eyes, wanting nothing more to do with this new world. A burning sensation builds and builds in my chest, threating to explode.

No one prepared me for this. Not only does my body feel pain, but my soul is slowly drowning in it.

Grandpas don't die. Goddammit! *Grandpas don't die!*

Two weeks later and here I sit on a cold, hard chair, watching as they lower my grandfather into his grave. I'm angry. Really angry. At everyone.

My parents cling to each other as my mom says goodbye to her dad. They look nothing like the people who raised me. They are shells of their former selves.

I thought they were strong. They told me they would protect me. But can I blame them? I was the fool who believed it. Now look, I have no fucking clue how to manage any of this. The pain. The sadness. The fear. Anger. Uncertainty. All emotions so foreign to me that I barely recognize one from the other. It's a vicious brew, stewing inside of me. The pressure of it all presses against my skull.

Nervous energy calls me to run. To scream. To tear the very skin from my bones. But I can't do any of those things. I'm trapped.

Mom hands me a rose and encourages me to stand and throw it on the casket that is now settled six feet in the rich dirt of the cemetery. Men and women in leather cuts approach one by one, tossing their roses on top of the shiny, black death box.

Rising from my chair, I stare into the hole.

My hand trembles as I hold it, suspended over his grave.

I turn around, taking my rose with me back to my chair. Jackson sits down and wraps his arm around me. I lay my head on his shoulder and squeeze the rose stem tightly in my hand. The pain of thorns digging into my skin helps release some of the pressure building inside of me. I sigh in relief and open my hand, staring as bright red blood pools in my palm. The open wounds drain the poison, diminishing some of my anger.

"It's going to be okay, Rosie," my cousin says, squeezing me tight.

I close my fist as my parents return to their seats next to us.

And that is how my secret begins.

Chapter One

Billie Rose ~ Nineteen years old

Have you ever watched Charlie Brown? Of course, you have. Everyone knows who Charlie Brown is. Anyhow, you know how all the adults talk funny? Wah wah wah… wah… wah wah wah… fucking wah wah wah. Whatever, you know what they sound like. That's exactly how my parents sound to me. Mom is doing it right now.

My dad reaches over and slams my book shut. "Did you hear what your mother said?" he asks, his eyebrow cocked.

I roll my eyes and nod my head.

"What did she say?"

Roses and Skulls

My fingers fly across my phone screen. I hit play and stare at him. **Saturday. Yeah, yeah, I'll be there,** the male, Australian voice relays my words through the speaker. I set it for this accent specifically because I know it grates on his nerves. I wave my hand at them in dismissal as I gather my things.

My phone is now my voice. I haven't spoken to anyone since the accident.

He grabs my arm as I try to pass by him. "I'm picking you up today."

I nod my head again, my eyes mockingly wide.

He swats me on the butt softly and pushes me from the room.

As I'm waiting for my aunt to pick me up, I listen for the chime hanging down by my old treehouse. The wind is light today, so no chance. I always have one hanging in the woods behind the warehouse. I pray every day that he will whisper to me through one. So far, no luck.

Great, my aunt must have sent Uncle Dan to give me a ride. And… the twins, lovely, just what I needed on this fine Monday.

The minute I get in the truck Carson and Cole both start in on me. "Rosie, are you going to be at the party Saturday?"

Shaking my head yes, I roll my hands, letting my uncle know to get this show on the road. He sighs and leans over me to grab my seatbelt. I take a deep breath as he buckles me in. "Sorry, no help for it," he says, shrugging.

Yeah, I get it. Buckle up, it's the law.

Lot of good it did my grandpa.

I dig my nails into my palms as the belt clicks shut.

"I bet you're excited," Cole continues.

Pulling my phone out of my pocket, I respond. ***Ecstatic.*** I roll my eyes, why the fuck would I be excited? The club has a damn get-together for every little thing. Nothing new.

"I need to drop these two knuckle heads off at school and then I'll run you to the shop. Lily is at the junkyard with Jackson today. JD got a bunch of stuff in over the weekend."

So, I'm at the store by myself today? my Australian companion asks.

Uncle Dan sighs. "Is that okay? I can stay with you if you want."

Quickly, I change the voice on my phone to that of an English-speaking woman and respond. ***Nope, that's cool. I just needed to know if I was going to be left to communicate with the customers.***

Carson starts laughing. "I thought you told your dad that you didn't know how to change the voice on your phone?"

Dan chuckles too. "You're fixing to get your ass whopped, little girl," he says as he pulls up in front of the school.

Like dad would lay a hand on me, please, I type, giving him my best bored as fuck look.

Both boys hop out, leaving Dan and I alone.

"Why are you torturing them, hun?" he asks, letting the truck idle.

I look away from him to stare out my window, biting my tongue. I so desperately want to tell him everything. This is exactly why I avoid him at all costs. Besides Jackson and Lanie, he is one of my best friends. And every time I'm with him, I just want to crawl up on his lap like I did when I was a little girl and share all my problems with him. He reminds me of grandpa. They both have a calmness about them. Well, grandpa had, he isn't around to be calm anymore.

He sighs again when I don't respond, pulling away from the curb. It's just a short drive to Aunt Lily's shop, Junkyard Treasures. She makes the coolest things out of, well, out of anything. My cousin, Jackson, and JD both work with her. JD also owns the local junkyard, so it all makes sense. I help around the shop when I can. The only things I make and sell at the store are my chimes. I make one, hang it up in the woods and when the damn thing doesn't speak to me, it gets brought here. They always sell out, but I've never been here when one has sold.

Thanks for the ride, I type as I open my door to hop out. Dan grabs my arm to stop me.

"Hey, I have something I want to talk to you about."

I sigh loudly and drop my head back against the headrest.

"Mama Bear finally found a buyer for the bar. The realtor gave them the keys yesterday," he says, watching my every move for any sign of discomfort. They all tiptoe around me now. Always trying to protect me. I'm sure if they could have gotten away without telling me, they would've kept me in the dark.

I thought grandma was just going to take some time off in Florida with Aunt Katie and Aunt Ally. How long has it been on the market?

19

He grimaces, giving me my answer.

I see.

Everyone is moving on.

Okay, good to know. I jump out of the truck before he can say anything else. This discussion is over.

I quickly unlock the door and hustle inside, watching through the window to see if he follows. I flip the lights on, and his head drops to the steering wheel. I pull my eyes away and head to the back to get things ready for the day. When I come back out, he's gone.

Part of me aches, the part that wishes he would have stormed in after me and demanded I talk to him. But the other half says, fuck him, fuck them all. The only thing I am to them is a fragile little MC princess.

The day moves slowly as I stew over grandma selling the bar. And don't tell me my parents didn't know about this. Or maybe they did tell me. I have a habit of tuning them out, so...

The little bell over the door dings and in bounces my best friend. "Where's Jackson?" she immediately asks.

Hello to you, too, my phone greets her.

She laughs. "Sorry, you don't have one of those dangly things between your legs." Lanie hops up on the counter, tossing my birth control pills at me.

Thanks for picking these up. I shove the pharmacy bag in my purse, good to go for another three months. And no, I'm not using them to protect myself against an unwanted pregnancy. I'm still getting zero *action*. They help with my cramps, that's all. I turn back to face my friend. ***And if you must know, he's helping Lily at the junkyard today.*** I shove her as hard as I can until she stumbles off the counter.

"Jeez, what has you in such a tude today?" she grumbles, taking a stroll around the shop to see if we have anything new.

Grandma sold the bar, I type, walking over and smacking her hand away from the jewelry. ***You're broke remember?***

"But Jackson made these."

I roll my eyes. ***Yuck, quit talking about him like that.***

"Okay," she says, taking a few steps away from me. "I'll just have to talk about Daddy D then."

That's it. I chase her around the displays and when I catch her, I knock her to the ground and sit on her, leaning over her face and drawing a loogy up my throat.

"Stop! Fine, I won't talk about your men anymore. You win."

I release my hold on her and roll off so that we are both lying on the floor, looking up at the lights above us.

She rolls her head to the side. "I do have something I need to tell you."

My eyes stay focused on the ceiling. I roll my hands, telling her to continue.

"I've met someone."

I slide my phone out of my back pocket. **What? Oh my god. Who? Tell me everything.**

She glances back to the ceiling. "I've been talking to him for a few years now. He's from Trap, he moved in with me over the weekend."

Lanie! A few years? Why haven't you told me before now? I reach over and grab her hand, squeezing it in mine.

"I… I don't know. You've been busy with… well, you know."

Turning to my side, I stare at her. **I'm never too busy for you, you can tell me anything, Lanie.**

When she faces me, a tear rolls down her cheek. "I know."

So, is him moving in with you a good thing or a bad thing? I ask, unsure of how she feels about all this.

"I guess we'll see how it goes."

I love you, I tell her, wrapping my arm around her shoulders. **I'll be here for you, no matter what.**

Lanie laughs, wiping away her tears. "It's weird not hearing the Australian. I bet Daddy…" she stops herself when I cock an eyebrow her way. "I bet Dirk is happy you changed it."

Oh, I didn't change it for him. It will go back as soon as I'm done here.

This makes her laugh harder. Once she controls herself, she turns to me. "Seriously though, I'm so glad I have you. He wants to meet you," she says, hopping up and offering her hand to help me from the floor.

Did you tell him about my problem? I point to my throat. She knows I'm nervous about meeting new people since I don't talk.

"Uh duh, you're all I talk about. You are my constant, the one who keeps me grounded."

Which is just about an impossible task, I tease.

"Why don't you come over for supper tomorrow and you can meet him?"

"Okay, I'll ask my parents."

She throws her head back, sighing. "Billie Rose, you're nineteen. I moved out of my parent's house right after we graduated. You shouldn't have to ask to go to your best friend's house for dinner. In fact, you should be moving in with me."

I grab her shoulders and push her towards the door. When we get to the threshold, I type out a message. ***You know how they are and besides, you just got a new roommate.*** I wiggle my eyebrows up and down.

Her eyes bounce over mine. "Yeah, but he wouldn't mind if you moved in too. Think about it."

I nod, shoving her outside. ***You're going to be late for class.***

She waves as she rushes to her car. "See you tomorrow night at six. Tell Daddy D I'm not taking no for answer."

If I had something to throw at her, I would, so instead she gets a finger.

She gives me one back before getting in and taking off down the street. I'm so happy for Lanie. Her parents never gave her much attention, all she's had is me and her Uncle Brody. Hopefully, this guy she is dating treats her right.

My mom pulls up across the street, headed to her tattoo shop. She waves at me; I drop the smile on my face and offer her a half-hearted wave back. Abruptly, I turn to go back inside.

You're thinking I'm a bitch, aren't you? Yeah, gone is the sweet little Billie Rose and in her place is the hardheaded and even harder hearted version.

Lily and Jackson come back right before my shift is over. One on each end of an old pickup bumper. **_Did you find some good stuff today?_** my phone asks them.

They set it down in the middle of the floor and Jackson turns, giving me a smile that brightens my day. "We did and wait till you see what I found for you." He grabs me by the waist and swings me around before placing a chaste kiss to my cheek.

Jackson is the town heartthrob. He's beautiful. A head full of brown hair that always seems to be perfectly falling in his eyes. He's tall and best of all, he's kind. Can't get much better than that. He always lets me tag along with him wherever he goes.

He sticks his hand in his pocket, his eyes sparkling from the lights above us. When he pulls it out, he opens his palm to reveal a handful of old skeleton keys. His smile widens when he sees the grin he just put on my face. I love them.

I run my finger over each key, already envisioning the beautiful chime I'm going to make. ***They're perfect. Thank you,*** I type before shoving my phone back in my pocket.

He dumps them into my hand, then helps Lily with the bumper, hauling it to the back. When he comes back, I have them laid out on the counter, admiring them. He stands behind me and wraps his arms around me. "Maybe this will be the chime to unlock whatever it is you're listening for."

I bite my lip and shrug my shoulders. He rests his chin on my shoulder. "Did Dan talk to you about the bar?" he asks.

Nodding, I try and pull away from him. He squeezes me tighter.

"Do you want to talk about it?"

The shake of my head makes him sigh. "You know, you can tell me anything, Rosie. Why don't you trust me?"

I pull myself away from him, pocketing my new treasures and then I type on my phone, letting him know that I do trust him. ***There's just nothing to talk about. It's a done deal.***

The little bell over the door interrupts us. My dad walks in, instantly eying the both of us. "Everything okay?" he asks.

Quickly, I change the voice on my phone back to the one that grates on my dad best and reply. ***Just peachy.***

His chest puffs up with the deep breath he just sucked in. Can you imagine the restraint this man must possess? Jackson laughs and heads over to shake his hand. "Just the usual, trying to get the dark one to open up."

My dad shakes his hand, but his eyes remain on me. "And…"

"No go, Prez," Jackson tells him before heading out to unload the rest of the stuff he and Lily brought back.

"You ready?" he asks.

Actually, Lily and Jackson just got back. Can I stay and help them unload? I'll catch a ride with one of them.

I can see his brain working, trying to assess the risk and reward of letting me stay. "Okay but remember your seatbelt."

Of course. I shove my phone in my back pocket. That was way easier than I thought it would be. He grabs me as I walk past him to help Jackson.

His face softens as he runs a thumb over my cheek. "Dan told me he let you know about the bar. We'll talk about it tonight. I'm sorry, I know you loved that place."

I roll my eyes, making his eyebrow cock in warning. I sigh dramatically before shaking my head yes, I understand that he will be torturing me later with talk about the knife they stuck in my back today. The look of pity on his face makes me look away.

He kisses my forehead and then follows me outside. I watch him walk across the street to mom's tattoo shop. Jackson nods for me to grab the other end of a dresser he's unloading off the back of his truck. I grab a corner and help him carry it inside.

Lily holds the door open for us before we set it down in the workshop. Her eyes scan it. I'm sure she already has something magical in store for it. She loves old things. "You can take off. Jackson and I got this. Thanks for holding down the fort today."

No problem, I type before heading towards the back door.

Jackson's eyes follow me. "You're not sneaking off are you?" He scratches his head, his brows creasing together.

No, I told dad I was going to Lanie's. You do know I'm nineteen. I stomp out, letting the door slam shut behind me.

I wait for him to follow but he must believe me this time. He knows how overprotective my parents are. It's rare they let me go anywhere without someone escorting me. It's annoying.

I shut my location off on my phone. Quickly, I make my way down the alley, looking left, then right before dashing across the street. I jog the rest of the way there, pausing only to admire a rose bush behind a home along the way. I stick to the alleys because chances of running into a Skull in town are high.

When I get to the trees behind the bar, I crouch down and retrieve the key I hid under a pile of old bricks. I peek around the corner to make sure there are no cars out front and when I find none, I head to the back door.

I haven't been back since that day. It's dark inside, dust motes float in the light as the door falls open. When I step in, they dance around me in welcome but as soon as the door shuts behind me, they vanish. I click the light on my phone and make my way to the freezer, popping it open to find the container of ice cream that my grandpa and I used to make our floats still there. Nothing has changed. It makes me wonder if grandma even stepped foot in here after the day he died.

As I'm closing the lid, all the lights click on. I cover my mouth to keep my scream locked inside. Adrenaline charges every cell in my body, and I fight to stay where I'm at. Men's laughter filters in from the front. Booted feet stomp through the bar, headed towards me.

Quickly, I dash into my grandpa's office, ducking under his desk. Just like I used to do when mom and dad would be ready to leave, and I wanted to stay. I think they always knew where I was hiding, but they pretended they couldn't find me. When they left, grandpa and I would share a root beer float and then he would take me home.

The door creaks open, and heavy boots stomp into the room. I hear the door close and then someone sets something on the desk above me. I hear a man sigh and the leather couch groans as he plops down on it.

My heart tries to beat its way out of my chest, clawing up my throat. Maybe I should just fess up. I'm sure the new owner will understand. I'll just explain I broke in for sentimental reasons, not to steal anything. It's not like they would press trespassing charges against me. Would they?

"You don't have to hide. I know you're here. I can smell you. Do you know you smell just like a bouquet of roses?"

My blood runs cold as the voice that haunts my dreams hits my ears.

"I've heard that you are a quiet little dove now. Why don't you come out here and let me see how much you've grown?"

Shit. Shit. Shit. I've waited for years to run into this man, but this is not how I envisioned it.

"I'm not going to hurt you. Come on now."

The couch squeaks again and soon I'm staring at his booted feet.

Roses and Skulls

He crouches down until I'm pinned in fear by eyes as dark as night. It's then I hear a loud squawk above me, making me jump out of my skin. I hit my head on the underside of the desk. What the fuck was that?

At this point, I'm sure I'm going to die. This is exactly how horror movies begin. I'm such an idiot. But how could I have known?

The man who killed my grandfather laughs. "Don't be frightened, if you feed her, she'll be your best friend." He holds out his hand to help me out from under the desk.

What choice do I have at this point? I don't take his hand, but I do scoot forward. He rises and takes a step back, giving me some space.

When I stand, his gaze slides over my body from head to toe. His dark eyes return to mine, and he smiles. "Very nice." He reaches out to touch the scar on my neck but pauses mid-air when I pull my head back.

He's just as frightening as he was all those years ago. He's tall, medium build, mid to late twenties, with black hair that is cut short, and he has a full beard, not unlike the men at the club. But the difference between him and the men I know, are his eyes. I glance away, afraid of what I'll see there. They are open pits that threaten to suck me in and then spit me out once he's finished with me.

I have so many questions. So many. Do I give this man my words, my voice? I've had it tucked away for so long. My grandfather was the last one to hear me speak and I was hoping to keep it that way.

A sudden ruffle of bird's wings and another loud squawk forces me to spin around. It's a bird, a crow to be exact, in a cage. My grandpa's words echo in my mind. Crow. It's a fucking crow!

"Do you want to feed her?" he asks from behind me.

I shake my head as I slowly slide around the desk, putting it between us. The door is just a few feet behind me now. I could run. I should run.

He chuckles and walks over to the bird, rudely tapping on her cage. She backs away from him, poor thing.

"I've always loved crows. They remind me of my father," he says before going over and taking a seat on the couch. He stares at me for a minute. "Go ahead, I don't bite. Ask away." He lays his arms across the back of the sofa, settling in.

Slowly, I pull my phone out of my pocket and type, **Why did you kill my grandpa?**

He throws his head back, laughing loudly, making the bird flap her wings and caw at the same time.

When he finally pulls himself together, he shakes his head. "Sorry, that was not the voice I was expecting." He tilts his head, shaking his finger in my direction. "You know, I'm real sorry you were there that night. You weren't supposed to be."

I bite my lip and look at the floor. He sounds sincere but the fact remains, he took my grandpa away from me.

"Your mother killed my father, so I killed hers." No beating around the bush, just an arrow straight through my heart.

My eyes snap to his.

"It's true. A life for a life, there isn't any other way in our world."

Roses and Skulls

My mother may be scary, but she isn't a murderer.

He tips his head, reading my expression. "You don't think she's capable? Awe, little dove, I think you need to open your eyes. Why do you think they keep you in such a tight little bubble? It's to protect you." He laughs. "From what? The boogeyman? Or could it be, she's worried she might have gathered a few enemies along the way."

I think about this, walking over to the crow. It is odd that I seem to be the only person in the club that is kept in the dark and protected. The crow hops over to me, her beady little black eyes tell me she wants out of this stupid cage.

My fingers fly over the screen. ***Isn't it illegal to keep a crow in a cage?***

"After everything I just told you, you're worried about the bird?"

My gaze roams over to his as I stick my finger in the cage, running it over her feathers. I shrug my shoulder and turn back to the crow.

"They don't see you do they?"

I ignore him and continue to stroke my new friend.

"You're a lot stronger than they think."

When I still don't respond, he stands. I make myself stay right where I'm at. Pulling my finger out of the cage, I type quickly, ***Why did you buy the bar?***

He reaches out and runs his palm down the back of my hair. I try to control the shiver that courses through my body but no luck. I think he mistakes my fear for something else.

31

His hand drops from my hair as he leans in and sniffs me, his nose brushing along my ear. "I bought it for you. You do want to see this place thrive, don't you?"

Again, my silence is all he gets.

He backs away, chuckling low and evil. "Together, we can make it something special. Do you know what I'm naming the place?"

I drop my head, sad that this is what has come of things. I should be here, running the bar with grandpa. Not standing here stroking a motherfucking crow, talking to a man who makes me want to crawl out of my skin.

The crow tips her head back and forth, studying me as I type. *So, are you offering me a job?*

He snorts, running his hand over his mouth. "You are a delightful little thing. Yes, I guess I am."

Well, let me know when you want me to start. I grab the handle of the cage and start to walk towards the door.

"The grand opening is this Friday. Come in after mommy and daddy go to bed. I'm assuming you'll have to sneak out to work here."

In case you're wondering, I have no idea what I'm doing. All I know are two things. The first is that I'm going to save the bird in this cage and the second thing is... I'm going to kill the man who put her there. And that makes me sad in a way.

I nod my head and take another step towards the door.

"Don't you want to know what the name of the bar is going to be?"

Roses and Skulls

I stop, waiting for him to tell me.

When he doesn't answer right away, I turn to face him, his grin widens. He taps his fingers over his mouth, a shiny ring on each finger. "I'm thinking The Black Rose. What do you think?"

We stare at each other for several minutes… and so the game begins. He's made the first move. Now, it's my turn. I set the bird down and type, the Australian accent delivering my message. **Perfect. See you Friday…** I wave my hand out, silently asking for his name.

"Draven, you can call me Draven," he says coolly, settling back on the couch my grandpa used to sneak naps on.

I bite my lip, halting my tears. **See you then, Draven.** I glance back down at the cage before picking it up. **Oh, and thanks for the gift.** I wrap my hand around the handle and quickly make my way through the door. His laughter follows me all the way down the hall.

When I push the door open to the outside world, I almost collapse, side-stepping to lean against the old picnic table out back.

My head feels like it's going to burst. I need to let the pain out. Just a bit before I make my way back to the warehouse. I kick my shoe off and dig for the blade that is hidden beneath the padding. When I pull it out, it glints against the sun. I drop my jeans and press it against the inside of my thigh. When the first red bead greets me, it's instant relief.

I look down at the bird, my image reflecting in her shiny eyes. I don't like what I see. In fact, I hate it. I hate all of it, but this is the only way I know how. I'm trapped, just like this stupid bird. "You should be thanking me," I tell her, my voice coming out scratchy and broken from unuse. I clear my throat and turn away from her, grabbing a tissue from my pocket to stop the pain from flowing.

While I'm buttoning my pants, I notice I'm being watched and not just by the crow. Draven is staring at me through the window of the back door. I pick up my new friend and run as fast as I can through the trees.

Chapter Two

Billie Rose

As I'm walking down the road, lugging this damn bird, a truck pulls up beside me. Jackson reaches over and opens the passenger door. "You are in so much shit. Your dad came back to the shop and when you weren't there, he went ape shit."

I slide in next to him, carefully placing the cage between my legs.

"What in the fuck is that?" he asks, his gaze going from the bird to me.

You know, when I woke up this morning, I had no idea how exciting the day would be. Funny, isn't it?

I found her.

"Jesus, Rosie, you're in so much trouble. And on top of it, you're bringing a fucking crow home? What the hell?"

I shrug my shoulders in response, looking down at the bird. She's starting to grow on me. But I need to let her go. *I'm letting her go out in the trees behind the warehouse. Give me a break, will you?* I close my eyes, laying my head back against the seat.

He hits his steering wheel. "Just once I'd love for you to fucking talk to me."

I open my eyes. *I talk to you every day.* The tone of his voice makes me sit up straighter. He's mad. He never gets mad at me.

He shakes his head back and forth as he puts his truck in gear. "No, you don't. Your damn phone does and even then you never tell me anything that really matters."

His words sting. For a brief moment, I think about talking to him but then I look at the crow sitting between my legs and just like her, I remain silent. Trapped. I sniffle a little and turn to look out the window.

"Ah hell, Rosie. Don't cry. Your dad is mad enough. He'll kick my ass if he sees I made you cry."

I type on my phone. *I'm not crying, dickhead.* I swipe angrily at my tears.

"Then what's that leaking out of your eyes?" he teases.

Glaring at him, I respond, *Maybe I'm allergic to the bird.*

He shakes his head, chuckling. "You're too stubborn. That's the problem. But you better get your story straight because Dirk has the whole club out looking for you."

Just drop me off at your mom and dad's.

He flips his hair out of his face before responding. "Do you think that's going to help? Dad is out of his mind worrying about you." He hands me his phone and I see message after message from Uncle Raffe.

I'm sorry, I hope they aren't blaming you for my disappearance.

"I can handle the heat, but it would be nice if you would tell me where you were. I sent a text to Lanie, and you were definitely not with her, she was in class."

Do you promise to keep it between us?

Jackson drums his fingers over the steering wheel. "You know, that's a tough one for me, Rosie. I took an oath to the club."

I roll my eyes and lean over to pet the bird. She's getting anxious being in the truck. She's scared.

"Fine, I'll keep it to myself. Tell me," he says, giving in rather quickly.

Sitting back, I decide I'll tell him the truth, some of it anyway. *I went to the bar.*

His face falls. "Rosie."

It's fine. I just wanted to see it the way it was before the new owner changes everything. Okay? It's no big deal.

"I would have gone with you. Why do you think you have to face everything on your own?"

The roar of bikes coming up behind us, interrupts our conversation. *You told them you found me.*

He chuckles. "I value my nuts, Rosie. I'm going to make some pretty awesome babies someday."

I drop my head back against the seat, typing while preparing myself for the storm that is coming. *Lame.*

My mom is already standing in the middle of the parking lot when we pull in.

When I hop out, she rushes towards me, wrapping me in her arms. "Thank god," she cries, pushing my hair out of my face to inspect me.

I just stand there and let her do what it is she does.

"Are you okay, sweetie?"

Yes, this tattooed, bad ass wife to the president of the Skulls, just called me sweetie.

"She's fine Aunt Jesse," Jackson answers for me. "She was at the bar."

Fucking traitor. I give him the finger before my dad pulls me out of my mom's arms and does the exact same thing she just did, patting me all over to see if I'm broken. I am, but not where they can see.

"I swear to god, little girl, do you think I need any more grey hairs?" he asks, his eyebrow at an alarmingly scary angle.

"She was at the bar, Dirk," my mom says quietly, squeezing his arm.

The entire club is gathering around. I fold my arms across my chest, determined to stand strong. No cracks, no cracks, no cracks.

My dad cups my face in his hands, kissing me on the forehead. He stays there for several seconds before pulling away. He turns around and thanks everyone for helping look for me. I feel five years old again, like the time I strayed off the path in woods behind the warehouse and got lost. Everyone came looking and thankfully my dad found me before it got dark. I felt guilty but grateful back then. Today... well, today I don't know.

I can't breathe with them hovering over me all the time. They think I'm right here, safe with them but what they don't see is I'm still lost. And I guess right now that's how I like it. It's fine. I don't need to talk to them about what happened, about how much I miss grandpa. It's easier being trapped inside the cage I built for myself.

Shit, the bird!

The crowd disperses except for my uncles, Jackson, and my parents.

I turn back to the truck and tug the cage out. The crow squawks loudly, frightened by the sudden movement.

My mom takes one look at me and turns a pasty white. Before my brain processes what is going on, she's lying flat on her back in the parking lot. My dad and Raffe hover over her, patting her cheeks and rubbing her chest. She blinks at them a few times, then starts to whisper feverishly, "Crow, it's a crow."

Jackson looks at me, mouthing silently, "What the fuck?"

I shrug my shoulders and look at the bird. Draven wasn't *letting* me take this bird… he was hoping I would.

"I'm…" My mom looks at the bird in the cage and then at me. She plasters a fake smile on her face. "I was just startled." She tries to get up, but my dad stops her, picking her up and setting her in the truck.

"I'm taking her to get checked out. She hit her head pretty hard," he tells us.

He gives me a look that I can't decipher.

"Dirk, I'm fine. Please," my mom begs, not wanting to go. She tries to get out of Jackson's truck but my dad slides in beside her, pushing her to the middle of the seat. Raffe heads around and hops in the driver side.

"We'll talk about this when I get home." He points at me then looks at Dan. "Don't let her out of your sight."

Are you fucking kidding me?

I take my crow and stomp away from them, heading around the back of the warehouse.

Jackson starts to follow but I hear Dan tell him that he's got me.

He's got me.

Great.

Roses and Skulls

I keep walking, heading out to my old treehouse. The one grandpa and dad built for me. Grandpa and I used to play out here all the time. He would be whatever I asked him to, a knight, a soldier, a pirate, he was always up for anything.

When I get there, I set the cage on the old wooden spool that I use as a table. I plop down heavily on one of my logs, resting my chin on my curled-up hand. The wind blows lightly, and my chime spooks the crow, making her flap her wings and screech.

I stick my finger in the cage and stroke her feathers. She calms instantly, tipping her head at me. I want to tell her it's okay, but Dan is taking the stump beside me, so my words are stuck right where they are.

After a few minutes of me staring into her eyes, trying my best to convey that the noise of the chime is not going to hurt her, she relaxes. I think she trusts me.

Dan doesn't say anything as I pet her. I know I need to let her go but I don't want to.

Whatever, let's just do it.

I learned a long time ago that you have to let go of things. Nothing is ours to keep.

I flick the latch and open the door. The crow looks at it cautiously before she hops over and perches on the edge of the doorframe.

She lets me run my hand over her back and when I pull it away, she flaps her wings, heading high into the trees.

The wind stills, the only sound now is that of an owl hooting nearby.

The sun is setting, and shadows begin to settle in around us.

I sigh loudly and stand, turning to walk away. Dan reaches out and snags my hand, pulling me towards him, pointing to his lap. Really? I'm a little old for this.

But I sit down on his knee. He wraps his arms around me from behind. "Where did you get the bird?" he asks calmly.

Biting at my nails, I wrack my brain, thinking of an answer. I try to reach for my phone, but he stops me. "No, no more games, Billie Rose. Tell me where you got the crow."

I shake my head no.

"Christ, you are just like your mom," he whispers, exasperated.

The look on my mom's face when she saw the crow was scary. She was frightened and I've never seen her like that. And now that I think about it, it's the same look grandpa had when he saw Draven at my window after the accident.

The day finally catches up to me. I haven't been able to go about it on auto pilot like I usually do. I've had to think and engage and... and... I need to let the pressure off. My thighs tingle with the thought of the blade giving me some relief.

Dan senses the shift in me. He hugs me tight. "It's okay. Use your phone. Just talk to me."

He leans back so I can reach for my phone but it's too late. Tears that I've kept buried for years erupt in an ugly way and I can't help the noise that comes from me, letting him know that in fact my vocal cords are just fine.

He forgets the phone and holds me tight, rocking us back and forth. I turn in his arms and burry my face under his beard, snuggling into his neck. And I let go.

It's dark before I finally stop crying and my eyes are so swollen I can hardly open them.

"I think you needed that," Uncle Dan says, breaking the silence.

I sit up and pull my phone out, still unwilling to share my voice with him. *Like a hole in the head.*

He laughs. "Glad to see you haven't lost your snark. Let's go back up to the warehouse."

We get inside just as mom and dad arrive. They look tired.

Now, I feel bad.

Are you okay? I ask, or my phone asks anyway.

Dad and Raffe usher her to the couch. "I'm fine, sweetie. Just a little bump on the back of my head. I've had worse."

Dan grunts beside me and goes to see for himself. He runs a giant hand over the back of her head. I watch as these three burly men fuss over her. I guess I haven't noticed just how protective they are over her too. Maybe I'm not the only one.

She huffs, shoving Dan's hand away. "I told you all, I'm fine. Just... just go figure this out."

A look of seriousness passes between the three of them and then their eyes are on me. I take a few steps back, but my dad's fucking

43

eyebrow halts me in my tracks. "You, table, now," he says, leaving no room for argument. For a few seconds I think he means *the* table but no, he points towards the kitchen. I'm kidding myself if I think I'll ever be invited to the table where all club decisions are made.

Think, think, think. I need a good explanation for that bird, fast.

I sit down and all three of them sit across from me. *Don't roll your eyes,* I remind myself. Don't do it. It will only make things worse.

My dad clasps his hands in front of him and then he leans forward, making me shift back into my chair. "Where did you get that bird?"

I type slowly, trying to buy myself a little time. Yeah, this could work, hopefully it works. I hit play, holding my breath.

"You expect me to believe you just bumped into a man behind the bar, who was releasing this bird back to the wild and you convinced him she would be better off out here," he says calmly.

I shake my head wildly. **Dad, town is no place for a wild animal. She'll be much happier here.**

"And why did he have the crow in the first place?"

She'd been hurt. He nurtured her back to health. I hold my breath, hoping the inquisition ends soon.

He nods, looking at Dan and then Raffe.

The latter doesn't believe me. "Who was he?" Raffe asks, knowing full well I know all of the people who live in this town.

Shit.

I shrug my shoulders. *He must have just been passing through.*

Raffe narrows his eyes at me. I look away, focusing on Dan but he isn't buying it either. Whatever this crow means to them, it's serious. Fucking Draven. Killing him is sounding better by the minute.

So, I decide to turn the table. *Why? It was just a stupid crow. You know I love animals. Why did mom freak out when she saw it?*

All three of them drop their heads.

This is more like it.

But my dad doesn't cower so easily. "It reminded her of someone. An unbelievably bad someone." He raises his head, a storm brewing in his eyes.

My mouth forms a tiny o.

"Now, how about you tell us what this man looked like?"

Dad, I was looking at the bird, not the guy.

He pounds his fist on the table, making me jump clean out of my chair.

Dan puts his hand on my dad's shoulder, his fingers digging deep in warning.

"Billie Rose, why don't you take your mom a bottle of water and check on her," Raffe says, nodding towards the door.

I nod jerkily, grabbing a water out of the fridge, making a quick exit.

But when I get around the corner, I pause and listen to their conversation.

"Do you think you can scare the answers out of her?" Dan asks angrily.

A chair scrapes across the floor and I hear someone stomping across the kitchen. "You don't think it's a little odd that she just happens to come home with a fucking crow?" my dad yells.

I quickly tuck myself behind the bookcase when JD rushes down the hall, heading for the kitchen.

"One of the Desert Dipshits bought the bar," he exclaims.

The silence that follows is deafening. Do they already know about Draven?

"Well, fuck. We need to know what this guy is up to," Dan says.

"You know what he's up to. It's always what the Devils are up to. He's probably planning to peddle their crap here," JD responds.

"Not on my fucking watch," my dad says, deadly calm.

"I hear he's trying to start up a new chapter of Devils. He even brought over some of the old fuckers from Trap County."

"Not good. Well then, we need to get someone on the inside. We need to keep our eyes on him."

I creep towards the door so I can hear better. What the fuck are they talking about?

"It's got to be someone none of them know," Raffe adds.

They're quiet for a minute.

Then my dad pipes up. "We send our new recruit."

"Oh shit, Dirk, Jesse won't be happy about that," Raffe says.

"I'll work on her. Don't worry about it. But this isn't our only problem. We still need to find out who gave Billie Rose that fucking bird."

I'm so confused.

"Don't you think it's an awful big coincidence that a new chapter of the Devils is starting up at the same time Billie Rose totes home a live crow," Dan chimes in.

Crap.

I hurry down to my mom, not wanting to get caught eavesdropping.

She has her eyes closed when I approach. I stand there, shifting my weight from one foot to the other, wondering if I should wake her.

"I'm not asleep," she peeks one eye open.

She pulls herself up and pulls her long silver-black hair over her shoulder.

I brought you something to drink, my phone tells her as I sit down on the coffee table in front of her.

"Thank you, baby," she says, taking the water from me. She leans over and pats my cheek. "I'm sorry I scared you."

I bite my lip. *I think I was the one that frightened you. I'm the one who should be sorry,* I tell her, dropping my face to stare at my shoes.

She grabs my chin and forces me to look at her. My mom has a way of reading me through my eyes. Her gaze scavenges mine. She says my eyes are just like my dad's. Just like a mood ring she used to say.

"Baby, please tell me where you got that bird."

Why does everyone keep asking? I don't know who he was. He was just releasing her after he rehabilitated the poor thing. I thought she would be happier here.

The tiny wrinkles around my mom's eyes soften. "Okay, honey. Go on to bed."

Why did she scare you so much? I ask.

"It's a long story. It's fine. I'm tired, I'll walk with you upstairs."

So, she's not going to tell me. Fine, whatever. And this is why I don't share anything with them. I'll figure it out myself.

I help her up and together we trudge upstairs. When we get to my parent's room, I remember I'm supposed to go to Lanie's for supper. *Can I go to Lanie's for dinner tomorrow? She's making my favorite.*

"I suppose that would be okay. Will she pick you up at the shop?" she asks, looking bone dead tired.

Yeah. That guilty feeling creeps back into my head but I ignore it, I know I'm taking advantage of her when she's down.

"Okay, then. Goodnight, honey." And she closes the door quietly in my face.

I rest my head against the door. What a fucking day. And all for what? I don't have any more answers today than I did yesterday. The only thing I have are more questions.

All I know is that whoever Crow is, he terrifies the toughest woman I know.

And that should scare the living crap out of me and make me spill my guts, but they don't trust me with the truth, so why should I trust them?

I know who will give me answers though and once I have them, I'm going to end him.

Chapter Three

Billie Rose

Well, after last night, I thought everyone would start the day hounding me but that's not the case. My mom started the morning off cleaning like a mad woman. She mumbled something about the party on Saturday. And dad called an early meeting with his officers, so... yeah, nothing out of the ordinary.

Seems my little escapade yesterday has been forgotten.

The day goes by quiet, and I spend my time working on my skeleton key chime. Maybe this time grandpa will talk to me through it.

Hey, can you give me a ride to Lanie's? I ask my aunt.

She raises her eyebrows.

I already cleared it with mom, I make an x over my heart, letting her know I'm being honest.

On the drive over to Lanie's apartment, Lily pulls over to the side of the road before we get there. Oh, man. Here we go.

"Billie Rose, I just wanted to let you know that I'm sad too. About the bar." She runs her hand over her brow nervously before continuing. "Bill gave me a job there when I first moved here. I had no idea what I was doing." She laughs lightly, swiping at her eyes. "Anyhow, I know change isn't easy. Especially, when it feels like everyone is moving on and you are stuck on that day. Am I right?"

I nod and look out the windshield. Aunt Lily is the sweetest person to walk the earth. She has a quiet resilience about her.

"The club wants to help you. I know it must seem suffocating but try to look at it from outside yourself. Everyone loves you, Billie Rose. You and Jesse are all we have left of Bill besides our memories."

My leg tingles. When I get to Lanie's, I'm going to have to sneak off to the bathroom and release some of the pain.

Lily reaches over and squeezes my hand. "Just think about it, okay?"

I shake my head that I will, hoping that she starts the car already. I need to get out of this little slug bug. It's cute and everything but I need some breathing room. When she pulls up in front of Lanie's, I look her in the eye and hit the button on my phone. *Thank you for sharing with me that you are sad too.*

Her big doe eyes tear up. "I love you, Billie Rose. I'll always be here for you."

Nodding, I reach for the door and hurry out and then inside the building. I burst into Lanie's. *I need to use your bathroom,* I type the minute I'm inside.

"Rosie, wait," she hollers, dropping the bowl she was holding into the sink.

But I ignore her and head down the hall to the bathroom. Just a tiny cut and then I'll be able to get through dinner with her and her boyfriend.

When I swing the door open to the bathroom, my eyes lock on Draven's. He's standing in front of the mirror, trimming his beard, in nothing but a towel.

What in the fuck?

A slow smile spreads across his face.

"Jesus, Billie Rose, you could have walked in on him bare ass naked," Lanie says from behind me.

I spin around, backing up. Wait a fucking minute. The cogs of my brain are moving at a snail's pace, but they are turning. Oh, no fucking way. No fucking way!

I'm... I'm sorry, my fingers fly across the screen of my phone.

Just as I'm about to make a beeline for the door, Draven reaches out and takes my hand, shaking it in his. "It's okay, hun. It's nice to finally meet you. Lanie's told me so much about you."

I blink at him in stunned silence.

"I'll be finished in just a second." He gives my hand a tight squeeze and then closes the door, leaving Lanie and I out in the hall.

She drags me back to the kitchen. "What's wrong? Do you not feel well?" Lanie pushes me down in a chair and pours me a glass of iced tea.

Can she see that my heart is about to beat out of my chest? Draven is her boyfriend. Lanie's boyfriend killed grandpa.

"Maybe I should call Daddy D and have him come pick you up. You look like you just saw a ghost." She presses the back of her hand over my forehead.

No, I'm fine. Really. I just had to pee really bad but I'm good now.

Her eyebrows crease together in concern. "Okay, I know there is something wrong now because you didn't yell at me for calling Dirk daddy."

That's the least of my problems right now, her boyfriend is the only one I'm concerned about. And I wish I had just seen a ghost and not a live man with a beating heart. Soon, though. My gaze travels from the hallway to Lanie. How can I do that to her?

"That's it, I'm texting him."

My hand darts out, stopping her. I shake my head no. *I just need to eat. The shop was crazy today and I didn't get lunch.*

She smiles big, clapping her hands. Lanie grabs a tray of dinner rolls and sets it down in front of me. "Here, try one of these. It's a new recipe."

I accept one, taking a big bite out of it, making her laugh. I nod in approval. They are good, they melt in your mouth. Lanie is an awesome cook. Living mostly on her own, she had to learn, or she would have starved.

Draven walks out in dark jeans and a black t-shirt, looking so good it makes me want to vomit. How in the hell did he become Lanie's boyfriend? How? I can't believe she's kept him a secret from me this whole time.

I guess I've kept him a secret too.

"Smells good, Lanie," he tells her, going over and snagging a piece of roast beef off the plate she is arranging her masterpiece on.

The smile that erupts on her face makes my heart sink to my feet. She's beaming at him like he is the best thing since sliced bread. He turns and winks at me. She has no idea how evil this man is. Should I warn her?

I watch as she bustles around the kitchen, clearly wanting to impress him with her skills. And she does have them, but he doesn't deserve any of it. He doesn't deserve to have her, period.

My blood is boiling. This motherfucker knew Lanie was my friend all along.

Lanie sits down, fixing him a plate. "Go on, Billie Rose, help yourself. I know this is your favorite."

It looks amazing, the man with an Australian accent tells her via my phone.

I chew on my bottom lip, wishing I could use my own voice. Suddenly, my silence feels different. It's like he's winning in some way.

The grin on his face makes me think he can read my mind. He strokes his beard, looking at the spread on his plate. "You're going to do great at culinary school, baby, it will be worth every penny to see you succeed."

Wait. What? I pause mid chew.

"Draven, I hadn't had a chance to tell Billie Rose yet," Lanie gently scolds him.

He runs his tongue over his teeth, his eyes narrowing in on me. "Oh, I'm sorry." Draven leans over and kisses her on the cheek.

"It's okay." She looks at him adoringly before turning her attention to me.

"I was going to tell you tonight." She bounces in her seat. "Draven is paying for me to go to culinary school. I'm leaving next week, I'm so excited. It's my dream."

I swallow and wipe my mouth with my napkin, trying to muster some happiness for her. *That's great.* I avoid looking at Draven. *Where are you going?*

"It's kind of far away." She frowns, looking at her lap.

Draven's fork scrapes across his plate. He continues to eat with gusto, enjoying the little skit playing out in front of him.

How far? I pick up my fork and stab a potato.

She taps her red nails on the table by me to get my attention. "Billie Rose, please don't be angry but it's the best school. It's… it's in New York city."

I cough into my napkin, laying my fork down on the edge of my plate. *I'm not angry, Lanie, this is your dream. You're right. I'm sorry, I'm just sad.*

"I know, me too but you could go with me," she suggests cautiously. "I don't want to go alone. Draven can't go with me because guess what?" She doesn't give me a chance to respond. "He bought the bar!" she exclaims. "When I graduate, we're going to make it into a restaurant. So, please come with me." My gaze shifts from her to Draven. He pretends not to care either way.

I think about it. I could leave this place behind. Forget about everything that's happened. Maybe I could find some freedom there.

He picks up his glass and looks at me over the rim. Excited for my response. I realize now that he has been the conductor of my life for the past three years. I offer Lanie a gentle smile. *I have a lot of unfinished business here.*

She leans back in her chair and shakes her head sadly. "When are you going to stop letting them dictate your life?"

If only she knew who has really been in charge.

Lanie turns to Draven. "Do you know this girl has never been kissed? She hasn't even held hands with a boy."

My mouth falls open at the abrupt change in her attitude towards me. She doesn't even sound like my friend at the moment.

Draven sits forward, giving her his full attention. This bit of information pricks his interest.

I grab her hand, but she pulls away. "No, this is ridiculous. You've let your parents and that club control every aspect of your life. You don't even have a fucking driver's license."

She tosses her napkin down on the table and stands up. "I'm sorry, I just had hoped…" she sucks in a deep breath, "never mind. I need some air." She rushes out the door.

Draven and I stare at each other quietly before I slam my fist down on the table and rush to the bathroom, locking the door behind me.

Kicking off my shoe, I slide my pants down to my ankles and drop the lid on the toilet, sitting down on the cold porcelain. Once I dig the blade out from my shoe, I pierce my skin and take a deep breath. My head falls back as blood runs down my leg, dripping onto the linoleum.

The door jiggles but I ignore it. I make another small cut for good measure.

Unbelievably, the door opens. Draven steps in, holding a bobby pin in front of his face. "Living with women taught me a lot of things." He kicks the door shut behind him and crouches down in front of me, holding my eyes hostage.

"You know, I have a better way," he suggests. He tips his head, studying me.

I've kept my secrets hidden for so long. Secrets of him, the cutting, my voice… the accident. Funny that one of those secrets was the first to discover another.

He reaches around to grab some toilet paper off the roll behind me. His chest brushes against mine. After he rips it off, he resumes his position and presses it against my thigh. We both stare as the paper turns crimson, then his gaze returns to mine.

Black pits focus on me as he presses his fingers into my soft flesh. No man has ever touched me there. I glance away, staring at the little window over the bathtub. It's dark outside already. I wonder what mom fixed for supper. Is she still cleaning? Has dad discovered that she let me go to Lanie's? Is he mad?

Draven's thumb brushes back and forth over my skin. I try to focus on anything but him. His eyes don't leave my face.

"There are other ways to feel good."

His hand slides up my leg, his fingertips reaching the edge of my panties. My hand shoots out to halt his advance. I grab his hand and hold it still. "Stop," I say quietly, my voice rough from unuse.

Neither of us move.

Great, another little secret reveled to my biggest one.

When I finally look at him, he slowly leans forward and presses his lips to mine.

I let go of his hand, pressing mine against his shoulders. He digs his fingers into the tops of my thighs, pulling me closer.

The fact he tastes like sweet tea is all I can think of as my mind scrambles to find a safe space.

Suddenly, the bathroom door swings open, and a loud screech comes from my best friend. Draven pulls his lips off mine but stays where he's at. I cover my mouth, tears springing to my eyes.

"You have to have everything, don't you?" Lanie's voice quivers but she continues to berate me. "You have everything I ever wanted and when I finally get something of my own, you have to go and steal it from me. You're nothing but a spoiled, fucking brat."

When neither Draven or I say anything, she storms out and I hear the front door slam shut.

I shove Draven away from me, making him stumble back on his ass. Shit, I need to talk to her. I need to explain. I'm buttoning up my pants as I rush out of the bathroom, headed for the front door when it swings open and in storms my dad.

I skid to a stop, my eyes wide. My dad glances around the room, stopping on the table, food still on our plates.

Draven steps around the corner. He pauses for a moment before stepping around me, holding his hand out to my dad. "You must be Billie Rose's father."

My dad stares at it like it's covered in shit, his eyebrow cocking to a level I've never seen. He looks past Draven to me. "I just saw Lanie run out the front door crying. Why?"

Draven answers for me. "Oh, the girls had a little disagreement at dinner. You know how women can be."

Dad's eyes cut to his and he cracks his knuckles. A big part of me hopes he puts his fist in Draven's face but part of me wants him unharmed… I want to be the one to hurt him.

"Lanie is moving to New York, to go to school. She wants Billie Rose to go with her," Draven says, not the least bit fazed by my dad's murderous glare.

My dad shows no emotion whatsoever. He holds out his arm, snapping his fingers for me to go to him. Normally, this caveman type behavior would piss me off, but I need a lifeline and right now he is my ticket out of here.

I practically run towards him and place my hand in his. He wraps his fingers around my hand, engulfing it in the safety of his own and tugs me close to him. He hugs me, pressing his mouth to the top of my head. I'm not sure what kind of looks are passing between the two of them and I don't care. Right now, I just want my daddy to shelter me from the world. Just for a minute.

He keeps me tucked to his side as he ushers me out the door. I glance over my shoulder. Draven is leaning against the wall. He holds up his index finger and I notice it's covered in my blood. Slowly, he sucks it into his mouth. I turn around, realizing that this little dinner gave Draven way too much ammunition.

If I'm going to fight him, I'm going to have to become someone else. Someone tougher. Someone who knows how to protect what's hers.

Chapter Four

Dirk

The day the midwife put Billie Rose in my arms, I knew what my sole mission in life was. And from that day forward, I vowed to protect her. I wasn't going to let her grow up like Jesse had, bouncing from home to home. Just trying to survive but getting knocked down and abused every step of the way. I didn't get to save that little girl, but I was damned sure not going to let anyone hurt her daughter.

Jesse didn't know her father until she was a teenager, so she made sure that Billie Rose and I were close. Were...

I glance over at my dark-haired, little girl. We aren't close anymore. She won't let me in. I know she's angry that I failed her. I let her get hurt. I didn't protect what was mine.

But I'm not giving up. My job isn't done. She has many years ahead of her and I need to make sure she doesn't get hurt again.

"Should we go look for Lanie?" I ask.

She shakes her head no, turning away from me to stare out the window.

"Do you want to go with her?" I ask, praying she shakes her head in the right direction.

That damn Australian answers instead.

No. You wouldn't let me go even if I wanted to.

She's right. No way in hell would I let her move across the country. The glow from her phone lights up her face and I notice the tears streaming down her cheeks.

"I'm sorry." It's all I know to say.

Did you know him? She asks.

Oh yeah, that was the whole reason for me storming over there.

"He's the fucker who bought the bar. I should have paid better attention when Candice sold it. He's a Devil. I don't want you anywhere near him."

Why?

Her big eyes swirl with a color I'm not used to seeing. Sometimes, it's like staring into my own. We've both been cursed with eyes that change color with our mood. And right now, I can't read hers.

62

"He's trying to start up a chapter of the Devil's here. That fucker is nothing but a low life drug dealer. I'm not having it here and I'm not having you hanging around him. He isn't here for Lanie. He's here to line his pockets and to make trouble."

I glance away from the road, catching her confused expression. "What's wrong?"

She runs her hand down her face, wiping it off on her jeans. *Nothing.*

"I mean it. You stay away from him, yeah?"

My daughter sucks her bottom lip between her teeth, nodding in understanding.

"Why don't you invite Lanie to the party Saturday? Maybe you two can work things out before she leaves. She has to understand your place is here."

Is it? she asks, pulling her shoulder up to her cheek. *You know she was the only person brave enough to be my friend.*

I press my hand over my heart, dammit she's just like her mother. She knows exactly where to put the knife. She's so innocent, she probably doesn't even realize it.

It's okay though. Who wants to be friends with a freak who doesn't speak and spends her time making windchimes?

And now she's going in for the kill, twisting the knife just right.

"Billie Rose," I breathe out.

She holds up her hand. ***It's fine. I'm fine.***

When we get home, she bounds up the stairs for her room. The slam of her door echoes through the entire warehouse.

Jesse comes out from the kitchen, her eyes going to the top of the stairs. "Is she okay?"

I grab my beautiful wife and pull her close to me. "She's upset. Lanie is moving to New York."

"What? Oh, no. First the bar and now Lanie. This is too much for her, Dirk. We should look at finding someone she can talk to." Jesse lays her head on my chest. "And I'm sorry about letting her go over there tonight. I didn't realize Lanie was dating one of the Devils."

"It's fine. I warned her about him. Now she knows. It won't be long, and the boys and I will have him and the rest of his crew moving on down the road."

Jesse presses her lips over my heart before pulling away. "Do you think he gave her the crow?"

Just hearing the word crow makes my blood pressure rise to a deadly level. Even though the asshole is dead, he still haunts my wife's dreams at night. If I could buy a round trip ticket to hell to watch him burn all over again, I would.

"It's possible he might be trying to distract us and rattle our cage. He knows it's an untapped market here and he's eager to fill his pockets with drug money. But he's just a punk. No worries, baby."

She pats my chest. "I'm going to try to talk to her."

Roses and Skulls

I watch Jesse walk up the stairs. My wife just gets more beautiful by the day.

When she disappears, I head out back to have a cigarette.

Fuck yes, I still smoke. I'm good at it, what can I say?

Well, well, my new prospect has arrived.

He smiles at me as he approaches, a fucking sucker hanging out of his mouth.

"Hey, Prez," he greets, smirking because he knows I'm not pleased to see him.

I shake his hand. I might not be excited to see him, but I do have a need for him. And better yet, it will keep him busy and away from the warehouse.

"You're early," I say dryly.

He pulls the sucker from his mouth, pointing it at me. "I just couldn't wait another day. I mean, look at this place." He holds his hands out and spins around. "Beautiful."

I snort. This kid annoys the fuck out of me.

"No time for sightseeing, I'm afraid. I've got a job for you."

He rubs his tattooed hands together, some of my wife's handiwork. "I'm ready, boss."

I flick my cigarette at him, making him jump back. "You better be." I turn and walk back into the warehouse.

Fucking prospect.

Chapter Five

Billie Rose

Lanie's blocked me on everything. She's not even giving me a chance to explain.

What am I going to do? I need my best friend.

I could sneak out and go back over there.

Or, maybe this is for the best. Because I'm going to kill her *boyfriend*. I don't know how or even when but it's just a matter of time. I need him to die.

My mom knocks quietly at the same time as she opens the door. Yeah, there is no such thing as privacy in this family.

"Hey, hun, dad told me about Lanie. Do you want to talk about it?" She climbs into bed behind me, wrapping her arm around me.

I pull my phone out from under my pillow. ***There's nothing to talk about.***

"Why don't you invite her to the party Saturday?"

Jesus, sometimes I swear my parents share a brain.

She blocked me.

Mom pushes me onto my back so she can see my face. "What? Just because you didn't want to go to New York with her?"

I roll back over, staring at the mural she painted for me when she was pregnant with me. It's beautiful. I wish I could run away to the place on my wall. I wonder if it's a real place or if it came from her imagination.

"Baby, talk to me."

It's fine, mom. She's leaving, people move on. People leave, it's a fact of life.

"I'll never leave you," she whispers in my ear.

I laugh silently. ***It's inevitable that one of us is going to leave the other. It's just a matter of time.***

She sits up, pulling me with her. Her eyes bounce over mine, searching. Mine do the same. I've never looked at her as someone besides my mom. Who is she? Is she capable of murdering someone?

"You are right. But while I'm on this earth, know one thing, Billie Rose, I'll be here for you."

Would you kill for me? My phone asks on my behalf.

Without hesitation, not even a blink of an eye, she responds. "Absolutely. I'd kill or die for you, Billie Rose. I protect what's mine, at all costs. Sometimes, things happen that are out of our control. Like the accident. But I would do anything for you." She runs a piece of my hair through her fingers before tucking it behind my ear.

One thing I admire about my mom, is that she's straight forward. She's true to her word and she always tries to protect me, but I don't know if that necessarily was the best thing for me. My parents didn't allow me the space to learn how to deal with problems or how to protect myself.

I'm going to go outside and work on my new chime, I tell her.

She nods, backing off my bed. "You know where to find me if you decide you want to talk."

I ignore her as she leaves, busying myself with putting on my shoes.

She pauses at my door. "I bought some new chain for your chimes when I was picking up paint. I left it on the bench in my art room."

Thanks, I tell her.

"Are you sure there's nothing else going on? Besides your fight with Lanie?"

I pull on the laces of my shoe before typing my answer. **There's nothing, mom. I'm fine.**

Before I head outside, I jog down the stairs to pick up the chain she bought. I hate it down here. It's creepy.

As I'm grabbing the sack from the art supply store, I let my eyes wander over her paintings. They are beautiful. She's so talented. I wish I had one ounce of her artistic ability.

When I close the door to her room, I notice the door across the hall is cracked open. Hm, that's strange. It's always been locked. I've never been in there. Once, I asked about it, she told me dad stored guns in there and it needed to stay locked for safety.

Maybe I should take one. I don't know how to use a gun but I'm sure I could learn by watching a video off the internet. You can learn anything there.

I'm going to kill Draven. A gun would be the easiest way to do that but probably the least satisfying option. Still, I could use it for protection.

I walk down the hall and glance up the stairs, making sure no one is around. After I slide into the room, I click the door closed behind me, then turn on the lights.

When the room illuminates, I cover my mouth to stifle a scream.

What the fuck is this?

I make my way to the center of the room, spinning in a circle as I take in all the colors swirling around me.

There are no guns here.

It's an empty room.

Roses and Skulls

It's hell.

No, it's my mom's version of hell.

My gaze stops on the black crow I'm standing on. The entire floor is covered with it. The crow's wings are going up in flames. But it's what is painted in the reflection of the bird's eyes that makes me shiver from head to toe. It's my mom, standing there watching the bird burn. Her face is painted like a skeleton.

Holy shit, what the fuck made her paint all of this? What darkness lives inside her? Maybe Draven was right. I have no idea what she is capable of.

I walk over to an image of a little girl kneeling in front of a cross, her feet bruised and cut. Her hair dirty and tangled. She's praying. Is this child my mom?

I'm so engulfed in the images painted from floor to ceiling that I don't hear my Uncle Raffe come in behind me.

He startles me when I turn around and find him standing by the door. I jump back, placing my hands over my chest.

He motions around the room. "Kind of scary, isn't it?" he asks.

I nod, worried that I'm going to be in trouble for being in here.

"Can I tag along on your walk tonight?" he asks.

Everyone knows I go for a walk out in the trees most nights. I've never let anyone come with me. Not since the accident. It's the only time I can get away from prying eyes.

"She gave me permission to share her story with you," he continues when he sees my hesitation.

The horror on the walls draws my eyes around the room. She left the door open on purpose. She wanted me to find this.

Why doesn't she just tell me?

He reaches his hand out. "Come on, let's take that walk."

When we leave the room, he locks the door behind us.

"What's in the sack?" he asks as we make our way through the trees.

I answer him, able to walk and type at the same time. I know this path like the back of my hand. **It's some new chain for my chimes.**

His footsteps halt as the trees open to my little fantasyland. The last chime I made is blowing in the breeze by the playhouse dad and grandpa made me.

Pretty cool, huh? I run the bottom of my shoe over the brush on the ground.

He steps out into the clearing. "This is incredible. Did Bill build all this?"

Yeah, and dad.

I head over to my wooden spool table and start laying out the keys in front of me.

He takes the seat beside me. "Jackson told me it was amazing out here. I guess I should have come out and saw it for myself. I'm sorry I haven't ever done that."

Shrugging my shoulders, I continue to work on my creation.

"I just figured you needed your privacy."

It's fine. I wave my hand out in dismissal. **What did you want to tell me?**

I'm trying not to be rude, but it will be completely dark in about an hour, and I want to get this done. I'm anxious to see if this one unlocks grandpa's whispers from Heaven.

He gets up and explores the playhouse as I try to figure out the design I'm wanting.

A crow perches in a tree a few feet away from me but I don't pay it any attention until another one lands on the table. Raffe stills behind me. The bird drops a bright blue bead from his mouth. No, not his, hers. It's the crow I saved.

She tips her head as I pick up the bead. It's beautiful and made of glass. I set it down in front of her, but she nudges it with her beak, giving it back to me.

"I think she's giving it to you." Raffe says quietly.

I put my fingers to my mouth and then pull them away, signing thank you. I don't use sign language much, but I've picked up a few small things over the past few years. She flaps her wings in response and then flies up to the tree to perch beside the other bird. It's bigger than she is. I wonder if it's a male. He caws a few times and then they both fly away.

The bead catches the light as I pick it up, rolling it around in my palm.

Raffe sits back down beside me, his eyes sliding over my face. I try with all my might to keep my expression schooled.

"I met your mom when she was just a girl, maybe a few years younger than you. I ignored all the signs that she was in trouble. I'm not going to overlook them with you. Something bad is happening. I feel it. She feels it too. That's why she asked me to tell you her story."

After I put the bead in my pocket, I respond. **Why can't she just tell me herself?**

He leans in close to me, taking my hand in his. "The same reason you have kept quiet for the past few years." I bite my lip and try to look away, but he grabs my chin. "Some things are hard to talk about."

He then begins to weave a tale so horrific, so unbelievable that I'm glad I don't have to speak because I feel sick.

I sit there as the forest grows dark, but the clarity of who my parents are comes into focus. The light is being shined on my mom's childhood. He doesn't give details. He doesn't need to. I get the gist. My mom was hurt by not one but many people throughout her young life. A man named Crow being the worst one of all.

Draven said my mom killed his dad. Was Crow his dad?

Raffe finishes, tears in his eyes. "You see why this might be hard for her to talk about?"

I nod as he leans over to wipe away the tears running down my cheeks.

"Oh, baby, we wanted to shelter you from all the ugly in the world, from this, but I think we're realizing that wasn't the way we should have handled things."

I busy myself, rearranging the keys on the table. *Is Draven, Lanie's boyfriend, is he related to him? To this Crow guy.*

"Is that where you got the bird?" he asks.

My uncle is one of the kindest men I've ever known. He's funny and he flirts with everyone, but we all know who holds his heart. My Aunt Rachel. She helped him rehabilitate after he'd been shot. I know this because he loves to tell the story of how they fell in love.

And that is where the first piece of the puzzle falls into place. *Was Crow the man who shot you?*

He leans back, studying me. "Goddamn, you're just like your mom. Ignoring my question to ask one of your own." He chuckles lightly.

So, everyone keeps telling me. I roll my eyes and go back to working on my chime. I grab my needle nose pliers and pinch a ring closed around the top of one of the keys, focusing on what I'm doing. But I decide to answer him, laying my tools down for a moment. *Draven had the crow on his desk when I went to take a final look at the bar. I couldn't leave her there in that cage.*

He sighs in relief. "Draven is trying to rattle our cages. He wants to start up a chapter of the Devils in our backyard and that means he wants to push drugs here. He's trying to distract us with all this crow shit."

75

You're the reason mom killed him. She wouldn't have done it for herself, but for you, for you she would live or die.

The shocked look on his face tells me everything I need to know. And my heart hardens a little more. My fate is sealed. I'm going to become a whole lot more like my mom. I just need to figure out how to get away with murder like she did.

"How did you get so smart?" he asks, realizing I've been thinking about all of this more than they thought.

I'm not but don't worry, I'll stay away from Draven, my phone easily lies for me.

"Good." He smacks his hands down on his knees. "I'm glad we got this all out of the way. Maybe things can start to get back to normal around here."

I shake my head mindlessly. Normal? Nothing's been normal since grandpa died.

"Can I stay until you finish?" he asks.

Again, I nod.

"I think that little crow was thanking you for letting her out of that cage," he continues.

Maybe, I type. It's then I notice I have a message from an unknown number.

It's fucking Draven.

Draven: Lanie left early for New York. I'm sorry about all that.

Roses and Skulls

Raffe gets up to explore again, leaving me to work.

I decide to text him back.

Me: I don't think you are.

I hit send, angrily.

Not waiting for him to respond, I put my phone away and finish the chime.

When I take the old one down by the playhouse and replace it with the one I just made, Raffe watches me with a curious expression on his handsome face. "Why do you hang them up here before selling them? Are you listening to make sure they sound right?" he asks, genuinely interested in my craft.

I flick one of the skeleton keys, sending it into another. ***None of them sound right,*** my phone tells him.

He looks at me even more confused. "It sounds fine to me."

I shake my head. He wouldn't understand. I start to walk away, and he jogs up beside me. "I guess artists don't see the beauty of their own work sometimes," he says, grabbing my hand and squeezing it. "Are you excited about the party Saturday?" he proceeds to ask as the warehouse comes into view.

I can hardly contain myself, I answer dryly, cringing at the thought of yet another party without grandpa. It's not the same without him. ***Anyway, thanks for telling me the truth for once.***

He winces. "Billie Rose, we just wanted to protect you. We weren't trying to hurt you by keeping these kinds of things from you."

I plop down on the wooden bench on the patio. *I understand you not telling me when I was a child but I'm a grown ass adult, Raffe.*

He runs his hand down his face. "I guess we forget how old you're getting.

My uncle looks up at the stars as they start to blink on. He shakes his leg nervously. "What about you?"

What about me?

"Do you have any truths you need to share?" His gaze leaves the Heavens to focus on me.

The patio door slides open and my dad steps out.

I turn my head to face Raffe. Maybe I'm being hypocritical but honestly, it pisses me off that he's calling me out. *It's been a long day. Goodnight, Uncle Raffe.* I lean over and offer him a kiss on the cheek, his whiskers tickling my nose.

He sighs, placing his hand over his cheek. "I love you, Billie Rose."

I dip my head and then make my escape. My dad's eyes are like a hawk on me the whole time. He stops me as I slide past him.

"You good?" he asks.

While I might understand them better, I'm still angry. Right or wrong. *Why wouldn't I be? I mean, Dan and Raffe have both given me the best of news this week, yeah?* I cross my arms across my chest, glaring at him.

He tries that scary expression to scold me for speaking to him like I just did, but it's not going to work tonight.

"Well, I'd tell you these things myself if you ever spent more than two seconds of your time with me."

Are you kidding me? You're always up in my space. Just admit that you didn't tell me about the bar, about this Crow asshole because you didn't think I could handle it and you didn't want to see your little princess cry.

He narrows his eyes. "Did you cry?"

I stomp my foot. **Not the point.**

"You're right. I don't like to see you cry. I didn't want to tell you about the bar, and I sure as fuck never wanted you to hear the name Crow. But the real reason I asked them to talk to you is that you never seem to listen to your mom or I."

I'm tired. I'm going to bed. I shove past him, but he reaches out and wraps his arms around me.

He whispers into my ear. "I'm not good at this. I'm not the father you deserve." And then he lets me go and walks away, down towards the lake.

I stare after him until Raffe gets up and follows.

My heart has sunk to a new level tonight. The pain is only getting worse, not better. I feel like I'm losing everything. My innocence, my friend, my dad. A few cuts might take some of it away.

Quickly, I make my way to my bathroom. As the blood drips on the floor, I think about how right Raffe is. I have so many hidden truths. They may have kept things from me but I'm doing the same. I could just tell them about Draven and the accident. I'm not sure why I keep calling it an accident. It clearly wasn't. But anyway, I can't share any of that with them. They would hate me. I know because I hate myself.

I glance at my phone to see Draven's response to our earlier conversation.

Draven: You're right. I'm not sorry. You see, Billie Rose, you and I are tied together by the past. Not even Lanie can break that bond.

I don't respond. I just delete the message.

After I clean up the blood, I sit down on my bed and hit play on the movie I've decided to watch. I knew I'd heard his name somewhere. Eric Draven, the main character in the movie The Crow.

Whoever named him is hilarious, or maybe just as crazy as he is.

He thinks he's avenging his father's death.

I don't know why my family doesn't realize who Draven really is, that he's Crow's son. But it doesn't matter. He's after my family, I feel it.

And while I might only be the Skull's MC princess, one fact remains, I'm still a Skull.

My mom's father was a good man, Draven's was a rapist. Maybe he doesn't know this, but my gut tells me he does, and he just doesn't care. If tonight was any indicator, the apple doesn't fall far from the tree.

I'm going to protect what's mine and in the process, I'll be doing society a favor.

Chapter Six

Billie Rose

I've been waiting to sneak out for over an hour. Usually, my parents are in bed by now, but mom's been cleaning all fucking night. I suppose for their stupid little party but whatever, I'm finally on my way and almost there.

When I walk up to the parking lot, a bright red, blinking sign tells me The Black Rose is definitely open for business. Unfortunately, his grand opening looks to be going well.

I decide to opt for the backdoor. I'm not ready to face a bar full of Devils. The minute I open the door, loud music, and the smell of weed greets me. I cover my nose as I push through. I'm going to have to shower when I get home, or my family is going to smell the smoke on me.

Roses and Skulls

As I'm heading to the office, the door to the main part of the bar swings open. I pause when a man steps through, the door swinging closed behind him. He pulls something out of his pocket. It's a sucker. He rips the wrapper off and sticks it in his mouth.

Holy shit, he's hot. I wish Lanie was here to see him.

He pushes it to the side of his mouth and then cracks his neck back and forth. An evil smile spreads across his beautiful face.

I swallow hard when he notices me, making me shrink back into the shadows. Our eyes lock and his smile widens. I take a deep breath as he walks towards me.

Shit, two seconds in and I'm already in a bad situation.

I push myself up against the wall to let him pass, but he stops when he reaches me. My eyes drop to the floor.

When he presses his body against mine, my gaze snaps up to meet his. The audacity. Who the fuck does this guy think he is?

Oh, he has the warmest brown eyes I've ever seen. He doesn't seem as scary if I just focus on them and ignore the rest of him.

He places one hand on the wall beside my face. The other pulls the sucker out of his mouth.

My heart is beating so hard, surely he can feel it thumping against him.

Then he surprises me by pushing his sucker in *my* mouth.

In my fucking mouth!

The sucker that was just in his.

My gaze drops to his mouth, hoping he doesn't have any communicable disease. He bites on the ball of his tongue piercing, and I whimper.

I know. I know!

This is so stupid.

My head tells me to run but my body wants to stay and see what these new feelings are all about. This feels, well, I don't know, good, tingly, definitely tingly.

"What are you doing here, sweetheart?" he asks, his eyes going to my lips as he pulls the sucker across my tongue before putting it back in his own mouth.

I shake my head, unable to speak. For real this time.

He chuckles and then pops the button on my jeans. My eyes widen but I do nothing to stop him.

The man keeps his eyes on mine as he takes the sucker out of his mouth and this time he doesn't place it between my lips... well, okay, so he puts it between my lips but... oh my god, please don't make me say it. You know where this is going.

He moves his stick of sin up and down, round and round, slowly, his gaze never leaving mine.

"Such a good girl," he whispers, his hot cherry scented breath blowing over my face.

Oh, oh no, the tingle is getting, oh. My eyes fall closed as my head drops back to the wall. I can't stop him. I can't even stop myself.

And then it happens. It happens so quick that I can't believe it. I've never been able to make myself come that fast and this man did it with a sucker in a matter of seconds.

My eyes blink open, just in time to catch him push the sucker back into his mouth.

And he moans.

My stomach does a little flip at the sound.

We both stare at each other as he buttons up my pants for me. His candy pushed to the side of his cheek.

"What are you doing here?" he asks.

And I find myself answering him, not with my phone but my own words. "I… I work here," I say quietly.

"Ah, so she can speak. Thought maybe the cat had your tongue." He grins from ear to ear, showing me his perfect straight pearly whites.

He taps the end of my nose with a tattooed finger and when the door to the office swings open, he tucks himself back in the shadows.

What the fuck kind of tall, dark, and dangerous is this man?

No one has ever touched me like that. Like… like he had every right to. Well, besides Draven but he obviously has a death wish.

I close my eyes and memorize everything about him. The way his head is shaved at the sides, and how he has some sort of symbols tattooed there in replace of hair. Then, I categorize every color that makes up his eyes. Like the bark on a tree, every shade blends perfectly together to make you feel safe and warm and cozy. Only he isn't safe. Is he?

He's probably in his mid-twenties, I would guess. He's tall and covered in tattoos. I told myself I'd never date anyone with them. Even though I have one, a gift from my mom on my eighteenth birthday, flowers that cover my shoulder. But I always envisioned finding someone opposite of the men in my family but maybe I could make an exception for this guy.

Shit! Wait till he finds out who I am. He will never give me a chance.

Anyone with half a brain would leave me alone.

He'll find out who I am and that will be the end of him sharing his candy with me.

"Billie Rose." Draven snaps his fingers, pulling me from my thoughts.

My gaze goes to the man hiding himself in the shadows. Maybe he'll wait for me.

Maybe it would be better if he didn't.

I walk slowly towards Draven. When I get within arm's reach, he places a hand around my elbow, speeding up the process of dragging me into his lair.

"I thought you might have chickened out."

Shaking my head no, I make my way to the far side of the room.

He closes the door and leans against it, crossing his arms across his chest.

I bite my lip and pull my phone out of my pocket. *Do you want me to go out and start serving?* I ask.

The sooner I get out of this office, the better.

Draven laughs and makes his way around the desk. "You're what, eighteen?"

I straighten to my full height, pulling my shoulders back. *I'm nineteen and I can tell you right now, I can work circles around any bartender or server out there.*

"Of that I have no doubt," he says, leaning back in his chair. I look around and notice nothing much has changed. He's kept the bar just the same as grandpa had it. "But I have something better in store for you. I want you to help me run the place."

I raise an eyebrow in question, moving to sit down on the couch. *What's your deal? Why are you really here?*

He rubs his hands together as he thinks about it. "I'm here to make amends."

I run my finger over the letters of my phone as I think about what to say next.

"Don't believe me?" He stands and comes to sit by me. I scoot to the end of the couch away from him. "I'm trying my best to clean up my life. I wanted to do something nice for Lanie, so I'm sending her to her dream school and for you… for you I bought this place."

That's a lie, you bought this place for her. You told her you were turning it into a restaurant when she graduates, remember? And then you ruined that by taking advantage of her best friend.

He laughs, running his fingers through his beard. "She'll get over it. I explained how I was only trying to help you, with you know, your little problem." He motions towards my thighs.

I squeeze my legs together and glance away from him, typing as I do. *It's not a problem.*

The leather squeaks as he leans back, laying an arm on the back of the couch behind me. "Why didn't you tell on me, Billie Rose?"

Because my dad would kill us both if he knew you touched me.

"You know what I mean, little dove." His fingers wrap around the hair at the nape of my neck, and he pulls back, forcing my face towards the ceiling. He slides close and stares down at me. "Why did you keep the accident a secret?"

I'm angry. I don't like being held down by him. Thoughts of sticking a knife into his throat pop into my head.

He wants me to talk to him. He knows I can, because I told him to stop when he was assaulting me at Lanie's. He wants me to do it again but I'm not giving him my voice this time, so I spit in his face in response.

Draven wipes it away, running a hand over his face. "I think you like defying them."

Roses and Skulls

I don't say anything.

"You're angry they let it happen. Aren't you? You thought they were these untouchable figures that could shield you from everything, but they can't, can they?"

I focus on the ceiling.

"Parents are human too. Look at my dad, he let a woman kill him. Pretty pathetic if you think about it. He died before I was even born, and he left me surrounded by women. Women are weak. Your mom is weak too. She hides behind that bad ass persona, but it's all a facade."

My silence keeps him going.

"But you," he runs a finger over the scar on my neck. I grip the edge of the couch, my knuckles turning white. "You are strong. You've kept our little secret all these years because you know there's something between us. The fates have brought us together."

I can't take it anymore, so I push him away from me.

He gives in, throwing his hands in the air in mock surrender. "Admit it, Billie Rose. I'm all that you've thought about for the past three years."

He's right.

His dark gaze tries to pull me in. "Think about it. How better to get even with them? Come to my side. Together, we will build this place up. Can you think of a better way to get back at them? They were ready to just hand Bill's bar over. They didn't even vet the man who was buying it."

Why did my mom kill your dad?

He stares at the phone in my hand, shrugging. "Does it matter? We've all done things we aren't proud of. Doesn't mean we should die for it."

I was right, Draven knows his dad was evil. A man like that is dangerous, one with no conscience.

What do you want me to do? I ask.

The smile on his face tells me he thinks he's winning. "Help with the ordering, the hiring, things like that. Nothing too strenuous." His eyes slide over me.

I stand up. **Fine, I'll do it but I'm not starting until tomorrow.** I shove my phone in my back pocket.

"Good," he says, watching me walk towards the door.

Before I head out, I turn towards him and open my mouth, all but choking on what I'm about to say. "I'll keep your secrets, if you keep mine," I say aloud.

He runs his tongue over his teeth. He nods once. "Welcome aboard, Billie Rose."

I step out, closing the door behind me. The man with the sucker is standing beside the door.

Was he eavesdropping?

My eyes narrow on him.

"I thought you might need a ride home," he says, stepping around me. He heads towards the back door, not even pausing to see if I'll follow.

When we get outside, I inform him I do not need a ride. He ignores me as he storms around the side of the building.

"Get on the bike," he orders, nodding his head towards the most beautiful bike I've ever seen.

"Jesus," I whisper, running my finger over the blue-black roses painted on the gas tank. I can't help it. I'm my father's daughter when it comes to bikes.

He shoves a helmet in my stomach. "Get on."

I push it back at him. "Why the fuck would I get on a strange man's bike?" I ask, taking a step away from him.

He tips his head, running a tattooed hand over his mouth. It's covered in black ink.

I take another step back.

"A stranger or a strange man?" he asks calmly.

Hugging myself, I back away even farther. "Both," I reply. "My car is right over there." I drag my eyes away from his and point. "Right there under that parking light."

Everything fades away as I stare at the light bouncing off the cement. A vision of my grandpa and I dancing there takes up the space in my head. I double over, groaning as the reality of everything comes crashing over me.

I'm so wrapped up in my memories that I don't notice the stranger approach me. He brushes a thumb over my cheek, snapping me out of my thoughts. "You don't have a car here, do you?" he asks. His brown eyes are softer now, kind. He hands me the helmet again, this time not as aggressive in his actions.

"I'll go fast," he coaxes teasingly.

I look past him towards his bike and then back at the spot where I left all my happiness three years ago. Jesus, I just need out of here.

I take the helmet and shove it down on my head as I walk to the bike. "You better not be a serial killer," I tell him.

He laughs as he straddles the bike, holding out his hand to help me on. I don't accept the offer. I've ridden on the back of bikes my entire life. I don't need anyone's help. Once I settle in behind him, reality of what I'm doing weighs on me. You can quit harping because I know how stupid this is but what is one more bad decision.

He rolls out onto the road and wraps one hand over mine, making sure they are clasped tightly around him, then he gives me exactly what he promised.

Yes, I tip my head back and stare at the stars as we fly down the open highway. I'm putting all my faith in a stranger, one that made me come on his sucker. I smile to myself. For the first time in so long, I feel alive. Truly alive.

After a while, he slows down and heads towards the warehouse. Wait, I didn't tell him where I live. But he doesn't take me there. He pulls off the road to a spot on the opposite side of the lake. He kills the motor. I slowly slide off, removing the helmet.

He stays on the bike, watching as I shake my hair out. "Feeling better?" he asks.

I nod shyly, the tough girl I pretended to be left behind at the bar. "Why did you bring me here?" I ask, hesitantly. Does he know I live just on the other side?

The stranger laughs. "I found this spot the other day. Don't you think it would be a perfect spot to build a house?"

This makes me smile. "It would, you could put the house right there." I point, before turning to face the water. "Then you could sit on the porch and watch the sun both rise and set.

He swings his long leg over the bike. I hold my breath as he gets off, still a little nervous. I mean, he could have brought me here to take advantage of me and then drown my ass in the lake.

I quickly point across the water towards the twinkling lights of the warehouse. "That's where I live, my family will be getting up soon. I should go."

The look on his face makes me pause.

"So, maybe you could put in a good word for me with the owner."

I'm confused for a moment but then I realize he's talking about the land. He wants to build a house here. "Oh, yeah. I guess I could do that but…" I let my words trail off. I can't do that. I just can't bring a strange man home and say hey, I met this dude at the bar, and he wants to buy the tract of land on the other side of the lake.

He laughs. "Hey, no worries. I get it. Your secret is safe with me."

My eyebrow shoots up and he laughs harder. Oh, he thinks he's cute, does he? "For your information, I don't have any secrets from my family."

He shakes his head. "Okay, sweetheart. Whatever helps you sleep at night. We can hash this out another time."

I watch as he gets back on his bike and fires it up. "Get on, I'll take you home."

I inch away from him. "I'm good. I can find my way from here." And then I take off running, dodging branches as I make my way through the trees to the other side of the water. I hear him take off down the road, so I slow my pace, breathing a sigh of relief. I survived. I went out into the big bad world all by myself and survived.

Chapter Seven

Billie Rose

"Up, up, it's time to get up," my mom singsongs, pushing the curtains back, letting the sun pour into my room.

I pull my pillow over my head. Ugh, I feel like I just fell asleep.

Maybe because I did.

She rips the blankets away from me and tickles the bottom of my feet because she knows I hate it. I kick at her but then a masculine hand grabs my leg. Great, dad is here too. Lovely, I toss the pillow I'm using to block the light at him.

My eyes blink open slowly as he catches it. But it's not my dad. I jump up and throw myself at the man standing at the foot of my bed. He laughs, taking a step back to steady us. "You're getting a little too big to be hurling yourself at an old man like me," he says, snuggling his nose into my neck.

I've missed him so much. When he sets me down, I race to my phone. *Uncle William! I didn't know you were coming.*

William is my mom's best friend. They were in the foster care system together when they were young. Uncle Raffe told me the other night about the abuse they suffered at the hands of a priest in charge of their care at a boy's and girl's home.

My mom crosses her arms over her chest. "Uh, hello. The party?" She grins at her best friend. "I told you, she never listens to me anymore." She throws her hands up in the air. "I'll leave you two to reacquaint. I've got to get the food ready." She pauses by the door. "Get dressed. I want you downstairs and presentable in an hour."

I nod, ignoring everything she just said. I'm rushing around, trying to find something to wear for the day. William sits on the bed, his eyes roaming over my room.

"It looks just like it did when you were a little girl," he twirls his finger around.

I roll my eyes, grabbing my phone off the dresser. *You think they would let me update my room? They still treat me like I'm five.*

He nods, he knows how they are. I don't have to explain anything to William. He's the best. I motion that I'm going to change in the bathroom quick. When I come back out, he's right where I left him.

96

I plop down beside him. *I'm so glad you're here. How long are you staying?*

His brown eyes roam over my face. "I don't know. Maybe a week."

My bottom lip pushes out. *Only a week?*

William chuckles. "Penny stayed back in San Diego. I can't leave her there to run the business alone for long. She'll kick my butt."

I doubt that. She doesn't even kill spiders that are in her house. I don't think she's capable of kicking your butt. I smile at him, leaning over to rest my head on his shoulder.

He pats my cheek, kissing the top of my head. "How've you been, kid?"

I run the pad of my finger over the cool glass on my phone before answering. *I'm here.*

He shifts on the bed, forcing me to look at him. "That's good. Sometimes, all we can do is just be. Is that where you're at?"

Nodding, I stand up and walk over to the window.

"Have you been talking to someone?" he continues, and I realize my mom has brought him here for me. She knows how much I love William. He is kindness incarnate. But I can't even share my problems with him. He wouldn't understand. No one will.

We should probably get downstairs. Mom will have my hide if I'm not on time.

He comes up behind me and wraps his arms around me. "They're worried about you."

We stare at each other in the reflection of the window. He continues, "Maybe you should talk to someone outside of the family."

I look down at my phone. *Like a shrink?* I wrinkle up my nose at the idea. Anger is slowly seeping into my muscles. She brought him here because she knows how much I respect him. How dare her?

"Billie Rose, take a deep breath, I'm not here to pressure you. It was just a thought."

Pulling myself out of his arms, I sit down angrily on my bed and grab my boots. I'm so sick of everyone trying to "help" me. Can't they stop already.

He crouches down in front of me. "So tough," he says quietly.

I hold up a finger, stopping him. *Don't even compare me to her. I'm so sick of everyone doing that. I'm nothing like her.* I stand up and storm out of the room. When I get downstairs, I plop down in a seat next to Jackson and busy myself in my phone, ignoring the lot of them.

Jackson bumps my shoulder with his. "I thought you would be happy today."

My eye roll and eyebrow cocking must be on point today because he throws his hands up in surrender and leaves his seat for one on the far side of the room. My gaze roams over the space, taking in all the bikers in their cuts. It must be a formal club party or some shit. My eyes stop on my dad's, and we begin a stare off.

Roses and Skulls

I win. He looks away as my mom rushes to his side in excitement, clapping her hands. "He's here! We can start the party now." She barrels past me when the door opens behind me. My dad looks irritated as fuck. Strange, because he's rarely annoyed by her.

Carson and Cole take the seats on either side of me. "This should put a smile on your face," Cole says, flicking me in the chest. I grab his hand and squeeze it, making him wince.

"Jesus, Rosie. I thought you would be happy that your crush is here."

What the fuck? Carson laughs when he realizes I have no idea what they're talking about. "Oh fuck, this is going to be good. And we've got the best seats in the house."

"Billie Rose, come here," my mom says behind me.

I give the twins a dirty look as I stand up and spin around to face my mom… and the stranger who made me come on his sucker last night. He smiles at me like the cat that ate the whole fucking canary.

What in the fuck is going on?

"Elijah, you remember Billie Rose," my mom says, bouncing on the balls of her feet. Clearly happy her nephew is here.

Fuck. It's Elijah. The candy man is Elijah.

To be clear, he's not her real nephew, it's just what she calls him. Just like I call his dad, William, my uncle.

Oh shit.

The stranger, aka Elijah, smiles wide. "How could I forget little Billie Rose." He steps towards me and before I can make a dash out of here, he wraps me up in a giant bear hug, ruffling my hair.

Jesus, he smells good. This is not fair.

A hand wraps over my shoulder and drags me away from him. My dads' fingers dig into me, holding me in place at his side. "I believe we have some business to discuss," he tells Elijah, a clear warning to stay away from me in his tone.

My dad takes his free hand and holds it up to his mouth, whistling for his officers. "Table, now."

Mom stomps her foot. "Dammit, Dirk, the food is ready. Club business can wait."

He shrugs, shaking his head. "Sorry, hun, if he is going to prospect, he's got to expect his meals a little cold."

And with a tip of his head, Elijah follows him, along with the others. The double doors to the meeting room slam shut behind them.

The women and remaining club members all make their way outside to the patio where I'm assuming the food is set up.

Prospect? I ask, mindlessly, turning in circles, my head and my heart struggling to make sense of it all.

Cole and Carson start laughing, punching each other. "Told you she didn't know," Carson says.

"Boys, go get yourself something to eat," mom shoos them out the door. "Billie Rose, I told you Elijah was coming to stay with us. That he was prospecting."

Did she? No, because I would have remembered any conversation concerning him.

My eyes lock on the doors he's behind. How did I not recognize him? Oh, maybe because it's been fourteen years since I saw him last.

I rush past her, and head outside. The world is spinning. Jackson calls after me, but I ignore him. This can't be happening. He's just arrived, and he already knows all my secrets.

When I get to the treehouse, I lock myself inside and rummage through my little box of treasures until I find the blade I've hidden there.

After shoving my jeans down, I pierce the soft flesh and breathe a sigh of relief.

Okay, everything is okay.

Yeah, sure it is.

Nothing is okay.

My chimes jingle in the breeze on the other side of the door. My head drops in shame as blood pours out of the cut I just made. Grandpa would be so disappointed in me.

I brush the blood away with my thumb, sucking it in my mouth. When the coopery taste hits my tongue, I cringe inwardly. I'm so stupid. So, fucking, stupid.

A knock on the door sends me scrambling to pull up my pants. *Hold on,* my phone tells my unwanted guest.

When I open the door, Jackson is facing away from me, staring at the forest floor. He backs up slowly, holding his arms out to his side in a gesture of protection. I just about trip as he continues pushing me back farther into the tree house.

"What in the fuck?" he whispers, turning around once the door is shut firmly behind him.

I hold my hand out in question, bored with his shenanigans already.

"There are hundreds of crows out there. Jesus, Rosie, it's creeping me the fuck out." He flips his hair out of his eyes, holding it in place on top of his head. I push past him and open the door a crack. "Don't," he yells, reaching around me to slam it shut again.

Sighing, I push him back and then turn and open the door. When I step out, I see why he is concerned. There are crows littering the ground. When I crouch down to their level, one hops towards me, and she drops another glass bead at my feet.

I sign thank you with my hands as I take in all the other black birds around us. Holy shit. When I stand up and walk farther out into the clearing, they flap their wings and flutter around me. I start to spin in a circle and smile. A full out smile. This is so amazing. My crow flies around my head.

The arrival of a stranger makes them caw and fly to the very tops of the trees. I stare up at them, my face warming as the sun kisses my cheeks.

"Hey, man, did you fucking see that?" Jackson asks Elijah.

When Elijah doesn't answer, I glance over my shoulder. He's pissed. I guess he didn't recognize me either. I'm sure he's shitting himself over the whole sucker incident.

"Can you give Billie Rose and I a minute. We've got a lot of catching up to do."

Jackson's eyebrows pull together, and he looks to me for an answer. He would never leave me. Never.

Sorry, Elijah, Jackson was just going to escort me back to the warehouse because I have to tinkle. Maybe we can hash everything out later. My phone throws his words from last night back at him.

I take Jackson's arm and when we walk past Elijah, he smirks. A full out smirk over his devilish face.

Now I see it. Yeah, I see the boy beneath the man. The one who got me in trouble more times than I can count. He was always conning me into doing something stupid with him. That is until my dad put a stop to the visits when I was five.

On our final visit, I broke my arm roller skating with him. He let me roll up his skateboard ramp and I fell backwards, catching myself with my left arm. I remember him saying, *"I can see your fucking bone, Billie Rose. That's so cool."* And then I passed out.

My dad never let me go visit with mom after that. He and I stayed home. I was sad at first because Elijah was my friend. He was the only one who ever let me do anything fun. Dangerous maybe. But fun, nonetheless.

When Jackson and I get back to the party, it's going full swing. I pat Jackson on the back in thanks and then high tail it into the house, jogging down the hall to the bathroom. When I get inside, I run my hand along the top of the mirror, snagging the only weapon in my arsenal. A blade.

Just one more. This will be the last time. I know I have to quit. My legs look terrible.

A knock on the door makes me jump.

Just a minute, my Australian friend tells whoever it is.

I quickly slide the blade under the soap dish and open the door.

I'm met with a hand in the center of my chest. He pushes me back, kicking the door closed behind him.

"Jesus, stop," I whine, thoroughly annoyed at this point.

"Whatcha doin?" he asks, his inked hand still firmly between my breasts.

My eyes roll high into my head. "I told you, I had to pee." I rise on my tiptoes, trying to get in his face.

"And did you?" he asks, not in the least bit intimidated by me.

"Did I what?"

He laughs. "Did you pee?" He steps back, nodding his head towards the toilet. "Go ahead. I'll wait."

104

Roses and Skulls

I take a deep breath and pull my dark hair high up on my head, wrapping a band from my wrist around it. I tighten the ponytail, giving me time to respond. "So, why don't you tell me about this new death wish you've seemed to have acquired over the last fourteen years."

Elijah tips his head as he pulls a sucker from his pocket. "What do mean?" he asks before pushing the candy in his mouth.

Not fair. Not fair. Not. Fair.

My nostrils flare as I try to shove past him. "You know my dad will kill you if he finds you in here with me."

He grabs my hands in one of his and spins me around harshly, pressing my back against the door, hands pinned high above my head. "I would be more worried about him finding you at The Black Rose some evening."

His leg pushes between mine and I glare at him. "Fuck you," I hiss. "I'm nineteen. I can go where I want."

"Can you though? It seems no one from the club knows you work there. Seems you are keeping a lot of secrets, Billie Rose." He dips his head, brushing his nose over the line of my jaw.

"Stop."

He pulls back, locking eyes with me. "You didn't tell me to stop last night," he says with a smirk.

I try to pull my hands away from the door, but his grip only tightens. Tears begin to blur my vision. I turn my head away from him. "I hate you."

"Hmm," he hums, not the least bit fazed by my admission. He releases my hands and steps away but not before plucking my phone out of my back pocket.

I try to grab it from him, but he shoves it down the front of his pants.

"Are you kidding me? You're acting like a twelve-year-old bully." I stomp my foot.

A loud knock makes me jump again. Jesus, can't people use the other fucking bathroom?

My eyes widen as I urgently hold my hand out for my phone.

"Billie Rose, I know you're in there, open up," Dan growls from the other side of the door.

Oh no! God, can this day get any worse?

"Give me my phone," I whisper yell.

Elijah points to his crotch. "You're free to get it yourself." His mischievous brown eyes taunt me.

"You have until the count of five and then I'm kicking this door down," Dan warns.

I almost cry out in frustration as I stare at the ceiling and delve into the front of the asshole's pants.

When I pluck it out, I quickly type, *I'm busy. It's my time of the month.* That should get him to go away.

"Wrong answer, little girl."

Sighing, I open the door and just as predicted, I catch Dan with his foot raised, about to smash the door to smithereens.

His gaze roams over me and then they focus on the man standing behind me. No doubt with a smirk on his face.

Dan's eyes narrow and he cracks the knuckles of one hand in the palm of the other.

Are you kidding me?

"Sorry, big guy, Billie Rose here clogged up the toilet and was too embarrassed to ask anyone for help. So, I rushed in for the rescue."

I'm going to kill him.

Uncle Dan doesn't buy it, I can tell by the way he grabs my arm and drags me out of there.

"You can thank me later, Billie Rose," Elijah calls down the hall as Dan continues to haul me out to the kitchen. He shoves my butt into a chair and then pulls one up to sit directly in front of me.

I raise my eyebrows, ready for the ass chewing to commence.

"I heard voices," is all that he says.

I hold up my phone, shaking it and then the thought of where it's been makes me drop it in disgust on the table.

Dan runs his fingers through his beard, taking me in. His eyes pause on my jeans and his brows pull together in concern. "Did you hurt yourself?"

I look down and see a spot of blood on my pants. Fuck. I pick up the phone and type, *I cut myself shaving.*

He seems to buy it. He glances over his shoulder and leans closer to me.

"I heard you, Billie Rose. You." His finger pushes directly over my heart. I'm sure he can feel the stupid thing trying to beat out of my body.

You know, you should see someone about that. Voices in your head aren't good.

Great, I hurt his feelings. His big shoulders fall. He's giving up on me. He was kind of the last man standing anyway. Everyone else gave up a long time ago.

And then he reaches out and plucks my phone from my hand and throws it against the wall beside us. I watch in horror as it shatters to pieces.

Slowly, I face him. Maybe I didn't hurt his feelings after all.

My dad is standing in the corner, watching the whole scene go down. He walks towards us and spins a chair around, straddling it. He looks from Dan to me. Laughter filters in from the outside but inside it's quiet.

I cross my arms across my chest, focusing on my knees, trying to tamp down the tears that are threatening.

"I heard *you*," Dan says again, this time much softer.

My mom walks in just then. Great, the whole family will be here for the show. She rushes over and starts scooping up pieces of my phone. "What happened?"

"Leave it, Jess," dad says.

She holds the broken fragments in her palm, taking us in. "Dirk," she begs.

"No. It's high time we stop coddling her and I'm sick of hearing that Australian fuck answer for my daughter."

I keep my eyes trained on my knees, not ready for any of this.

I've been longing for them to push me. To stop treating me like a broken doll but now that it's happening…

My mom slams the broken phone down on the table and leaves the room, sniffling as she goes.

"Go, I'll take it from here," my dad tells Dan.

Dan stands to go after her. "Talk, goddammit," he says, tugging gently on my ponytail as he walks away.

"Why are you so angry?" Dad asks once we're alone.

I turn my stormy eyes his way, silently asking if he really wants to go there.

I'm met with his calm ones. Clear and blue as a quiet summer sky.

"Let it out," he says, resting his chin on his arms that are folded across the back of the chair.

When I glance down the hall, I see Elijah leaning against the wall. He's weaving something back and forth through his fingers. When the shiny metal catches the light, I close my eyes. He found my blade. He's not letting me out of here without speaking. Because if I don't, he's going to tell them everything.

His fingers halt and we stare at each other for a moment before my dad realizes what has captured my attention. Elijah straightens, grinning at my dad as he salutes him, then he spins on his heal and walks back down the hall.

"Stay away from him," my dad says as he turns his attention back to me.

I'm not sure where the laughter comes from. I suppose from that little place deep inside where I keep my crazy. We all have it. It's like a freaking jack in the box. You crank on that fucking handle, spinning slowly, hoping that it won't make an appearance because you know it's going to scare the shit out of you when it does. You know it's going to eventually rear its ugly head.

And then pop, there it is and sure as shit, you jump a mile. Why? You know it's coming, so why is it such a surprise?

The sound of my laughter filters outside as Uncle Raffe opens the sliding glass door. He pauses on the threshold.

I stand up, doubling over, holding my gut, I'm laughing so hard.

And then the world stops spinning, and I shove the jack in box right back down where he belongs. Slowly, I straighten, wiping the tears from my eyes with the palms of my hands. "Oh, dad, sometimes you're priceless. Elijah is the last thing you should be worried about."

My dad's eyebrow cocks.

Not this time, dad.

"You want to know why I'm angry?"

"I asked, didn't I?"

I pull my shoulders back and then with as much venom as I can muster, I spew word vomit all over the place. "I'm angry because this entire club has seemed to have forgotten their fucking oath."

My dad stands slowly, his eyes never leaving mine.

I take a step towards him. "You throw a party for everything under the sun while Bill rots in the ground."

"Be very careful what you say next," he warns.

Narrowing my eyes, I take another step forward. I tip my head, looking up at him. He looks down at me, and I can already see the disappointment forming. I wonder how let down he was when he found out he was having a daughter and not a strong son. Someone who could take his place someday.

"I'm angry because the club failed him, they failed me… *you*, you failed me."

Elijah returns and is literally at my back. "Billie Rose, not like this," he cautions.

"But it is like this. Can't you see? I'm trapped. You might as well have left me in the pickup to die right alongside grandpa, because it would have been better than living like this."

My dad flinches, his mood ring eyes turning a sad black.

I back away from him, bumping into Elijah before shoving him away. "I have to go get ready for work." I wave a hand in dismissal as I head towards the stairs.

It's then I notice the entire club just heard my rant, thanks to Raffe leaving the door wide open. I drop my face towards the ground and leave them all behind. Just like they left grandpa and me.

While I'm putting makeup on for the first time since the night of my last high school dance, I ignore my mom standing behind me. She watches as I work meticulously to turn myself into the woman who's going to set things straight. I'm going to get justice for Bill.

When I finish, I stand up and pull my leather pants a little higher over my hips. I stare at my reflection in the mirror before finally shifting them to look at the older version of myself, her arms crossed over her chest.

"Whatever is going on, you don't have to do it alone," she says quietly.

"I'm just going to work. Hard to believe, I know, but I actually got a job all by my little ole self."

She smiles sadly. "Oh, how I've yearned to hear your voice."

My thighs tingle, the urge to cut courses through my veins, the blood begging to be freed.

"Where are you working?" she asks as if we're just two friends bumping into each other on the street.

I sling a bag over my shoulder, answering shortly, "The Black Rose."

She wraps her arms over her stomach. "The bar," she whispers to herself.

"The bar," I repeat. "Lanie's boyfriend, Draven, offered me a job when I was there the other day, you know, rescuing the crow," I remind her.

"Billie Rose," she breathes out. I know she came in here prepared to back me up. She wants to be the good cop so to speak but there is no good cop in this situation.

I hold my hand up. "I know he is a Devil. I don't care. I want to work there. It reminds me of grandpa."

The lines under her eyes soften immediately. "I understand, hun, but men like Draven are dangerous."

I struggle to keep the color of my eyes steady. Any flicker of change and she'll pounce. She's good at reading them. She's had years of practice with my dad.

"He offered me a job. He's Lanie's boyfriend. Do you really think he would cross a line with me?" I ask, knowing full well the answer is yes, yes he would. Will. Has.

She doesn't hesitate. "Yes. Yes, I do. Billie Rose, trust me, I know all about men like him."

Well, me too, mom. Me too.

"I understand that you and dad aren't going to give me your approval on this, so I'll be getting out of your hair soon. I just need a few paychecks and then I'll move out."

She runs her finger over the rose tattoo that is hidden behind her ear. I can't see it because her hair is covering it, but I know it's there. "This isn't how I envisioned this." She says, walking over to stand in front of the mural she painted on my wall. "But do what you have to do."

I pause with my hand on the doorknob, wanting to get this over with. I'm openly defying my parents. I know there is no coming back from this.

"I know you don't listen to me very much anymore but listen to this." She looks over her shoulder at me. "Trust your gut."

"Mom," I breathe out. I already see the worry dragging her tired shoulders down.

She faces me fully and points her finger towards me. "You remember who the fuck you are. You are a Skull. We won't forget. Don't you." She locks her hands behind her head, struggling to get the rest of her speech out. "When you feel it, you'll know. Don't make the same mistake I did. You have a whole club behind you. I'm not telling you anything you don't know. You're smarter than I am. I hope you prove it."

Part of me is doing this for her. I believe her story. I do. And I know that she would beat herself up if she thought I got hurt because of the choices she made all those years ago. It would destroy her to know that those decisions played a part in her dad's death.

I can't let her take the fall for that. Only one person deserves the blame, and he is waiting for me at The Black Rose.

"I need you to trust me for once," I say quietly, catching her nod before I leave the room.

Chapter Eight

Billie Rose

Jackson and Elijah are waiting for me when I get outside.

"Forget it. I'm out of here. Go away." I shoo them with an exaggerated wave of my hands.

Elijah wraps his arm around my waist. The dark scruff on his face, brushes against my cheek as he picks me up off my feet and dumps me on the back of Jackson's bike. He shoves a helmet on my head before I even get a chance to complain.

Jackson's bike roars to life and Elijah heads over and starts his. Oh my god, are they fucking kidnapping me?

I have no idea where we are headed until we pull up in front of Brody's house.

"What are we doing here?"

"I think you know," Jackson says, taking the helmet away from me.

I stomp my foot. "I have no idea what you two jackasses are up to. I'm leaving. I need to get to the bar."

"Not tonight you aren't." Jackson says. He bends over, wrapping his arms around the backs of my knees and heaves me over his shoulder.

My feet kick out, trying to catch him in the nuts. Who does this oaf think he is?

He tightens his grip with one hand while his other slaps my ass. Hard.

"Oh my god. I'm going to murder you in your sleep," I scream at him.

Jackson laughs. "God, I've missed hearing you chew my ass."

Elijah chuckles too and raises his hand to knock on Brody's door. It opens before his fist connects. Brody holds the door open wide. He runs a hand through his dirty blond hair. "I'm sorry, Rosie," he says as Jackson and I pass by him.

Jackson tosses me onto the middle of Brody's couch.

Elijah sits down on the coffee table in front of me. "This is an intervention."

I chuckle low, the goddamn nerve of him. If he told Jackson and Brody my secrets, I'll skin him alive. I run my hand over the 60's floral print of the couch. Brody's place is like stepping into a time warp. Not because he's making a fashion statement. It's just because he bought the place off an older couple who hadn't updated in 60 years and Brody could give two shits less about home décor.

"Where is Lanie?" Brody asks me.

My first response is the mean one. "She's your niece. You tell me."

Elijah's hand snaps out and his fingers wrap around my neck, dragging my ass to the edge of the couch. He gets in my face. "Not the time, Billie Rose."

I wait for Jackson or Brody to step in but neither do. What in the fuck? Elijah literally has me by the throat.

"Answer," he orders. His brown eyes pierce mine, letting me know he isn't messing around.

"I… I don't know. I thought she was at culinary school in New York," I say when he loosens his grip.

His fingers squeeze gently this time, letting me know he's happy with my response.

I close my eyes when my lady bits signal just how much power this man has over me. Not good. Not good at all. I'm tired of people controlling me. But with him…

"She's not there, Rosie," Brody groans, running his fingers through his hair.

I try to turn my face towards him, but Elijah keeps me in a firm grip, forcing me to look at him and only him.

"Her boyfriend gave her the money to go. She has to be there. Are you sure she isn't just ignoring your calls?"

Brody plops down beside me on the couch. "I called the school and they said they didn't have any Lanie registered there. Will you try to call her?"

Elijah's eyes bounce over mine.

"I... I can't, she blocked me."

"Why? What happened?" Jackson asks.

"It... we just had a falling out, okay? She wanted me to go with her and you all know I couldn't do that. Did you call the police? The hospitals? Did you try her mom?"

I reach for my back pocket and remember I don't have a phone anymore. "Goddammit!"

Elijah rips a wrapper off a sucker and leans over and pushes it in my mouth. I stare at him, dumbfounded by the audacity. It's the same flavor as last night. Was that just last night? It seems ions ago.

"Shut up and listen. Jesus, you don't talk for three years and now you won't shut up," he says, resting his forearms on his knees, pushing himself in my space.

I lean back and rip the sucker out of my mouth, drawing the flavor across my tongue. It prompts me to cross my legs and scoot back, resting against the cushions.

An evil smile spreads over his face, the dimple I remember adorning the twelve-year-old version of him makes an appearance.

"That's better," he says, pleased with my visceral response to him. "Let's not jump hurdles here. Let's get right to the finish line." I stare at the ink on his hand as he runs the tips of his fingers over the stubble on his chin. My eyes roam over his neck, caressing the dragon tattooed there. They follow a strand of ivy until it stops at the collar of his shirt. "Focus." He taps me under my chin, drawing my eyes back to his.

"Brody here is wondering why Draven would send Lanie away when he just moved in with her. Seems a little strange, don't you think?"

I roll my head towards Brody. Brody is about ten years older than Lanie and I've always felt safe with him. "Brody, I don't know," I answer honestly. I glance around, looking for an escape. I don't want anyone to know what I know. If they figure out who Draven is, they'll ruin all my plans for him. I stand up and try to slide past him.

Brody snags me around the waist and pulls me down onto his lap, wrapping an ankle over his knee to keep me locked in place. His big arm wraps over my chest, holding me firmly against him.

"Lanie hasn't talked to me much since she got her own place. Please help me, Rosie. Elijah told me that you are working for Draven. Maybe you can find out where she went."

I glare at Elijah.

He bites the ball on the end of his tongue piercing, shrugging.

"You said you would keep my secrets," I accuse.

Jackson sits forwards. "What secrets?" His face falls in hurt. "I thought we were friends," he pouts.

"I haven't disclosed all your secrets, so you better behave," Elijah points out.

I roll my eyes and turn to Jackson. "There are things that can't be shared between cousins," I say, trying to ease the betrayal I see on his handsome face.

He flips his hair with the shake of his head. "I'm not any more cousin to you than he is." He nods towards Elijah.

True but…

I shake my head. This is all too much.

"I have to go. Sorry guys, you'll have to figure all this out on your own."

"You're not going anywhere," Brody tells me, his breath hot on my ear.

I thrust my head back hard, hitting him square in the chest. The air rushes out of his lungs, giving me just the time I need to shimmy out of his grip, but Elijah tackles me to the floor, pinning my hands to each side of my head.

His dark brown hair falls into his eyes. "We are not your enemy." He drops his forehead to mine. "You know more about Draven than you're sharing."

I don't say anything.

"Come on, Rosie. We aren't letting you go in there alone. He's dangerous," Jackson says from somewhere nearby.

"I'm just working there because I love the bar," I pant, trying like hell to shove this buffoon off me.

"I didn't say we were taking that away from you. But we're going to have your back, Rosie."

"Why are you even here?" I ask Elijah, ignoring Jackson.

He smiles. "Someone from the club called me. They knew I'd send you for a loop. Set you off balance."

I don't know who called him, but it pisses me off. He's ruining everything. "I need to get to work. Get off me."

"No. You're going to get me in. We're going to see what he's up to, together," Elijah says.

I roll my head back and forth on the floor. "No, you're prospecting for the club. Draven will see right through that shit."

"Wrong. I'm working for you first and foremost. The club second."

I glance up at Jackson. He nods. "Me too."

"The club comes first," I whisper, turning my head away from them.

Jackson runs his hand down my hair, playing with the ends. "Not anymore, Rosie. I've watched you suffer for the past few years. I know you think I didn't see over your walls, but I did. I just didn't know how to knock them down."

122

I bite my lip, watching him and Elijah in my peripheral vision.

"Curtain left, in comes the wrecking ball." He chuckles sadly, pointing to Elijah.

Elijah releases me and sits back on his heals, pulling me up with him into a sitting position. I hug my legs, protecting myself and my few remaining secrets.

My forehead falls to my knees. "I can't have you guys distracting me. It takes all my concentration to stay ahead of him."

Elijah's big palm cradles the back of my head. "Dirk hates me. We don't even have to lie about that to Draven. You introduce me as your boyfriend and ask him if he could give me a job somewhere in his club or at the bar. I'll kiss his fucking ass if I have to but I'm not letting you do this any other way, so it's this or I tell Dirk everything."

I raise my head with tears in my eyes. "Back to blackmailing? I wish you would have stayed in California," I say quietly.

"Hate *me* if you need to hate someone," Jackson says, drawing my attention to him.

"Oh, I do. I hate both of you." I shove off the floor and point to Brody. "And don't think I don't hate you too."

"You're not going to the bar without Elijah," Brody reminds me.

"Whatever, fuck all of you. Tell my dad whatever you want." I flip them the bird on my way out, letting the door slam shut behind me.

I walk the few blocks down to The Black Rose. Standing in the parking lot, I notice a dark figure hovering in the shadows across the road. I salute the president of the Skulls before walking inside.

Draven stands behind the bar, a half-dressed woman draped over one arm. When he notices my arrival, he smiles and shoves the woman to the side. I head straight to my office and lock the door behind me.

The doorknob rattles and Draven starts laughing like a hyena on the other side. "I'm glad to see you made it in tonight."

"I've got work to do."

"Well then, I'll leave you to it," he says rapping a little tune on the wood before walking away.

Good. Finally, some peace.

The first thing I do is rummage through the desk, hoping I can find something, anything. No clues as to what Draven is up to or where Lanie might be.

Maybe I'll just ask him straight up.

The door swings open, interrupting my thoughts. Draven walks in, twirling keys around his finger. "You have a visitor."

Elijah steps in behind him.

"Baby, I told you to wait for me." He leisurely strolls around the room, running his fingers over everything.

Draven looks at me. "He says he's your boyfriend."

124

I snort, slamming the file in front of me closed. "No, he's not."

Elijah throws himself down on the couch, dramatically. "Okay, so maybe she isn't my girlfriend yet. But that's only because her asshole father is in the way."

My fingers drum over the folder. I really want to hurt him.

"Is this true, Billie Rose?"

My gaze slides from Elijah to Draven. "Yes, my father is an asshole, but I believe you already know this." The chair squeaks as I lean back, relaxing.

Draven looks slightly jealous... maybe. The wheels are turning fast behind his eyes as they bounce between Elijah and me.

"I had to sneak in the backdoor because he's hiding out in the trees like a creeper. I mean, for real, man, her dad is a straight up psycho. And don't get me started on her uncle. The dude threw Rosie's phone at the wall today and it shattered in a million pieces." Elijah shakes his head, stretching his long legs out in front of him. "I'm telling you, man, it's not going to be long before they're busting in here to..." Elijah uses air quotes for the next words out of his mouth, "rescue their little princess."

Draven sits down beside Elijah. "You mean Dirk is outside right now?"

"Yeah, man, dude is cray cray." Elijah twirls a finger beside his temple.

I sit forward, making my chair creak again. "He's not going to bust in here. Quit being so dramatic."

"Don't let her fool you, man. Tell him, Rosie. Tell him how your dad's kept us apart for the last fourteen years."

I take a deep breath. If this fool doesn't quit calling me Rosie I'm going to lose my ever-loving mind. Draven's eyes light up with all this insider information.

"Elijah," I warn. "My boss doesn't want to hear about the skeletons in my closet."

"Ah, but I do." Draven says, getting up and walking behind me. He places his hands on my shoulders and Elijah visibly bristles. Draven chuckles. He gives me a light squeeze before letting go and perching his ass on the corner of the desk. "You know, Billie Rose, I would do anything for you. If you and your boyfriend want to hang out here, that's fine with me. Hell, you both can come over to the apartment and hang out if you want. I'm sure you'd like a little alone time." He winks at Elijah before turning back to me.

My stomach coils tight as I realize this is just another game for Draven and I don't like that he's invited Elijah to play. I haven't forgotten just how dangerous he is, and I don't want him messing with my… my friend. Yes, he's my childhood friend.

I look at Elijah. He looks boyish sitting there, hanging on every word Draven utters. Like he's someone to look up to. But when his eyes meet mine, there, hidden behind every shade of brown, is no boy. He's all man, one who came in here with intent.

Well, they can both kiss my ass because this is my game. And I intend on winning.

"No, thank you. My dad is already upset that I'm working here. I wouldn't dare think of involving you in... well, in whatever this is." I motion between Elijah and me.

Elijah scoots to the edge of the couch. "It's love, Rosie. You've always had a soft spot for me."

I roll my eyes and glance at Draven. He's amused. "Whatever, Jesus, I have work to do." I shoo Elijah with my hands. I focus my attention solely on Draven. "The distributor you used ripped you clean the fuck off. I've pulled the file for the one my grandpa used. It's half what you paid your guy. Do you know anything about running a bar?" I ask.

"No. Which is why I hired you. I knew you'd get things back on track." He glances over his shoulder at Elijah. "What are you good at, kid?"

I snort because Elijah is anything but a kid. In fact, I think Draven and Elijah are about the same age.

"I fix things," Elijah says, running his hand through his hair.

Hmph. Fix things. All he's done is destroy things as far as I'm concerned. Everything was going fine until he showed up and now it's all a damn mess.

"I noticed your back door is falling off the hinges. I'll start there, that is if you're offering me a job?"

"He's not," I say, focused on the paperwork in front of me. "Go home, Elijah."

"Now, now, your friend needs a job and I think it will be good for the two of you, to... reconnect."

127

I sigh loudly. I guess this is the game now. "Fine, I guess you both really do want my dad barreling in here."

Draven waves for Elijah to follow him. "Let's have a chat. She'll come around. Just give her time."

When they close the door, I throw a book at it for good measure. Their laughter filters through from the other side.

Fucking assholes. All of them.

I sit there, tapping my forehead. Think, Billie Rose, think. What is it you want? What's the purpose of all this?

One, I want the bar. Plain and simple, she's mine.

Two, I want the man who murdered my grandfather to die while I watch the life slip from his eyes. I want him to know that I didn't give him a pass.

That's what he thinks. He thinks I hate my family so much that I let him get away with murder. And he loves that. It's just one more way to make my mom suffer.

But now Elijah is involved. And Lanie.

What if I'm wrong? What if I should have just told my dad what had happened, the minute I opened my eyes at the hospital?

And that right there is the kicker. I know deep down that's what I should've done. But then again, it would have killed mom.

Draven opens the door and pokes his head in. "Is it safe to come in?"

I cross my arms over my chest.

He slides in. "Listen, I'm just trying to help you out here. You have to admit your family is a bit controlling and I want to give you an outlet. A place where you can be yourself." He tips his head.

I stand up, stretching. "Why is Lanie not at school in New York?"

He pauses and pinches the bridge of his nose. "You know about that?"

"Yeah, her uncle is a Skull. Didn't you think I would find out eventually?"

Draven motions for me to sit on the couch.

"I'm heading out. Just give me an answer, Draven."

He leans against the wall, unfazed. "She asked me to keep it a secret. She didn't want you to know that she had decided to try a new... profession."

My blood pressure rises but I remain cool. "Funny that upon your arrival, she just decided to try something... new," I say with a hint of malice in my voice.

He laughs. "At some point all women have an interest in trying something new. I mean, look at you." He points to me. "I'm sure you never thought you'd be working here, for me. And besides, you've kept a few secrets from her too."

"It's not the same," I whisper. "Something had to have happened to make her change her mind."

Draven walks towards me slowly. "She's fine."

I swallow hard and take a step back, shaking my head timidly.

His eyes darken as he closes in on me, forcing me back into the corner.

"Do you really think I would put Lanie in harm's way?"

I stare at his chest, too scared to look him in the eye.

"I'm sorry," I say quietly, pretending to be ashamed that I thought the worst of things.

He brushes my hair away from my face. "You need to trust me, Billie Rose."

"Maybe I could go see her. Where is she staying?" I open my eyes wide and blink my long lashes, trying to look innocent. But I really need a visual confirmation of her wellbeing.

Draven smiles and dips his head. "She's still angry with you. Give me some time. I explained that I was just trying to help you when she found us in the bathroom. She'll come around."

"Is… is that what you were trying to do? Help me?"

He runs his hands down my arms. "I told you. I'm going to make it up to you. I didn't mean to hurt you." His gaze settles on my scar.

"I'm just worried about her. She's my best friend. I… I wasn't accusing you of anything."

He trails a finger over my shaking bottom lip. "I think you were. But that's okay. How about I walk you out to your car?"

"Um, no, I don't have a car. I've been walking."

His head pulls back in shock. "What?"

"Maybe Elijah is still here. I can catch a ride with him."

Draven stares at me. "He's still here but it sounds like he's scared of Dirk. I'll take you home."

I shake my head back and forth. "No. No, my dad really is outside."

"Well, I wouldn't want him thinking I would let you walk home. I insist."

Oh, fuck. This isn't good. Not good at all.

And I was right, the minute I step out in the parking lot with Draven, dad is in front of us.

"Dirk, I was just getting ready to give Billie Rose a ride home."

I stare at the ground, letting the "men" hash it out.

"I'm here to pick her up. Just like I will be every night she decides to work in this hell hole."

My head bops up. "Take that back. It's not a hell hole."

Dad doesn't even grace me with a glance. "Like I said, I will be here. Every. Night."

Draven laughs. "Jesus, man, you're going to give yourself a coronary. I can see you're upset about her working here. I just wanted to give her a piece of her grandfather back."

My dad shoves him, knocking him to the ground. "Don't pretend to know what my daughter needs." He grabs my arm, but I spin out of his grip.

"I don't need anyone to tell me what I need. I'm walking." I storm off, leaving them to yell at each other.

Men are so stupid. I don't know how mom has put up with so much testosterone over the years. The gravel crunches beneath my feet as I continue walking down the road. I bet Elijah got a kick out my dad and Draven going nuts over me. I'm sure he was watching safely from a window somewhere.

A truck pulls up beside me.

I stop and stare at the moon. Peace, I just want a little peace.

"Can't you just let me live my life?"

My dad doesn't say anything.

I drop my shoulders and open the door. "If you're just going to yell at me, I'm not getting in."

He hands me a box, wrapped with a pretty red bow on top.

I climb up in the truck and accept the gift. "What's this?"

He shifts the truck into gear. "It's a new phone. But just so you know, I specifically asked for a model that won't talk back to me."

I chuckle lightly.

"I love hearing your voice," he says quietly.

"Yeah, well, it doesn't sound the same." I run the soft satin bow between my fingers.

My dad pulls off the road at the very spot the accident occurred. My stomach falls. What's he doing?

He kills the engine. "Of course, it sounds different. You sound like a woman."

I bite my lip and stare at the gift in my lap. "I want to go home."

"I know that just because we forced you to speak, it doesn't mean you're ready to talk, so don't. I just need you to listen."

"Dad, I don't like it here," I say nervously, trying my best not to lose my shit.

He reaches over and grabs my hand. "I don't like it here either. It reminds me just how close I was to losing you."

He doesn't start the truck though.

"That night, I was supposed to pick you up from the dance, but I got a call from one of my guys saying some chick told him someone was selling dope down by the high school. So, Bill said he would give you a ride, he told me to go take care of business."

He squeezes my hand before letting go to run his hands through his hair. He sighs loudly, shaking his head. "I was sitting across the street

133

from the school when Bill picked you up. I watched you and Lanie climb in the truck with him."

I glance at my dad, he looks tired.

"I never did find anyone selling drugs." He looks at me. "When I got home that night and you and Bill weren't back, I wanted to go looking for you, but mom said you had probably stopped off at the bar. I… I should've trusted my gut. I should have looked for you right away." He turns to face the windshield. "It should have been me that picked you up. I fucked up, Billie Rose. I should have put you first. I'm sorry." He buries his face in his hands and cries, "I'm so sorry. I'm so, so, sorry."

My dad is the scariest motherfucker out there and he is sobbing, letting me see a part of him I've never seen. I don't know if he's ever let anyone see this side of him. I've been so selfish, thinking that night had only trapped me… I think he's been trapped too.

"Do you remember that time I climbed a tree when we were visiting Uncle William in San Diego?" I ask.

He wipes his eyes with his tattooed hands before running them down his ripped jeans. He pinches the bridge of his nose and stares out the windshield, still unable to look at me. "Yeah, the one that fucking punk talked you into climbing?"

I giggle and my dad finally tuns to face me, his eyebrow cocked high.

"That would be the one, but it wasn't Elijah's fault. He did try to talk me out of it and when I started to climb he followed me up so that I wouldn't slip and fall."

My dad snorts. "Don't think I'm giving him a good guy award for that."

134

I offer him a smile. "Wouldn't think of it."

He thumps me on the nose but returns my smile with one of his own.

"Anyhow, I wanted to see what the birds could see. What was beyond the fence of Elijah's tiny little yard. So, I climbed and climbed until I couldn't."

I let my gaze wander to the windows, looking out at the moonlit road. To the ditch where we landed…

"It was scary, but it was amazing. The wind, the view, all of it. I loved every minute. I could see all the way to the beach." I close my eyes, remembering that day, tasting the salt on my tongue. When I open them, my dad is staring at me, hanging on every word. "I think I could have gotten down on my own, but I knew you would come save me. I guess a small part of me wanted you to. I'm always going to try to climb the tallest tree, dad, but I know you'll be there to get me down."

He turns away from me. "I wasn't there the day of the accident," he whispers gruffly.

"But you were. You came. Grandpa told me you would… and you did. I guess what I'm trying to say is that you have to let me be brave enough to see what's on the other side. You can be there to get me down, to catch me if I fall but you can't keep me fenced in.

"I know. I know." He hits the steering wheel, making me jump. "I had a hard time before, but now…" He chuckles sadly. "Now, I can't do it, Billie Rose. I hate it when you're out of my sight. It about killed me tonight, waiting outside the bar for you to come out. Not knowing what was going on inside."

"What if I help you?" I ask quietly.

Dad tugs on his lip ring, his gaze settling curiously on me. "How would you do that?"

I sit up tall in the seat beside him. "What if we work together."

He tips his head, his interest peaked.

"Just let me climb and I promise I'll tell you when I need help down."

"Billie Rose," he starts.

"Grandpa and I stopped at the bar for root beer floats after the dance. He wanted to talk to me about boys." This makes my dad grunt. I roll my eyes and continue, "I should say lack thereof. Nobody asked me to dance that night."

My dad gets a satisfied look on his face. "I don't see any problem with that. No boys needed to be touching you."

"You see? This is the problem. Dad, do you really think no boy is ever going to touch me?"

He grips the steering wheel, taking a deep breath. "Has a boy touched you?"

I huff, getting out and slamming my door shut. "I'm walking home," I yell, flipping him off over my shoulder.

He gets out too. "Wait, wait. I'll keep my mouth shut. Please finish the story. I'm sorry."

Roses and Skulls

I turn around, the headlights shinning right in my face. My heart starts beating fast. Lights, headlights, that's how it all started.

"Billie Rose?" Dad takes a step towards me.

I hold up my hands, stopping him.

"We had root beer floats and we talked about boys... and he danced with me." I spin, looking for his truck. "We were almost home and then there were lights and we rolled and the noise." I cover my ears, hearing the metal and glass crash around me.

Warm arms pull me in close. "It's okay, baby girl, I got you."

I look up into my dad's handsome face. His beard containing more silver strands than dark these days. "He... he told me you would come," I cry, holding onto him tight.

We stand there holding each other for a long time before my dad speaks. "Bill was gone when Dan and I found you. I thought you were gone too, but then you opened your eyes." He chokes on his words and hugs me tighter.

When the chill of the night air has me shivering, dad walks us back to his truck and helps me inside. We don't say anything on the short ride home.

Mom is waiting by the door when we get there.

"I'm tired. It's been a long day," I tell her.

She nods before giving me a kiss on the forehead. "Go on, get some sleep." She slaps me lightly on the butt and shoves me towards the stairs.

When I get to the top, I look down and see them holding each other. I swallow the lump in my throat and head to my room. I leave the light off and walk over to the window seat, pushing the curtains aside. The moon is reflecting off the lake. It's so bright I can clearly see the dock. "I wish you were down there fishing. You always had the best advice, and I could use some about now. Today was a mess," I whisper aloud.

My bedside lamp turns on, revealing William sitting on the side of my bed.

"Shit! You scared me," I squeal.

He chuckles. "I'm sorry. I thought you would turn the light on when you came in." He moves over to sit with me, looking out the window as he does. He sighs loudly before speaking. "When my dad passed away, we didn't have any family to take me in. So, I went into the foster care system and all the places my dad and I shared were taken away. I wondered if it would have been easier if I could have stayed in the home he raised me in. But now, seeing you, I realize it must be hard seeing him everywhere you go."

I pull my legs up and hug them. "He used to fish off the dock every day. It was one of his favorite places."

We both stare out over the lake. "When will it end?" I ask, my eyes glued to the spot I want him so desperately to be.

William places his hand on my knee. "It never ends, Billie Rose. Grief is a funny thing. It comes and goes in waves. Sometimes, you will remember him, and pure joy will fill your heart but other times, it will feel like a punch to the gut. And the shitty thing is, it will come out of nowhere. Grief isn't a destination, it's a journey. One you will be on the rest of your life."

I can't feel like this the rest of my life. No. Oh my god, I need a blade.

The rest of my life?

My fingers tap frantically over the tops of my thighs. I need relief.

"I'm… I'm sorry, Uncle William, I'm really tired. It's been a long day." I uncurl my legs and stand.

"It has been. Go lie down and I'll sit here quietly until you fall asleep," he says.

My eyes bounce over his moonlit face. He has the same warm eyes as Elijah, but his face is smooth and shaven. His hair is cut and styled to perfection. I bite my lip, shifting from foot to foot. "That's a very nice offer but I'm sure it's been a long day for you as well. Traveling here and…"

"I'm not leaving, Billie Rose." He rises and cups my cheeks in his hands. "Elijah asked me to come and watch over you tonight. He was very concerned with your well-being."

My first instinct is to run because my adrenaline just spiked to a dangerous level. William senses my anxiety and pulls me close to him. "He didn't tell me why and I didn't ask. Elijah didn't betray anything you might've told him. But I know my son, and he wouldn't ask for something like this if he didn't think it was warranted."

I don't move a muscle, holding my breath to the point of passing out. He's not going to let this slide.

"So, I want you to go lie down and get some sleep. Tomorrow, we'll talk to your parents."

My entire body begins to tremble when I realize what he just said. I can't talk to them. No.

His tone doesn't change. He doesn't coddle me. "You're going to talk to them about how you're struggling on a deeper level than they're seeing."

I grip his shirt, whispering, "I can't. I can't." My forehead rolls over his solid chest.

"The Billie Rose that you've let take over probably can't. But the girl you were before..." he pushes me away from him, looking me directly in the eye. "That girl can. The one who fished with her grandpa down at that dock." He spins me around and forces me to look down at the lake.

He shakes my shoulders gently. "She can do it. You just have to let her out."

I angrily swipe at my tears. "I'm not pretending to be anyone else."

"No, I never said you were. But you're hiding behind anger, bitterness, and irritation. I see how you stomp around here. You do that in hopes everyone will stay away and not notice what you're really feeling."

A hiss of air escapes me as I spin around him and stomp to my bed. "I'm not hiding." I throw the blankets back, and irritably slide into bed, huffing as I lie down and pull the covers over my head.

"I'm not going to fail you like I did your mother. I see you, Billie Rose. Elijah sees you too. You can hate me if that helps. It's okay because I'll still love you.

I lie there, still, waiting to see if he leaves but he doesn't. When it feels like what must be an hour, I offer up a small, faint snore. Even then, he doesn't budge. I peek over the blanket and see he's sitting tall in front of the window, looking down at the lake.

"Go to sleep, Billie Rose. I said I'm not going anywhere."

I shove the covers down and stomp over to the bathroom.

"The door stays open," he says calmly.

My feet pause mid step. "Look, I don't know what kind of impression Elijah gave you but I'm fine. He just likes to make trouble for me. You know this."

He turns to face me, tipping his head. "Do you think he is making trouble for you now?"

I roll my eyes. "Um, yeah." I point to him. "He asked you to sit and watch me sleep. Don't you think that's kind of creepy?"

Instantly, I regret my words. Jesus, I'm a terrible person. My uncle is the farthest thing from creepy there is. And Raffe just told me about what happened to him and my mom at the religious half-way house they were sent to.

William stands up indignantly. He storms across the room and pushes me up against the wall, holding me still with one arm while he bites the cuff of his shirt at the wrist. He tugs it down his arm with his teeth, exposing scar after scar. "I see you, Billie Rose. You can't hide from me."

My eyes fall closed.

"Do you know why Elijah picked up on it?"

I shake my head a fraction.

"He walked in on me, while I was in the bathroom. Elijah had to see his father purposely hurting himself."

William drops his hand away from my shoulder. "He saw the signs with you."

My head falls. "I thought you said he didn't tell you."

"He didn't. I saw the look on his face when he asked me to keep an eye on you tonight. It's the same one I saw the day he walked in on me. I'm sure he would have rather not come to me, but he knew if Dirk caught him up here, it would only make things worse."

"How could things get any worse?" I ask sadly.

William sighs. "It's only going to get better from here on out."

He takes my hand and leads me back to the bed. "Lie down and close your eyes."

I do as he asks, feeling the bed dip as he sits down beside me. Then he starts to sing, quietly. Relief washes over me. For the first time since the accident, I don't feel like I have to carry everything. William knows. He knows.

When I pictured my parents finding out, I thought it would be because I had gone too far, cut too deep, or I would get an infection. Not because Elijah would come back into my life and stir things up.

Elijah and his perfect fucking face.

And his warm autumn eyes.

With his sweet candy...

I drift away. Far from the physical world. Dreaming of sitting around a fire, a warm body snuggling me tight. The fire pops, and I raise my eyes, seeing it reflect off the lake. I'm happy, my heart light. If only this was real.

Chapter Nine

Elijah

My old man is taking the night watch. Not like I couldn't have done it, but I think the day was long enough. I didn't want Dirk finding me there and blowing his stack. But don't for one minute think I'm scared of the asshole. Not even close. I like fucking with the man to be honest. It doesn't take much to get him riled up.

Dad thinks I've spotted something going on with Billie Rose because of my experience with him and his self-harm but trust me that's not how I figured it out. He's giving me too much credit. It was the night I had my hand shoved down her pants. My knuckles brushed over her thigh briefly and I felt the raised lines.

Roses and Skulls

And then I saw her looking back and forth before she ducked into the bathroom yesterday. She looked guilty as sin. So, I followed her and sure enough, I found a blade after she left.

Now, back to the fact I had my hand down her pants. Judge all you want but I thought she recognized me. The way her lips parted, and her big galaxy eyes widened. What the fuck was I supposed to think?

I was on my way to see if I could secure a place in the Devil's club per the asshole's orders but then I saw my girl. When did she become *my* girl? Well, I guess she's been mine since we were kids.

Firm believer here in unseen forces. I mean, why else would my dad and Jesse have had to endure so much shit in their lives? It was for us. For Billie Rose and me.

We are destiny.

She's the only woman who will be able to keep up with me, or maybe I should say put up with me. Same thing.

When we were kids, she followed me around like a little puppy. I didn't mind. She made me feel good. Like I was a fucking rockstar or something. Her parents tried to keep us apart, but she would always find a way to sneak out of the house and follow me outside.

She has a lot of firsts with me. Her first time climbing a tree, riding a skateboard, catching a squirrel, jumping off the shed onto a trampoline, you know, all the fun things.

I run my tongue over my teeth as I watch her haul ass down the stairs and slide into the board room. I crack my neck from side to side before shoving a sucker in my mouth. I'm trying to quit smoking and so far this seems to be doing the trick.

As I follow behind her, I think about how her eyes lit up the first time I taught her to light a firecracker. I mean, maybe it wasn't such a great idea to let a five-year-old light a m-80 but you know, she begged me to let her try. You try saying no to someone with eyes like that. It's literally impossible.

Anyhow, I've been waiting for Billie Rose to grow up my whole life.

This girl is going to make all my dreams come true.

I close the door quietly behind me. Her eyes raise to mine as she sits like a queen in her father's chair. Her palms are face down on the table. One slides over and she picks up his gavel and without taking her eyes off me, she whips it at my head.

When I catch it with one hand, her eyes widen.

I shake my head and circle the table, going the long way around to get to her. I trail the gavel across the wood as I make my way around.

Her eyes track me, and when I get to a point where she thinks she can outrun me, she jumps from her chair. I leap on table and hurl myself at her, launching us both against the wall. A woosh of air rushes out of her pretty little mouth as her back bounces off the wall.

Tiny hands push against me. "You're such an asshole. What the fuck do think is going to happen when I tell them?"

I step back, pinning her to the wall with only my gaze.

"What do *you* think is going to happen?" I return her question with one of my own.

"They're going to lock me up," her voice cracks as she pleads with me. "I have things I need to do first. Please talk to your dad. I'll tell them. I will. Just…" A tear slips down her cheek. "Just buy me a little more time."

"Things that involve Draven?"

She nods.

"Let me see where you cut yourself," I tell her, pulling the sucker out of my mouth and pointing at her legs.

Her brows pull together in distress at my request. "Elijah."

When I don't respond or move, she knows she has no other choice. If she wants me to buy her some time before telling her parents, then I need to see. I want to know just how big this problem is.

Chapter Ten

Billie Rose

I shouldn't have let him trap me in here. Dammit, why didn't I high tail it out of the warehouse the minute William turned his back on me?

Truth is, I know there is no way around this. It was always going to happen. It was just a matter of when. I'm hoping that if I show him, he'll think I trust him, and it will give me time to make things right before they find out.

If I can make Draven pay for grandpa's death, then maybe they won't hate me as much when they find out the truth.

Roses and Skulls

The truth. That they are right and I'm just a worthless princess who needs everyone to keep her safe. Someone who needs others to slay her dragons.

Elijah takes my silence as acceptance of his request. He shoves his sucker in my mouth and once again, I find him unbuttoning my pants. Only this time, he drops to his knees in front of me as he slides them down my thighs.

His fingertips dig into the back of my legs, his thumbs brushing over the raised lines that cover them.

I squeeze my eyes shut tight as humiliation floods my system. My cheeks heat to crimson as he takes in the extent of my pain.

His breath is hot over my skin as he leans in close. "Never again," he whispers, pressing his mouth against the angriest of all my scars. His tongue sneaks out and he runs his piercing along its length.

An unbidden whimper escapes my lips and then it happens. The moment I've been waiting for the last three years.

The sky falls.

I stand frozen as Elijah quickly rises in front of me, trying to shield me from the shocked eyes of my family.

In a split second, my dad's fist is connecting with Elijah's cheek. His head whips towards me, blood splattering over my face. He stumbles back, reaching out for the wall to remain upright and to avoid knocking me over. And then my father's eyes drop to my legs, and he sees my exposed secret.

We are both unable to move, suspended in time until my mom's pained cry breaks the barrier. I quickly reach down and haul my jeans up over my ass. I rush past my parents and my Uncle Dan. He tries to snatch my wrist, but I dart away from his grasp.

I grab my mom's keys off the hook by the door and push my way to the outside world. My dad roars and I hear his booted footsteps following quickly behind me. Rachel and Raffe are just pulling into the parking lot and Raffe joins the pursuit, not knowing what has happened but he would follow my dad into the bowels of hell without question.

Just then, a murder of crows blots out the sun above me. I skid to a stop and turn, facing my family. They halt too, staring as the birds lower their flight. Some land on the sun beaten pavement between us. My little crow chooses to perch herself on my shoulder, her black eyes reflecting the look of disappointment on their faces.

"I'm… I'm sorry," I say, taking a step back.

My dad attempts to follow but the birds flap their wings, keeping him where he's at.

I open the door to mom's rat rod, the little crow hopping off my shoulder as I duck inside. She hovers outside my window until I fire up the engine and take off, skidding sideways as I turn out onto the road.

Grandpa's secret driving lessons are finally paying off. I wonder how long the birds will hold them off. Not long I'm assuming.

I need to get away. Far away.

Somewhere that I can go and let all this new pain out.

Roses and Skulls

The drive takes me higher and higher. When I was a little girl, I felt like we were driving into the clouds when we came up here. The naivety of a child. But wouldn't that be nice? If mountain roads took you to Heaven's door. Maybe then I would hear him.

The sun is high when I get to the cabin. I kill the engine, my hands shaking as I unlock the door and rush to the bathroom. I don't even take time to shut the front door behind me.

I kick off my shoe and pull the blade out, falling to the floor. My thumb runs along the edge as I stare at my wrist. They all hate me. They're going to hate me even more when they find out this isn't the only secret I've been keeping from them.

I've been so angry. So angry.

"It's over grandpa. I can't do it anymore. I've made such a mess of things. There's no coming back from this. They know. They have their proof now. Proof that I'm just as weak as they suspected."

I drop my head, tears and snot pouring out of my mouth and nose. With the blade pressed to the center of my wrist, I tip my head back and close my eyes. Just push and pull.

The warm summer breeze wafts in from outside, bringing with it whispers from Heaven.

My eyes fly open and my heart stops. I drop the blade and tip my head, straining my ears, positive that I'm hallucinating but praying I'm not.

The wind encourages the old souls to speak again.

I jump to my feet, staring into the mirror. My face is streaked with tears and snot.

"You're the best of both of them. You just don't see it, but you will." His voice counteracts the words I've been telling myself, that I'm weak.

"And you're not angry, you're just sad, baby girl."

That is what he had said to me the first summer my dad and I stayed home while my mom went to visit William in San Diego.

"Am I angry now?" I ask the mirror.

The tears streaming down my face answer my question.

I'm so sad, grandpa. So sad.

The chimes pull me away from the mirror. The melody draws me outside and I fall to the ground, sobbing when I see all of my chimes hanging from trees and shepherd hooks around the property.

A gust of wind whips my hair around my face as the chimes play a tune in unison. The sound lifting my broken soul.

I cover my mouth with both hands not wanting to break the spell. His voice infiltrates the present. Memories, or whispers from Heaven? I'm not sure.

"This is where I keep all my treasures and my secrets," he tells me in his best pirate voice. He digs in the dirt with his fake hook hand.

I crouch down beside him, squealing in delight when he pulls out a shiny gold box. He wipes off the dirt and turns the latch, revealing all the things that mean the most to him.

He smiles wide, tugging on his beard with one hand, his other holding a picture so we can look at it together. "This... this right here was one of the best days of my life."

I crawl onto his lap and take the photo from him. "Is this mama?" I ask.

"No, that little burrito is you." His warm, rich chuckle shakes us both.

I set the photo back in the box and pull out a book. "What's this, papa?" I hand it to him and dig right back in his box of wonders before he has a chance to answer.

"This," he shakes the book in front of my face, "holds all of my secrets. Sometimes, there are things you can't tell anyone. So, I write them down here."

My gaze drifts down the path now lined with chimes. My feet follow and when I'm standing under the tree, I let my eyes trail over the valley below. I take a deep breath and listen.

"Isn't it bad to keep secrets?" I ask softly, lifting a pocket knife out of the box.

My grandpa wraps his hand around mine, helping me pop the blade out. The sun glints off it, momentarily blinding me.

"If they're secrets that might hurt someone, then that is bad but sometimes, secrets can protect those we love."

My gaze drifts around till it lands on a sturdy stick. I launch myself at it and begin digging in the dirt.

"Skulls protect what's theirs. And occasionally, that involves burying the truth."

"Does mama know where you bury your secrets?" I ask.

He takes the knife from me, closing it before wrapping his fist around it.

"Your mama is the one I'm protecting. I would do anything to protect her." He looks down at me, thumping me on the end of my nose. "And you."

"But I get to know where your secrets are?"

He grins at me. "Because I trust you, baby girl."

I nod enthusiastically as I jump off his lap and jump around him. "I will help you protect mama. I'll never tell her where your secrets are."

Grandpa sets the knife and the book back carefully in the box after he riffles through the other odds and ends he has hidden there.

"I have a secret too," I tell him. He raises his eyes to me, running his fingers through his beard.

"Do you want to know what it is?"

He nods, so I go over and cup my hands over my mouth and lean into his ear. "I have a secret boyfriend."

Grandpa pushes me away from him. Worry pulling his brows together. "Who?" his eyes dart back and forth over mine.

"Elijah is my boyfriend, but daddy won't let me go see him anymore," I say sadly, picking up a stick and drawing a heart in the dirt.

Grandpa smiles at me kindly. "Your dad is just trying to protect you. Elijah seems to cause you a lot of trouble. And don't you think he's a little old for you? You know dads don't like that kind of shit."

I stomp my foot. "Elijah is only twelve and he's the only one who lets me do anything fun."

Grandpa laughs. "Oh, Billie Rose. I love you, girl. Don't let anyone ever steal your spark."

"Does that mean you're going to keep my secret?" I ask shyly.

He pinches his thumb and finger together and draws them across his lips. "These lips are zipped. Your secret is safe with me." He ruffles my hair as he stands, picking me up. He squeezes me tight, brushing his whiskers across my cheek, making me giggle in his arms. "I love you, baby."

When the stick hits something hard, I freeze.

I finish uncovering the box and pull it onto my lap.

My cell buzzes in my pocket again. I pull it out to see Elijah's name flash across the screen. I lay it on the lid and answer the call on speaker phone.

My gaze shifts to the horizon as it absorbs all the colors the sun is leaving behind for the day.

"Tell me where you're at and I'll come get you," he says calmly.

I glance down at the box. What secrets did grandpa have? Are they bigger than my own? Or are they one in the same. I bite my lip.

The chimes ring down the path, reaching my ears as I run my thumb over the latch.

"Do you hear them?" I whisper, so softly I don't know if Elijah heard me.

He remains quiet on the other end.

I stand up and follow the path with the box clenched under one arm.

"Everyone is looking for you," Elijah says on the other end of the line.

I'm sure the little black crow and her family held them off for a little while anyway. I wish I had a family of black crows standing behind me. I pause in front of one of my chimes. But I do have a family at my back. Don't I? Gruff, bearded men with black cuts and boots that wouldn't hesitate to stomp the face of anyone who hurt me.

My knees buckle and a groan escapes me as the realization of how much I've been hurting my family hits me in the gut.

"Billie Rose?" Elijah's voice rises in concern.

The crystals on a chime catch the sun as the wind picks up, sending rainbows littering the ground. I spin in a circle. What have I done? Why did I push them all away?

"Dammit, if you don't tell me where you are, so help me god I'm going to beat your ass."

I run into the cabin. This time slamming the door shut behind me. When I get to the bathroom, I slide to the floor, setting the box in front of me.

I take my cell off speaker and bring it to my ear.

"Please, tell me where you are," he coaxes.

My fingers grip the phone tightly. "You... you wouldn't be able to find me without their help and I can't see them right now."

Elijah sighs on the other end of the phone. "You're so stubborn."

"They hate me, Elijah. And I don't blame them. I would hate me too."

"Jesus Christ, they don't fucking hate you." I hear him moving around on the other end, car doors slamming and hushed whispers. "I'm coming for you. Stay where you're at."

I scoot down on the floor and lay my head back on the cool porcelain edge of the tub. "I've really made a mess of things."

"Listen to me. Things are not as bad as you think they are. I'm going to find you, Billie Rose. Just promise me you won't hurt yourself."

My eyes roam over to the blade I dropped on the floor earlier. I almost ended it all and then I heard them... *whispers from Heaven.*

I choke on a sob. "I... I promise." And then I disconnect the call.

My finger scrolls over all of the messages from my family.

They don't sound mad, but how could they not be? I'm not strong like the rest of them.

Mom: Baby, come home.

Cole: Carson and I will steal dad's truck and come get you. We can be outlaws, together. Tell us where you are.

The thought of the twins stealing Dan's truck makes me chuckle. I have no doubt they would do it too.

Dad: Baby girl, I'm not mad. Please come home.

William: I'm sorry I pushed you when you weren't ready. I can't handle seeing your mom so upset. Please call her.

Dan: I'm going to turn you over my knee, little girl. Pick up the phone.

Rachel: Honey, please call me. I'm here for you.

Message after message keeps coming in and the longer I sit here the more scared they sound.

Jackson: I'm sorry. I'm sorry I didn't see it. You must hate me. Please don't do anything stupid. I'll never forgive myself if you do.

Oh, Jackson. I could never hate you. You've been my best friend my whole life. But how do you not hate me? I've been a terrible friend.

Swiping at my eyes, I sit up straighter. Elijah will never find me. I made sure to shut the location off on my phone when I got in the rod. My finger runs over the metal box, stopping on the latch. I flip it and open the box in one swift movement, leaning over it to peer inside.

I smile at the knife. It's beautiful. It's gold, and black with a bald eagle painted on each side. I flip it open and run the flat side of the blade over my jeans, and then I pull out the book, opening it up.

The first pages are revealing. Grandpa had been in prison. Is that why he missed so much of mom's life? Oh, my god, he killed Crow's brother. I flip through, seeing her name scribbled on the edge of the pages. It must have been so hard for him… and her.

And then the ugly stories that Raffe told me about my mom come pouring from the pages.

I want to kill them. Every single one of them. But how can I leave my baby girl again? Especially, when she's hurting so badly.

Licking my finger, I flip farther in his story, not wanting to read the horrors that my mother suffered and then I see my name.

I didn't think I could love anything as much as I love Jesse but then she gave me a granddaughter. What a beautiful thing she is. Her name is Billie Rose. I made a promise to her, that I would always be there for her.

So, I'm laying my secrets here, along with all the trinkets that remind me of the man I used to be. I need to be better for this new little girl. She is going to change us all, for the better. She is the innocence that we all crave. My only concern is that life is going to come along and steal it from her.

Her tiny eyes sparkle with something special… I hope she never loses it. We're all going to do our darndest not to let that happen.

And that is where it ends. No! There has to be more. Where are all the secrets?

I dig through the box, pulling out a skull ring, some old concert tickets, brass knuckles and a joint. At the very bottom, I find receipts to a place called Bell's House of Tail. They are for hundreds of dollars, every month, for years.

Bell's House of Tail? What the heck is that? Whatever it is, Grandpa spent a lot of money there.

Then it hits me.

No.

I google it and sure as shit. It's a whorehouse over in Trap County.

Nope. No way did my grandpa cheat on my grandma. He was devoted to her.

This just can't be. That's not the kind of secrets I thought I would find here.

I shove everything back in the box except for the knife. I take the box back down to the tree and bury it. I can never tell anyone about what I found here.

My eyes take in the scenery around me as I shove dirt over it. How could he do this to grandma?

The hundreds of chimes play an eerie melody.

"You know me, baby girl. You know me."

"I don't know anything anymore," I say aloud, standing and stomping on the dirt to pack it down tight.

After his secrets are hidden, I run back and hide in the bathroom. The sun is setting and it's scary out here all alone. I sit on the floor and rock myself back and forth, staring at the blade lying on the floor.

I squeeze my eyes shut tight and rest my head on my knees. Elijah made me promise I wouldn't do it. I've never broken a promise to him. Never.

Roses and Skulls

He'll never find me. He doesn't know about this place.

If I just make it to morning, then I can leave and find somewhere else to go. I've wanted my grandpa to talk to me and now that he has, I don't understand. I'm more confused than I was before. Nothing makes sense.

I'm tired of feeling so alone.

Yes, I know it's my own fault.

"Please just give me something. Work your magic up there and let something go my way." I groan in the space between my knees and my chest.

And then the bathroom door slams open.

I raise my head slowly and in the doorway stands the most terrifyingly, beautiful creature I've ever seen.

He blinks, his gaze scanning me from head to toe. When he sees I'm fully intact, he lets out a harsh breath.

I continue to rock back and forth. "I didn't do it. I didn't do it," I cry, tears streaming down my face.

Elijah sits down in front of me and pulls me into his arms. "I know, baby. I know. You did so good. So good." He kisses me on top of my head, and I whisper a little thank you to grandpa. I don't know how much longer I would have been able to hold on.

Chapter Eleven

Dirk

I was both relieved and pissed as hell that the only call she answered was his. My fist was just about to connect with his ugly face when he held up his hands and said he knew where to find her.

I'll never get the image of him kneeling in front of my daughter out of my brain.

But right now, I'm focused on what I saw after that. The brutal scars that covered the tops of her legs. How did I not pick up on how much she was suffering?

Elijah sits next to me, pulling out a fucking sucker and shoving it in his face. God, how I would like to hurt him again.

Roses and Skulls

The little fucker tricked me. Got me to jump in my truck with him by my side and he had no clue where she was. But he did hear something, windchimes. I knew right where she was when he told me. I tried to shove his ass out of the moving truck once he was no longer useful, but Dan wrapped his arm around my neck and kept me in the driver seat.

"She answered him. Let's see if he can talk her down," he said.

I'm her dad. I'm the one who should be talking her down. But then again, I've obviously failed her.

And now Raffe, Dan and I are all standing in the living room, listening to their conversation. The kid was kind enough to leave the door open.

"I didn't do it. I didn't do it," she cries.

My baby girl is crying and it's not me in there to soothe her.

I take a step towards the bathroom door when Raffe's hand slaps across my chest. We stare each other down, memories of the past flashing between us.

"You did so good, baby. So good," Elijah says to her.

She continues to cry, and it takes everything in me to stay where I'm at.

"It's okay, I'm here. Shh, everything will work out. You'll see."

"They all know. I c-can't g-go back," she stutters, trying her best to calm herself.

"What? Do you think none of them have destructive ways of easing their pain? We all do, Rosie. Don't you dare feel ashamed for it. We just need to find you a better way, and we will. I'm going to help you."

I catch a glimpse of them in the mirror on the door. As hard as I try to tear my eyes away, I can't. My daughter peeks up at him and turns in his lap so that she is straddling him. I clench my fists by my side. Raffe keeps his hand on my chest.

Tears continue to streak down her cheeks as she runs her fingers over the cut on his cheekbone, courtesy of me.

"I'm sorry he hit you."

The little fuck laughs, wrapping his arms around her and pulling her close. Too motherfucking close.

"You have nothing to be sorry for. Besides, I would take a thousand punches from him to be with you."

She looks away. "You don't even know me," she says quietly. "I'm not the same girl who used to come visit you in San Diego."

He grabs her chin, forcing her to look at him and I just about lose my shit. Dan rests his hand on my shoulder.

"Listen to me. You are the same girl. Sure, you seem a little angry, but you know what?"

She shakes her head sadly in his grip.

"Grief masks itself as anger. I don't think you are as angry as everyone thinks you are... you're sad."

She burst into tears again at his words. "I've been so mean to everyone and I don't want to be, I just…"

He wipes tears from under her eyes with his thumbs. "You were just trying to keep them away so that they didn't find out," he finishes for her.

She nods and drops her head to his shoulder, her body shaking as she cries it out.

I watch as he rubs his hand lightly over her back. He shushes her in a way that actually seems to help calm her down.

"Do you remember on your last visit when you and I snuck out in the middle of the night? We walked along the beach because you wanted to give everyone in the entire club a souvenir from your trip."

Billie Rose doesn't lift her head, her voice coming out muffled against his shoulder. "I was so worried dad would catch me. He was so mad about my arm."

"Anyway, I still have them."

She sits up and stares at him while wiping at her eyes. "I was so upset I had forgotten them."

He takes her face in his hands. "You knew then that your club was your family. They don't hate you; I promise. They love you more than anything. Especially, that old grouch you call dad."

My eyes narrow and Raffe shakes his head.

And then a sound I haven't heard in so many years filters out from the bathroom.

Her laughter grows and grows.

I rub my hand over my chest. It's music to my ears.

"Did you see his face?" she chuckles, wiping at her eyes.

Elijah throws his head back. "Yeah, I'm glad he didn't have his gun on him, or I would be dead right now."

She smiles at him. "I think he thought…" Her cheeks turn pink, and she looks away from him shyly.

"What?" he asks, teasing her. "What do you think he thought?"

Billie Rose leans forward, her lips entirely too close to his ugly mug. "You're lucky he didn't see you a few nights ago when you…"

That's it. Game over. Dan wraps his arm around my shoulders and literally lifts my ass off the ground, tossing me outside.

I gain my footing and barrel back towards the door. Raffe follows us out, shutting the door firmly behind him.

"Let's go home," Raffe says, twirling his finger in the air.

This makes me stop dead in my tracks. "Are you fucking kidding me? No, I'm taking her home, right now."

Dan folds his arms across his chest, moving in front of the door, blocking it like the fucking wall that he is.

"Didn't you just hear them?"

He shrugs his shoulder. "They were flirting, so what?"

My fingers grip my hair as I spin around. "Has everyone lost their fucking minds? She is my daughter and there is no way I'm leaving her here all night with him." I stop and spit on the ground, showing them what I think of the situation.

"Do you remember bringing Jesse here?" Raffe asks, leaning a hand on the side of my truck.

"What does that have to do with…"

"Sometimes, girls need more than their dad," he says, sticking a knife in my back.

"Listen, Dirk, I'm not trying to twist the knife after everything that's happened but," Raffe continues.

"No. Stop. I don't want to hear it."

The wind picks up, rattling the chimes that I've hung here over the years. I've bought every single one she's made.

The sound deflates me.

"Remember how mad Jesse was at Bill. And you saw how that turned out in the end. Trust your daughter, Dirk."

"I'll let Elijah know we're leaving. They can come back down tomorrow," Raffe says, turning to go back inside.

"Argh!" I yell at the Heavens. How did all this happen? I had everything under control until that fucking accident.

Chapter Twelve

Billie Rose

Elijah puts his finger over my lips, stopping me from finishing my sentence.

"Your dad is here," he says quietly.

I stare at him for a second. What? They came up here, together?

My feet propel me out of his lap. Elijah stands slowly, reaching for me. "It's okay, Billie Rose. He's not mad at you."

My heart feels like it's going to beat out of my chest. Of course, that's how Elijah found me. He heard the chimes.

Just then, a knock sounds on the wood trim of the door. I jump back, finding Raffe standing in the doorway. "Hey, I think you need a little time to… to think about things, so we're going to head back down the mountain and we'll see you tomorrow."

Elijah nods, reaching out to shake Raffe's hand. "I appreciate that, man. I'll take good care of her."

Raffe remains near the doorway after their exchange. His eyes remaining on me, he nods. "Tomorrow."

I give him a little nod back, wringing my hands together.

"I love you, Billie Rose." And then he turns to walk away.

My heart feels like it's being ripped out of my chest. "Wait," I rush after him, catching him at the front door.

He pauses with his hand on the handle.

"Is… is dad outside?"

"He is." His gaze bounces between me and Elijah.

My fingers nervously curl around the bottom of my t-shirt. "Um, could you show Elijah where all the kitchen stuff is. I'm hungry and we all know I can't cook."

His shoulders drop. "Yeah, I think I can handle that. I'll get Dan to help."

I squeak when I hear that Dan is here too.

He chuckles quietly. "Did you really think we would let your dad come up here alone with Elijah?"

A small smile breaks out over my face. "No." I look back at Elijah who is leaning casually against the door frame. "I'll be right back."

He grabs the back of my neck and pulls me towards him. "You can do this," he whispers in my ear, then he lets me go.

Raffe watches us and I'm not sure what he thinks of the way Elijah touches me. He's rough yet gentle. Whatever he thinks, he doesn't say anything.

I take a deep breath before opening the door. When I open it, I'm greeted to a wall of muscle. I reach out and place my hand on Dan's arm. He turns and stares down at me, a puff of air leaves his mouth when he sees me. "Billie Rose."

"Hey, I was wondering if you could help Raffe in the kitchen. I'm a little hungry." My gaze falls on my dad who is pacing back and forth in front of his truck.

"Sure thing, baby girl." He ruffles my hair and walks around me, heading inside.

It's then my dad notices me. He stops dead in his tracks. His chest heaving as if he just ran a marathon.

We stare at each for a long moment. Neither of us knowing quite where to begin. "Do you want to sit for a minute?" I ask.

He nods and throws out his arm, pointing to the bench Lily made for us. It's made of an old pickup tailgate. It's the coolest thing ever.

When I sit down, the night air makes me shiver. Dad promptly takes off his jacket, wrapping it around my shoulders. "I'm fine," I protest but he ignores me. It smells like him, like leather and smoke. It brings back memories of me curling up with it and napping when I was little. At one time, I could curl my whole body inside, like a little pill bug. Anyway, it makes me feel safe.

He takes the seat beside me, staring out at the darkening forest.

"Who taught you to drive?" he asks, breaking the silence.

I let out a long sigh. "Grandpa. He used to let me sit on his lap. But I don't know if that makes me a qualified driver."

My dad shakes his head, chuckling to himself. "I should've known."

"Was it you?" I ask, bringing my foot up to the bench and resting my chin on my knee.

He glances at me. "Was what me?" His head hangs low as he stares at his hands dangling between his legs.

"The chimes."

Slowly, he looks at me. I fight to not glance away. He nods.

"Why?" I ask, hugging my leg to me.

He leans back on the bench. "I don't know. I guess because you made them. You don't draw me pictures to hang on the fridge anymore. I'm proud of them." He shrugs. "And it made me feel close to you." His head turns away from me so I can't see the emotions playing out over his face.

The wind blows gently, and I close my eyes. I know what I need to do. I have to start somewhere. Maybe this won't hurt as bad as I think it will. But I must do it. I owe this man something.

I rub my hand over my throat, the words feeling stuck there.

The chimes jingle in the wind and I look up, taking it all in. "The night of the accident, Grandpa asked me if I heard them. I was so confused because I didn't hear anything. Then he told me that he could hear wind chimes and that they were whispers from Heaven."

My dad slides closer, putting his arm around me. He pulls me into his chest.

"I thought maybe I could hear him through them, but none of them worked."

He squeezes me tighter.

"Until I came here." I sit up and turn to fully face him. "I... I was so embarrassed at what you saw today that I didn't even notice the chimes when I got here. I just rushed for the bathroom to..." I wince and look away from him.

"What are you saying?" he asks calmly, a slight crack to his voice.

I rub my lips together, struggling to find the right words. "In my mind I didn't see a way past what happened today."

He makes a strangled noise beside me. I know I'm hurting him right now, but I have to start somewhere. I can't even look at him. I just can't stand to see how much pain I might be causing. But I need to finish what I started. "But then I heard them, the chimes." He places his hand at the back of my head, pulling me towards him, resting his chin on the top of my head. "I heard him but not like he was a ghost or anything. I just heard his words from the past." My fingers wrap around his t-shirt as it catches my tears.

"I'm sorry. I'm so sorry, dad," I whimper.

"It's okay, baby. It's okay. We're going to get through this. I promise."

I push off his chest and stare into eyes that mirror my own and I see his sadness. "I have more I need to tell you but..." I shake my head. "Can you give me some time? I need to sort things out in my head."

"This is a start, baby, it's a start. God, I've missed you so much, Billie Rose."

I swipe at my eyes and offer him a smile. Not the usual smirk I give him, but a real, heartfelt smile. One that I hope reaches my eyes.

He leans forward and kisses my forehead.

"Now about that boy," he jokes.

I give him my best eye roll. "He's not a boy and no..." I hold up my hand, "he's not my boyfriend. He pisses me off way too much."

My dad's eyebrow goes up, but I ignore it. That look may bring grown men to their knees, but it only makes me want to give him a harder time.

"I'm going to trust you here, for tonight, with him," he chokes on the last word. "But I need you to come home tomorrow, yeah?"

I nod as I slide his jacket off my shoulders, ready to go back inside.

He stops me. "No, keep it, you might need it." I see the internal struggle pulling his eyebrows together. This is hard for him. I can't hold that against him. He would shove a knife in his own heart for me. I know he would.

"We'll be safe. I promise," I tell him, bumping my shoulder against his.

He stands up and pulls me into his arms gruffly. "I love you so much. Don't ever doubt that. There's nothing we can't work through. Okay?" He leans down, staring straight into my eyes.

"Okay," I say, still amazed he is letting me stay here with Elijah.

Dad squeezes me one last time before shoving me towards the door. "Tell the boys I'm ready to head out."

I walk to the door and then look back, watching him climb in his truck. "I love you, dad."

He taps his fingers over his heart and then jumps in the cab.

Chapter Thirteen

Elijah

Every time she looks at my cheek she winces. "I'm fine," I tell her for the hundredth time since we sat down to eat.

The guys left a while ago. A-fucking-mazing that her old man left her with me.

There is no way the dude trusts me and if he does, he shouldn't.

I tip my head as she glances away from me, her cheeks turning the cutest shade of pink. It's got me wondering if she's used to being alone with a man. And when I say man, I mean someone other than her family.

"Do I make you nervous, Billie Rose?" I finally ask, curiosity winning out over my love of seeing her like this.

Her tiny fists wrap around the bottom of her t-shirt, curling it up so I catch a glimpse of the porcelain skin beneath.

It's adorable how shy she is all of a sudden.

She covers her mouth with her hand, swallowing hard. "No," she lets her hair fall to the side of her face, shielding herself from me.

I lean over and brush it behind her ear. "Don't hide from me."

"I'm not," she says grumpily, her brows pulling together.

"Come here," I tell her, patting my leg.

She pulls her head back. "Um, no."

"What are you so afraid of?"

She looks away. "I'm not sitting on your lap, Elijah."

I run my hand over my leg, catching her glance towards my lap. She turns herself around in her chair, avoiding me completely.

Oh, Billie Rose. Does she really think that just because she let her emotions get away from her today that I'm going to treat her any differently? Fuck no.

Slowly, I rise to my feet and walk up behind her, wrapping her hair around my fist before she realizes what's going on. She struggles to turn around, but I hold her still. Her hands fly up to mine. "Owe," she whines.

I tug her head back, so she's forced to look up at me.

"What the fuck are you doing? My dad trusted you to stay here with me." She tries to unwind her hair from my grip, but I just force her head back farther. She grabs the seat of the chair, breathing through her nose at the pain I'm causing.

"Oh, he doesn't trust me." I lean over, brushing my nose along hers. "He just had a weak moment."

Her breath catches in her throat and her legs squeeze together.

"Because he definitely shouldn't have left me alone with you. I'll admit, it was a pleasant surprise."

I pull away a few inches, watching the rise and fall of her chest.

"W-what do you mean?" she pants, trying to sit up but realizing I have her pinned with nowhere to go.

A slow smile spreads across my face. "We're going to play a little game," I tell her, noticing how big her pupils get at my suggestion.

She squirms in the chair. "What kind of game?"

My fingers loosen in her hair as I gently massage my fingertips over her scalp. "We are going to play a little game of show and tell."

Immediately, she tries to get up and run but I tighten my grip and whip her back into the chair.

"Shit, you fucking asshole. That hurts."

I round the chair and crouch down in front of her, pulling her face close to mine. "But you like pain. Don't you?" I ask, running my thumb over her trembling bottom lip.

Her pupils are full blown now as her eyes dart over mine. She's trying to figure me out. When she doesn't answer, I let go of her hair. "I'm not like everyone else, Billie Rose. I'm not going to make things easy for you."

She swallows but doesn't look away. "What does that mean?" she asks breathlessly. The tension between us is palpable. I feel her fear with each beat of my heart just as she senses my need for her. It frightens her.

"Has anyone besides me, touched you here?"

I press the palm of my hand against the seam of her jeans, pressing down hard. The little gasp that she makes, pumps blood straight to my cock.

"Elijah," she pleads on a whimper.

"Answer me," I demand, pressing harder against her.

Her knuckles turn white as she wraps her fingers around the seat of the chair. "No," she finally responds.

"That's good." I slide my hand down her thigh. "Because I would have to kill anyone who had touched what's mine."

She looks up at me through her lashes, her eyes blinking rapidly.

"What about here?" She shivers as I brush my knuckles over the swell of her breasts.

"No."

When my thumb runs along her bottom lip, she turns her head away, my finger trailing across her cheek.

The clock ticks on the wall beside us. Tick, tick, tick. My gaze scours her face, searching for answers to her reaction.

"Your lips belong to me."

Her eyes drop closed.

"I want a name, Billie Rose."

She sucks her bottom lip between her teeth, biting down hard. I reach out and grab her by the cheeks.

Billie Rose releases her lip, indentions from her teeth left behind. Leaning over, I run the tip of my tongue over them and then I kiss her.

My parents are soul mates. I know most think that sounds cliché. But I was lucky enough to witness the phenomenon that is true love. And if I'm being honest, I think Billie Rose has seen it too. I believe Jesse and Dirk love each other fiercely.

I remember the first summer she didn't come to visit. Jesse said Dirk was busy and couldn't make the trip and that he didn't want to be away from Billie Rose for two weeks. And then the next year was just another version of the same lie.

For a few years, I didn't think much about it. I was young and busy with my friends. I mean, sure, I missed the little girl who followed me around with stars in her eyes, but I had my life. It wasn't until after her accident, when Jesse came and showed me pictures that my heart began to ache.

The carefree girl she'd been had vanished. Her soul was buried so deep that very few traces of her remained.

So, I spent the next few years turning myself into the man she was going to need. One that would unapologetically reach in and pull her out.

After several minutes, I allow her a breath. When our eyes lock, she pulls back slowly. The fear in her eyes, makes my heart soar. She understands now. I'm going to drag her kicking and screaming out into the open.

"Give me a name, Billie Rose. I'll get it out of you, one way or another."

Her hand comes up and presses half-heartedly against my shoulder. "I don't... I can't... Elijah, just stop. Please. I can't do this now."

I sigh and rub my fingers through my beard, not giving her an inch.

"If..." she stops, taking a deep breath. "If I tell you, it doesn't change anything. I'm not going to stop working at the bar."

She crosses her arms across her chest when I don't respond, the whoosh of blood pumps in my ears as my anger soars.

"Did that asshole, Draven, touch you?" I ask, deadly calm. I'm already picturing how I'm going to peel the skin away from his body.

"Elijah," she reaches out and touches the side of my face. "It's okay, he didn't. I mean, it was nothing, really." Again, her teeth pinch her bottom lip. "He just, well, he pressed his lips to mine. Just once, and I stopped him." She pauses and drops her head. "It was no big deal," she finishes quietly.

There are several ways I could handle this. A call to any member of the club would be the easiest, less messy way, for me that is. But I believe in handling my own business. Not that I'm above asking for help. Just like tonight, I needed to find her, and I wasn't above asking Dirk for help to do that.

I place my hand on the back of her head and she releases a tiny sob. It sure doesn't sound like no big deal. In fact, I think it was quite the opposite.

Her fingernails dig into the skin on her arms.

"Let me erase him from your memory," I tell her.

She shakes her head back and forth, swiping angrily at her tears. "I don't think you understand. My dad will literally kill you if he finds out about the other day at the bar. You're crazy if you think we can do more," she coughs.

But I saw the flash of electric blue that sparked in her eyes. She might be able to hide from everyone else, but I see her. Oh, do I see her. They have no idea just how powerful this woman is going to be. I knew it was going to take a strong man to walk beside her.

I should thank Dirk for doing such a good job of keeping her locked away for me and only me.

Draven is just a little annoyance. A blip on the radar. One I'm going to eliminate.

"Oh, we're going to do more." I grab her around the neck and hoist her up and out of her chair. "Much more," I say as I drag her face towards mine.

Chapter Fourteen

Billie Rose

Elijah is backing me up the stairs with his hand around my throat.

"The next little game we will be playing is called truth or dare," he says, content with the pace he's set for us.

"Um, I think you've gotten the wrong impression of me," I tell him, my mind skittering through the pros and cons of letting this continue. Because I know he'll stop if I ask him to. Yeah, yeah, he'll stop. Won't he?

When we get to the top of the steps, he flips the light on and glances around the room.

"Elijah, I can't do this," I whisper quickly, my stomach doing a huge flip at the sight of the bed.

I'm out in the middle of nowhere with a man I'm not sure I know.

His warm brown eyes meet mine. The satisfied grin he gives me, makes me feel funny. "Good girl," he says, walking me over to the bed and gently pushing me down on the mattress.

I'm so confused. Why is he praising me for telling him no?

He rolls me to my side and then curls up behind me. He reaches over and flicks the switch by the bed, shutting the light off.

I lie there, frozen, his body is pressing into mine with each breath he takes. I wait and wait and when several minutes pass, I break the silence.

"Is that it?" I ask, starring at the wall.

He raises his head off the pillow and lays his cheek against mine. "Billie Rose, I will never force you to do something you're not ready for. I'm happy you told me. I was hoping you would stop me. It's easier than me having to stop myself."

"But you were so…"

"It was a test." He kisses me on the temple. "I want to do bad things to you, Billie Rose, and I will… when you're ready."

A test? A fucking test?

I flip over on my back, ready to give him a piece of my mind but his palm covers my mouth before I can open it.

He stares down at me. "You were testing me too. Don't lie."

Was I?

His hand slides away from my mouth. And then his lips are covering mine. This time it's slow, and gentle and nothing like the one he laid on me downstairs. That one was possessive, and it stole my breath. Both are... absolutely toe curling.

I squeeze my legs together as a slow burn begins in my nether region and he chuckles in my mouth, catching the slight movement.

My phone has been quiet ever since my family figured out where I was but now it's buzzing again. Elijah slides his hand under my ass, not breaking our kiss as he slips it out of my back pocket. He holds it over my head before breaking away from me to see who it is.

No, I don't want to stop. Ever. He could kiss me forever and I wouldn't complain. He seems to be the only thing that can shut my brain off. His eyes meet mine in the dark and he growls, sitting up, his fingers flying across the screen of my phone.

I sit up and try to grab it from him but the look he gives me pauses my hand mid-air.

Then my phone starts to ring, and he places his finger over my mouth, telling me to keep quiet.

"Hey, man. Yeah, you know, her old man is an asshole, they had a blow-out, but everything's cool. She'll be back to work in a couple days, sorry we forgot to call you." He narrows his eyes at me when I part my lips. "Naw, we got a place to stay tonight but we'll be back in town tomorrow. She just needs a little time to regroup."

185

Then his eyes drop to my thighs and his gaze turns murderous, making me whimper and scoot back on the bed. His hand darts out, grabbing me around the knee, keeping me in place.

"She's good. I promise. We'll be in soon. Sure, man, I'll tell her. Yep."

Elijah drops the phone on the bed before crawling over the top of me, forcing me to lie back. "How, may I ask, has Draven seen your legs?" he growls.

I swallow hard. Shit, this is worse than facing my dad.

"It-it's not what you think," I stammer. "He, well, he caught me cutting myself and..." I thought my dad had an intimidating look but it's nothing like Elijah's. His brows are furrowed together, his dark hair falling over his forehead and his brown eyes are hard, unrelenting as he glares down at me.

I whimper again, whispering softly, "I'm sorry."

He blinks a few times, shaking his head like he's coming out of a fog. "So, he didn't touch you?" he asks, brushing the hair away from my temples with his thumbs, his weight fully on me now.

I shake my head. "I told you, no one but you has touched me... there," I finish, glad that it's dark so he can't see my cheeks flush with my admission.

"I wish you would trust me enough to tell me why you are working there. I can see that he scares you."

My eyes squeeze tightly shut. *Please don't force me to tell you. Please don't.*

186

It's as if he can read my mind. "I'll figure it out soon enough. You've had a long day, try to get some sleep." He rolls off me and shifts us back into our original position.

My breath whooshes out in relief when I realize he isn't going to push me on this.

"Goodnight, Billie Rose," he says against my ear.

I try to wait for him to fall asleep first, because, well, I'm nervous. I've never slept beside a man before. What if I drool, or worse yet, snore? But he is so quiet behind me, the only way I know he's awake is by the soft touch of his fingers, rubbing gently over my stomach. My mind starts to wander, going through all the events of the past few days.

Everything seems to be unraveling at the seam but then again, it kind of feels like maybe it's all coming together. I'm so confused. The timing of Draven showing up and then Elijah. I smile to myself in the dark, remembering his lips against mine. He effectively erased the feel of Draven's. And he did it without even knowing. Or did he?

Chapter Fifteen

Billie Rose

I woke up early, before him. I moved over to the chair so I could just sit and stare at him without the fear of reaching out and touching him. The sun is pouring in through the windows and he looks like a dark angel being bathed in light.

He's fucking gorgeous. I'm trying to separate the man I see before me from the boy I knew all those years ago. But they are one in the same. My chin rests on my knee as I hug my leg close to me.

For the first time since the accident, I slept all night and I actually feel rested.

The wind is blowing this morning, and I can hear the chimes calling to me through the walls. Today's message is screaming at me to open up to him. To tell just one person my secrets. I know this sounds weird, but I feel grandpa today.

It was the first time I woke before dawn and didn't need to run to the bathroom to release the pain. It's still there but it's not screaming to be let out. It's just simmering beneath the surface. I keep waiting for it to roll to a full boil but nothing yet.

He told me that someday a boy would come along, and he wouldn't let anything stop him from being with me.

I didn't believe him at the time but now… Elijah is here with me. Alone in a cabin, hours away from the warehouse where no doubt my dad is pacing the floors.

Grinning to myself, I pull my other leg up.

His tattoos are beautiful. I suspect the handiwork of my mom. My eyes trail over the dark ink covering his arms and running over his hands. A shiver courses up my spine and I close my eyes, remembering the first night I saw him at the bar, before I knew who he was.

Last night, he said he still had the shells that I collected in San Diego. He carried the bucket for me and shined the flashlight over the sand as I cradled my broken arm. I mean, it was kind of his fault but not really. He warned me that it was a bad idea. My actions, my consequences.

Elijah stretches one hand over his head and the other dips below the waistband of his jeans a tiny bit. My mouth suddenly becomes dry. The tip of my tongue comes out to wet my lips when his eyes open, instantly connecting with mine.

He doesn't pull his hand out of his pants. No, instead, he shoves it down farther and I see it wrap around his, um, yeah, that thing.

Quickly, I jump to my feet, embarrassed for him and myself.

"Where are you going, Rosie?" he asks, his voice rough from sleep.

I stop and fist my hands at my sides. "I'm going to make breakfast."

"I've got something you can eat," he taunts. And with that I'm flying down the stairs.

He's much easier to deal with when he's asleep. I know he's going to end up getting me in so much trouble with dad. My stomach tightens. My dad. I've forgotten all about what he learned yesterday. Who knows, I could walk back into the warehouse and right into an intervention. What if they make me go back to that dreaded therapist?

I hated it there. It made me feel broken.

My hands rub over my thighs. I am damaged. Not on my legs but in my damn head. I think too much. It's all I do. Think. Think. Think.

A hand slaps my ass, making me screech and rise to my tiptoes. I turn around with my hand raised, ready to slap him across the face, but his fingers wrap around my wrist, holding me there.

"What are you thinking about?" he asks.

My eyes narrow. Does this man have some kind of weird intuition, one where he can read my thoughts?

"Let me guess. You're worried about going home today."

I spin myself out of his grip and go back to the sink, rinsing out the mugs I retrieved from the shelf. "Wrong," I quip, shaking the water from my hands.

He laughs, making his way over to the cupboard, pulling out the container of coffee. "I doubt that but let's hear it."

Crossing my arms over my chest, I scowl at him. "Well, first of all I'm not going home. I have to work at Junkyard Treasures at ten this morning, so I'll drop you off on my way."

"No can do, Rosie. Dad says I have to have your ass to the warehouse by ten. I'll text Lily and let her know you'll be late."

My heart stops. Maybe my fears are valid. William told him to take me home. They are probably waiting with guys in white suits and a straitjacket in just my size.

Elijah continues working on our coffee while I sit in the chair, planning a way out of this. Okay, so if I drive, maybe I can make that hairpin turn at the bottom of the mountain and throw his ass out. I mean, I'll tell him to tuck and roll right before, so maybe he won't get hurt.

My shoulders drop. I can't hurt him. So, I could just get to the warehouse, shut the engine off and then the moment he gets out I'll lock the doors and run.

To where?

Aunt Katie is in Florida. Grandma just joined her. I could go there.

Elijah snaps in front of my face.

When I blink at him, he grins. "Come on, let's go sit outside."

He guides me to the bench where dad and I sat last night. It's so beautiful here. I hadn't been here since…

I sigh loudly and turn away from the view to stare into the cup of coffee Elijah placed in my hands. All my memories are either before or after that night. It's the moment of time that I define everything else around.

"Why are you scared to go home?" Elijah asks, reminding me that I'm not alone.

My fingers nervously tuck my hair behind my ear. "Isn't it obvious?"

"No, it's not. That's why I asked."

My gaze slides over to him, he has his fingers steepled in front of his mouth. An ankle propped across his knee. I giggle. He looks just like my old therapist. Minus all the tattoos, the brown eyes, and the dangerous glint in his eye.

I shake my head and bite my lip, looking away from him.

"What do you think is going to happen?"

"They aren't going to be able to trust me."

He drops his foot and leans forward, resting his arms on his legs. "It's probably going to take some time, yes. But I think the road goes both ways. You all need to learn to trust each other again."

The wind blows gently and suddenly there are a thousand little rainbows surrounding us. Elijah stands up and walks over to the first chime I ever made. It's made out of crystals. It really is beautiful in the morning sun.

"Your mom told me about how you started making these after your accident." He pauses before flicking one gently with his finger.

"Grandpa told me that the sound from wind chimes were whispers from Heaven."

"Do they work?"

I wonder if he is making fun of me but the way his shoulders tense, I know he's being serious.

"I didn't think so until yesterday. I don't think I had been ready to listen before that."

He spins in a circle, his gaze roaming over my dad's collection.

"What did you hear?" His brown eyes stop on mine.

I pull my legs up and hug them to me. "He told me to trust you."

The corner of Elijah's mouth tips up. "I think we have a ways to go for that, huh?" He gives me his back as he stares out over the amazing view.

"It wasn't an accident," I say quietly, my heart thumping loudly in my ears. I'm risking everything right now. It was one thing when he made me talk, and then showing the world my scars but this... this, he could use to crush what's left of my soul.

He spins around.

"Rosie," he whispers, covering his mouth with one hand while the other grips his hair.

No going back now. "That night I saw the headlights first, and then the truck hit us." I slowly uncurl myself. "I still hear the sound in my dreams." I snort, shaking my head. "I guess they aren't dreams, more like nightmares."

He makes his way back to my side, sitting down and giving me his full attention.

"When everything stopped, it was so quiet. And then a man came up to the driver's window. He smiled at grandpa." I bite my lip and kick my feet back and forth over the rocky ground. "I couldn't figure out why he was smiling. Grandpa was broken."

Elijah doesn't move. Doesn't speak.

This is the first time I've said any of this out loud and I realize just how awful it all sounds.

"He fucking smiled," I say louder. I jump up and grab a rock off the ground, throwing it as hard as I can and then I pick up another and another. "He smiled. He fucking smiled!"

After several minutes of throwing rocks, the size of my fist, I fall to the ground.

Elijah finally moves, coming to sit on the ground beside me, pulling me onto his lap, wrapping his arms around me.

I begin sobbing. "And then he walked away. I heard him yell at someone, telling them that grandpa wasn't alone. They started cursing and I didn't understand," I cry into Elijah's shirt.

My fingers wrap themselves tightly in the fabric, holding him close so when the final words come out of my mouth he doesn't abandon me.

"Then another man came to my window."

Roses and Skulls

Elijah's fingers stoke lightly over my arms.

"It... it was Draven."

His fingers stop, his breathing stops. "Please don't hate me," I whisper, into his shirt. "Don't leave me."

His arms tighten around me. "Rosie, I could never hate you and I'll never leave you. Never." He rocks me back and forth as I sob uncontrollably, letting it all out.

Years of pent-up emotions pour out of me. I don't know how long it goes on. I did feel Elijah shift me in his lap to pull his phone out but other than that he's just held me, letting me cry, snot, and spit all over him. I would be embarrassed but it's too cathartic for me to care.

When I quiet down, he asks the question I've been dreading. "Why didn't you tell anyone, baby?"

My heart squeezes at the endearment in his tone. "I don't know. I didn't know how to deal with grandpa being gone and it was just too hard to talk. And then as time went on, I got angry, and I took it out on everyone but the one person who deserved it. But I see that now."

"Let me help you," He presses his lips to the top of my head.

Something shifts inside me. I lift my head and stare into his eyes, trying to figure out if I made the right decision. His fingers trail down the side of my face, he captures his tongue piercing between his teeth before running it along the bottom of them. "I want to watch you make *him* bleed."

A gust of wind echoes its approval.

I'm listening, grandpa.

I hear you now.

My eyes go back to the first wind chime I made. It's time to remember who I really am. I let Draven steal my spark. Grandpa wouldn't like that.

I reach in my pocket and send my dad a text. Elijah nods his head as he reads my dad's instant response.

"I think this is a great start, Rosie."

My heart feels a little lighter, the girl I used to be stretches, finally awakening after three long years. I take Elijah's hand and we begin to gather up all the wind chimes. It's time for *me* to make amends.

Chapter Sixteen

Elijah

When Jesse called me, I knew I was their final straw. *Finally.* I was up.

I'd been planning and preparing for this since I saw the pictures of her broken body. I'll admit this is not what I expected but it's fine. I'm going to hold that motherfucker down while she guts him.

In my mind, I thought the whole bar thing was just a way at getting back at her parents. My girl is a rebel at heart.

She may forever be daddy's little girl, but she will always be my little rebel warrior.

She sits beside me in her mom's rat rod. The first car my dad ever customized. It's fucking cool and is as old school as you can get.

I've taken after him, my old man, except my taste lies in custom bikes. It's my dream to start up my own shop someday. But first, I need to earn the respect of my girl and her club. All good things come to those who wait.

Don't believe me? I've waited a long time for her and now here she is, sitting right beside me with her tiny hand curled in mine.

She's nervous but I'm going to be with her every step of the way. I'm not going to let her slip back into old behaviors.

By the time we get back to the warehouse, she's shaking.

"You have to trust them, Rosie," I say, shutting off the engine.

She glances around the parking lot, looking for any signs that this might be a trap.

"How much are you going to tell them?" I ask.

Her eyes are swirling with emotions. "I… I can't tell my mom about Draven. She will blame herself. I have to protect her from that."

I reach out and run my hand down the side of her neck. "Do you want me to go in with you?"

She nods but doesn't make eye contact with me. "I can talk to them alone but if you could be around, just in case…"

Roses and Skulls

I lean over and press my lips to hers. "I'm yours for the day," I say, pulling away from her. "You can do this and then we will go from there, okay?"

Billie Rose takes one last deep breath, nodding. I jump out and open the door for her before she gets a chance to do it herself. She peeks up at me, her beautiful blue eyes sparkling in the sun.

The warehouse is quiet when we enter. A breeze blows in from the back, the patio doors open wide. Dirk and Jesse are sitting at a picnic table, their backs to us. Jesse has her head on his shoulder. His fingers scratch gently over her scalp as they stare out towards the lake.

Billie Rose clears her throat to get their attention. I press my hand to the small of her back and guide her towards them as they turn. Jesse tries to rise but Dirk places a hand on her shoulder, keeping her in place. I'm sure he's scared that his daughter is going to spook easily.

She did just runaway yesterday, so I don't blame the guy.

Rosie sits down across from them, and I set the chimes down in front of her and then squeeze her shoulder, letting her know she's got this and then I turn to walk away.

"Wait," she squeaks. "Please stay."

When I spin around, I catch the glare that's being thrown my way, but I don't give a fuck. If my girl wants me to stay then that's exactly what's going to happen.

She gives me a little smile as I sit down beside her, then turns and focusses on her parents.

"First of all, I'm sorry for running," she begins, shifting in her seat. "I know that's not the club way."

Neither of them says anything, letting her continue.

She picks up the chime made of crystals, sending rainbows over the patio and she focusses her gaze on her mother. "I made this one because it reminded me of you. You know, with the rainbows and all."

Jesse is an artist and many of her paintings involve rainbows. My dad said it fit her personality. Her young life was a dark storm, but she always expected a rainbow at the end.

"It's the first one you made," Jesse notes as her daughter hands it to her.

Billie Rose glances at me nervously. I give her a reassuring smile. "Grandpa told me that he could hear wind chimes after the accident. He said they were whispers from Heaven."

Dirk drags his eyes away from his daughter and focuses them on his wife. It's scary just how much he loves them. I have no doubt he would do anything for them. Anything. And I'm coming to find that I feel the same.

Jesse blinks, tears falling to her cheeks. "He... he was alive?"

Billie Rose drops her head, nodding. "I thought maybe I could hear his whispers through them but none of them worked, so that's why I sold them at the shop."

Dirk glances away.

"Oh, baby, how did you get them back?" Jesse holds it up in front of her face, admiring the beauty of her daughter's imagination.

Rosie sits up a little taller. "I got them back because of you."

Jesse shakes her head, confused. "I don't understand."

"You chose a man who always looks out for his daughter."

Dirk covers his face with both of his hands as Jesse looks over at him. I've never watched someone fall in love with someone they're already in love with but I'm witnessing it right now and holy hell do I want it for myself. If I can get Billie Rose to look at me like that, I'll die a happy man.

Rosie pushes the other chime made of silver and labradorite stones. "This one I made thinking of you, dad. It reminds me of our eyes."

He runs his hand over his face before looking down at it.

"I've always loved that I inherited your mood ring eyes. It's my biggest flex," she teases, trying to lighten the mood.

Dirk runs one of the rocks between his thumb and finger. "I don't think that's true. It's your heart, baby girl, that's your biggest flex. It always has been."

Billie Rose looks at her hands in her lap. "I'm sorry about everything. I've been in so much pain." She rubs her hands over the tops of her thighs.

Jesse leans forward. "Tell us how we can help you," she says, her long silver-black hair falling over her shoulder.

Rosie looks up at them through tear filled eyes. "Just know that I'm trying. I… I don't want to hide anymore, and I don't want to hurt myself."

Dirk and Jesse exchange a look.

"We don't want you to move out. If working at the bar helps you feel close to grandpa then…" Jesses pauses. "Then that's okay, just don't leave us. Not now, not after we're finally getting you back. We've missed out on so much the past few years."

"You're not going to lock me up?" Billie Rose asks, her body tensing at the thought.

Dirk reaches across the table and tilts her face with a finger under her chin. "Promise us you won't hurt herself again. That you'll reach out to someone. I don't give a fuck who it is. It can even be this dipshit. But promise me you will never take a blade to your skin again."

I pull a sucker out of my pocket, thinking that a cigarette would be really good about now. Sometimes, I'd like to clock this motherfucker. When I slide it into my mouth, I catch my girl's mouth quirk up on one side.

"I promise," she whispers. When her old man lets go of her, she turns to me, her eyes going to my mouth. "This dipshit has actually been very…" her cute little tongue runs over her lips before she finishes, "he's been very helpful."

Dirk flexes his hands on the table but otherwise remains calm. Jesse jumps up and walks over to the edge of the patio, hanging her chime on a hook that is sticking out from a beam. She stares at it admiringly and smiles to herself, tears streaming down her face, then she closes her eyes and raises her face to the blue sky.

Billie Rose turns back around to face her dad. He raises an eyebrow. "I... I need to talk to you. Later, in private," she says quietly so that Jesse doesn't hear.

He nods.

"I'm going to go change and then Elijah is giving me a ride to Lily's."

His gaze goes back to his wife, who is still smiling up at the sun. She really is stunning. Her daughter equally so.

"Is this something the others should hear?"

Billie Rose chews on the inside of her cheek which is just another way of hurting herself. I reach over and tap there, to stop her.

Dirk doesn't know whether to thank me or punch me for touching his daughter.

"I don't know." She looks to me for guidance. I give her a quick nod. This is definitely something the others should know about. Billie Rose won't be safe until that fuck is dead. I would feel better knowing that the others were watching her back while she brings him down.

But it has to be her... it's the only way she's going to be able to put this to rest and move on.

"Yeah, maybe you should call a meeting but..." her eyes dart over to where Jesse is standing. "It has to be a secret."

Dirk's jaw works back and forth. I'm sure there is very little he keeps from his wife. But I get why Billie Rose wants to keep her out of this, Dirk will too.

"We'll meet at Dan's at six. Don't be late," he tells her.

She rises from the table, and he stands too, pulling her into his arms and hugging her before shoving her towards the sliding doors. Jesse seems to be in a daze as she wanders down to the lake, leaving Dirk and I alone.

"Is she going to be okay?" I nod towards Jesse.

He follows her with his eyes. "Yeah."

And then as quick as shit, I find my back slammed against the wall, her dad's ugly mug right in my face. He's spitting mad. "You better remember who the fuck is in charge real fucking quick."

"She is," I tell him, turning my head and spitting the sucker out of my mouth.

He shoves himself off of me. "This isn't a game, you dumb fuck."

"Never said it was."

He paces the patio.

"You need to trust her. She's just being who she was raised to be. She's trying to protect her," I nod down towards the lake.

Dirk stops and glares at me.

"You're not going to be around forever. You've been setting it up for men to watch her back her whole life. Jackson, the twins, JD, hell, the whole club. I want to be included in that group. I'm not going to hurt her, Dirk."

His eyebrow climbs and he straightens to his full height. "If you think I can't crush your skull right here, right now, you're wrong. I'm not dead yet, kid."

I stand up and walk out to the grass. "Let's go. I'm willing to do what it takes. Even if that means taking a beating from you."

His eyes follow me, his nostrils flaring. Instead of fighting me, he flips over a whole damn picnic table, making enough noise to draw the attention of his wife. And then he charges me, knocking me to the ground. I jump to my feet and manage a solid punch to the side of his face.

He reaches up and runs a finger over his now busted lip. He offers me a bloody grin right before his fist connects with my gut. Oh god. For an old man he's fucking insanely strong.

I right myself as he circles me. "You think you have the balls to date my daughter?" he asks.

Keeping him in front of me, I turn around, noticing Jesse hasn't moved. Her arms are crossed over her chest, but she doesn't appear to be interested in stopping us.

"I think you know I do. Has anyone else ever gotten this far?" I ask, smirking at him.

His eyes narrow before he takes another swing. This time I'm ready for him. I duck, catching him with an uppercut right under his jaw. It doesn't faze him. He just spits blood and spins around, clocking me right in the eye.

This dude is fucking crazy. But here I am, so maybe we're both nuts.

We duke it out for a few more minutes before Big Dan steps between us. I'm not sure where he came from but I'm kind of glad he showed up, because I think Dirk and I would both fight to the death for her.

"I'm not fucking around, Dirk. I want her. And I'll do anything to have her."

He breathes heavily. "She's too young."

Dan stands between us, his eyes sliding to me. "Do you have a fucking death wish, kid?"

"No, I want a life with her. I'm willing to do whatever it takes. I promise. I promise I'll always put her first."

When neither of them responds, I throw my hands up in the air. "You trusted me with her last night."

Dirk glares at me. "What did she talk about?"

I shake my head back and forth. "Oh, no way, I'm not going to betray her."

"Not even for my blessing?" he asks.

Shoving my hands in my pocket, I turn to walk away. "No. Whatever she said to me, she said in confidence. Jesus, I just got her to start talking again. Kick me out, do what you gotta do but I'm not divulging her secrets."

"Stop," he says as I reach out to open the door to the warehouse. "Don't fuck up, cause with her… well, I won't do second chances."

"I don't plan on it." And without looking at him, I head inside with the biggest fucking smile I've had on my face in some time.

Chapter Seventeen

Billie Rose

I was watching my mom make her way down to the lake when it started. My first thought was to run down there and stop my dad from murdering Elijah but then my mom looked up at me. I can't explain how her eyes stopped me, calmed me even. Eventually, her gaze went back to the brawl and so did mine.

My dad isn't hitting near as hard as he could. I've watched him fight many times. The men in the club need an outlet and I've never really questioned it, growing up around it my whole life.

But is Elijah going full out? I don't know, I've never seen him fight.

It's a little unnerving watching them go at it like this. Is this all over me?

Roses and Skulls

"Someday, a boy is going to come into your life, and he isn't going to be afraid of your dad. Nothing will stop him from stealing your heart. Not even Dirk."

"Oh, grandpa, I wish you were here to see this." A smile breaks out over my face as I watch Elijah take a punch to the face. And he just keeps taking it, but don't get me wrong, he's not afraid to fight back.

Dan steps out from the patio and throws his hands out, shoving them off of each other. I start to giggle because it takes him no effort at all. Words are still being thrown but I don't think Dan is going to let them do any more physical damage to each other.

Mom is still watching from the dock. She won't let things get out of control. I drag myself away from the window, trusting that they will work it out. When I get out of the shower, Elijah is perched on the end of my bed.

I lean against the door and stare at his beat-up face. "Come here," I say, waving him into the bathroom. He follows me and sits on the toilet lid while I grab some things from the medicine cabinet to patch him up. I've watched my mom do this for my dad many times.

"Why do you keep doing this to yourself?" I ask him.

He pulls me between his legs and stares up at me. I wipe my thumb over his busted lip.

"I'm not worth it, Elijah."

"Stop."

I bite my lip and continue to clean the blood off his face.

"Your mom has known for a few years that I was coming for you."

My hand pauses over his cheek bone.

"It was her who kept us apart. Dirk took the heat for it, but it was her decision to stop your visits."

I focus on what I'm doing, wondering why my mom would do that. That makes no sense. It's always been my dad who chases the boys away, not her. And Elijah was my friend. My only one. Yeah, I made a new friend in Lanie when she transferred to my high school, but no one could ever replace Elijah.

"You're angry?" Elijah asks as he follows me back into my bedroom.

"I don't know what I am anymore. Here I'm finally ready to tell everyone my secrets and…"

"She saw something we didn't. She said she didn't want to put us in a situation where things progressed before you were old enough."

I shake my head. "Elijah, that makes no sense."

"Doesn't it?"

"No, we were just friends back then."

He nods his head slowly. "We were, we still are." He walks over and sits down in my window seat. "I wanted to come back with her when she visited after your accident. She showed me a picture…" his words trail off.

"Why didn't you?"

He laughs lightly. "Because I would have done something stupid. I wasn't ready for war." He tilts his head to the side. "I needed to become someone worthy to stand by your side."

"But there was no war. There was nothing. Not a single damn thing. Everyone just assumed it was an accident. No one even asked me what happened." I shove off the wall and storm over to my dresser. I open the top drawer and throw all of the newspapers I collected about the "accident" to the floor.

He doesn't even look down at them. "I saw it in your eyes. The war. It killed me that you were going through it alone."

"But I did and don't think I need anyone to help me fight it now."

The fucker smirks. "Don't think I'm saying you can't. I'm saying you don't have to."

My mom bops her head in as she knocks. "Is everything okay in here?" She steps inside, her eyes focused on the newspaper clippings scattered across the carpet.

"Yep, everything is good. She got me all patched up," Elijah says, tapping the bandage over his eye.

Mom bends over, picking up an article, her eyes scanning over the words. "That's good, I just got Dirk cleaned up as well," she says mindlessly. She gathers up all of the rest of them, her brows pulled together.

"I was just showing Elijah what the papers wrote," I say nervously, dropping down beside her to help.

"Yeah, yeah," she scratches her head and then she looks at me, really looks at me. She stands up abruptly. "I... I have to go, are you going to work tonight?" she asks.

"I'm going to the shop to help Lily this morning, but I don't think I'll make it to the bar tonight. I have an apology tour I need to focus on."

She pulls me close, hugging me tight. "You have no need to apologize to anyone."

"But I do. I've been awful," I say, breathing her in. I've missed her so much, but I still feel the separation. It's as if we're standing on opposite sides of the canyon, yearning for each other.

My mother kisses me on the cheek before pulling away. "I'll see you both later then."

When she walks out of the room, my gaze crashes with Elijah's. "Do you think she heard us?"

He shrugs his shoulders. "I think she feels like you are still keeping something from her. But I get it, you're trying to protect her from the truth."

I rub my hands over my thighs. Elijah pulls a sucker out of his pocket and throws it at me. I catch it in one hand.

"It will help, trust me." He winks at me and just like that, poof, my mind is elsewhere.

He reaches behind his head to pull his t-shirt over his head, and I about drop over dead.

I take a step back, steadying myself against my dresser. He tosses it in the trash. "We need to stop by my room so I can grab a new shirt."

My eyes are roaming over all the ink on his chest.

He snaps his fingers, drawing my eyes up to his. The smile he's giving me makes goosebumps erupt over my skin.

I clear my throat and shove the newspapers back in the drawer. "You go on. I'll meet you downstairs."

Elijah just laughs and comes over, smacking me on the ass. "Don't run away this time," he scolds before grabbing my cheeks and pressing his lips to mine.

My hands land on his chest as my eyes fall closed. He's warm and firm. My fingertips curl into him, my nails pressing lightly into his skin.

When he pulls away, he runs his hand down my neck, holding my shoulders to keep me upright. "Isn't this exciting?" His eyebrows raise as he backs away, letting his hands fall from me slowly.

Jesus. I can't think when he is around.

Shit, I didn't ask mom if we could borrow the rod. I have it full of the chimes I'm going to give to my family.

I try to get Elijah out of my mind as I jog downstairs. My dad is sitting at the bar with a drink in his hand. "Hey, where's mom? I forgot to ask if Elijah and I can borrow the rod."

"She's painting," he says, not looking at me.

Okay. I head down to the basement and peek in her room. She's staring at a blank canvas. "Hey," I say quietly as I push the door open.

She spins around, a paintbrush in her hand.

"I was wondering if Elijah and I could borrow the rod?"

"Oh. Yeah, yeah, that's cool," she answers, giving me her back once again.

"Okay, thanks." I pull the door behind me, but I don't close it. I watch as her brush chases the light away. Whatever she's painting, it's going to be dark. I glance behind me at the door that holds most of her darkness.

"Mom?"

She doesn't turn around. "Yeah?"

"Are you mad at me?"

This has her rushing over to me. "No. No, of course not."

"I know I've been a brat."

She pulls me into her art room and sits me down, crouching in front of me. "I'm mad at myself. I promised your dad I would be a fierce mother and I think I failed."

I roll my eyes. "You've been fierce. I promise. You kept Elijah and I apart all these years."

She rests her head on my knees. "I'm sorry. I'm so sorry. I just... I saw how you looked at him and I knew." She looks up at me with tears in her eyes. "I didn't want you thinking about boys."

"Mom," I run my fingers through her soft dark hair.

"I looked at your dad like that when I was too young. Like he was already mine." She swallows. "I didn't want you to grow up too soon."

"But you brought Elijah back?"

"I wasn't going to keep him away from you forever. I just wanted you to grow up without all that." She glances away, grimacing.

"Hey," I grab her cheeks and turn her to face me. "I get it. It must have been hard having a daughter after all you went through." I point to the room across the hall, letting her know I understand.

"I don't know what normal is, Billie Rose. I thought I was giving you normal by keeping you close to the family, surrounded by people I trust. And now, I see how wrong I was."

"Elijah is... well, I wouldn't say he's one hundred percent good. But I think I can trust him. Don't you?"

"Of course, you can trust him," she whispers. "It wasn't him... it was me."

She lays her head in my lap as I stroke her hair. I notice my dad leaning against the wall outside the door.

"We've all made mistakes. But nothing we can't recover from, yeah?" I ask softly.

215

"Yeah," she says, closing her eyes. She's tired. Her long lashes hide the dark circles of exhaustion. I've been so wrapped up in my own pain that I've failed to see hers. I continue to run my fingers through her hair as she weeps in my lap.

My dad comes in and pulls us to our feet. He wraps his arms around both her and I, his eyes meeting mine. All this time I thought it was him keeping me away from boys. And I'm sure it was but I understand now. She was trying to protect me from the horrors she went through. And my dad was only trying to make sure the same thing didn't happen to me.

"I've had the best life," I whisper into her hair, keeping my eyes on my dad. "You did it, mom, you kept me safe. Nobody's touched me. I'm whole. I promise, I'm whole. The accident wasn't your fault. I didn't know how to cope with the loss but I'm learning."

She sobs louder and my dad and I continue to hold her.

After a few minutes she pulls herself together and straightens, pulling away from us. "I'm... I just need to be alone for a bit," she tells us as she picks up her paint brush.

"I'll be upstairs," my dad tells her. He drapes his arm around my shoulders and tugs me out of the room, closing the door behind us.

When we get back upstairs, Elijah is waiting for us.

"Dan's, six o'clock," dad reminds me.

Elijah sees the look on my face, letting him know I need a moment with my dad. "I'll meet you outside," he tells me, heading for the door.

As soon as he steps out, I'm hugging my father.

"I'm sorry, I didn't understand. I just assumed you all thought I was weak. But I understand now."

He hugs me tight. "I've never thought that. If anything, I think you're too tough for your own good." He kisses me on the top of my head before releasing me. "Please be careful."

I nod before waving to him on my way out. The sun is bright today and I feel like the world is at my feet. I haven't cut myself for an entire day and the best news is my parents aren't locking me up. It's been my biggest fear. Ever since I was trapped in the pickup, I've been claustrophobic. Just having the seatbelt on gives me anxiety.

"Ready?" Elijah asks, opening the passenger door to the rod.

"As ready as I'll ever be."

When I give Lily the chime I made for her, she starts crying. She's known for making things out of motorcycle parts. It's her signature collection. This chime is made of old bike springs. "This one has always been my favorite," she says, running her fingers over it.

I tell her the reason behind my making them and the tears fall harder. I don't mean to make everyone sad, but Grandpa Bill belongs to them too and they deserve to know his final words. Maybe it will help them somehow.

"I'm sorry I've been so rude and that I lied about not being able to speak," I tell her, rubbing my hand over her back.

"I understand. We all hold onto our secrets as long as we can."

My gaze bounces over her face. I can't see Lily having any secrets. She's the most honest person I know. But I guess you never know what someone's been through. Just look at my mom.

"Do you need me today?" I ask. "I can work, but if you don't need me I have a few more chimes to deliver."

She smiles at me. "I've got it today. I think I'm going to close down early. Your mom and I are going out for drinks tonight."

I pull my head back. "Oh, well, I hope you have fun. She was a little sad when I left her."

Aunt Lily pushes me towards the door. "Don't you worry about her. I'll have her cheered up in no time."

Elijah smiles at me when I get back in the rod, his arm resting on the back of my seat. "Your face looks brighter with each chime you deliver."

We spend the rest of the afternoon making the rounds to club members. Every single one of them forgives me for the way I've been acting. Most just saying I reminded them a lot of my mom.

I usually brush it off but the more I hear it, the more I wonder if it's true. God, I wish. She's beautiful and courageous and strong. Yeah, I say she annoys me and sometimes she does but if I could be like anyone, it would be her.

Dan sits across his table from me, staring at the chime I'm gifting him. This one is made of tattoo gun parts. I didn't realize until I saw them all hanging together on the mountain that they each reminded me of someone in my family.

The twins took Elijah out back to do a little practice shooting. Uncle Dan and the boys cleared some of the trees out back for a shooting range a few years ago.

Finally, Dan speaks. "Your mom came to me when she was fourteen, dumping a whole can of change on my counter, wanting a tattoo." He knocks on the wood of the table. "I didn't realize how much that little girl would change my life."

"Did you give her a tattoo? Because if so, she's going to have some explaining to do since she made me wait until I was eighteen."

He chuckles. "No, not when she was that young, but it was the start of our friendship."

I bite my lip and look down at my lap. "I'm sorry I haven't been a very good friend lately."

"That's life, kiddo. Sometimes, we do things we aren't proud of but you're making it right."

My hands rub over the tops of my jeans nervously. "I'm worried about the meeting. I don't know how you guys are going to take what I have to say."

"Sweetheart, there isn't anything you could tell us that would make us stop loving you."

Eventually, the guys come back inside, and the rest of the club officers roll up one by one. The rumble of each bike pulling in only tightens the knot in my stomach.

I walk out to the kitchen and pour myself a glass of water, the quake of my fingers sending water over the edge of the glass. A warm body presses against mine. Elijah braces his arms on each side of me. "Relax," he whispers, his breath hot on my ear.

I take a drink. Easy for him to say. He's not the one who lied to the club for almost three years.

My Uncle Raffe clears his throat. Elijah shoves off the counter, his warmth leaving me. My uncle's concerned expression makes tears burn in the corner of my eyes. I don't know if I can do this.

"You got this, Billie Rose," Elijah says, going out to join the others on the porch.

My fingers strangle each other as I stand there, contemplating an escape out the back door.

"Trust us, baby girl," my uncle says, wrapping his hand around mine. "It's time."

There was a time I would have run to these men, spilling my guts if someone wronged me. Not one time did I not trust that they would take care of me. Nothing changed after the accident. I've always known they've had my best interest at heart. Maybe it wasn't them I didn't trust, maybe it was myself.

I felt weak. Unable to help myself let alone grandpa.

Elijah reminded me how brave I used to be. How I loved the thrill of trying something new, even if it was dangerous. But I don't blame my parents from keeping me from him. I understand now. My mom was scared for me. Her whole life she has had to live with her childhood influencing how she parented me. I also understand why they couldn't tell me. They wanted me to keep my innocence as long as possible.

I'm grateful for that. I would have never guessed the horrors she had gone through. Because of her, I had an amazing childhood. I owe it to her to take it from here.

Straightening my shoulders, I squeeze Raffe's hand and let him lead me outside. A dozen pairs of eyes turn our way when we step out. He releases my hand, and I remind myself whose daughter I am. My mother is the one who keeps this club, this family together. She is the queen of the Skulls, and I'm their fucking princess.

I straighten my crown as I walk over and take the seat beside Elijah. My dad's eyebrow raises a fraction, but he holds his tongue.

"I know I've apologized in person to all of you today, but I want to reiterate that apology. I'd forgotten who I was and who you all were." My eyes roam across the highest-ranking members of the club.

This is the first time I'm speaking to them as a member. I'm sticking my white flag in the soil, at the same time claiming my position here.

So, I don't beat around the bush. I handle this exactly how my father would.

"The accident wasn't an accident. Someone hit Bill and I on purpose," I say as calmly as my body will allow, a slight tremble in my voice. But hey, not even a week ago, did I have one.

Their non reaction has me tipping my head. No yelling, no gorilla like pounding on their chests, no racing for guns or bikes. What the actual fuck?

My dad levels his gaze on me. "We know."

"You know?" I repeat. Elijah and I exchange a confused look.

221

Dan taps around on his phone and then holds it out to me. "We did a little police work of our own and came across some video footage of a man driving the truck that hit you that night. The guy was a nobody. A known drug user who probably stole it to flip the thing. These types will do anything to feed their addiction."

Elijah takes the phone for me, noticing how bad my hands are shaking. He holds it so I can see an old mug shot of the man.

"It was easy to put together," Jackson says, running his knuckles over his jacket. "A little computer work and I was able to find the fuckers mug shot on some old drug charges. Dirk found him over in Trap and the rest is history."

The man that smiled at my broken grandpa stares back at me. I remember the shocked look on his face when he saw me in the passenger seat. And how he and Draven had yelled at each other. I wish I could remember what they said.

I push Elijah's hand away, dropping my head between my shoulders. This is the reason they never asked me what happened, they knew. Jesus, you're an idiot. Did you really think these men would let it go that easy? At the word of a police report that deemed it an accident.

Elijah hands the phone back to Dan as his other rests against the back of my neck.

"Did you see him?" my dad asks.

I nod, keeping my head hanging. Elijah's fingers gently brush over my skin, keeping me grounded.

"You don't have to be afraid of him. He no longer exists."

I suck in a huge amount of air at the implication of his words. He crouches down in front of me, gently drawing my face upwards. "He's never going to hurt you again, baby."

My bottom lip rolls between my teeth as a tear slips down my cheek. Elijah's hand falls from my back and he braces himself for what is about to go down.

My father blurs as water pools in my eyes. I'm about to break his heart and it kills me. It's one more reason that Draven is going to pay.

"He wasn't the only one I saw that night." My heart slows as I stare into my dad's eyes. The clear blue is getting muddier by the second as understanding settles in and he realizes he missed something. That someone is walking this earth who hurt me.

Dan stands up and puts his fist right through the wood of his front door.

Oh shit.

My dad closes his eyes and when they open again, I pull back. Jesus Christ. They are as black as coal.

Abruptly, I stand and slide away from him, jumping off the porch.

"Billie Rose," he warns.

It's then I decide to put them right the fuck in their place. I spin around, daggers shooting from beneath my brow. "Don't even fucking think about it," I growl, my voice low and full of venom. "He is mine. Mine." I shove a finger in my chest. "You got the satisfaction of taking one down but the other, well, he is off limits."

Raffe rises slowly, holding his hands out. "Let's all just calm down." He motions for me to take my seat as my dad starts pacing like a caged animal.

"Who is he?" Dan snarls, ready to rip someone's limbs from their body.

Oh, fuck me, why did I think they would let me do this my way?

"I'm not telling any of you anything until you promise me that I get to handle this my way."

My father pauses, his gaze sliding to mine. "And how do you want to handle this?" he tips his head.

I rub my palms together before steepling them in front of my mouth. How do I put this? "This man thinks I'm giving him a pass. I want him to trust me and then I'm going to smile in his face when he realizes just how big of a mistake he made by letting me live."

Dan's head is immediately snapping back and forth, and the other officers lean back in their chairs, unsure what to think.

"It's him. Isn't it? That fucking little prick, Draven. Those fucking Desert dipshits just don't fucking learn. I'm going to burn every one of those motherfuckers to the ground." My dad grinds his teeth together.

"He did it to hurt mom," I say quietly. "He says he's the son of Crow." I place my hands on my hips, watching these men closely.

Gazes bounce off of each other. They are stupefied. This is news to them.

"No way. Crow didn't leave any spawns behind. I made sure of it," my dad says, running his hand over his head. His face contorts as he tries to figure out what is going on.

I throw my hands in the air. "Well, that's what he believes. A father for a father he said."

"We have to find out everything we can about this dude," Travis, our very own club hacker, announces as he pulls his laptop out of his bag.

My phone is buzzing in my pocket and when I pull it out, I see it's the man of the hour himself.

"Can I trust that you guys will keep quiet for five minutes?" I ask, my gaze bouncing over the men.

They all nod, my dad hopping off the porch and coming to stand a few feet in front of me.

This is my chance to show them just how good I can be at this.

He's video calling me, so I tilt the phone so that all Draven can see is the bright blue sky behind me.

"Hey," I answer, pulling my hair out of my mouth as the wind whips it in my face.

"Hello, little dove," Draven greets.

I open my eyes wide, giving him my best innocent look, and sniffle. "I'm sorry about last night. I should've called."

"No worries. How're you doing?" He's at the bar, laughter and music filters out through the speakers on my phone.

I rub my fingers over my head. "I-I'm okay. My parents are so pissed at me."

"That's what I heard. What did you do or not do this time?"

My bottom lip sneaks into my mouth and I bite down on it, my cheeks staining crimson. "Well, my dad caught Elijah, um, he caught him with his face between my legs."

I can see my dad balling his hands into fists at his sides.

Draven's eyebrows shoot to his hairline. "Damn, Elijah is really asking for it, isn't he?"

I plop down dramatically on the ground. "Yeah, wait till you see his face," I pout.

"So, I take it your dad saw your other little secret."

My heart jumps to my throat. Great, now I'm going to have to explain how he knows about my scars. I don't risk a look at my dad, but I do manage to push a couple tears out. I rub my eyes with my free hand. "Yeah," I whisper.

Draven stops walking. "Did your parents happen to learn about *our* secret?" he asks, tension tightening his voice.

My brows pull together at his sudden change. "No. Why?"

He shifts the phone so that I can see what is hanging behind him on the wall in the bar. Oh fuck. It takes everything in me not to react. "That's cool," I simply say.

Draven stares at me through the glass on my phone.

"What? You said they remind you of your dad. Where did you get it?"

"Where did I get it?" he repeats. "Well, let's see. I think you may know the artist. She's still here." He flips the camera and there at the bar sits my mother and Aunt Lily.

My eyes widen in surprise as he turns the camera back on himself.

"Care to explain?"

My eyes go back to the painting of the black crow behind him, his wings engulfed in flames, a panicked look in his beady little eyes.

I shrug. "You fucking tell me."

He storms back to his office, slamming the door shut.

"Don't play games with me, little girl," he shouts, making me flinch.

I notice from the corner of my eye, a few club men rising to their feet on the porch.

I jump off the ground. "Fuck off. If you think I told her about you then you're sadly mistaken. I don't have time for this shit. My dad just saw Elijah's face shoved in my fucking cunt, Draven. Just fuck off," I yell again.

He takes a deep breath, grinding his teeth. "Then what the fuck is up with her and her little welcome to the neighborhood gift?"

My head tips back and I laugh. "You're kidding me, right? Helloooo. I toted a fucking live crow home, dumbass. She thinks you're fucking with the club. They're pissed. They think you and your club are selling drugs here. This is Skull territory. How did you think she would fucking react?"

Draven releases a long-drawn-out sigh, running his fingers through his hair. "You're probably right. You think it's just a warning?"

"Yeah, I mean, come on, Draven," I say with a little less anger. "She doesn't like your club. That's not private information. And then you add the fact her daughter is working there. She's letting you know that she's watching you."

He settles back in his chair. "Well, what the fuck should I do?" he asks.

I shake my head and chuckle. "My advice, stay away from her and if you do go near her, watch your nuts. Oh, and if you see her with anything flammable, run." I give him my best smile and then end the call.

When my attention finally goes back to the men in front of me, Jackson stands up and starts clapping. He whistles. "Damn, Rosie, didn't know you were such an actress."

I flip him off not taking my eyes off my dad. He doesn't like any part of this. Draven is a dangerous man.

"What's the point?" he asks. "I can go over there right now and end him."

I've thought about this myself. What is the point? What do I want out of this? If I'm being honest, I want him to feel comfortable. Like I did, sitting in the truck with my grandpa and then I want his world to come crashing down around him. I want, no scratch that, I need to watch him suffocate with the realization that I'm the judge, jury, and executioner.

My dad's eyebrow rises slowly, he reads me like an open book. I'm sure staring into my stormy eyes is like looking into a crystal ball. "I see," he turns to the others before narrowing his gaze back on me.

In no way do I blame them for the way they're all looking at me. It must be hard to accept the fact that even their little kind-hearted Rosie has thorns.

"What if I say no?"

I want Draven's pain so bad. It's all I've thought about for three years. But I'm not just Billie Rose, I'm a Rebel Skull. With tears threatening, I hold my head high, before dipping it slightly in his direction in submission. "Then I will respect that."

He shifts his head to the side, speaking over his shoulder. "You used her to get in?" His query is directed towards Elijah.

"Yes, sir. I found her working at the bar the first night I went over there. It didn't take long to gain his trust. He thinks you hate me."

"I do," my dad deadpans. Focusing once again on me, he pins me with eyes so black, I have no doubt he could suck the soul out of his enemies.

"Three things." He holds up three fingers, his eyebrow at a ridiculously scary angle. "This dipshit is now your shadow." He nods towards Elijah. "Second, you promise to pull the fucking plug the second something doesn't feel right and third, never, and I do mean never, talk about that little prick being between your legs again."

229

The smile that breaks out over my face counteracts the scary look on his. If this doesn't end well, you may as well call me Rapunzel because he will keep me locked up in that warehouse the rest of my life.

I squeal and rush him, throwing myself in his arms, hugging him tight.

"God, I hope I'm not making a mistake," he whispers against my hair. "But it's nice to see you smile again."

Chapter Eighteen

Billie Rose

My excitement is short lived when I realize that I'm now stuck with Elijah. He's wonderful to look at but he's bossy and annoying and he's going to get me in trouble.

He winks at me from the porch.

The scowl on Dan's face makes me take a step back. "Is my wife with your mom?"

"Um, you know, I didn't…"

Dammit, my hesitation was all the answer he needed. He heads towards his bike, nodding for my dad to follow. "I need to hit something. Let's go get our wives out of there and see if there are any Devils hanging around that need their faces rearranged."

"Wait…"

Dad throws his head back, laughing, he follows his friend, swinging his leg over his bike. "Jesse hasn't given me a reason to redden her ass in a long time."

My face scrunches up. "Eww." I gag at the thought, making a big show of it.

Uncle Dan howls with laughter. "Let's go raise some hell, brother."

Their bikes roar to life, and I close my eyes, relishing in the sound.

Everyone slowly follows, all except Raffe. He's sitting on the porch, deep in thought. Elijah excuses himself to get a few more rounds of practice shooting in before the sun fully sets for the day. He senses that my uncle is having a hard time swallowing the pill I just gave him.

I nod silently, taking a seat on the porch step. Raffe gets up and sits beside me.

We watch a group of sparrows flit from tree to tree for several minutes. "This makes me nervous, Billie Rose. What's his game?"

Shrugging my shoulders, I pick at a hangnail. "He says he's sorry I got hurt. I wasn't supposed to be in the truck that night. Maybe he feels guilty." I'm not sure if I'm trying to convince myself or him. I suppose it's true that Draven didn't know I was going to be in the pickup that night. But men like him don't usually possess empathy.

He picks up a rock and tosses it out into the driveway. "He wants something from you. Either he wants you dead or..." he turns away from me, letting his thoughts die on his tongue.

Flashes of memories flip through my mind. The way he looked at me as grandpa sat dying next to me. The way his fingers brushed against my panties. The way he pressed his lips to mine.

I shove it all away, kicking it to the far corners of my mind. "He knows I have a boyfriend. Well, I don't have a boyfriend, but he thinks Elijah is... my boyfriend," I spit out.

Raffe isn't budging. "It doesn't make sense."

"I know," I finally admit. "But I want to hurt him so bad."

"You already know that he wants to hurt your mom and he was successful. He hurt all of us." Raffe stretches his long legs out in front of him. "If he thinks Jesse killed his dad, he isn't going to let it go or he wouldn't be here. And that's if he's telling the truth and he really is Crow's son."

"Well, it makes sense. You said mom shot up a bunch of his guys as they came out of a whorehouse. It's not like Crow didn't sleep around." My pulse quickens, my mind racing. "What did you say the name of that place was?"

"I don't think I did but it was Bell's House of Tail," he says, rolling his eyes at the ridiculous name. "Your mom spray painted dicks on their bikes first. When they came out and stood around freaking out about their new paint jobs, she popped them all right in the head. All but Crow and I told you how he met his demise."

Maybe grandpa wasn't a cheater after all. What if those receipts I found in his box of secrets are somehow tied to Draven?

Raffe notices I've checked out of the conversation. "What's going on in that pretty little head of yours?"

"Nothing, I just remembered that I have something I need to do." I hop up and head to the rod.

"Billie Rose, where do you think you're going? You can't drive."

I turn around and walk backwards. "Oh, but I can. Just not legally."

"Billie Rose," he warns, his muscles poised for a chase.

"Chill, uncle. I'm not going to do anything dangerous. Promise." I run my finger over my chest, drawing an imaginary x.

"You're missing your shadow. Dirk just told you the rules no more than ten minutes ago."

I tip my head back and forth as if weighing my options. "Rules are made to be broken."

Quickly, he puts his fingers in his mouth, whistling loudly for my shadow.

"Tell him I'll be back by midnight," I holler over my shoulder as I take off running.

My mom's rod is getting quite the workout lately as I spin the tires, sending gravel flying everywhere.

I don't plan on going very far. All I need is to get picked up without a license. And the rod is hard to hide, it sticks out like a sore thumb.

But I happen to know that there's a bus that goes through Trap County on its way to Vegas and it should be leaving soon.

I knew Grandpa wasn't a cheating dog. This is the break I've been waiting for.

The sun settles behind the mountains in the distance as the bus rolls down the highway. Surprisingly, my phone isn't blowing up. Huh. Weird. I thought Raffe would have the whole club after me again. Could it be that they are finally going to let me be a grown up?

Before I know it, the bus is pulling up on the edge of the shithole that is known as Trap County.

My foot catches on a small rock as I step away from the bus. Strong arms catch me before I face plant onto the desert floor.

"Oh, gosh. Thank you," I tell the stranger as I tug on my shirt and run a hand over my hair, smoothing it down.

"No problem," a familiar voice says from behind me.

I spin in the dirt, creating a puff of dust around my boots. "Elijah!" I take a step back.

He shoves his hands in his jeans. The veins in his forearms bulge as if he is restraining himself from dragging me back home by my hair. "Whatcha doin?" He tips back on his heels, nonchalantly.

Taking a big, deep breath, I square my shoulders. "I have a meeting over there." I point across the road towards the whorehouse where my answers await.

His big brown eyes follow the direction of my finger. His eyebrows raise and he takes a step back. "No. Oh fuck no." He pulls his hands out of his pants. "I'm all for you being free to do what you want but no. Nope." He shakes his tattooed hand at the neon sign of a woman blowing a giant kiss to the desert as if it's the most ludicrous thing he's ever heard.

"Christ, I'm not getting a job there. I just have a meeting."

He runs a hand through his gorgeous hair. Fuck, he looks like a model standing against the backdrop of the darkening sky. I lick my lips, suddenly wanting to taste him."

"No."

My fantasy snaps. I narrow my eyes at him. "I took a big risk coming here today. I'm not leaving until I get my answers."

He twirls the ring in his nose as he processes my words. "Answers to what?"

When I don't answer, he snaps, his hand striking out, his fingers wrapping around my throat. He gruffly pulls me towards him. "I've been tiptoeing with you, but now I have your father's blessing. We," he squeezes, cutting off enough of my oxygen to make my eyes go wide. "We are in this, together."

His fingers loosen, letting me suck in a breath before tightening again. I claw at his hands. Jesus.

Elijah drags my face to his, bumping his nose against mine. "Comprende?"

I nod with a jerk, not able to move much with his goddamn giant hand wrapped like a python around my neck. Something about the way he's looking at me, holding me helpless in his grip, makes strange things start to brew low in my gut.

When he releases his hold on me, I bend over, coughing, trying to suck precious oxygen into my lungs.

"So, if there are any trees you want to climb, any planes you want to jump out of, or any whorehouses you want to visit, you will make sure I'm by your side."

I rub my hand over my throat, glaring at him. "You do know I lived the last fourteen years without you."

He tips his head, staring at me down his perfect fucking nose. A clear warning to shut my mouth before he shuts it for me.

"Fine, jeez, I've just traded one jailer for another," I grumble, stomping away, headed down the road towards my destination.

Elijah jogs to catch up. "I think you'll find I'm a much more pleasurable gate keeper."

Rolling my eyes, I snort.

"Who are you meeting with?" he asks, turning serious as we approach the building.

I called from the bus on the way over for a meeting with the owner. They may or may not be thinking that I'm coming in for an interview but I'm not telling Elijah that. At least not until I'm in the building.

"The owner."

"And?" he prompts.

"And I have a few questions for them. Like why my grandfather had been paying a lot of money to their establishment."

Elijah halts in his tracks, the gravel crunching beneath his feet. His hand snags mine, pulling me to a stop with him. "Billie Rose," he says softly, looking at me all sad and shit. "Some things are better left unknown. Do you really want to know why your grandfather was spending money at a whorehouse?"

"It's not like that." I shake my head, pulling away from him.

"Then what's it like?" he asks, reluctantly following me to the doors.

I ignore his question and step inside. It's mid-week, so there are only a few men and women milling around when we walk in. A young woman bounces over to us and when I say bounces, her tits almost hit her in the face. She eyes Elijah up and down, sticking the tip of her tongue out to run over her top lip.

I glance at him, but he's unaware of her interest, his eyes darting around the room. A growl escapes me before I can reign it in and I step in front of him, forcing her eyes to me. Of course, the deep rumble that came out of me draws his attention back to us. He chuckles quietly behind me. Dick.

Taking a deep breath, I manage to force a smile on my face. "I called earlier, I'm here to see the owner."

Her shoulders drop, clearly disappointed that we're not here to enjoy the services of the establishment. "Follow me," she says on a sigh, mumbling under her breath about none of the good ones wanting to play.

I roll my eyes as we make our way down the dimly lit hallway. Obscene sounds emanate from behind closed doors, staining my cheeks bright red. She knocks on a door at the end of the hallway. "Bell, that girl that called is here to see you," she hollers through the door.

"Well, show her in."

She turns to look at me, smacking her gum loudly before turning the doorhandle and pushing it open for us. As we walk past her, I glance back, catching her eyeball Elijah's ass. A restless energy bubbles in my veins, she's really pushing it.

Why am I letting it get to me? I don't even like this asshole half the time. He's done nothing but rock my world since he came to town.

When the girl closes the door behind her, I relax, taking my first look around the room. Red walls and black lace sum it up. An old woman with stark white hair, piled high on her head, sits in a high back chair by a fireplace. "Come here girl, let me see you," she says, motioning with a hand full of big gaudy rings. "One thing you need to know right now is I don't allow boyfriends to be hanging around." She narrows her eyes at Elijah. He stands where he's at, looking completely terrified to be in her private room.

Quickly, I take a step towards her. "Oh, I'm not here for a job. I just had a few questions if you would indulge me."

Her eyes widen when I move into the light. She rises from her chair slowly, her body trembling with the effort. "Jesse?" she whispers.

"No, I'm her daughter, Billie Rose," I offer kindly. I feel bad, she looks like she just saw a ghost.

Elijah is behind me in seconds as if he needs to protect me from her. His hand rests on my back as she reaches out and runs a crooked finger over my cheek.

"My god, you are just as beautiful as she was." She eases herself back down in her chair, motioning for Elijah and me to sit as well. "Your mother was the sweetest child. She used to work for me, you know?"

My eyebrows shoot so high I think they might have left my face. Bell cackles at my reaction. "Not that kind of work, hun. She used to help me around the place, take the trash out, run and pick up my cigarettes, things like that. She was skinny as a rail that girl. I found things for her to do so that I knew she had money to eat on. Her aunt was a worthless piece of shit." She taps her bright red nails on the arm of the chair, tilting her head at me curiously. "Anyhow, what can I do for you child?"

I breathe a sigh of relief. I'm not sure why but the thought of my mom being a prostitute didn't settle as well as her being a killer. "Thank you for giving me a few minutes of your time," I say, beginning to nervously pick at my nails. "Um, I found some receipts of my grandfather's…"

She cuts me off. "Oh, honey, that isn't what you're thinking either. That man was a saint and a loyal one to boot."

All of the tension I had been holding releases. I knew he wouldn't cheat on my grandmother; I should have never doubted him.

"What were the receipts for?" Elijah asks, leaning forward.

The old woman isn't easily intimidated. She ignores him, remaining focused on me. "One of my girls got knocked up and I took the child in. Bill graciously helped me out financially with him when she took off and left me with the baby."

Why?

"Why would he do that? You said he didn't frequent your establishment, so the kid clearly wasn't his," Elijah continues to interrogate the old woman, voicing my thoughts out loud.

"I'm sorry," I say, elbowing him in the ribs. "But I am curious myself."

She doesn't seem bothered by either of us, waving a hand in front of her face. "Let's just say he felt an obligation to help. I can't say more than that. He tasked me with helping to make sure the little one didn't end up in the foster care system and he offered to take care of the expense. I never had a child and figured it was my last chance to experience motherhood, so I agreed."

Elijah stills next to me. Both of us coming to the same conclusion at the same time.

"Was the baby Crow's son?" I ask.

Her eyes widen but she recovers quickly, shaking her head. "I should have known you'd be a smart girl just like that mama of yours. I can't say for sure who his daddy is. Like I said his mother worked for me."

I fall to my knees in front of her, taking her gnarled hands in mine. "Please, my grandpa passed away, so I can't ask him. Anything you could tell me might help me understand why he would want to help this child."

She pulls her hand away and pats my cheek as I stare into her makeup caked face. "I didn't know Bill had passed. I'm sorry." Her eyes well with tears.

"Please," I beg.

She pulls at a hair on her chin, and just when I think she's considering giving me answers, she presses her lips together. "Bill was a good man, one who was trying to protect his family. He made me promise I would never speak of any of this. I'm sorry, hun, but I'm a woman of her word. I've said too much already."

"But.." I glance around, searching for clues.

"Sweetie, do your mama a favor and let this one go," she says quietly. "I'm leaving all this behind in a few weeks." She waves her ringed fingers around her room. "There's a beach on the west coast and a margarita just waiting for me. It's time for me to move on and leave this shithole behind. I suggest you do the same." She presses a button, and a big, bald man steps out of a room behind her. "Reuben, can you please see my guests out."

"Yes, ma'am," he says, walking towards the door, holding it open for us to follow.

Slowly, I rise to my feet, more confused than when I arrived.

Once we're outside, I pull away from Elijah and walk down the sidewalk running along the building. He follows closely behind, then I hear a familiar voice coming from behind us.

"Hey, when are you getting in?" I hear Lanie ask.

Without thought, I spin around and grab Elijah by the front of his shirt. I kiss him at the same time shifting so my back is against the brick building.

Elijah pulls his head back a few inches to stare down at me, his eyebrows raise in question. I place my finger over my lips.

"No, it's just me, she wouldn't come with." Lanie lights up a cigarette. "Yeah, I know I failed but did you really think her family was going to let her leave with me anyway?"

Elijah doesn't miss the opportunity and gently places his lips against mine, his hand roams down my side, rubbing lightly against the side of my breast. My eyes widen in warning. He smiles against my mouth.

"Draven's lost his fucking mind. Like I don't get the hold they have over men. Like what the fuck?"

Elijah freezes and every muscle in his body tenses against me. I grab his shirt, keeping him tethered to me or maybe to keep myself upright, I'm not sure right now.

"She's such a spoiled brat. I gave up years of my life for this *plan*," Lanie says dramatically. "I said I was sorry about that. Yeah, I'm letting him handle it but... yeah, I know I betrayed his trust by setting her up to be in the truck that night."

I glance around Elijah's shoulder and find a scantily dressed Lanie, leaning against the building.

"If you were in my shoes, you'd want her dead too. Yeah, yeah, I know. Like I said I'm just waiting for you to get here, then maybe you can talk some sense into him."

My heart drops into my stomach. Lanie wanted me dead. My best friend.

"Shit, okay. Yeah, I got a customer coming in twenty." Lanie drops her cigarette and stomps on it. "I'm trying to trust him." She sighs and leans her head back against the bricks. "Does Bell know you're coming?" She pushes off the building and heads towards the entrance. "Okay, I'll talk to you later."

Once she's gone, I try to push Elijah away from me. He stands his ground, pinning me to the building. "Was that woman the same one you call best friend?"

Nodding, I turn away, blinking rapidly to stall the tears of betrayal from running down my face.

He cups the side of my face and I lean into his hand, unbelievably grateful that he's here.

"Let's go home, baby," he says quietly, kissing my temple.

I nod and let him place a helmet on my head, his long fingers making quick work of the strap. He hops on and pulls my hands around him. Once he's satisfied I'm hanging on tight, he heads out onto the open road.

My mind runs through every memory of Lanie and me. The hurt builds and builds until I think I might combust.

Strangely though, the one thing I hold onto is the fact that Draven didn't lie. I wasn't meant to be in the truck with grandpa that night.

Grandpa wasn't supposed to give us a ride that night.

The call, dad said he got a tip about someone peddling drugs near the school.

Was it Lanie who provided the tip?

Oh my god, my best friend wanted me dead.

Elijah reaches around and grabs hold of my leg, brushing his hand back and forth over my thigh. Can he sense that I'm about to lose my goddamn shit?

He doesn't take us home. He pulls into the spot across the lake from the warehouse and kills the motor. I hurry off the bike and toss the helmet to the ground. I need… I need… I start to rip my pants down my thighs, kicking my shoe off at the same time, completely forgetting where I am or who I'm with.

Elijah lets me shimmy them down and then once my legs are trapped in my jeans, he tackles me to the ground.

I stare up into his beautiful fucking face, wanting to rip it off him. "Let me go." I struggle under him, trying to roll him off me.

"Let me help," his minty breath whispers over my face.

My lungs are burning from my inability to breathe. I'm losing the battle with each second I don't get some relief. Electric currents skitter to the tips of my fingers, and I let out a little sob. "Hurry," I tell him, admitting my own defeat.

He instantly slides off me and tosses my other shoe to the side and then he makes quick work of getting my pants the rest of the way down. When his hand goes for my panties, I grip his wrist with a force I didn't know I possessed.

"I'm not going to go all the way. This isn't going to be how your first time goes down. Not when you just found out your friend is an evil bitch who wanted you dead."

Slowly, I let go of him.

My reaction does make him hesitate though and he leaves me in my panties, instead he stretches out beside me. "Look at me, baby," he says, brushing hair away from face.

"I-I can't," I admit, the shy Billie Rose taking over.

Chapter Nineteen

Elijah

She's so goddamn beautiful even when she's falling apart. She's shy, inexperienced, and like I've said, thank God for that. I'm glad I'm getting all her firsts. I'll take them greedily. But right now, I just need to stop the panic rushing her system and turn it into something else.

"That's okay, just look at the stars and breathe," I instruct.

She nods and every muscle in her body tenses when my fingers trail beneath her shirt, sliding under her bra. Her nipples are pebbled and perfect for what I'm about to do. I pinch hard enough that she arches her back off the ground, her mouth falling open. Her eyes roll back in her head before closing and I know she's getting her first dose of relief.

My hand slides over to give her breasts equal attention, only this time when I clamp down on the little bud, I lean over and kiss her neck gently, balancing her pain with a little burst of pleasure.

Her throaty moan goes straight to my cock.

I move higher and suck her bottom lip into my mouth and I bite down, hard enough that a tinge of copper erupts over my tongue.

"Jesus," she whispers.

Then without warning, I plunge my hand straight the fuck into her cute little pink panties, cupping her hard against my palm. Our gazes clash, her chest rising and falling quickly as I hold myself still. When she doesn't stop me, I move on, rolling her clit between my finger and thumb, gently, ever so gently and then I pinch down, her pupils widen, and I drown in the depths of them.

Her cheeks pinken with embarrassment when she realizes I can tell just how turned on she is.

"Do you like this?" I whisper in her ear, letting my tongue snake along the edge. I bite down on her lobe at the same time pleasuring her little clit.

"Shittt," she groans in desire, her eyes rolling back in her head again.

This isn't going to take long. Billie Rose came after riding my sucker for five minutes, she doesn't waste time. She's right there, but this time I'm going to draw it out, make her suffer. It's what she needs.

"Answer me, do you like it when I make it hurt so good?" I hover over her, halting the movement of my hand, relishing in the fact that her hips are now pushing off the ground as she tries to grind herself into the palm of my hand.

"Elijah," she begs, lifting her ass again.

"Tell. Me," I demand, pulling my hand out of her panties, making her let out a little whine. I smack her, right over her drenched panties.

She yelps, her eyes narrowing on mine.

She might as well learn right now who's in charge. Billie Rose is strong, wild, and untamed. She needs a strong man to keep her grounded and balanced. She's not even aware just how strong she is. But she will.

I grab her around the throat, the scent of her arousal on my hand makes me groan. Oh, what I would give right now for a taste but that's not what she needs. She needs it to hurt. Again, her cheeks pinken as my wet fingers tighten.

"Yes. Yes, I like it," she confesses.

"Such a good girl." Her eyes flutter closed at my words. "I'm the only one who gets to hurt you. Do you understand."

She nods feverishly.

I make my way back down her body, stopping to give her perfect tits a harsh squeeze before diving back into the promise land. Except this time, I'm gentle. Her breathing picks up and I know she's getting close as my finger swirls and then I let it dip lower, the very tip entering her.

Her eyes are full blown galaxies, beautiful and limitless. She breaths out slowly, her body stills except for the trembling of her legs.

I slide in another inch before pulling back and then slowly, ever so slowly, shove it all the way in till my knuckles bump against her.

"Oh," she breathes out, her eyes focused on the sky.

Giving her time to adjust, I lean over and kiss her, dragging the ball of my tongue piercing over her bottom lip. When I withdraw my finger, I decide that she's ready for another. She whimpers into my mouth as I slowly press into her and oh my god do my balls tighten as I swallow the sound. I can't wait to take her as mine, but not yet. Not tonight.

Her whole body begins to tremble when I curl my fingers, finding her sweet spot. I increase my pace, letting my thumb press down on her clit with just the right pressure. Her body tenses, her mouth falling open. Long lashes flutter against the creamy skin of her cheeks as she leaves this world for the one I'm giving her.

So much promise.

I lick my lips as I watch this pretty little creature ride out her orgasm on my hand.

When her ass drops to the ground and her breathing slows, I gently pull my hand out of her panties. Her gorgeous eyes focus on my face as I bring my hand up and shove my fingers down my own throat. My head falls back, she tastes so good.

Billie Rose covers her eyes with her hand. Her bottom lip caught tightly between her teeth.

"Hey." I pull her hand away and she screws her eyes shut, shaking her head. "Don't be embarrassed, you come so beautifully for me."

Her head falls to the side, but I grab her chin and turn her to face me. "You better get used to it because it's going to happen again and again and again. You'll never be able to escape me."

"But what about you." She frowns, glancing down between us.

"Don't worry about me. I'm a patient man. Remember? I've been waiting for you for a very long time, Billie Rose. I can wait a few more days."

Her eyes widen, half with fear and half with excitement. "Days?"

The corner of my mouth turns up in a smirk. "Or less, depends."

"Depends on what?"

"How long you're going to make me chase you."

The little lines that appear on her forehead as she ponders my words, make me smile.

I roll on top of her and roughly grind myself against her core. Her hands press against my chest. "I like a chase, Billie Rose. Are you going to run from me?" I tip my head, then jump to my feet, staring down at her.

Fear mixed with excitement flashes against the starry night of her eyes. She sits up and quickly pulls her pants on before grabbing her shoes and cradling them to her chest.

"When I catch you, you're mine." I bare my teeth at her.

"You're crazy," she says, her voice trembling as she rises to her feet.

251

"And you love it." I tip my chin to her.

I head back to my bike and pat the seat.

She eyes it warily and then just like last time we were here, she whips around and runs. Her blue-black hair flowing behind her.

I laugh loudly.

So much fun.

Chapter Twenty

Billie Rose

My feet carry me around the lake but as I near the warehouse my sudden burst of energy depletes.

I stop and smile up at the stars. I've missed this. The pure exhilaration of being with him. Pushing things to the very edge, knowing he'll reach out and catch me if I fall. I guess he didn't catch me when I broke my arm, but we were just kids then. He'll catch me now. I know he will.

My body tingles from the orgasm he just gave me. It was wonderful and intense. I've never... well, I've done it that way to myself, but holy shit is it better when someone does it for you.

And best of all, it stopped the noise in my head.

I'm so wrapped up in my own thoughts and post orgasmic bliss that I don't think about the fact the lights are on in the kitchen as I open the back door.

My parents both pause as I step inside.

"Oh!" I jump back, startled by their presence. "Are you guys..." I scratch my head, "mopping?"

My mom has a mop in her hand and my dad is following behind her with a bucket. I glance at the clock on the wall.

"Yeah, couldn't sleep with the thought of waking up to a dirty floor," my mom replies, going back to running it over the tile.

Crossing my arms over my chest, I wrinkle my nose at them. "Were you waiting up for me?"

My dad doesn't lie. He may omit but rarely does he tell even the tiniest of fibs. A man like him doesn't need to. "You think we can just shut that shit off overnight? It's going to take a while, baby girl." Then, his eyebrow slowly climbs its way up towards his hairline. "Where's your shadow?" he asks, his eyes raking up and down my body as if he's trying to read exactly what I've been up to.

"Her shadow?" My mother's mouth falls open. "Please tell me you didn't?" she snaps.

Dad leans back against the counter. "Hey, your dad assigned me to be the stink on your shit, and you didn't have a problem with it. No different, Elijah is now her," he turns to me, "shadow."

Now that I think about it, it's not like this is something new. I've always had a shadow. Dan, Raffe, Jackson, JD... the list goes on and on.

"Dirk." My mother's face turns red as she glares at him. "We're just getting her back," she seethes.

"It's okay, mom, I don't mind. In fact, it's been kinda fun." I walk over and grab an apple out of the basket and rub it over my shirt before taking a big bite.

Both their heads swivel my way. "Wait. What?" my dad stammers.

Just then, Elijah comes barreling in from the other door, not realizing the floor is wet because why would it be at two a.m. He throws his arms out to steady himself.

Was he just trying to "catch" me?

His wide eyes go from my parents to me.

This is the most fun I've had in forever. I smile at him sweetly, grabbing another apple off the counter and tossing it to him. "Beat you to the apples," I tease. He owes me for this.

He catches it with one hand, his eyes alight with mischief. "Damn, you're faster than I thought. I'll have to remember that next time." He scratches under his nose with two fingers. Asshole.

I can feel the flush run up my neck, so I turn my attention back to my apple, biting it a little too aggressively.

My parents watch our entire interaction with a look of confusion and something else that I can't put my finger on.

Elijah shifts his focus to my dad. "Mission accomplished, sir. The princess has been safely returned to the castle for the night." He salutes my dad and hightails it out of there.

Gee, thanks for leaving me with them.

"Welp, I'll leave you two to your mopping," I say, pushing myself away from the counter.

As I walk past them, dad stops me. He plucks something out of the back of my hair, and then my mother reaches over, joining him.

Leaves, several of them, are stuck in my hair. Shit.

"Thanks. Um, we were looking at the stars," I say, not turning around to look at them. It's not a lie. Not only was I looking at the stars, but I was also floating amongst them. My feet move forward, and I pray that they don't ask me anything else. "Goodnight."

"Goodnight, sweetie," my mom says. My dad grunts but doesn't say anything.

I breathe a sigh of relief as I jog up the stairs. Once in my room, I throw myself on my bed and let my head fall to the sunset my mother painted on my wall. I think I finally found something that makes me feel as good as that mural.

Chapter Twenty-One

Billie Rose ~ five years old

The sun shines on my face as Elijah pumps his legs back and forth.

"Higher," I squeal, gripping the chains on the swing, right above his hands. My head falls back, and I pretend I'm floating in the clouds. I've never swung this high. My daddy wouldn't like that I'm sitting on Elijah's lap, facing him as we swing together but it's the best. Way better than doing it alone.

When my head tips back down, Elijah smiles at me. "Do you like this, Rosie?" he asks, not even a bit breathless from all the work he's doing.

"So much," I say, biting my lip and encouraging him to go even higher.

"Billie Rose," my mom hollers. Elijah instantly drags his feet, creating a dust cloud under the swing set. The jerky stop makes me lose my grip and I start to fall backwards but he catches me, preventing us both from falling off the swing.

"Caught you," he teases before setting me on my feet. He helps me to right myself and then takes my hand, leading us back to where mommy is waiting for us. I look up at him as we walk through the grass. I like that he's so much taller than me.

He holds my hand out for mommy to take.

"Thank you for watching her while I ran to the store," she tells him.

"No problem, Aunt Jess." He ruffles my hair and then a boy from his class hollers across the park from the basketball courts asking him if he wants to shoot hoops. "Can you tell my mom I'll be home by six?" he asks.

"Sure, we'll see you later." My mom drags me away as Elijah jogs over to his friend.

My heels dig into the ground.

"Come on, sweetie, you can play at the park again tomorrow."

"I wanna stay with him," I pout, dropping all my weight to the ground.

My little fit doesn't deter my mother. She picks me up and tosses me in the backseat of Uncle William's minivan.

258

Roses and Skulls

I cross my arms over my chest after buckling myself in, my eyes fixated on Elijah through the windshield. It's not fair, I could have sat on the ground and watched him. I love watching him. He's funny and I'm never bored when I'm with him.

"Come on, Billie Rose, we have to get back to the house. We're baking cookies with Penny today. Won't that be fun?"

My lips curl between my teeth. I'm not talking to mommy the rest of the day. All I wanted was to stay with Elijah. He could have walked us home. Even I know how to look both ways before crossing the street and they only live a few blocks from the park.

My mother sighs. "Hey, I know you like to spend time with him, but he's a lot older than you and he has friends. You can't tag along with him everywhere he goes."

This makes no sense to me. Why does it matter how old we are? Elijah is my friend and I know that daddy is a lot older than mommy. So, I tell her exactly this.

Her eyes meet mine in the mirror as she shuts the engine off after pulling into the driveway. My heart drops when she brushes a tear off her cheek. I didn't mean to make mommy cry. "You're right, baby, age doesn't matter when you're friends," she says. "Elijah will be home in a few hours and Penny really wants to bake with us. Maybe you can bake a special cookie just for him."

And that's all it takes to get me hopping out of the van and skipping into the house. I know exactly what kind of cookie I'm going to make him. One with extra chocolate chips because Elijah loves anything that's sweet.

My five-year-old self doesn't recognize that in this moment, my mother decides it will be my last trip to visit William and his family. A decision made with the best of intentions. She was only protecting what was hers. At all costs. Even from threats that only existed in her mind.

Chapter Twenty-Two

Elijah

So, the dirty looks that I've received from both Dirk and Jesse should concern me, but they don't. Billie Rose and I have gone past the point of no return. Anyone who tries to keep her away from me will be eliminated from our lives. Whoever and however it needs to be accomplished.

Billie Rose is sitting a few feet away from me, a granola bar hanging from her hand as she watches me do my morning workout on the patio.

"Want to grab a bite to eat before we head to the bar tonight. I'll pick you up at the shop at five."

She snaps out of the trance she's in, quickly righting her granola bar as it's about to slide out of the wrapper. "Like on a date?" she asks, squishing up her cute little nose at me.

"Don't act like you don't want to go on a date with me, but no, you'll know when I take you on a date. It won't be to some little hole in the wall pizza joint, which is about all there is around here."

She giggles. "So, where will you take me?" Her eyes turn a shade of purple as her head tips back to look at me. Grabbing the towel beside her, I wipe at my brow. Her lips part as her eyes roam below the waistband of my sweats, my junk hovering just above her.

"To Heaven, baby. I'll take you to Heaven," I say, dropping my eyes to stare down at her.

Her gaze slowly climbs up my torso and I flinch. She smiles. Dammit, what this girl does to me. God, I want to tie her up and make her regret the way she is looking at me right now. Like she's in control.

She jumps to her feet, dusting her ass off. "You know, I've never been convinced such a place exists."

Time stops as we size each other up. She's challenging me.

The ball on my tongue slides between my teeth and her breath hitches. I step into her, trailing my fingers down her arm. "Well, aren't you lucky, because I know the exact coordinates to Heaven."

Her eyelids drop a fraction, her muscles tense. She wants to step away from me, but it can't happen. We're magnetized. That is until the sliding door shoves open, and she falls backward. I wrap my arms around her, catching her seconds before she loses her balance.

"When I catch you, I'll punch your ticket and you'll see just how real Heaven is," I inform her.

"Billie Rose, come inside and eat," Dirk says, grinding his teeth.

She holds out her granola bar, not taking her eyes off me. "I'm good." The wrapper rattles as she shakes her hand.

Dirk takes a step out, finally drawing our attention to him. He stands with his hands on his hips and points to the kitchen. "A real breakfast. Now," he points to the door.

"You've got time, go on. I'll shower and meet you in the kitchen."

Billie Rose nods at me, sucking her bottom lip between her teeth.

Once she's inside, I wait for the ass chewing to commence. Billie Rose already told me how her parents found leaves in her hair last night.

Dirk doesn't scold me. In fact, the advice he gives me resonates deeply in his stormy eyes. "Don't let your dick distract you so much that you miss something, and she gets hurt."

I nod my head once, dropping my eyes to the ground.

"I'll kill you if that happens," he warns.

I meet his glare. "I'll kill myself if that happens."

Later that day, after I pick her up from Junkyard Treasures, Billie Rose and I decide to go to a quiet little ice cream shop for corn dogs and shakes. It's the first time we've actually had to just sit and talk. I told her about my dream to open up a custom bike shop. She listened just like she did when we were kids, hanging on my every word. And I like that.

Lily pulled me aside when I picked her up and said she hadn't seen Billie Rose smile this much since before the accident.

It makes me happy to be part of the reason for that smile.

I've enjoyed it all evening and that's why it's so noticeable when it falls from her face as we walk into the bar.

Grabbing her by the back of her hair roughly, I pull her into my chest, growling into her ear, "Am I going to have to shove my fingers back into your tight little cunt?"

A whimper falls from her lips.

"You've got this."

Draven rounds the corner and spots us. He raises his brows and whistles. "Wow, he sure did a number on your face, didn't he?" He whistles, his gaze bouncing over my face.

Billie Rose nervously glances up at me.

I smile wide. "Still got all my teeth," I joke.

Draven laughs, he steps forward and places his arm around my girl, guiding her back to the office. "Anyhow, I'm glad you guys are back. The bar is fucking killing it. I'm going to need your help deciding if we need to increase our liquor order." He snaps his fingers over his shoulder, indicating I should follow like a goddamn dog.

Roses and Skulls

Flopping myself down on the leather couch, I listen as they discuss business and wait for my orders.

Honestly, the dude doesn't seem to be interested in her for anything other than her knowledge and expertise at making him money.

Maybe it was Lanie all along. Dude still needs to be punished for taking Bill out but maybe he was bamboozled by the crazy bitch and really didn't know that Billie Rose was going to be with him that night.

Billie Rose told me that she had never heard Lanie talk that way. It was as if someone else had taken over her body. I asked Rosie if she knew who Lanie could have been talking to on the phone, but she didn't. At least it sounds like whatever plan they might have; it doesn't involve killing her.

"I saw Lanie at her new job." She says unexpectedly, looking up at Draven.

He genuinely looks surprised. "You did?"

Billie Rose looks down. "Yep."

Draven glances over his shoulder. "Hey, can you take a look at the jukebox? The things not working, and fuck knows I don't want to buy a new one. Those things aren't cheap. See what you can do, yeah?"

I'm really interested in what he's going to say about Lanie working at a whorehouse, but I guess I'll just have to hear it from Rosie later. I stand up slowly and stretch. "Sure thing, boss."

"See you after a bit, baby." I lean over the desk, pulling the sucker out of my mouth and then I hold it out to her.

I've never considered myself a jealous person. In school, I was always the first kid to speak up to share a toy, my lunch, whatever anyone needed. But all that changed when I saw her here that first day. I want to make it very clear to fuck face over here that she's mine.

Her cheeks turn bright pink because she knows what I want from her. I can see the word "fine" hidden within her stormy gaze. She leans forward and oh sweet lord, she wraps her lips around my sucker.

Slowly, I back away from them with an *I just won the lottery* smile on my face.

As I'm making my way down the hall to go take a look at the jukebox, I notice the trash needs taken out, so I grab it and head out back. When I get to the dumpster, I notice a painting face down amongst the bags. My curiosity gets the best of me, and I flip it over.

I tip my head back and laugh. Seems Draven didn't like Jesse's little welcome to the neighborhood gift.

Chapter Twenty-Three

Billie Rose

When the door shuts, I grab the sucker out of my mouth and toss it in the trash bin. Asshole. Could he make it any more obvious?

"So, I'm assuming I can officially call him your boyfriend now?" Draven asks, his arms folded lazily across his chest.

Rolling my eyes, I ignore him. "So, why didn't you tell me she was working at a whorehouse?"

"Maybe because you wouldn't have approved. And why were *you* there?" he asks, leaning over, trying to catch my gaze.

"You're right, I don't approve." I grab a folder and open it. "And it's none of your business, why I was there."

He gently slides it away from me. "You and I don't keep secrets from each other."

"Don't we?" I ask a tad bit too angrily.

He searches my face. "Why don't you just tell me why you were there. Let's try that," he suggests, ushering me to the couch.

Draven doesn't even have to ask me another question before I spill my guts. I would make a terrible detective. No finesse. None. "I found Bill's receipts. I know he was paying Bell to take care of you. Why?"

He chuckles angrily. "Could it be that he felt responsible for killing my uncle and then to top it off, his daughter killed my father?"

I glance away. He's got me there. That is exactly why. My grandfather was a good man, Draven was an innocent child. He wouldn't have wanted him to end up in the foster care system like my mom, no matter who his parents were. "Funny that you repay him by murdering him."

"So, a few bucks are supposed to make up for the fact that I had no family because of the two of them?"

I ignore that comment. "Do you want me dead?"

His dark eyes widen, and his mouth falls open. He stutters, "Billie Rose, no."

"Does Lanie?"

He sits back, his brows pulling together. "No," he whispers to himself.

Lanie sounded so hateful last night. How did I miss it? Has she always hated me? "I heard her talking on the phone to someone about me... and you."

"My mother..." he growls, running his fingers through his dark hair.

My knee bounces and I begin picking at my nails, slowly ripping off a hangnail. I close my eyes, wishing I would have kept my mouth shut.

"But there's no way. She didn't know that Bill was going to be picking you up that night. He was supposed to be coming home from the bar after closing." I'm not sure if he is trying to convince me or himself. "No. She definitely didn't know."

He turns to me, and I can see he wants some sort of confirmation from me.

"My grandpa gave her a ride home too. If she knew what you were up to, she would have had time to call you. Did she know?" I bite the inside of my cheek hard enough I can taste blood. "Did she know what you were doing that night? Has she been in on this the whole time?"

He sighs loudly before jumping to his feet. "Why didn't I see this before?" he says more to himself than to me.

"Did... did you make her be my friend?" I ask, a knot forming in my throat. In my heart I already know the answer.

"Women," he mutters to himself. He wanders around the room aimlessly, ignoring my question.

I'm assuming that means yes, she became my friend on purpose.

I grab another hangnail and tug at it, trying as hard as I can to shove down the hurt I'm feeling. Lanie was my only friend in school. We laughed together, shared embarrassing stories, and now it's almost as if she died. Only worse.

Draven punches the wall, making me jump.

He's breathing heavily as he stares at the hole he just made in the drywall. "All my life I've been deceived by women, why would I think Lanie would be any different." He turns to look at me with a sadness in his eyes that matches my own.

Hesitantly, he comes to sit by me, pulling me into his embrace. Tears track down my cheeks as he holds me close to him. I should push him away and tell him this is all his fault, but I don't.

"I'm so sorry, little dove. So sorry." He grabs me by my shoulders and pushes me back so he can look me in the eye. "Stay away from her, okay? Promise me you won't go back there."

His gaze bounces frantically over my face and I see his genuine concern. My mournful reflection rests there in the pit of his dark eyes.

"I promise," I say softly, turning away.

"If it's any consolation, I really did give her the money to go to culinary school… it was why she agreed to help me in the first place."

My fingers press into my temples as I try to figure all of this out, "So, you aren't really dating? It was all a ploy?"

He grimaces. "We had a mutual understanding. But it seems she has had a secret agenda of her own. My heart skitters when he continues, "I'll take care of it, yeah?" he dips his head, making sure I've heard him. "You're the only girl I've ever been able to trust." He grips my chin and smiles at me.

Me.

Little ole me.

The one who will be the very last woman to deceive him.

And I don't know how I feel about that anymore.

Chapter Twenty-Four

Elijah

Tink. Tink. Tink.

Slowly my eyes blink open.

Tink. Tink. Tink.

My head lulls over to see the bright red numbers on my alarm clock, telling me that I've only been asleep for an hour. Groggily, I sit up and rub my eyes with the palm of my hands.

Tink. Tink. Tink.

Whipping the covers off, I stumble over to the window just as a tiny rock hits the glass. I lean over and spy a little minx taunting me from the ground.

She gives me a shy smile before she takes off running. I watch as she crosses the lawn and disappears amongst the trees.

I shake my head as I swipe my joggers off the floor. Oh, she wants to play, does she?

The full moon lights the path to her secret hideaway, which isn't all that secret. I slow when I enter the space. The only sound is the chime hanging outside the little fort built around a giant tree. I smile before I shove the door open. It's dark and empty. Slowly I spin around, jumping when I find her right behind me.

"Boo!"

The deep chuckle that begins low in my chest makes her take a step back. "So, you wanted me to chase you."

"No," she denies, taking another step back. "I-I couldn't sleep." She nibbles on her nail, refusing to meet my gaze. "You said I could come to you when," her words die off and she huffs. "Never mind," she waves. "It's late. Sorry to…"

I take two steps before I'm wrapping my fingers around her neck and pulling her to her tiptoes, capturing her lips against mine in a brutal kiss. "Shut up," I say against her mouth. My tongue explores hers as I carefully drag us back towards her playhouse.

When I feel the doorway at my back, I spin us around and shove her inside, slamming the door closed behind me. Darkness engulfs us. Christ, it's dark in here. I hear her rummaging around and soon the light of a small lantern chases some of it away.

She slides to the floor, and I notice the edge of her nails, they are bloody and sore.

I don't say anything about it, she doesn't need me to tell her what she's done to herself. I sit down cross-legged in front of her and take her hands in mine, kissing each finger gently.

"This is harder than I thought it was going to be," she says quietly.

"You know, my dad has some really good tips for curbing the urge. I think you should talk to him."

She rubs her cheek over her shoulder. "Okay."

"But until then, I would be happy to help take your mind off of it." I gently start to push her back, but she stops me.

"Wait, wait." Her face turns fire engine red. "Are we going to…"

Oh, how I wish but I'm saving that for something special. Not that this isn't an intimate little space but no. My girl deserves better than to be taken in a treehouse her first time. When I shake my head, the disappointment is evident on her face.

I try to encourage her onto her back once more.

"No. Wait, Elijah. I. God, I don't know anything about sex, okay? There, I said it." She slides away from me.

"Baby, I know that. We had this discussion at the cabin. I like that you haven't been with anyone else," I admit, grabbing her ankle and pulling her back to me.

She kicks at me. "Stop, you're not listening. Let me finish."

I pause but keep her ankle locked in my grip.

Her eyes are wide and beautiful. I could stare into them for days.

"I want you to tell me what will happen, and I want to see it." She nervously points to my groin.

My hand releases her and she slinks back against the wall. "You don't know what happens?" I ask cautiously.

Her face is so red it's almost purple. "How would I?" she whispers.

My head pulls back, and I blink at her. "Well, haven't you, um, you haven't looked things up on the internet?"

She shakes her head back and forth. "No. I mean, I get what happens." She rolls her eyes. "I get the gist, but I don't." She sighs and rests her head against the wall. "You know how my parents are. Do you think I would risk them finding out I was watching porn?"

When Jesse came to me, asking for my help, she apologized for keeping Billie Rose and I apart. She said she didn't want to risk anything transpiring between us before its time. I understand, she had been abused. Violently. And as a mom, she felt it her duty to thwart any potential threat, even if there was no viable danger to her daughter.

But now here sits said daughter, on a completely different end of the spectrum. Where Jesse knew too much, too soon, Billie Rose knows nothing.

Clearly, I can see how embarrassed she is. I don't want to make this anymore awkward for her than it needs to be.

"If I take my dick out, he's going to wake up and want to play," I tease, tipping my head and giving her an *I want you to be my play date* sort of smile.

275

She sits forward, her eyes going wide.

I run my hands through my hair. "Have you really never seen one?" I ask.

She grimaces as she continues to stare at my crotch.

With my knuckle, I tip her chin, raising her face. "You've been around plenty of boys and men. All of which pee outside any chance they get, and you've never accidentally caught even a glimpse?"

"They don't pee around me. One time a guy came to a barbeque. He wasn't one of the regulars, so he didn't know the *rules*. Anyhow, he started to take a piss by a tree near where I was playing. He wasn't facing me or anything and to be honest, I wouldn't have even known had my dad not drawn attention to him. I don't know if it's true or not, but Jackson told me that my dad beat him so badly he pissed blood for an entire month."

Jesus.

"Great, now I scared you and you're not going to show me yours either." She tries to stand but I catch her around the wrist and pull her back to the ground.

"Take him out," I order, rising to my knees and pulling my shirt off over my head.

Her eyes slowly climb up my frame until locking on mine. She swallows hard. Her innocence is going to be the death of me. I want to corrupt her. Just for me. I want to make her my own personal plaything.

Gently, I stroke her face. "I'm going to do bad things to you, Billie Rose."

"Tell me," she whispers, her lips parting.

A small thrill runs up my spine. Her hungry gaze drops to my chest, eyes curious as she notices that my body responds much in the same way hers does. She's getting under my skin, and she's finally realizing it.

I grab her cheeks in one hand and slowly tip her head back. For a long minute I stare into her eyes, wondering how long she's waited for this. There's a look of longing on her face. One of desperation. She's a woman who wants to be touched, kissed, chased... caught.

"Open."

She does without hesitation, and I lean forward and spit into her mouth.

The look on her face, doesn't change. Billie Rose slowly sticks her tongue out, showing me my own spit.

"Swallow it."

She does.

"Good girl. Now, you know what to do next."

Without taking her eyes from mine, she allows her hand to slide down the front of my sweatpants. Her eyes widen in awe, fear, and fascination. A combination of emotions plays over her face as her fingers wrap around me.

"I'm going to use that cock to fuck every one of your pretty, little holes," I tell her.

I'm not sure if she believes me but she wanted to know what's going to happen and I'm not about to lie to her. Her eyes fall away from mine, and she uses both of her hands to slide my joggers down my hips. When my dick springs out in her face, she starts to slide away from me but stops herself.

"It's okay, you two are going to be best friends soon, don't be afraid of him." I run my hand through her hair.

Gently, she wraps her hand around the base of my cock, making my eyes roll back in my head. This was probably a terrible idea. I want to throw her on her back and sink my dick in her so deep she forgets her name.

A hiss escapes me as I feel a hesitant lick of her tongue around my tip. I open my eyes and stare down at her. Eyes as blue as the deepest part of the ocean peek up at me, seeking approval. "Such a good girl," I gather her hair and wrap it around my fist, encouraging her.

It's clear she has no idea what she's doing and fuck if that doesn't turn me on. Mine. All fucking mine.

When her lips wrap around me, she takes me farther, gagging about half the way there. She tries to pull away. I don't let her. "Keep going, baby, just relax."

So, she does. Billie Rose wants to please me and fuck if that doesn't make my balls tighten. My other hand hits the wall as I hold myself upright. It's been a long time since I've been with a girl, and it's never felt like this.

I let her pull away for air and those damn sapphires catch the look of pleasure on my face. She smiles wickedly before shoving my cock back down her throat, wrapping those tiny fingers around the base. She slides them up and down as her mouth works me. Jesus, a porn star is being born right before my eyes.

She truly is beautiful. A unique blend or exotic and simplicity, rolled into one tiny little package. Her long, dark hair, clutched tightly in my fist and my dick in her mouth, is a sight I could get used to.

"Billie Rose, you need to stop or I'm going to come right down that pretty little throat of yours."

A challenge sparks, one dark eyebrow rises, announcing that I will indeed be doing just that.

If that's what she wants, I'm happy to oblige.

Her tongue swirls and her pace increases. God, it's too much. Her cheeks hollow out as she sucks. I tighten my grip, unable to hold back. Her hands fly up to my thighs as I shove her head down as far as I can, her nose pressing against me. The sound of her gagging, does me in.

Billie Rose's nails dig into my thighs before I finally release her and let her take a breath. She sputters, wiping the back of her hand over her mouth.

Unease creeps over her features as she sees the intent in my gaze. "My turn," I flip her on her back and have her pants down before she has time to stop me.

I stare at the wet spot on her white cotton panties as I pull up my own pants. Don't want him to think he's getting seconds. In fact, I wasn't even expecting to get my dick wet until my big surprise for her. But I'm not complaining.

"You look scared," I say quietly.

"I'm… no, it's just…"

My hands slide up her legs and I hook my thumbs around the edge of her panties. "I want to see you." I run my nose along her, sniffing loudly. "I want to smell you." My tongue flattens out over the soft cotton, and I lick her right over her underwear.

She jerks her hips in response, lifting her ass off the ground. It gives me just enough time to slide her panties right off her.

"And I want to taste you."

I let her keep her shirt on even though I want to see her tits. I'm betting they are just as pretty as the rest of her.

My fingers wrap around her thighs and push her legs back and then I burry my face in her delightful little pussy. When I moan against her, she lets out a garbled noise from the back of her throat. I smile against her. She is very responsive, and I know it won't take her long. But I don't want this to be over quickly.

I run my tongue piercing over her clit and her legs begin to tremble.

"Elijah," she groans, grinding herself into my face. "Please," she begs.

My hands slide under her ass and squeeze her plump cheeks. I want to explore all of her but there will be time for that later.

Slowly, I slide a finger inside of her and then another. No longer able to contain herself, she cries out, "God, oh god."

I give her the pressure she needs to hurl herself over the precipice. My tongue continues to tease her while my fingers curl, giving attention to the spot that will make her erupt in my mouth.

"Elijah. Oh. No. Something's not right." Her hands press on my shoulders but I'm not quitting, not even to explain to her that it will be okay and to let go.

My fingers continue their brutal assault, while my tongue soothes away the hurt and then she starts speaking nonsense right before her body tenses and she fucking comes hard all over my face, just like I was hoping.

Tremors wrack her body as I slide myself up beside her, pulling her close so that her head rests on my chest.

As her body starts to come back down to earth, I stroke my hand over her hair, down her back, along her hips.

"That was… different," she says quietly.

"You're fucking beautiful when you come for me," I tell her. "Don't ever be embarrassed and don't ever hold back."

She shifts so that she can look at me. "I just have one question," she says shyly.

"What's that, baby?" I ask, my fingers combing lightly through her dark locks.

"How is that thing going to fit inside me?"

I bop her on the end of her nose with my finger. "You're adorable."

"I'm not joking, Elijah, I don't think it's going to work." Her eyes change color, her eyebrow cocking in warning.

So cute. I shove her head back down on my chest. "It will fit, stop worrying."

Chapter Twenty-Five

Billie Rose

If my family noticed the change in me, nobody said anything. There's just something about knowing I'm Elijah's girl that makes me stand taller. Gone is the girl that hid her voice from the world. I feel powerful... I feel like a woman.

We haven't had sex yet but that's okay. It's the way he looks at me. It doesn't matter where we are, his eyes follow me everywhere. I pretend not to notice but I do.

I'm making my way around the club members, saying hello as we host yet another party. This one is for JD and his fiancé. They are getting married in a few weeks and instead of having a separate bachelorette and bachelor party, the club decided to do it all in one. I've never seen JD so happy.

I can feel Elijah's eyes on my backside as I approach my father. My father's gaze is fixated behind me, his lip curled up in a snarl. "The party seems to be going well," I say as I reach him.

He focuses his attention on me, the lines around his eyes softening. "It sure is, baby girl." He pulls me into a hug and pats me lightly on the back.

When he releases me, I shift so that I'm standing beside him, looking out over the guests milling around the yard and down by the lake.

"How are things going at the bar?" he asks.

I kick my foot up behind me to rest against the wall. "Actually, it's going really well. The bar is doing great. Our revenue is awesome."

His forehead wrinkles in confusion. "Did you forget why you are there?" he asks.

"No," I huff. "But it's going to be mine soon and I want it to be making money."

He laughs quietly. "I get that, but we need to end this soon. It's been several weeks now and I'm getting nervous."

"I don't know dad, maybe it was Lanie all along. Draven hasn't done or said anything inappropriate lately. It's been strictly business."

My dad lights up a cigarette. "Never let your guard down, baby girl. He is a Devil, and they're definitely trying to set up shop here and I can't let that happen. I'm going to have to step in soon."

Roses and Skulls

I watch as a girl I don't know walks towards Elijah. Of course, he doesn't notice because his eyes are glued to me. "I know dad. I just, I don't know. I'll wrap it up."

"You just tell me when to pull the plug." He blows a veil of smoke around us. "You know, you don't have to be the one to do it. I'll handle it."

The girl that I watched approach Elijah is trying to get his attention. He's being polite but I can tell he's irritated as fuck that she's interrupting his ogling of me.

"Billie Rose," my dad says, trying to get my attention.

"Hold that thought." I hold up a single finger.

I march across the lawn as the pretty blonde lays her hand on Elijah's chest, blinking up at him all innocent like. I don't know where this bitch came from or which one of these bikers brought her here, but I don't give one single fuck. This is my home. My club. My man.

Elijah sees me coming, his brow raising slightly. He tells her something and she turns my direction. But it doesn't deter her. She smiles sweetly and shifts back to Elijah, not moving her hand. I guess I'll have to do it for her.

I hear Elijah tell her, "I tried to warn you." Amusement twinkles in his mischievous brown eyes.

Asshole.

When I tap her on the shoulder, she ignores me. "Sorry, sweetie, we're busy. Go find yourself a boy, this guy here is too much man for someone like you."

Without thought or feeling, my hand snags her hair and pulls her away from Elijah. I drag her across the lawn as she screams, reaching up, clawing at my hand, attempting to get me to release her.

"You bitch, let me go. Brody is going to kill you for this," she seethes.

This makes me pause, letting her go. She jumps to her feet, and we stare at each other. Brody brought her here?

Brody comes running over just then. "I'm sorry, Rosie." He grabs the woman's hand and tries to pull her away. "Lanie asked me to give her friend a place to stay for a few days. I didn't know she would go and cause trouble." He glares at her.

The blonde laughs. "You think you are woman enough to handle that," she taunts, tossing a look back over her shoulder at Elijah. She snorts when she faces me.

Everyone is quiet.

I pull my hair over my shoulder. "I hope you and Lanie have good insurance at Bell's."

Bimbo says nothing. She just stares at me, rubbing the back of her head where I pulled her hair.

"You're going to need it for a new nose," I tell her calmly.

She laughs when she finally realizes what I'm saying. She looks me up and down, rolling her eyes.

Roses and Skulls

I know I'm tiny, but she must have short term memory loss because I just drug her ass across the lawn by her hair. Did she forget that already?

My eyes roam behind her. Elijah sticks a sucker in his mouth and winks, a relaxed, somewhat bored expression over his face.

The woman thinks I'm distracted, and I am, but I'm not stupid. She charges me and without taking my eyes off my man, I rear back and my fist clashes with her nose as she approaches. The crunch of bone sends a shiver up my spine. Blood spurts over the both of us.

She bends over, holding her nose and crying. I take a few steps towards her and muster up the best loogie of my life and spit it right in her eye. "I hope she's a better friend to you than she was me."

Brody helps her to her feet, apologizing the entire time. "I'm so sorry, Rosie. You won't see her again." He drags her away.

It's then I notice the entire club gawking at me, their jaws dropped open in surprise.

"Just for the record," I say loud enough for all the women to hear, "he's mine." I point to Elijah. "I'll knife anyone who so much as looks at him wrong."

And with those parting words, I make my way into the warehouse to clean up.

My mom follows me inside. When we get to my room, she pulls me into her arms. I'm shaking. From anger, adrenaline, I'm not sure. "I take it you don't consider Lanie a friend anymore. Why would she send someone here to hurt you?"

I pull away, a new worry entering my thoughts. Lanie knows about Elijah. How? Is she in town? Draven told me he would handle her. I didn't ask what that meant but maybe I should have.

"She's jealous. She doesn't like that I'm working for Draven."

Mom nods sadly. "Okay, I'll leave you to clean up." She stops at the door. "That was one hell of a punch."

"You aren't mad?" I ask, hesitantly.

"No, baby. I'm not mad. I would have done exactly the same." She gives me a wide smile. "Don't beat yourself up over it. You're a Skull." She nods her head towards my hand. "Put some ice on that."

I glance down, noticing my knuckles swelling slightly.

The pain feels good. Punching that bitch felt good. I wonder how it would feel to kill someone. Can I do it? I heard my dad before Ms. Bimbo put her hands on what was mine. He said he would handle it. I just need to tell him when to pull the plug.

As the days go on, I wonder if it's Draven I should really be angry at. I mean, he was there that night, but he didn't drive the truck and he didn't know I would be there. He's been so nice to Elijah and me the past few weeks. Like he really is trying to make amends. Does today prove who really has it out for me?

After a quick shower, I sit on the edge of my bed and send Draven a text.

Me: She's at it again.

Draven: What now?

Me: She sent a friend in to make the moves on Elijah.

Draven: No way.

Me: Yes way.

Me: I thought you said you would handle her.

Draven: She's a female, nuff said.

Me: Well, I'm just warning you that I'll handle her myself if you don't.

Draven: What's that supposed to mean, little dove?

Me: Ask her friend.

Draven: Don't know her friend. Tell me.

Me: I'll give her and her friend matching face lifts.

Draven: …

Draven: …

Draven: Okay, I'll try again.

Me: You do that.

Draven: I don't really like the way you're talking to me.

Me: I don't give a fuck what you like. Keep her away from me and my family or I will.

I toss the phone down on my bed, feeling better than I have in a long time. If I'm not mistaken, I think my balls have finally dropped. I'm not going to be walked on ever again.

Chapter Twenty-Six

Billie Rose

"I really needed you to work this weekend," Draven says, thoroughly annoyed that I'm off the next two days.

My feet shove off the floor, sending my chair sliding over to the filing cabinet. "Don't care. I've been here every weekend for over a month. You can live without my help two days."

"Where are you going?"

"Don't know." I shift the cherry sucker in my mouth to my cheek. "I'll be back Monday."

He flops down on the couch, the leather groaning beneath him. The intensity of his gaze on my back makes me spin around to face him. "What?"

"I can't protect you if I don't know where you're at."

"Protect me from what, Draven?" I roll my hands.

He crosses his arms across his chest and focusses his attention out the window. "Sometimes, I wish you were still afraid of me."

A million swarming bees invade my stomach. I haven't had this feeling in a long time. The wheels on my chair squeak as I slowly make my way back behind the desk. Draven's mood is one I haven't encountered before. I'm not sure what he's feeling right now. "What do you mean?"

"It was easier when you were afraid of me."

My hands begin to shake, so I tuck them under my legs. "You want me to be scared of you?"

"Yes, because then maybe you would listen to me. I don't think it's a good idea that you go away this weekend. In fact, if you were my daughter, I'd lock you in your goddamn room. I thought Dirk was smarter than this."

Lanie is busy plotting ways to stab me in the back, maybe you should worry about that.

But I don't say this to him.

"I'll be fine. Elijah would never hurt me. You know this," I offer quietly. "And as far as my dad is concerned, it's none of his business where I go. I'll be twenty in a few months. I'm an adult, remember?"

He eyes me for several long minutes as I ponder what is going on in his head.

"I'm sorry, I just worry about you is all." He waves it off, pretending that the last few minutes never happened.

"Are you worried about me because of Lanie?" I ask.

He runs his hands through his dark hair, laying his head back on the couch to stare up at the ceiling. "No."

"Then what is it?"

"Nothing," he jumps to his feet. "I just wanted you to be here for the band this weekend. It's going to be crazy, and I need you."

I stand up and head towards the door. "I'm sorry, Draven, but Elijah has been planning this trip for a while now. I don't want to disappoint him."

Life has been clicking along for so long that sometimes, I forget who Draven really is. And actually, I'm not really sure I know him at all. Is he Crow's son? Grandpa's? No, he couldn't be grandpas. Bell all but confirmed it.

But I've been studying Draven when he isn't looking and there are moments of familiarity. His mannerisms sometimes remind me of my mother. They have the same dark hair too. I shake my head and sigh.

When I walk into the main bar, Elijah spots me and waves me over. He finally got the new part in for the jukebox. I'm glad he was able to fix it. "Are you almost done?" I ask, looking at the clock on the wall. I'm ready to get out of here. Draven's mood has me rattled.

"Yep." He stands behind me as I look at the music selections, his breath hot on my ear. "When you walk by the table behind us, look at their jackets. They have a new patch."

I nod slightly and turn around to face him. He stares down at me, and I can see anger simmering in his brown eyes.

"I'm going to go wash up and I'll meet you out back," he says, grabbing me by my shoulders and placing a kiss to my forehead.

He walks away from me, and I allow my gaze to follow him until he disappears. Slowly, I let my eyes fall over the leather jacket that is draped on the back of a chair.

My heart drops to my stomach. The new patch is of a woman held hostage by a devil, his tail wrapped around her torso, pinning her arms to her side.

A woman who looks an awful lot like me.

No.

Jesus Christ, is this just another way to taunt my mother?

Draven meets my gaze from behind the bar. One of the men at the table whistles, drawing my attention to him. "Hey, princess, you gunna let your boy prospect for us?"

Roses and Skulls

It's Draven's second, his VP. And he's always looked at me with a loathing that makes my skin crawl. "You mean, Elijah?" I ask.

He nods, leaning back and pulling his cigarettes out of his pocket. "We'd take real good care of him."

"He's a grown ass man. Ask him yourself," I say on my way past him.

The man reaches out and grabs my arm. As I begin to pry his fat fingers from my elbow, he releases me. I stumble back and see why the asshole let go so fast. Draven has a gun pressed to the man's temple.

"What did I say about her?"

The man laughs, a gold tooth shining against the lights from the bar. "Yeah, yeah, don't touch the little MC princess."

Draven lifts the gun away from the man's head and slowly moves it across the room, making sure to run it over every member of his club that is here. "Never. Never touch her or I will paint the walls of this bar with your blood."

I swallow hard and rush behind the bar. Draven follows me to the back. He tries to pull me into his arms, and I let him, because, well, because he still has his gun out.

"They know better, it won't happen again."

My head bobs up and down as I try to gently pry myself away from him. "Elijah's waiting for me," I say quietly.

"I know." He spins me around. "What my VP said back there. Would you be okay with that?"

"Y-you mean, Elijah prospecting for the Devils?"

"Yes. I think it's time you both break away from the warehouse. Things are going good for us here. My club is the strongest it's been in years thanks to you and the profits from the bar."

My heart is still swimming in bile as I try to wrap my head around what he's asking. "Draven, Elijah can do what he wants. You don't have to ask for my permission."

His dark eyes spark. He runs the back of his hand over my cheek. "I just want you to be happy here."

"I am," I assure him. "It's just, that guy scared me."

"I'm sorry about that. Like I said it won't happen again. You're safe with me, little dove."

I back away and offer him a small smile. "I know."

"You guys could even move in with me. It's lonely without Lanie at the apartment," he offers.

Tucking my hair behind my ear, I start to walk away. "I'll think about it over the weekend."

He smiles wide. "Sounds good. We'll talk more next week."

As I'm walking out, I feel his eyes on my back.

When I get outside, Elijah instantly pulls me into his arms. "Did you see it?" he asks, nuzzling into the side of my neck.

"I saw it," I whisper. "Take me home."

Roses and Skulls

Once we get the warehouse, Elijah tells me that he has some things to finish up for our date weekend. I smile up at him. "Come on, give me a hint." I rub my hand over his chest, sliding it lower, hoping he will give me what I want.

He takes my hands in his. "Don't think you can weasel your way around me, Rosie. I know you better than anyone."

My bottom lip pushes out. "But.."

"But nothing. Go on, I'll wait until you get inside safely and then I've got things to do." He gently pushes me away from him, swatting me on the behind.

"Fine," I stomp away from him. But I squeal to myself when I get inside. I'm so excited to be going away with him for the weekend.

The warehouse is dark, but I know where to find him. He secretly waits for me to get home every night. I'm sure the thought of us going away for an entire weekend is killing him.

I push the door open and flick the light on.

My dad is sitting at the head of the table, his fingers steepled in front of his mouth.

He doesn't even jump in surprise. His stormy orbs climb up my frame, making sure I'm in one piece.

I drag my finger over the table and take the seat beside him. "You know you don't have to wait up for me?"

"Who says I'm waiting up for you?"

My eyebrow cocks at the exact same angle as his. He chuckles lightly and sits forward, tucking my hair behind my ear. "Old habits, remember?"

I nod. "Old habits."

"How was work?"

Biting my lip, I glance at the wall behind him, fixating on a picture of him and my mom on his Harley. Both are smiling wide, her arms locked around his waist, her head resting on his back. They look young and happy. I want that. I'm tired of feeling unease at every turn.

He follows my gaze with his stormy eyes.

"That's all I've ever wanted," I whisper.

"What did Elijah do?" my dad asks in a low growl.

Shaking my head, I sit back. "Nothing. He didn't do anything. Jesus, you jump fast."

"Then why the melancholy?"

My gaze goes back to all the photos on the wall. My club. My family. I want more than the life I've been living.

"What if I can't do it?" I ask, pulling my legs to my chest and hugging them.

My dad grabs the arm of my chair and pulls it so I'm right in front of him. "It's something that changes you forever. You can't take it back. It's permanent."

I start to speak but he stops me.

"I'm not saying that you don't understand all of this. What I'm trying to say is that I've tried my whole life to keep you from having to experience it. I won't think you're weak. No one will. Let me be your dad, let me take this burden from you."

My feet drop to the ground, and I stand up, walking over to the pictures. I run my finger over one of grandpa and me. A sound somewhere between a laugh and a cry escapes me. I'm riding on his shoulders at a local biker event. I remember how tall I felt. I could see over everyone's heads. His hands were wrapped around mine, holding on tight.

Dad wraps his arms around me from behind, resting his chin on my head.

"I miss him," I sniffle, wiping my nose on my shirt sleeve.

"Me too, baby girl. He wasn't just my father-in-law; he was my best friend."

We stand there quietly, looking at all the memories from years past. It's then that I make my decision. It's time for me to move forward. Grandpa wouldn't have wanted me to live with this pain for as long as I have.

"I think it's time to pull the plug," I say quietly.

My dad squeezes me, letting me know he understands what I'm saying.

"Draven asks me every night if I need a ride home, but I always decline. I do this in front of others. No one will expect me to catch a ride with him next Friday night. I'll ask him for a lift after everyone leaves."

My dad straightens and turns me to face him.

"I'll tell him I have a cramp in my leg and ask him to pull over. When we get off his bike…"

The scary eyebrow pops up.

"Then you will show up," I explain quietly.

He breathes a sigh of relief. "He will know that it's you who is holding him accountable," he reassures me.

"I know. I-I just want him to die the same way grandpa did. Can you do that?" I ask.

Dad nods slowly and then pulls me into his arms, hugging me tight. "What happened at the bar tonight?"

"Nothing, it just doesn't feel like Grandpa's bar anymore."

He nods, scratching his fingers through his greying beard. "Your mom is driving back with William and then flying home. They leave Thursday morning, so this should all work out nicely."

Dad sits back down and immediately is on his phone. No doubt, preparing the troops for battle.

"I'm going to head to bed. Elijah and I are leaving tomorrow morning. We'll be back late Sunday."

The only sign of aggravation is the clench of his jaw. "I'll be here when you leave."

I nod once and turn to walk out.

"Billie Rose."

Resting my shoulder against the door jamb, I pause and wait for his lecture about staying safe while I'm away. But that's not what I get.

He gives me a small smile. "Don't tell Elijah this but I do hope you both have a good time this weekend."

I rush over and wrap my arms around him and kiss his cheek. "Thank you. I'm so very excited!"

My father, the big bad biker, pats my arm. "I know, baby girl."

I think he finally realizes that he has to let me experience life.

Even if that means he might not be there to protect me.

But I know in my heart, no matter what befalls me, as long as he lives, he will always have my back.

Chapter Twenty-Seven

Billie Rose

Being on the back of Elijah's bike is the best feeling in the world. I've ridden on bikes my whole life, but this is different.

Smiling up at the blue sky, I take a deep breath.

Free.

I feel free.

It doesn't matter where we're going. I would go anywhere with him. I'm still amazed my parents let me go without any hassle.

My dad did do a quick inspection of Elijah's bike but found nothing that concerned him. He held me extra-long before letting me hop on behind Elijah. I can't blame him though. He loves me and one thing I'm learning, is that his love language is taking care of me and mom. Making sure we are as safe as possible.

When I realize where we are, I get excited. I've been here once before with my Uncle Dan. There is nothing better than races on the salt flats.

But there are no other people around as we speed across the wide-open space. And then we come upon two things. My mom's rod and Aunt Lily's Volkswagen bus.

We slow down and stop beside them. "What's this?" I ask as I take my helmet off.

"This is our very own little piece of Heaven." He waves his arm around us.

I bounce on the balls of my feet.

The bus is decked out just like a small camper. Everything we need all right here.

"You're not disappointed we aren't staying in a fancy hotel somewhere?"

I spin in a circle with my hands out. "This is perfect!"

He laughs and busies himself at the back of the bus, pulling out chairs and everything we need for our own little outdoor sitting area. "Your mom let me borrow the rod. I thought we could see how good your donut game is."

The thought of driving my mom's rod over the flats makes my heart skip a happy beat. "I can't believe everyone agreed to all this."

Elijah looks up at me as he sets up a little fire pit. "They want to see you happy."

And I am happy.

Life is definitely looking up. I think a lot of it has to do with letting go.

I've realized that I don't have to carry the pain of that night with me everywhere I go. I don't have to introduce it to every single person I meet.

"What can I do to help?" I ask, rubbing my hands together.

"Nothing." He points to one of the chairs. "Sit, this weekend is my early birthday gift to you."

Don't have to tell me twice. Watching Elijah do anything, is like a live and in stereo thirst trap. He pulls his hair back into a bun, showing off the tattoos on the sides of his head.

"Let's get crazy while it's still light out." He motions for me to follow him to the rod.

We determine that he is in fact the donut king. I laugh so hard I'm afraid I'm going to pee my pants. There's nothing like having an open space to drive fast and spin-out, without fear of hitting anything. By the time we've almost burned through a tank of gas, it's starting to get dark out.

Roses and Skulls

He tells me that he has an outdoor shower set up for us behind the bus. He takes his first as I sit and watch the sun dip behind the mountains. It's so beautiful out here and not a soul in sight. When he finishes, he comes around the bus in nothing but a pair of boxers.

I swallow hard, slightly nervous about the night that is to come.

"So, I have something for you to change in to after your shower. There is a mirror back there and everything you need. Your mom helped me with this part of the surprise."

"Okay," I say nervously. What is all this about?

I get up and walk around the back of the bus, finding a little vanity set up and I see my makeup and things lying out across it." I run my hand over the black bag that must contain my outfit for the night. Slowly, I unzip it to find a beautiful, sparkly blue dress.

My hand flies to my mouth. This is all so unexpected.

"Do you like it?"

Elijah is leaning against the back of the bus watching me.

"It's beautiful."

"I have a lot of regrets in life," he continues. "Not taking you to your prom is one of them."

Tears pool in the bottom of my eyes. "I didn't go to prom."

"I know, your mom told me. Hence all of this." He waves his arm out.

One thing I didn't expect from the beautifully, brutal looking man standing in front of me, was romance. Elijah just checked another box. Can he be any more perfect?

He backs away. "I can't wait to see you in it," he says and then with a wink he disappears around the back of the bus.

For some reason, when I sit down after my outdoor shower to do my makeup, I begin to feel a sadness settle deep in my heart. I miss my mom. She had begged me to go to prom. I didn't have a date, but I knew Jackson would have taken me in a heartbeat. But I wouldn't indulge her. Instead, I simply informed her that there would be no more dances for me.

Draven stole so much from me. From her.

I set my phone on the vanity and hit video call.

She picks up on the first ring, my dad hovering over her shoulder. "What's wrong, baby?" she asks.

I smile at them and instantly they both drop their shoulders in relief. "Nothing is wrong." My chin settles in my hand as I stare at my parents through the screen "I'm sure you both know that Elijah is giving me a mini prom out in the middle of nowhere." I laugh and rub my hand over my forehead, watching as they both nod. "Well, I thought maybe you would want to, well, I thought you might want to help me get ready."

My mom tears up, but answers right away. "Yes, baby, I sure do." She gets up to assumably grab some tissues.

My dad picks up the phone. "Everything is going okay?" he asks.

"It's perfect, daddy. Thank you."

He nods, biting at the ring in his lip. "Thank you for doing this for your mom."

I pull the towel off my head to dry my hair. "I think she did this for me but whatever." I roll my eyes, pretending to give him the sass that he had become accustomed to.

"She needed this, Billie Rose," he says in all seriousness, adding, "I think you did too."

"He's so good to me, dad."

He sets the phone back down. "Here comes your mom. Just, please be safe," he reiterates, his voice cracking. "I'll leave you women to it." And he's gone before I can say anything else.

My mom comes into view with a glass of wine in her hand and a box of tissues. "Okay, I'm ready," she says, setting everything down on the desk in front of her. "Now, what are we going to do with your hair."

"I was thinking of leaving it down. What do you think?" I ask, smiling ear to ear.

"Well, our hair is one of our best assets," she states, winking at me. "I think down would be perfect."

As we go back and forth about eyeshadow colors, our relationship slowly morphs back into what it used to be before the accident. Maybe even better, now that we are both women.

"So, do you have any questions for me? I feel like I haven't prepared you enough for an intimate relationship." Her cheeks turn to fire as she looks around her bedroom.

"Mom, look at me." She turns with sad eyes. "I might not know everything but trust me when I tell you that I'm figuring it out. I think it's more exciting that way, don't you?"

She runs her hand over her face. "I'm sorry I projected my trauma on to you. I learned everything so young..." she shakes her head as if trying to shake the memories away. "I didn't want you to know too much too soon."

"It's fine. Elijah likes it this way," I tease.

My mom covers her ears. "I don't want to hear it," she scolds but then smiles. "I'm glad we can talk like this again."

"Me too."

"Go on, get the dress on. I want to see the whole look. I'll go get your father."

Quickly, I move out from in front of the camera and slide the dress up and over my hips. It's so soft, and it fits me perfectly.

I don't have shoes because my mom thought of everything and since we are on the salt flats, she sent some sparkly barefoot jewelry.

"Are you guys ready?" I ask.

"Yep, we're both here."

Roses and Skulls

When I step into view, they both gasp. "Beautiful," my mom cries. My dad pulls her head into his chest as she weeps.

I shift back and forth, trying to see myself in the camera. It's been a long time since I dressed up like this.

"Baby girl, I knew I should have locked you up and threw away the key the day you were born. You're gorgeous, honey."

My eyes slide to his. He's giving me a look that literally melts my heart. And I start to envision a day when this man walks me down the aisle.

My mom sniffles and raises her head to give me another once over. "You better send pictures."

"I will. I should go now. Thanks for all your help."

We say our goodbyes and before the phone disconnects, I catch my dad cradle my mom's face in his hands and kiss her tears away.

I sigh dreamily as I make my way around the bus, stopping dead in my tracks.

Elijah is standing under a canopy covered in twinkling white lights. He slowly turns around as if sensing my presence. He's in a tux. A fucking tux, people. He smiles and the whole world breaks off around us.

Music starts playing from a speaker and it's then I notice he has a remote that he shoves back in his pocket. He holds out his hand for me. I take a step but then hesitate, remembering the last conversation I had with my grandfather.

Elijah tips his head in question.

"This is all too much," I whisper.

He closes the distance between us and stares down at me. "Nothing is too much for you."

I place my hand against his chest, fighting tears that threaten to ruin all the hard work on my makeup.

"What is it?" he asks gently.

Gripping his jacket in my fists, I answer. "I prayed for this Elijah. All of this. Boys were so afraid of my dad, they never asked me to dance. No one had big enough balls."

He tips my chin with his knuckle. "Are you saying my big balls are the answer to all your prayers?"

I bust out laughing. "I guess they are." But then I turn serious. "The last time I danced was with my grandfather. It was the night of the accident."

Elijah pulls me into his arms, finally understanding.

Slowly, he starts to move to the beat of the music, letting me savor the moment. Then he spins me away from him. "I'm sorry but you are so goddamn sexy in that dress," he tells me, flashing me a toothy white smile.

"You aren't so bad yourself."

We dance the night away, stopping only to warm up the delicious meal my mom made for us.

Roses and Skulls

I lie back on the blanket after we finish and stare up at the dark sky. "The stars are beautiful here," I tell him. "Thank you for all of this. I don't know when I've had this much fun."

"This is just the beginning. Some day we will be bringing our kids out here."

My head falls to the side. "Kids? You want to have children?"

"Don't you?" he asks.

"Well, yeah."

He gives me a panty melting smile. "I want to experience everything with you, Rosie." Elijah pushes up on his elbow. "Do you remember when we would sneak out at night and sit on the beach and watch the waves roll in?"

"Yes. I loved it there. The water was so powerful, it scared me, but I always felt safe with you." I run my fingertips over the tattoo on the side of his head. "I still do."

A slow smile begins to form on his face. "Are you sure that's wise?" he asks before running his tongue along my bottom lip, catching it between his teeth.

My hips rise from the ground. Elijah possesses some serious voodoo magic when it comes to the invisible string between us.

"I want to see you," he growls into my mouth.

We've done a lot of petting and kissing since the day in the woods but tonight is the night I fully give myself to him. I've tried to prepare and it's not that I'm scared, but I am anxious.

He helps me to my feet and spins me around, slowly unzipping my dress, his breath hot on my ear. "I've waited for this for so long, Billie Rose. But tell me if any of this makes you feel uncomfortable, and we'll stop. Okay?"

"Okay," I say, a bit breathless as my dress pools around my feet.

He makes quick work of unhooking my bra. The cool night air is such a contrast to the heat at my back. His heat. A shiver courses through me as his hands slide around to cup my breasts. The groan that he releases makes my stomach do a little flip.

"So, perfect," he whispers, teasing my nipples between his thumb and fingers. My head falls back against his hard chest. Little ripples of pleasure course through my body. His hands are rough, and he is anything but gentle. He doesn't handle me like a princess, no, he treats me like I'm his little slut. I love it.

One of his hands leaves my breast and slides down my stomach, dipping into my panties. His finger glides up and down, just like he did with a sucker that first night in the bar. Only this is so much better. Knowing who he is this time around makes it so damn good. He's my Elijah.

"Who do you belong to, Billie Rose?"

"You," I moan as he shoves two fingers roughly inside of me, making me rise up on my toes.

He brushes the stubble of his beard over the side of my cheek. "I want you to come on my fingers, baby."

He works me harder and harder until my head presses into his chest, and I cry out to the stars above. My knees give out. Elijah holds me close to him, keeping his fingers buried deep inside me, allowing me to ride out the bliss under the inky night sky.

Once I come down from my high, he lays me on the blanket. He towers above me, slowly removing his own clothes, letting me enjoy the show. When he slides his boxers down his legs, I unconsciously slide back. Okay, so I might be slightly scared.

He drops to the ground between my feet and pulls me back down to him. "Shh, I'm not going to draw this out the first time because I can see that you're afraid. But know that after this time, there will be no holding back. I will destroy this little pussy of yours."

My stomach does another flip at the crassness of his words. Like I said, I'm a sucker for this side of him. He's the only one I'll ever let talk to me this way.

He's the only one brave enough to.

Elijah settles between my legs, his arms braced on each side of my head. He reaches between us, and I feel the length of him slide against me. My eyelids flutter closed because it just feels so damn good. He starts kissing my neck, his hand sliding between us.

When he lines himself up at my entrance, my eyes fly open. "Elijah," I choke.

"It's not going to be as bad as you think," he says quietly, his eyes meeting mine. It's then I notice the gold flecks in his eyes. "Breathe, baby," he coaxes as he slowly pushes inside of me.

Just concentrate on his eyes, I tell myself.

"Jesus, you feel so good," he praises not looking away from me.

I'm so glad I waited for this, with him. I can't imagine doing this with anyone else. Once he's fully seated inside of me, he stills, brushing his thumbs over my temples.

"You good?" he asks.

I give him a smile and nod. "You were right, it's not so bad," I say shyly.

"Your pussy was made for my cock." He pulls back completely, and I groan at the loss of him.

He pushes back in, faster this time and my back arches off the ground, shoving my tits against his smooth chest. "Such a good girl," he growls as his mouth descends on mine.

And then everything evaporates around us. It's just the two of us, tasting, feeling, devouring each other. We both become frantic with our need to be close. I can't get close enough. "Elijah don't stop. Don't ever stop," I beg.

"You're mine forever," he soothes, sucking my skin into his mouth, making me groan in a heady combination of pain and pleasure.

I want to feel him everywhere. My hands claw at his back, sliding down to his firm ass. He's mine. I'll kill anyone who tries to take him from me. I dig my nails into the hard flesh of his ass as I come, screaming his name to the dark Heavens.

"Fuck," he says hoarsely. "You're gripping my dick so good, baby."

And then I feel him swell inside of me and he comes with one last brutal thrust, shoving us both up the blanket.

His head drops to the crook of my neck. We lie still like this for a long time, both of us breathing hard but then I begin to tremble and no matter how much I try to control it, I can't. He raises his head, his brows pulled together. "Hey." He pulls out of me and sits up, taking me with him.

I curl up on his lap as he reaches over and grabs another blanket, wrapping it around us.

"I'm s-sorry," I say. "It's n-not you. I p-promise. I don't know w-what is h-happening." My teeth chatter so hard it's giving me a headache.

He rubs his hands over me, warming me up. "It's okay, baby. That was pretty intense." His gaze catches mine. "I have a feeling you and I are going to take each other to the very edge and beyond," he says. "It will be important for us to take care of each other after, yeah?"

I nod and burry myself into his chest. "It was amazing, Elijah. I didn't know how much I would feel. I was prepared for the physical part, but it was so much more than that," I whisper quietly against his skin. Slowly, I start to relax. The shivers wracking my body subside as I breath in his scent.

When I feel better, I sit up awkwardly, wondering if he could feel what I haven't been able to bring myself to say.

He takes my face in his hands and levels me with a look I'll never forget as long as I live. A promise is woven in every shade of brown god ever created. "I love you, Billie Rose. And I know you may not be able to say it back right now, but I felt it. Your soul wasn't able to hide the truth."

315

We spend the rest of the evening lying side by side, staring into each other's eyes, our hands still exploring each other with light touches.

The next morning, I wake up to another bright and sunny day. I stretch, rubbing my hand over my stomach when the smell of bacon wafts into the bus.

Elijah has set my robe right beside me, so I slide it on and make my way outside. He's standing over the fire, flipping pancakes.

"Why didn't you wake me? I would have helped," I say, drawing his attention away from the food.

The smile that breaks out over his face warms my chest. I smile back, dropping my gaze to the ground, slightly embarrassed and a little insecure about last night.

"Come, eat." He coaxes me closer with the promise of food. When I get within arm's reach, he grabs me around the throat and pulls my face to his, kissing me hard. He smacks my butt, making me yip and then points to a chair. "Sit."

"Awfully bossy this morning, aren't we?" I snip. But I do what he asks.

He just laughs and hands me a plate and a bottle of syrup. "You haven't seen anything yet." He shrugs, sitting down next to me with his own plate.

I let my eyes wander around the landscape, still amazed by the vastness of the salt flats. It's beautiful in its simplicity.

"So, did you bring what I asked you to?" he asks.

"Yeah, I think so."

After we finish cleaning up the breakfast mess, we sit down in front of each other, our knees touching.

When Elijah asked me to bring at least five things that are important to me, I thought it was a great idea. He said he wanted to get to know me again and that he would also bring parts of his life to share with me. Conversation starters he called them. Who knew this heavily tatted, pierced, gruff looking hottie was also sentimental?

"I'll go first because I can already see you're nervous. Stop picking at your nails. There is nothing to be nervous about." He pulls a stuffed, brown puppy dog out of his bag.

I cover my mouth.

"Don't laugh, Rosie. I've slept with this thing since I was a kid. When we share our bed, he'll be there with us."

Elijah is the sweetest man alive because I know he chose this first to put me at ease. I grab the puppy from his hands and look him over. "He's adorable. How long have you had him?"

"Since I was born. My dad got him for me. I have pictures of Boris and I in my hospital bassinet together."

"Boris?" I raise my eyebrow.

"Yes, Boris sounds tough, doesn't it? I wanted him to have a bad ass name," Elijah says, grinning at me.

"Well, he's cute and I would be happy to snuggle with him at night."

I set Boris down beside me and reach into my bag, pulling out my little treasure chest. I hand it to Elijah. "My grandpa made this for me. We went on many treasure hunts over the years, and I stored all my favorite finds in here."

He opens it and smiles when he pulls out a black rock. He sets it beside him and takes out the next thing, a little ceramic frog that looks like it was painted by a four-year-old and it was. Elijah laughs. "I didn't peg you as a reptile sort of girl."

I snatch the frog from him. "This is Miles, and we call him that because he's traveled many miles." Smiling at the small trinket wistfully, I flip it over and show Elijah the Velcro strip on the bottom. "The other half is on my dad's bike. Every time I rode with him, Miles went with us."

Elijah reaches for him. "This is exactly why we're doing this." He stares down at it. "We've missed the last fourteen years." He sighs loudly. "I wish I could have been there to see you on the back of his bike." He places the frog and rock back carefully in my treasure chest and sets it aside.

His words make my heart long for the same thing, we've missed so much.

We continue to laugh and poke fun at each other as we share all of our items. As I'm putting my grandpa's knife back in my bag Elijah says, "I only have one thing left but I want to go last."

"Okay." I nervously tuck my hair behind my ear. I pull out the sketchbook my mom gave me, she never knew I actually used it. "Before I show you these, remember, I'm not my mom. I don't have her artistic ability or anything. This is just some doodling I do when I'm trying to..." my words trail off.

"To not hurt yourself," he finishes.

I nod, giving him an anxious smile, handing the book over to him.

Elijah's eyebrows shoot straight up to his hairline. "Rosie, fuck, these are cool!" His gaze bounces to mine before resting back on one of my sketches. "Did you copy these from photos?"

"No, they're all my design. I know some of them are a little crazy. I've always loved bikes. I'm not sure if any of them could ever be a reality."

"This is..." He rubs his hand over his jaw, his eyes narrowing on me. "Take your clothes off."

What?

The surprise must show on my face because he's on me in a second, pushing me back with a hand to the center of my chest.

"Who do you belong to?"

"You," I say, my eyes widening.

His nostrils flare and his eyes almost roll in the back of his head. When he drops his gaze back to me, I see a man who's on the verge of consuming me. And it's the hottest thing I've ever seen.

"You are perfect for me, Billie Rose. God made you just for me."

Then he is stripping me of my pants at the same time unbuckling his own. As he pulls himself out, he warns me, "This isn't going to be gentle."

"Good, I don't want it to be."

And with that, he thrusts into me. And just like last night, the world around us could be burning to the ground and neither of us would notice.

"Fuck," Elijah grits as he explodes right after me.

This time, he immediately pulls me onto his lap and wraps me up. "I'm never going to get enough of you, baby," he says, kissing my temple. He's prepared for my trembling this time and I recover much quicker than I did last night.

"You said you had one more thing to show me," I say quietly, rubbing my hand over his.

Without hesitation, he pulls the last item out of his bag. He cradles it in his hands in front of us, letting me run my finger over it.

"I bought this for you, for your sixteenth birthday. I saw it in a gift store and immediately thought of you. I was going to give it to your mother when she came that summer but then you got in the accident and when I saw the pictures…" he pauses. "God, Rosie, I was so angry that you were hurt. I went back to my apartment and furiously swiped everything off my dresser. The rose fell to the ground and broke in a hundred pieces."

He kisses the back of my head before continuing.

Roses and Skulls

"I sat on my floor and cried, Rosie. A grown-ass, twenty-three-year-old man, crying on his bedroom floor. I knew right then I wasn't going to let anything stop me from getting to you. Not your dad, the club, nothing was going to stop me." He twirls the long-stemmed glass rose in front of our faces, holding it up so the sunlight catches it. "It took me months to put it back together, but it was worth it. It taught me patience. And I needed that. I knew I had to wait a few more years to be near you."

I run my finger over the tiny gold cracks.

"It's called Kintsugi, it's the Japanese art of fixing broken pottery with gold. It can also be used on glass. It's based on the idea of embracing one's imperfections, the gold making it stronger and more beautiful."

He places it in my hands, leaving me speechless.

I turn around in his arms and wrap myself around him like a little spider monkey. My fingers twirl the glass rose as I stare at it over his shoulder. "It's the prettiest thing I've ever seen." I lean back and meet his eyes. "I love you, Elijah. Thank you for this," I say, pulling my arms from around him and holding it between us.

"Now, are you ready for your next surprise," he asks mischievously.

"Yes," I say excitedly, bouncing on his lap.

"Okay, please stop bobbing on my dick or it's not going to happen. I'll keep you here with me all day."

I ignore his sexual inuendo and squeal, "Where are we going?"

"Do you want to jump out of a plane?"

"Ab-so-fuck-ing-lutely," I say without hesitation, the adrenaline already kicking in.

He flashes me a brilliant smile. "We never tell your dad about this."

I draw a cross over my chest before linking my pinky around his. Elijah is helping me find that spark that grandpa made me promise never to lose.

Chapter Twenty-Eight

Billie Rose

When we get back to reality, I'm on cloud nine. Literally, my head is in the clouds. I'm going through the motions of daily life, but my mind is back on the flats wrapped in big, tattooed arms.

My mom snaps in front of my face. "Billie Rose, are you listening?"

Yawning, I lean back in my chair. "Yeah, casseroles in the fridge, make sure the guys clean up their mess after poker night and last but not least make sure dad stays out of trouble. Got it."

"I'm being serious here, Billie Rose. It's been a long time since I left you all alone."

I roll my eyes. "Mother, we will be fine."

I'm happy she is actually leaving. She's been going back and forth all week. I know she wants to be here because she thinks I'll eventually open up and tell her about my trip with Elijah but I'm greedily keeping it to myself. For now. Eventually, I will share with her but right now I just want to savor it. Every. Delectable. Minute.

After her and my uncle, no not uncle, I need to stop that now that I'm sleeping with his son. Anyhow, after her and William take off, I head to the bar with Elijah. Tonight, I just need one final signature and then tomorrow will be my last day working at The Black Rose. It will also be the last night of breathing for Draven.

As I'm adding up all the profits from the previous weekend, Draven comes into the office and tells me the vendor for our alcohol is on the line. I look at the phone in the office. He laughs. "The phone isn't working in here. Phone company said they'll be out on Monday."

I roll my eyes and push my feet off the floor, sliding my chair out. "There better not be any serious issues," I grumble, heading out the door.

The guy on the phone tells me the truck with our order is broke down about twenty miles away and he can't find a tow truck anywhere around us.

"Jesus, okay, let me see if my boyfriend can take a look at it." I set the phone on the bar and go to the back, finding Elijah under the men's sink. He tells me he'll go and to tell them he just needs to drop me at home and then he'll be right there.

"Elijah, I have things to finish up here, I can't leave now. I'll text Dan for a ride." I turn and walk out not giving him a chance to argue.

I finish up the call and then go back and find Draven sitting in my chair. He's looking over the numbers on the desk as I pick up my phone and text Dan, asking him for a ride. I'd ask dad but he's over in Reno, putting the final touches on our plan to bring down the Devils. A few seconds later, Dan's reply comes through. Perfect, I think to myself.

I relay the news about the distributor to Draven. "Shit, that sucks. I might see if Sadie needs me. If not, I'll ride along with Elijah."

Elijah comes in soon after he walks out. "Did you find a ride?" he asks, rubbing his dirty hands over his jeans.

"Yep," I say, rearranging the papers on my desk.

He snaps his fingers. I glance up at him. He holds his hand out. "Phone."

I pull my head back. "What the fuck do you mean, phone?" I ask haughtily.

He crosses his arms across his chest. "I want to make sure you have a ride."

I'm not even in the mood to argue with him. I hand it to him, not even watching as he goes to my messages and double checks that I indeed sent a text to my uncle, and he replied.

He sets it back down in front of me. "Happy?" I ask.

"Very," he replies.

Elijah leans over and plants a kiss to the top of my head before turning and walking out. "Love you," he says.

"Love you too. See you tonight," I say, biting my lip, giving his retreating form one final look of appreciation.

"You know it."

Draven catches him at the door. "Hey, are you heading out to meet up with distributor?"

Elijah nods.

"Mind if I ride along?"

Elijah visibly relaxes, happy that I won't be left alone with him. "Sure, man, I might need a hand."

Both of them turn and Elijah gives me one last wave before the door closes shut behind them.

A few minutes later, Sadie, one of the new bartenders, bops in. I made some jalapeño poppers. I brought you some. She sets a plate in front of me and takes the chair across from me, setting her drink down in front of her.

Mindlessly, I grab one and pop it in my mouth. "Oh. Oh, shit that's hot," I say, waving my hand in front of my mouth.

She pushes her glass across the desk to me. "It's just coke with a splash of rum."

I take it because I don't give a fuck what it is as long as it puts out the fire in my mouth. "Goddamn," I choke, taking another large drink. I finish it off and slide the empty glass back to her.

She laughs, picking up the glass. "Thanks for saving me some."

"I'm sorry, I didn't know it was going to be that hot."

Giggling, she heads towards the door. "No problem, I can easily make myself another."

After she closes the door, I carefully tuck the papers I had Draven sign earlier in the bottom drawer of the desk for safe keeping.

One more day and this will all be over.

I gather the rest of my things, checking my phone to see that Dan won't be here for another hour.

Leaning back in my chair, I worry that maybe I'm being too harsh on Draven. He does seem like he really wants the bar to be successful. I rub my eyes, it's been a long week, I think it's finally catching up to me.

I sit forward, my head spinning at the sudden movement. Groggily, I grab my phone and try to focus on the screen.

The door to the office opens and when I glance that way, I do a double take. "Lanie?" I ask, my eyelids drooping with exhaustion.

"It's time," she tells me as Sadie steps in behind her.

My last thought before darkness claims me is, time for what?

Chapter Twenty-Nine

Billie Rose

When my eyes blink open, a headache assaults me. Jesus, what the fuck happened? My eyes are blurry as I try to make out where I'm at. There are papers taped to the wall across from me. I rub my hands over my face as I continue to try and make sense of what I'm seeing.

They are drawings. Dragons, skulls, hearts, flowers, and then my gaze stops on one of a young girl. She looks just like me. I try to sit up to get a better look but the pain in my head stops me. I moan, lying back against the pillow. I squint and see that each drawing is signed Jesse. These are my mom's drawings.

Slowly, I roll over and see that I'm in a tiny room. The only other piece of furniture in the room is a single long dresser with a mirror. It's covered in dust. The room smells dusty but the sheets on the bed look clean.

I groan again as I try to sit up. The door opens and a woman I've never met before walks in. She stares at me for a long time before speaking. "I've got something to make you feel better."

The bed dips as she sits down beside me. "Give me your arm and close your eyes."

I slide away from her. "No," I tuck my arms close to my chest as I watch the flame she's lit, warm the bottom of a spoon.

"Lanie," she yells.

The girl who used to be my best friend walks in.

"Hold her down."

Frantically, I try to get away but between the two of them, they overpower me. I'm still weak from whatever they gave me the first time around.

Warm tingles slowly make their way down my body. Tears begin to stream down my face because I can't make sense of what's going on. "No," I whisper.

"Not so tough now, huh?" Lanie sneers.

The woman beside me pats my leg. "It gets easier. Soon, we will be able to get you set up at Bells. The men are going to love you."

My eyes fall closed. This was the plan, to make me into the very thing my mother loathes, a drug addicted whore. This will kill her.

Lanie's phone dings with an incoming message. I pry my eyes open, taking them both in. Somehow, I need to get out of here.

"Oh, shit, Renee! We've got to go!"

"What? What is it?"

"Sadie says Jesse is at Bell's."

The woman, Renee, quickly rises and rushes out of the room, coming back with a couple of silk scarves. She tosses one to Lanie. "Tie her wrists."

My mom is at Bell's? That can't be right. Mom should be in San Diego with William by now.

They each take one of my arms and quickly tie me to the bars on the headboard. My head lulls to the side as I stare at my friend. "Why do you hate me?" I slur.

She doesn't look at me, yanking hard on the scarf so that it digs into my wrist. "You had everything I ever wanted."

Had.

Lanie continues, "Parents, family, a stable home, Jackson... you had Jackson." She sits back, looking me in the eye.

"Lanie," I whisper. "He's my cousin."

She shrugs. "Doesn't matter, they all fawn over you. Especially, Jackson. Do you think he ever gave me more than a second glance?"

The woman tries to draw the attention away from me. "Lanie, we need to get back to Bell's. They'll be time to torment her later. First, we need to deal with Jesse."

"How do you think she knew to look at Bell's?"

"I don't know, but we can't let her see me or she'll look here next."

Here. Where is here?

Once they're gone, I struggle with my bonds but with each tug, the scarves only tighten.

I'm so tired. So tired.

My eyes fall closed.

When they open again, someone is urgently trying to free my hands. "Draven?" I croak, my throat dry and my lips chapped.

He frowns, his hands pausing. "Little dove." He runs his fingers down the side of my face. "It's okay, I'm going to get you out of here. I'm sorry they took you."

I glance down my body and notice that I'm naked from the waist down. My eyes immediately go back to Draven. He guilty looks away.

I blink at the sketches on the wall, slowly remembering where I'm at. I'm so confused. Is Draven saving me or is he still working with Lanie? And that woman, Renee. Who is she?

This cannot be happening. I was so careful. Wasn't I? Where did I go wrong? I thought I was the one in charge. Just one more day and it would have been over.

"Did we?" I can't even bring myself to say it.

He releases my hand and moves over to the other side. Pain skitters along my fingers and shoots down my arm as I attempt to cover myself.

"Hey, it's going to be okay. When Elijah called and told me you were missing, I knew they had you. And then I saw you here so vulnerable and..." He shakes his head as if to clear his thoughts. "I'm not like him. This is different. Elijah will understand," he finishes with certainty. "We are destined. Linked by the past."

The blackness threatens to take over again, but I fight it with all my might. I do not want to be asleep around him again.

Suddenly, Draven sits up, turning his head like he's listening for something.

A woman pushes the door open. "What in the fuck are you doing?" she screeches when she sees what's going on.

Renee. It's the woman who drugged me.

"Get out," he orders.

"Draven, you dumb shit, you can't be serious. You fucked her?" she asks, putting her hand to her head. "Jesus Christ, why didn't I abort you?"

This woman is his mother? I slowly slide back to the wall when Draven releases my wrist. He shifts in front of me, shielding me from her.

"It's none of your business who I fuck, mother."

Roses and Skulls

"Didn't Bell teach you anything, you idiot? You can't have sex with someone you're related to. Do I need to fucking spell it out for you?" she sneers, sending a look of disgust my way.

Family?

Oh. Oh no. He is… no… he can't be grandpa's son.

"I don't fucking care," Draven yells. "I've done everything you asked. This is the one thing I want. I want her." He points at me.

"You can't have her," the woman says, shaking him. "You are a sick fuck. Just like your father."

I'm just about to shout that grandpa wasn't sick when Lanie pushes her way into the room.

"Tell him he's lost his ever-loving mind," the woman says to her.

Lanie looks at Draven before letting her gaze fall over me. A look of horror that must match my own, passes over her face, then she turns and glares at him. "The plan was to ruin her, turn her into an addict, not your own *personal* whore."

"I'm not giving her up," Draven says.

"Get the fuck out here," the woman says, pulling the door wide open and pointing for him to exit the room with her.

Draven turns to me. "I'll be right back, little dove. No worries."

I'm pretty sure I'm losing my mind. I feel it fragmenting off into gigantic pieces. Nothing makes sense.

333

Lanie stares daggers at me.

"You just have to have everything, don't you?" she shakes her head and sits down on the bed, shifting to face me. "Was it all worth it? Getting Draven into bed?"

"Lanie, *you* kidnapped me. *You* tied me up," I say, trying to scoot closer to her. I don't care how mad I am. She may be the only person who can save me. "He... he..." I can't even say it.

She looks at her bright red nails. "Do you know I've always wanted to be you," she says quietly.

"Why? I'm so messed up and you, you've always been strong," I try to smooth her hurt away.

I jump up from the bed and stand in front of her when she doesn't respond. "Look at me, Lanie. Look. At. Me."

She can't. She turns her head away, but then sees something that catches her attention, her face lights up. Before I can stop her, she has the gun Draven must have left behind clenched tightly in her hand.

I back away, holding my hands up. "Lanie, please don't do this. Please, you're my best friend."

Her head falls and she begins to cry. "They fucked with my head, Rosie. I was supposed to lure you away from your family, but you never strayed from them. Nor they from you. Never. Why couldn't I have had a family like that?" she whispers.

"It's okay. Help me get out of here and let's go home. My family is yours too," I promise, taking a step towards her.

She lifts her face to me. "I've never had a home. Not like you, Rosie. All I ever wanted was for someone to watch my back."

"You've always had Brody and me... we are your family. It's not too late. I promise, it's not." I reach for the gun, but she quickly pulls it away and places the barrel to her temple.

"Don't," I begin to beg.

Blood splatters across my body as Lanie's head gets ripped apart by a bullet.

My ears are ringing when Draven and his mother rush into the bedroom.

"Oh, fuck me," the woman says, slapping Draven over the back of the head. "Now look what you've done."

Draven stares at Lanie's body, she's lying across the bottom of the bed, half of her skull missing.

I lean over, gagging.

"None of this is going as planned. Did you know that Jesse kicked all the girls and their clients out of Bells and then preceded to burn the building down?"

"What?" Draven asks, confusion all over his face.

"If you would have listened to me from the very beginning, her daughter would be a drooling crack head at Bell's by now and Jesse would know what it feels like to lose everything. But you messed it up, just like your fucking father did."

"Get rid of her and meet me in Vegas. We're done. It's over. Jesse will never stop now that you've touched her. We need to get across the border." The woman gives me one last disgusted look before she walks out.

Draven stands beside me, both of us silent and then I begin to feel sick to my stomach again.

He grabs me by the arm and drags me out of the room, taking me into a bathroom. He lifts the lid on the toilet and holds my hair as I dry heave. While I'm busy retching, I feel a sharp stick in the crook of my arm as he pumps more drugs into my system.

"No," I rasp, struggling to pull my arm away.

"It's okay, baby. Everything is okay. I'll take care of it." He rubs his hand lightly over my back as my body trembles in shock. "I'm not getting rid of you. That was never my plan, don't listen to her. The only thing I ever planned on was turning you into mine."

When I'm done getting sick, he gently guides me to the floor.

"Just rest here." He leaves but comes back with my clothes. "Get dressed while I make a few calls. Look at me."

I raise my eyes to him.

"It's okay," he says, staring down at me. "She's in a better place."

Nodding, I rest my head on the toilet.

I know she is.

Anything has to be better than this.

Roses and Skulls

When he closes the door, I manage to pull my pants on and then I open the door. I can hear him on the phone in the other room. Glancing around, I see we're in a trailer. The door to the outside world is right there.

Without thought, I make my way to it and surprisingly it opens. The cool night air makes me gulp in a large breath. Oh god, I don't even know where I'm at. I stumble down the steps, looks like a trailer park, but everything is dark and most of the other trailers have broken windows and look vacant.

So, I walk.

I've got no clue where I'm going.

I feel as though my brain is fracturing. It can't really break, can it? My body feels nothing though. Just a numb sense of calm while my mind spins with the image of Lanie lying across the white sheets covered in bright red blood.

Time no longer exists as I wander farther and farther away.

My surroundings show me that I'm in a place somewhat resembling a town but not quite. Houses are scattered and most look like they're about to fall in. There is an orange glow on the horizon.

My vision is blurry and my limbs so heavy. It takes extreme effort to put one foot in front of the other. Suddenly, I stop, tilting my head to the side. Is it a windchime or just the ringing in my ears? I make my way towards the sound as I empty my mind. I'm trying to compartmentalize everything and lock it away for safe keeping.

I turn the corner and walk alongside a brick building when I find the source of the sound. It is indeed a windchime, hanging from a broken-down porch across the street.

When I hear Draven yelling for me, I glance around, looking for a place to hide. My eyes widen as I backup, staring at the brick wall that was beside me. It's a sunset, just like the one on my bedroom wall. I choke, covering my hand with my mouth. Mom. Oh God, mom. I need you.

It happened to me too. I'm so sorry. I'm so sorry. I let it happen to me too.

"Jesse?" a man asks from behind me.

When I spin around to face him, his eyes widen. "Shit," he whispers.

I don't say anything, I just stare at him in confusion.

He looks confused too.

"Are you Jesse's daughter?" he asks cautiously.

As I'm nodding, we both turn our heads abruptly, hearing Draven's call for me.

The man acts quickly, taking me gently by the arm and hurrying us behind the building. His hands shake as he uses his keys to open a door. He ushers me inside, closing and locking it behind us.

It's dark and I start to shrink away, blinking when he turns the light on.

"Shit," he says again.

He follows my gaze to the locked door.

"I'm not going to hurt you, honey. I'm friends with your mom. I'll call her, okay?"

I don't say anything.

"Here, why don't you sit, and I'll get you some water." He urges me to a chair, smiling kindly as I lower myself onto it.

He walks into another room and comes back with a bottle of water. I take it and sign thank you, not able to find my words.

The man seems to know what I'm saying.

"You're welcome, hun. I'll call your mom now."

My eyes roam over the space and see there are paint cans and boxes of tools, it looks like the back of a hardware store.

"Hey, this is Samuel over in Trap, not sure if you remember me." He pauses. "Yeah, I'm looking for Jesse and this is the only number I could think of to reach her."

Samuel seems like a nice guy. I set the bottle of water on the floor and notice the blood on my hands, I pull my knees to my chest and tuck them between my legs. And then I rest my head, trying my best to keep it together in front of Sam.

"Her daughter is here... um, I found her outside the store." I hear him sigh. "Yeah, Dan. You know I'd do anything for Jess. I'll keep her safe. See you soon."

When he gets off the phone, I feel him sit down in the chair next to me. "Dan is coming for you, hun."

I nod against my knees.

He doesn't try to talk to me after that. I hear him roll his chair over to a desk and shuffle papers around.

I try to think about what I'm going to tell Dan when he gets here.

I have nothing.

How do I explain what happened?

The blood.

The drugs.

Maybe they won't be able to tell anything else happened.

I'm good at keeping secrets. What's one more?

Chapter Thirty

Dan

I slide the shop cell out of my pocket, wondering who's calling it at this time of night.

"Hello."

A man's voice greets me, it's familiar but…

As Samuel reminds me who he is, my heart drops to my stomach. I can tell by his voice something bad has gone down. He has Billie Rose. She's in Trap County.

On one hand, I'm relieved that we know where she is. On the other, well, my other hand wants to punch something because I know nothing good happens in Trap.

I get off the phone and turn to Raffe. "She's in Trap."

He doesn't say a word, just backs out and flies down the street. His knuckles are turning white from gripping the wheel so hard. When we get to the highway, he looks over at me.

I raise my hands. "All I know is she's at the hardware store with Samuel. He said he found her in the parking lot and that he would keep her safe till we got there."

He hits the steering wheel.

My phone vibrates. It's the kid again. He's going out of his fucking mind. I pick up.

"Jackson and I didn't have any luck up at the cabin. I know he has her. He fucking has her," he yells.

I didn't think she would be at the cabin, but I sent them up there to keep them out of the way, hoping one of my contacts came through with some info.

"I'm going to get her right now. You and Jackson head back to the warehouse. If Dirk shows up before I get back, you don't fucking say a word to him. I need to figure out what's going on and then I'll call him. You got that?"

"Fuck no. Tell me where she's at. I'm going to kill that fucking son of a bitch," he roars.

I know the kid is worried and hurting and I know that he loves my niece, but he needs to calm the fuck down.

"She is safe with a friend of mine."

He gets quiet. "What happened to her?"

"I don't know, son. Just prepare for the worst and hope for the best. That's all we can do. The important thing is she's safe. The rest we can deal with when we get her home." Raffe looks from me to the road, shaking his head.

"Yeah, okay. Just tell her I love her and I'm sorry I left her there alone."

"We've been through that. It's not your fault. The blame lies in one place and one place only. Now get your asses back to the warehouse."

"Yes, sir," he says sullenly. He knows there is nothing he can do. I'm not a man that budges. I'm a man of my word.

I hang up and Raffe curses under his breath.

When I went to pick up Billie Rose from the bar and found it dark and quiet, my heart sunk, I knew something was terribly wrong. I broke in, finding her phone lying on the desk.

I drove to the warehouse, hoping that she had found another ride and just forgot her phone at the bar. Elijah walked in minutes after me, telling me that the truck he went to look at was a simple fix. Just a loose battery cable he had said. When he looked around, expecting Rosie to be with me, I saw the look of panic in his eyes. We've all spent the last few hours looking for her. Thank god Samuel thought to call the shop phone.

"This is all too familiar, Dan," Raffe says. "I can't bear it. If he hurt her…"

"If he hurt her then we will deal with it."

343

He slams his fist into the steering wheel again.

"Get it out now," I tell him.

"I know. Goddammit, I know." He runs his hand over his face.

When we get to the hardware store, it's still dark outside.

Samuel lets us in the back door. He nods for us to follow him, not saying a word. He pushes the door to an office open and there she sits, all curled in on herself.

Raffe clenches his fists beside me.

"I came in early to do some inventory and I found her staring at the mural outside. I thought it was Jesse for a minute." He shoves his hands in his pockets. "I heard a man yelling for her, so I brought her inside."

"Thank you," I tell him, watching as Raffe cautiously makes his way over to her.

He kneels in front of her. "Hey, baby girl," he says softly, lightly touching the top of her head. She lifts her face and I close my eyes. Lord, please help me keep my shit together.

Raffe handles it much better than I could have imagined. He cups her face in his hands as she stares through him. Her eyes glassed over. "It's okay, sweetheart. Uncle Dan and I are here. We're here, okay?"

She doesn't say anything, and my heart sinks.

"Do you know which way she came from?" I ask Samuel.

He scratches his head. "No, but the man was yelling from the north, maybe four blocks away."

I'm not waiting for orders this time. "Raffe, wait here. I'll be back."

It takes me two seconds and I'm pulling into the trailer park. When I storm into the trailer, Draven barely gets a look at me before I knock him clean the fuck out with one hit. After that, I find two cleanup assholes in the bedroom with Brody's niece, she's dead and lying on a black tarp. At least that's who I think it is. The only thing recognizable is her blond hair.

"Who the fuck are you?" one of them asks, reaching for his gun.

"Get the fuck out of here," I tell them.

Both scatter when I turn my back to them. Seeing my patch was all it took. I walk back out to the living room and tie up the soon to be dead man. I wrap him in a blanket and toss him as hard as I can in the back of Raffe's truck. He whimpers.

"If you so much as make a peep, I'll really give you something to whine about."

Someone steps out from the shadows; I pull my gun, pointing it directly at the dark figure.

"You gunna shoot me, big guy."

My hand instantly falls. "I thought you were in San Diego?"

"And I thought you were home, in bed with your wife," Jesse replies smartly.

345

She follows me back inside. Immediately, she walks over and picks up a pack of cigarettes off the table. "Only one bitch I know who smokes these skinny little things. Where is she?" She tosses them on the table and then her nose turns up.

"Is someone dead in here?" she asks.

"Jesse, what the fuck are you doing here?"

"Same?" she tips her head at me.

I cross my arms over my chest, and she caves.

"Okay, fine. I burnt down Bell's tonight."

My mouth falls open, but I recover quickly. "I thought you had recovered from your pyromania." I shake my head, taking in the skull makeup on her face.

She chuckles sadly and walks over to the kitchen sink. Jesse continues her tale as she scrubs the paint away from her skin. "Me too, but Bell called me a few weeks ago. She told me quite the story about Crow and my aunt... and the spawn they left behind. The spawn that bought dad's bar. He also bought Bell's House of Tail. Bell was only a week away from leaving it all behind and retiring to the beach when Billie Rose paid her a visit. Renee arrived shortly after. Bell put two and two together and began to worry that Rosie might be in danger, so thank god she did the right thing and called me. After we spoke, I knew what had to be done. So, I left with William and then ditched him along the way. I was just going to pay my aunt a visit. When she wasn't there, I decided to torch the place."

Roses and Skulls

She shakes the water from her hands and wipes her face on the bottom of her shirt. "Logically, I thought this should be my next stop. And then, even though I hate to do it, I'm going to burn down the bar."

I shake my head, this fucking girl. I nod for her to follow me to her old room. We should have known Jesse would figure out who Draven was.

She takes in Lanie's body, then her eyes slowly roam around the room. Her gaze catching on the two scarves still tied to the posts on the headboard. "What happened here?"

"I don't know but Billie Rose was here. Someone, we're assuming Lanie, took her from the bar. It wasn't Draven because he was with Elijah. They were helping one of the liquor distributors who broke down on the road. I was supposed to give her a ride home but when I got to the bar it was dark. The boys and I have been looking for her all night. We got our break when Samuel called, he found her outside the hardware store. She's there right now with him and Raffe."

Jesse wraps her arms around herself, her face falling. I continue telling her what I know. "Samuel said he heard a man calling for her from this direction. I headed straight over here and found Draven and a clean-up crew. He's alive, he's in the back of Raffe's truck. Don't know where the old hag is. After what you just told me, I'm sure she isn't far."

We're both silent as we stare at the wall in Jesse's old bedroom. She was just a kid when she first started showing me her drawings. Her art was the only thing that kept her sane. She suffered tremendously in this shithole. It was supposed to have been her home.

"Take care of my baby, Dan. I'm going to find Renee." And then she's off before I even get a chance to stop her.

My fist slams into the mirror, shattering it. Blood runs down my hand, I wipe it on my jeans and make a call.

"Brody, I've got some bad news for you, man, are you sitting down?"

After the call, I carefully wrap Lanie and carry her outside. I'll send one of our own crew out to burn the place down. I'm sure they'll be happy to do so. We haven't had much business for them lately but that's all about to change.

And then I call Dirk...

Chapter Thirty-One

Billie Rose

My uncles are here. Well, one of them is here. Uncle Dan stormed out and said he would be back. I wonder where he went. Raffe is talking with Samuel in the corner, both of them look over at me from time to time.

I wish Uncle Dan would come back. I'm tired.

You know, I think all I need is a good night sleep and then I'll feel good as new.

And a shower.

Definitely a shower.

Uncle Raffe crouches down in front of me. "Are you hurt, sweetheart?"

Hurt?

I glance down at my body, dropping my feet to the floor. There's blood all over my arms and my hands and my bare feet. Did I cut too deep? My head tips to the side in confusion. I start to scratch at my arms, the dried blood suddenly itching my skin.

Raffe grabs my hands in his. He dips his head, trying to catch my attention. Wait. This isn't my blood. Is it?

"Do you hurt anywhere?" he asks again, saying each word at a snail's place.

No. Yes. No, I'm not hurt. No.

I shake my head answering his question, not really believing my own conclusion.

He sighs and stares deep into my eyes.

"Have you taken any drugs?"

Again, I shake my head because I don't do drugs. My family has a zero-tolerance policy.

My uncle turns my arms over and runs his thumbs over each crease. He stares at my right one, so I follow his gaze. His thumb runs over a bruise that is forming. Raffe and I look at each other. "Did Draven give you something?"

Roses and Skulls

I scratch at my nose, it's so itchy. Did they bring a truck? I'm so sleepy, I just want to lie down. My gaze scours the room, looking for a place to rest. It stops on Raffe, he's looking at me like he is expecting me to say something. What did he ask? Oh, yeah, did Draven give me something? I search my pockets. Nope. Nothing, he didn't give me anything.

Using my hands, I tell him no.

Then I sign, my fingers flying, that I'm tired and want to go home.

Anguish washes over his face as he watches my hands. He swallows and drops his head, pressing his thumbs into his eyes.

I can't take it anymore; I need to close my eyes. My feet push off the ground, sending my chair back. Raffe startles, his head darting up.

I slide off the chair and lie down on the cool cement floor. This is nice, this will work fine. My eyes fall closed.

I'm not sure how long I've been asleep, but someone is picking me up and settling me on their lap.

He presses my head into his neck and his beard tickles my cheek. Oh, it's Elijah.

Elijah.

Elijah feels like home.

I want to go to sleep but I'm straddling that place between here and there.

Where am I again?

Oh, I'm with grandpa. I love his beard. He looks just like a pirate with his dark hair. No, his hair is silver now. I should make him some tea.

"Do you want tea?" I say aloud.

No. Grandpa doesn't like tea. He likes root beer floats. Yeah, we love ice cream. And dancing. And rainbows. And...

Something doesn't feel right. I must have had too many floats. I groan, holding my stomach. I just need to sleep. Keep my eyes closed and sleep.

Why can't I go to sleep? I don't want to dream. No dreams.

One sheep, two sheep, this little piggy went to market.

Oh god, I need to find a bathroom.

My eyes fly open, and I sit up covering my mouth.

"Pull over," Uncle Dan says urgently.

He hauls me out of the truck and holds me from behind as I crouch down on the desert floor, emptying the contents of my stomach which isn't much, but I heave for so long I think my ribs are breaking. Squinting my eyes, I shield my face from the sun coming up in the distance. Like a pink diamond on the band of the horizon.

"We're not far from home, hun," Dan says, holding me close to him. I drop my head back on his chest, wiping my mouth on the back of my hand.

Roses and Skulls

Raffe comes around the side of the truck with a bottle of water. "Here you go. Just sips," he instructs.

I cough after a few gulps.

"I said sips," he scolds gently.

They both help me back in the truck and it's then I see the two forms in the pickup bed. I turn around in my seat and stare out the windshield. My mind desperately tries to clear away the fog. Everything is right there through the mist. What happened?

I feel like shit, and it hurts to think. Uncle Dan settles his arm around me and pulls me close to him, resting his chin on my head.

Raffe hops in beside us and fires up the engine of his pickup, with a quick look behind him he pulls back out onto the interstate.

My eyes fall closed again as the truck and my uncle's warm embrace ebbs the nausea I was feeling.

A few miles from home, I start to rouse again. Dan lifts his arm when I sit up straight, blinking against the bright sun. Neither of my uncles say anything as we pull into the lot.

I glance around. Not too many people here today.

"You ready to go in or do you want to talk for a minute?" Dan asks me.

Shrugging my shoulders, I stare blankly at him.

The door to the warehouse opens and my dad steps outside. Daddy. I scramble over Dan, reaching for the doorhandle. My dad must see my frenzy to get to him because when I get the door open, diving out headfirst, he catches me.

He catches me.

Swinging me up into his arms as if I weigh nothing more than a feather, he cradles me to his chest. I burry my face into his t-shirt.

"It's okay, baby girl. I've got you." He kisses all over the top of my head as he carries me inside, repeating that he has me.

Once inside, he sits down on the couch, keeping his arms tightly wrapped around me. "Does she need a doctor?" he asks over my head.

No!

I sit up and face him, shaking my head feverishly. No doctor.

He pushes my hair away from my face and cups my cheeks in his hands. "Are you sure, baby girl? You're not hurt?" he asks.

No.

He stares at me, finally seeing the elephant in the room.

His grey eyes bounce back and forth to the men standing behind me. Then they return to me. "Say something, Billie Rose." He lets go of my face and grabs my shoulders, shaking me lightly. "Please," he begs, a mixture of sadness and panic etched in the lines around his eyes.

I open my mouth and then snap it closed. What do I say? But I can't stand the look on his face, so I try, for him. "I-I'm confused," I tell him honestly.

He swallows back a sob. "Okay. It's okay, we'll figure this out, together." He hugs me tight.

An electrical current stirs the air. Shivering, I feel Elijah enter the room. I squirm, uncomfortable to be seen on my dad's lap like a scared child. I slide off, keeping my head lowered, my hair shielding me from everyone. A shower. I need a shower.

"I-I'm fine. I'm going to go to my room now," I say quietly, scooting to the edge of the couch.

Uncle Dan stands in front of me as I try to rise, gently pushing me back down to the soft cushions. My dad leaves my side and I detect the sound of retreating footsteps. My uncle sits down heavy beside me, making me roll towards him.

I scoot away and then slowly let my eyes lift. We are the only two people in the room. My mind races as thoughts of last night flood my brain. The last bit of the drug Draven gave me slips away. The dried blood is driving me nuts. I have to get it off.

"Dan," I say, my voice tight with panic.

My dad comes back at the exact moment I'm about to lose my shit.

Jumping to my feet, I head to the stairs. "I-I'll be back. J-just give me a minute." And then I race up the steps two at a time.

When I get to my bathroom, I slam the door shut before shoving my pants down my legs. My feet get caught up in my jeans and I fall against the counter, banging my hip. My fingers scramble over the top of the mirror, finding my pain reliever.

When I sit down on the toilet and press the blade to my skin, I pause. It's already bloody. Dried blood. Lanie's blood.

"You don't want to do that," a familiar voice calls from the other side of the shower.

Fingers wrap around the edge of the curtain and shove it back. He's sitting in my bathtub. Why is he in my fucking tub?

"Your dad told me to wait for you up here. Said this is where you'd be headed next."

I look away from him, setting the blade down with shaky hands. Elijah stands and steps out. He reaches back and turns the water on, adjusting the temperature, then he undresses himself. I watch out the corner of my eye, but keep my gaze focused on the tile floor.

When he's done, he reaches for me and helps me to stand. He pulls my shirt over my head and then helps me untangle my jeans from around my ankles. Gently, he guides me to the side of the tub and helps me in.

Instantly, I move to the shower head and let it run over me, entranced by the amount of blood swirling down the drain. Elijah turns me around and holds my head under the water, careful to keep my face from under the spray.

Gently, he brushes my hair away from my face. He gathers some shampoo in his hand and then begins to massage it into my scalp, never taking his eyes from mine. I want to look away. It hurts my soul to stare into his warm chocolate eyes after everything that has happened.

Roses and Skulls

After he conditions my hair, he takes a washcloth and gently washes my face, and then his hands cautiously move down, roaming over my torso. His gaze holds mine hostage. "Who do you belong to?" he asks.

My eyes fall closed. He pulls my hair harshly, holding me still. I blink back water and tears.

"Who. Do. You. Belong. To?" he grates out.

"You," I whisper.

He pushes my head down with one hand, the other tracing the fingertip bruises over my breasts. He pushes on them. "This doesn't change that," he says sternly. Then he pulls my hair again, forcing me to look him dead in the eye. "Do you understand?"

I try to nod but I can't, his hold on me too tight.

"Don't ever feel ashamed in my presence again. What you felt downstairs when you felt me enter the room, it ends right there. When we walk out of this shower you will fucking straighten that fucking crown. Your revenge awaits. There will be time to break down later. Do you understand?" His chest rises and falls, his nostrils flaring. Elijah is right. This is not the end.

He continues, "Dan has him. He's here. You need to decide what happens next."

"He's here." My body begins to tremble without permission.

Elijah caresses my cheek. "He's here, baby. But he can't hurt you. Never again will he hurt you."

My eyes follow a water drop down Elijah's shoulder as he goes back to washing me. His hands cautiously search my skin for wounds, only finding light bruises.

When he guides me back to my room, I sit down on the bed heavily. "I want him taken out to the forest," I say, clearing my throat. He hands me a bottle of water that was sitting near the door. I take it and greedily start drinking.

He gently pulls it away. "Not all at once, baby. Take it slow."

"I'm sorry," I whisper.

He sits down beside me, handing the bottle back to me. "No apologies. From either of us. What happened was neither of our faults."

"But…"

"But nothing."

"Our new bartender, she, she brought me poppers and a drink. She must have been friends with Lanie. They drugged me."

Elijah takes the water bottle from me. "Billie Rose, listen to me. There will be time to hash all this out but right now, I'm going to go tell them your wishes, okay. He will be tied up in the forest and then what, Rosie? Then what do you want us to do?"

"Us?"

"The club," he says calmly. My eyes roam over the Viking tattoos on the side of his skull, a rose weaved around one of the symbols. I reach out and run my fingertip over his head, the slight stubble of hair scratches against my soft skin.

I think about my mom and William and what they've overcome in their lives. I can conquer this. I can. Tipping my head, I tell him what I really want, "I want it to be me."

But I know I can't face him as me. I have to become someone else. I have to become her.

He starts to shake his head. I grab his face in both of my hands. "Take him out to the forest and tie him up in a chair. I will be there soon."

I walk over to my closet and pull out my leathers. Elijah sighs but walks out to fulfill my wish. As I'm doing my makeup my dad appears behind me in the mirror. "Do I have it right?" I ask.

His eyebrow rises. "No," he smirks. He sits on the edge of my vanity and takes a makeup wipe out of the package. "She always left one eye unpainted."

The colors swirling in his beautiful eyes fight for dominance as he contemplates what is about to go down. "My offer still stands. I'll take this burden from you."

I tap my fingers nervously over my knees, holding still so he can draw death upon my face. "I need this."

He nods. "I'm proud of you, baby girl. Your grandfather would be too."

"Proud of me for getting myself drugged and kidnapped," I snap. His brows instantly shoot to his hairline at my outburst. "And I'm not sure how I feel about grandpa anymore."

He sets the makeup stick down and runs his tattooed hand over the top of his head.

Then he leans forward and pushes his nose right into my face. "Proud of you for standing up and not shutting down. Proud of you for getting away. For fighting."

I roll my lips between my teeth, keeping them pinched there. He leans back, my comment about grandpa finally registering.

"What don't you know about Bill?"

Tears begin to pool in my eyes. "I think he's Draven's dad."

My dad grips my chin in his hand. "That's not possible."

I pull my face away from him and walk over to the window, staring out towards the forest. "Draven was raised by Bell," I glance over my shoulder. My father nods, information I'm sure he already knows. "Grandpa was sending lots and lots of money to her, to help with him."

When I sit down, my dad joins me in the window seat.

"I went to Bell, and she told me she couldn't tell me who his father was. When I asked about the money she just said grandpa was a good man."

My dad wraps his fingers around mine. "Billie Rose, that doesn't mean that Bill fathered him. It just means he felt the need to help out. Your grandfather was dedicated to Candice."

Big crocodile tears begin to roll down my cheeks, smearing my makeup. "Draven's mother was there last night. She yelled at him. Told him he had committed incest. That we were related." I cover my mouth, desperately trying to push everything down.

Dad stares at me, blinking wildly.

"And Lanie was so mad, she pointed a gun at me, dad," I sniffle, rubbing white and black makeup all over his t-shirt. "Then she..." I gulp down a few breaths, swallowing hard. "Then she turned it on herself, and I tried to stop her. I tried but she did it. She killed herself, dad!"

Dad continues to rock me. He doesn't say anything, still reeling himself I'm sure from the shock of all that he's learned.

Then a thought comes to me. I sit up straight. "I-I didn't g-go with them. Lanie drugged me, and I woke up in a room w-with m-mom's drawings on the w-wall. I s-swear I d-didn't go w-with them." I stutter, my teeth clattering together.

"Billie Rose, look at me," he says sternly. "Not once did anyone think you went willingly. Stop, right now."

My eyes fall closed, and I whisper quietly. "I don't remember any of what he did to me but..." God, how do I say this? But I have to get it out before it eats me alive. "I don't remember any of it, but I know what happened."

"Billie Rose, I don't even know what to say. God, I wish your mother was here."

My hands curl into the soft material of his t-shirt. "Just tell me this isn't going to kill me, that it will somehow make me stronger."

"It will. It will, baby. You and your mother are the strongest women I know."

After a minute, I risk a peek at him. His eyes are blue as the lake on a calm day. Eerily calm. He grabs my hand and takes me back to the mirror, fixing my makeup. His jaw ticks and I know that the furry building up in his muscles is going to need to go somewhere soon.

When he's finished, he stares at me for a minute. "You look exactly like her," he whispers. "I'm so lucky to call you both mine." And then his eyes turn black as the midnight sky over the flats. "You go down there, and you show no fear. You have a club at your back. He has nothing."

And then he walks out of the room, leaving me to stare at the broken girl in the mirror. I grab my gold eyeliner and highlight the lines on my face.

Stronger more beautiful, Elijah had said. What did he call it? Kintsugi. He said it worked on pottery and glass.

I wonder if it works on flesh and bone.

Chapter Thirty-Two

Billie Rose

As I walk down the hill towards the forest, I shake off any unease I have. When I get to the clearing, several of the club members are leaning against trees. Their eyes widen as my boots crunch over the dead leaves of the forest floor.

My dad nods to me as well as my uncles. Jackson falls in step with me. "You've got this, Rosie. You're a Skull through and through."

Elijah has his back to me as he crouches down in front of Draven, no doubt trying to intimidate him. He's wearing a leather cut with the Skulls logo on it. I turn my head to my father. He shrugs. Elijah senses my presence and stands, slowly spinning to face me.

He grabs a sucker out of his pocket and shoves it in his mouth with a smirk, looking me up and down. I walk past him to stand in front of Draven. His shocked face stares up at me as Elijah presses his chest to my back. We both stare down our noses at the asshole.

"Dan was kind enough to bring you a present, Rosie," Elijah says, rubbing his hands over my stomach lightly.

"Little dove," Draven croaks. His throat dry, his lips cracked and bleeding. Looks like someone has already gotten in a few punches.

I don't even get two words out when hushed whispers breakout behind me.

When I spin around, giving Draven my back, a prospect comes running through the trees. He slides in front of my dad, catching himself before falling on the ground. "Shit, Prez." He's breathing hard. He takes a deep breath before continuing. "It's your ole lady. She's back and she's dragging some red headed bitch by the hair."

My dad glances over at me. And then I hear a woman screaming. "Owe, stop, Jesse! Let me explain!"

I recognize the voice and my blood runs cold.

I glance back at Draven, his face turning white. I'm sure he never expected to hear his mother's voice either.

Everyone stares down the path as my mom's form comes into view, and she is indeed dragging the red headed woman through the dirt.

Our eyes lock when she gets to the clearing. Her black hair is down. She hasn't even broken a sweat. She continues to make her way towards me, ignoring the older woman's cries. She tosses her roughly to the ground beside Draven, kicking her once in the chest with her boot, making the woman topple over onto her back.

It's quiet for several long moments. Draven starts laughing manically, breaking the silence.

My crow flies over their heads, squawking loudly before settling on a branch nearby.

Draven glances back at it, his burst of merriment fading. "Do you remember her?" I ask.

He turns back to me, his face slowly falling. Both of us know the end is near.

My dad speaks up. "Why is she here, Jesse?"

"Bumped into her at the airport. She was trying to buy a one-way ticket out of the country. When she saw me, she freaked," my mom says, looking down at her nails. "Made me a little suspicious. Isn't that right, Renee?"

"Jesse, I can explain. We're family, let's talk about this reasonably."

My mom rolls her eyes.

Family? I'm so confused. Does mom consider her family since grandpa got her pregnant? She's just some whore who worked at Bell's.

"You won't let them hurt me. I'm your aunt. I took you in when no one else would. Where was Bill then, huh?" The woman sneers up at my mom.

Hold the fuck up. She's my mom's aunt? The one who neglected her?

"You are bound by blood to protect me." Renee glances at me nervously. "You won't let her hurt me will you, Jesse?"

I cock an eyebrow and the lady cowers. Me? Is she afraid of me?

"Protect you? Like you did for me when you let your boyfriend and his club rape me," my mom says deathly calm.

The woman, my mom's fucking aunt, snaps her mouth shut.

"Well, what a wonderful family reunion," I announce, holding my hands out. "Seems we have a lot to unpack. Where should we start?"

My mother takes a few steps away and leans her back against a tree.

"So, Bill isn't your dad?" I ask Draven.

He spits blood on the ground before answering me. "Fuck no, I told you my dad was Crow, and that bitch…" He jerks his head towards my mother. "That bitch killed him. Like I told you, Billie Rose, an eye for an eye. Which, by the way, was all her idea." He nods towards his mother.

But that means Draven is my second cousin. A wave of nausea assaults me, and I take several large gulping breaths. Elijah runs his hand over the side of my neck, whispering in my ear. "I've got your back, baby. Breathe, just breathe."

My mom directs a question to her aunt. "I thought you were with Jimmy. How did you end up with Crow's bastard?"

Roses and Skulls

Renae looks back at my mom, shaking her head. "Did you think I really wanted Jimmy? He was just a way to get to Crow. I wanted the president of the Devils. I wanted to be his old lady. But then you killed him and ruined everything. And then I found out I was pregnant. I knew I should have gotten rid of the baby, but I waited too long. So, I came up with a plan. I was going to take everything away from you, just like you had done to me."

Draven looks at me sadly. "Fucked up, isn't it, cousin?" he says with a bloody frown. "You and I are both victims of their fucked-up past."

"But I told him, Jesse. I told him it ain't right to go fucking one of your own family. That was never part of my plan. I wasn't going to hurt her, just turn her into the very thing you loathe. Evidently, the idiot doesn't know what incest is."

My mom pushes away from the tree.

"Shut the fuck up," Draven yells at her, squirming in the chair once again. His eyes dart over the men of the club. I think he was hoping we could keep what happened between him and I at the trailer a secret.

"Why are you looking at them?" I ask, stepping between his legs. "They're not who you should be worried about. Look at me."

"Little dove, you know we're meant to be together. From the moment we met. Don't let them taint what we have. We made love..."

I grab him by his shirt, spitting in his face as I yell, "Don't call it love! When someone is unconscious that makes it rape, Draven."

Both our heads snap towards my mother when she releases a roar. She grabs the back of Renee's head and reaches around, drawing a blade across her throat. His mother's blood projectiles from her body, splattering over us.

Renee's surprised eyes glass over and when my mother releases her, she falls to the side with a thud.

My little crow shrieks in excitement. Her wings flapping wildly.

Draven starts sputtering. "Fuck, fuck, oh my god. Please don't let her near me," he wails.

Slowly, my eyes go back to him. I let go of his shirt, patting it back down in place. I straighten to my full height and point to my mother. "You see that, Draven. That's what having balls looks like." I tip my head, the smell of piss assaulting my senses. A large wet spot darkens the front his jeans.

"Listen," he says quietly for only me to hear. He nods for me to lean closer. "You need to think of our child."

Leaning in so close his hair tickles my nose, I whisper, "I'm on the pill. There will be no child."

When I lean back, his eyes narrow on mine. "You *thought* you were," he says, a slow smile spreading across his face.

My mind scrambles to make sense of what he just said. And then I remember asking Lanie to pick up my pills. "She wouldn't have."

"She didn't… but I did," he leans back and stares up at the sky.

His face contorts in confusion as he stares Heavenward. He blinks a few times as if he can't believe what he's seeing. I follow his gaze. There amongst the treetops are hundreds of black crows.

When his head drops and our eyes meet, he starts rambling again about the family we could have, the bar, his club.

"Elijah, Jackson, hold his head for me, yeah? I'm tired of hearing this asshole."

Both men jump towards Draven. He starts thrashing in his binds. "I love you, Billie Rose. Don't do this."

When they have him secure, I reach down and pull grandpas knife out of my boot. I dive into his disgusting mouth and pull out his tongue. The sharp blade rips right through it in a matter of seconds. My mind doesn't even pause to think about what I'm doing. I need him to shut up. He's been feeding me shit for the past three years. I'm done. I'm just done.

I toss the foul object to the ground.

"You stole my voice for three years. Fitting don't you think?" I crouch down in front of him. The guys let go of his head and his chin falls to his chest. I watch as blood runs out of his mouth, mixing with the tears and snot running down his face. I wipe my blade off on his jeans, staring into his black soulless eyes.

"We should set him on fire, burn him alive," my mother says anxiously by my side.

Draven casts her a nervous glance and starts mumbling, straining against the ropes. More blood flows from his mouth.

My crow flies over and perches on Draven's shoulder, pecking at his lips as blood continues to stream from between them.

I rise slowly from the ground. "No, I think we've had our revenge. I think it's time for my little friend and her family to get theirs."

A few more crows fly down from the trees, poking at Draven as he struggles to free himself.

"I think we should leave them to it."

My eyes meet my mom's, she nods her head and whistles for everyone to head out. She joins my dad and heads up the path.

Elijah wraps his arms around my shoulder, guiding me away. My feet abruptly stop. I step away from him and crouch before Draven one last time. Several more birds have landed on him. "Oh, and if you're wondering if anyone will miss you? They won't. The DEA will be arresting every member of the Devils tomorrow morning. Seems someone ratted them out and went into the witness protection program but not before selling his bar."

Draven's eyes widen, his anger overriding the pain the birds are inflicting on him. He knows I've won. That I've been gunning for him since the minute he arrived in town. He thought I was weak. He was wrong.

"I bet you regret not killing me that day. My only regret is that I should have pulled the trigger one day sooner."

He starts screaming, blood and spit flying out of his mouth, splattering my face.

I wipe it off with one hand, smearing blood and makeup over my hand. When I rise, his eyes follow my movement. "You want to know what I'm going to name the bar?" I ask.

Roses and Skulls

"Oh, sorry. You can't answer." I tap my finger over my mouth. "On second thought, I think I'll keep the name. The Black Rose fits, don't you think? Didn't you know that even the black ones have thorns?"

And with that, I turn, meeting Elijah at the end of the path. We walk away, listening to his screams as my friends tear the flesh from his body.

The club is up at the warehouse. Their bloodlust calling for a party. In this club everything calls for a party. Even death.

"I'm going to sit here for a while," I tell Elijah, ducking out from under his arm.

He stares at me as I plop down on the grass just beyond the forest, my back to the warehouse. Screams break through the trees.

"Then I'm sitting too," he says, hauling his ass right down beside me.

Neither of us say anything.

I'm numb.

There is so much to process.

Elijah pulls at the grass, the music firing up behind us as I continue to stare into the trees.

Gone are the days of magical fairytales, knights in shining armor and dragons needing slayed.

The only thing left is this gapping black hole that is threatening to suck me in.

Elijah bumps my knee lightly with his. "You okay, baby?"

"Not really," I tell him honestly.

He runs his hand down the back of my hair. "I'm not going anywhere. I'll be here when it all comes crashing down. I promise."

A loud scream pulls my gaze back to the trees. "How long do you think it will take?" I ask, desperately trying to hold everything in.

"As long as it takes," he answers, wrapping his arm around me and pulling me close.

Silence falls over the forest, but I continue to sit, my eyes blurring from exhaustion. My parents join us on the grass. My mother sitting on the other side of Elijah, my dad beside me. None of us speak.

"Do you think it's done," I rasp, my mouth dry.

"I'm sure it is, hun. Why don't we go up and get you something to eat and drink? You're getting dehydrated."

"I-I want to see," I start to rise but falter back on my butt.

"Not happening," my dad and Elijah say in unison.

A flutter of wings lands in front of me. My little crow hops to me as I hold my hand out, urging her to come closer. She drops a bloody ring in my hand, then hops away from me, her beady black eyes leery of the others sitting around me.

I close my fingers around it. "Thank you," I whisper.

The larger black crow that always seems to be watching her back caws and my little bird gives me one last look before flying away.

"You two take care of her," my dad says, jumping to his feet. "I'll get the boys and we'll clean up the mess."

Elijah helps me to my feet.

"Go on and take her upstairs. I'm going to grab something for her to eat," my mom says once we reach the warehouse.

The club members are very respectful as I walk by them, all giving me a nod or a soft squeeze to my shoulder.

When Elijah gets me to my room, I stare up at him, suddenly embarrassed by everything that has happened. He kneels in front of me as he takes off my boots.

"Do you believe in Heaven?" I ask quietly.

He shakes his head, focused on what he is doing. "I don't know what I believe, Rosie."

I glance to my right, staring at the sunset on my wall. "What have I done?"

Elijah lays his big hands on my thighs, squeezing. "You rid the world of a bad man, baby. Don't do this to yourself right now. You're tired."

My mom knocks before opening the door. The smell of the food she has brought in makes me feel nauseous.

"I've got her, Elijah, you can see her again in the morning."

He takes a deep breath, not wanting to leave me. But when he opens his mouth to argue, I grab his hand. "It's okay," I whisper. "Can you... can you please go down and make sure he's really gone."

"Sure, baby." He leans down and presses his lips to my forehead. "I'll be back at first light," he glances over to my mom, making sure she knows he won't stay away for long.

Chapter Thirty-Three

Jesse

I realize my first mistake was not taking out Renee when I had the chance years ago.

For some reason, I always gave her the benefit of doubt. Thought maybe she didn't know that Jimmy was hurting me. But now I know the truth and my father and daughter paid the price for that miscalculation. How could she have known and not stopped it? She was my aunt.

When I saw her at the airport, her face fell when she spotted me. I knew right then something bad had went down at the trailer. She let me drag her out of there with little fight. But once I got her out in the middle of the desert she word vomited all over the fucking place.

"Mom, I'm sorry we didn't tell you," my baby says as I cradle her in my arms. Both of us lying on her bed.

I run the washcloth over her face, washing away blood and makeup. "Shh, it's okay. I understand. Sometimes, we keep secrets to protect those we love."

Her multi-colored eyes, ones that look identical to her father's, swim with unshed tears. "I... I thought I had it handled. Even though I knew what he had done, I thought he really felt bad for my being in the truck that night. Do you know about Lanie?" she asks me.

Brushing hair away from her face, I see my little girl, the one I held in my arms nineteen years ago. "Yes, I'm sorry."

Billie Rose shifts her eyes away from the sunset I painted on her wall. "Your aunt hurt you, didn't she?"

I nod. "I don't think I knew how much of that hurt I was still holding on to. When I was young, she had an opportunity to be my savior but instead she became my enemy. I'm sorry she sent her son here to hurt you. You and grandpa paid the price. I didn't know how much of a threat she would end up being," I tell my daughter. I sit up, crossing my legs in front of me. She also rises, mirroring me.

"I didn't think she could hurt me anymore than she already had, but when she started talking about incest and..." I look at Billie Rose, her soulful, trusting eyes blink back at me. Blowing out a long breath, I continue, "I saw red, Billie Rose, I'm sorry you had to see that."

My eyes drop to our bloody hands, and I let out a mirthless laugh. "Some mother I turned out to be."

Her gaze drops to where mine is. "You are the best mother any girl could ask for," she whispers.

"I've kept you sheltered in this warehouse, using your father to keep you secluded from the rest of the world, all in the name of keeping you safe. It was all for nothing." I drop my head, ashamed, thinking about all the things my baby girl missed out on. All because of my own fear.

My daughter and her old soul, lifts my face with the pad of her finger, forcing me to face her. "Don't give them any more power over you. You've suffered long enough for the sins of others. You did not kill grandpa and you did not rape me. Draven did and there is not one other person to blame."

"How did you get so wise?" I ask, cupping her chin in my palm.

"Well, if you must know, I was schooled by a whole club of outlaw bandits," she says, wiping her eyes.

My daughter is brave. Braver than I've ever been. She is better than me.

I place my hand on her knee, squeezing gently. "Do you want to talk about it?" I ask hesitantly.

She shakes her head. "I don't remember what happened," she admits. While that brings me some relief, knowing that she will not have to see the images when she shuts her eyes each night, it worries me. Will she spend the rest of her days fighting with her mind, knocking on doors, hoping to find the one that holds those memories?

"After Jimmy and his friends hurt me," I say, pausing to swallow the bile rising up my throat, "I was lost, the only thing that saved me was Dan and the guys. Mostly Dan though. He's saved me so many times,

I've lost count. He even bought me a morning after pill. I hadn't even thought to think about the consequences of what had happened to me…" my words trail off.

Billie Rose sucks in a quick breath.

"It was a hard decision. One that I still think about today. I know it does no good to contemplate all the what ifs…" I stop myself. "But after that, everything fell into place, and I married your father and then I got you." I let my fingers trail over her cheek.

She grabs my fingers and squeezes them. "Dan is one of my best friends too," she tells me with tears in her eyes.

"Just please don't shut down," I beg of her. "I can't bear the thought of you losing your voice again. When you need someone to talk to, find someone you can trust. It doesn't have to be me, just someone safe." My heart beats fast in my chest, the furry I felt before, banging against my rib cage. I need to paint. I need to let the pain out through my brush.

She nods, her eyes drooping sleepily. "I'm tired, mom," she says as she falls back against the pillows, her dark hair fanning out over the crisp white pillowcase.

I finish cleaning the rest of the blood from her skin as she drifts to sleep, then I move over to the window seat. I'm not leaving. Tonight, I sit vigil over my daughter, wondering why there has to be so much evil in the world.

An answer never comes but it doesn't matter, because tomorrow the sun will rise. And we will all be stronger for it. Even my baby. She is hurting but each crack to her kind heart will strengthen her. Some day she will have a child of her own and she will be better than me. And that makes everything I've been through worth it.

With each generation comes an opportunity to make this world a better place and I still have hope that someday there won't be so much evil residing here.

I'll always be that young girl, holding on to roller skate dreams and rainbow beginnings.

Chapter Thirty-Four

Billie Rose

My eyes blink open as a ray of sunshine cuts across my face. The curtains billow as a soft breeze blows in through the window. I sit up to find Elijah sitting in the window seat, a lit cigarette hanging out his mouth.

The corners of my mouth turn down in a frown. I don't think I've ever seen him smoke. He must feel my eyes on his back because he flicks the cigarette from his fingers and pulls the screen closed.

When his eyes meet mine, he smiles wide. "So, what kind of crazy shit are we doing today?" he asks.

My shoulders fall in relief, he's still the same Elijah. He looks at me just like he has our entire lives. "Oh, well, I thought we could go shooting at Dan's. I think I would like to learn."

Elijah jumps to his feet and claps his hands together before pulling his phone out and texting, no doubt, my uncle. "Done." He slides it back in his pocket and stalks over to me, taking my mouth like he owns it. And I guess he does… for now.

"Let's shower and then we'll head over there." His phone dings and he glances at it quickly. "All set up." His fingers wrap around mine as he pulls me from the bed.

I know what he's doing. What they will all be doing, keeping me on my toes, making me put one foot in front of the other. I've heard my mother say it many times over the years, it's engrained in my brain. To be honest it was all that got me through some of the early days after my grandfather passed.

"Elijah, I can shower alone. Please." I stand up and press my hand against his chest, his heartbeat betraying him. I know why he's worried. I do. So, I make it easier on him, without giving up my dignity entirely.

He runs his hand through the top of his hair, his thumb running over the bare skin on the side of his head.

"I'll leave the door open," I promise. "I just need some privacy."

His warm brown eyes run over my face; his brows pull together. "Okay," he says, rubbing his hands down both of my arms. "You sure you feel okay?"

Nodding, I pull away from him to gather my clothes. He watches me with hawk like eyes.

When I step into the bathroom, I do as I told him and leave the door open. Quickly, I step into the shower and rip the clothes away from my body. I turn the faucet on, welcoming the ice-cold water. My shaky hands roam over my body as I strain my mind, trying to remember where he touched me, how he touched.

There are faint bruises over my breasts, along my ribs and over my thighs. The only thing the dead man left behind are his fingerprints on my skin.

My teeth clatter together as I wash myself in the freezing cold water. I need to numb the itch of my skin, cool the blood thumping against my veins.

I quickly wash myself and when I step out, Elijah is standing there with a towel. He immediately wraps it around my shoulders and pulls me into the warmth of his embrace. Shivering in his arms, he gently rubs his hands over my back.

"I know I don't have to tell you this but exchanging one form of pain for another is not the answer."

Shoving away from him, I grab my shirt and slide it over my arms, tossing it over my head. "You don't have to tell me," I snip. My panties slide up my legs next. He blatantly watches me, a clear message that he doesn't think anything has changed between us.

After I'm dressed, I feel somewhat better. I run the brush through my hair, my eyes connecting with his in the mirror.

"We need to talk," he says into my ear as he leans forward, his arms caging me against the counter.

I bang the brush down hard. "And we will."

Our gazes hold each other hostage, neither of us willing to back down. He breaks first. Normally, I would smile, except I don't feel like I've won. "Listen, I… I don't remember what happened, okay?"

His knuckles turn white as he grips the counter.

"Can we just go to Dan's?"

He drops his arms and steps back, letting me slide past him. He grabs a strand of my hair as I walk by, letting it slide through his fingers. "I'm not going to lose you over this."

My feet pause. "Elijah, you're not obligated to be my shadow anymore. The threat is gone. You should go back to your life in San Diego. I will survive." I find my footing again and take a step forward but a hand wraps around my throat and pulls me back roughly.

Elijah has never been gentle. He didn't treat me like glass before this and it looks like that hasn't changed. It makes me smile, my cheeks betraying my need to cling on to the hurt of the last twenty-four hours.

"I will always be your shadow, Rosie. And not because some club elders tell me I have to be. I will always stand behind you, trapped in your shade. I welcome it. It's where the parts of you that no one else can see reside. I love all of you. Every single piece." His hot breath whisps over my cheek and I feel a slight stirring in the pit of my stomach.

It's still there.

I inhale a deep breath and steadily release it. Elijah's fingers dig into my skin in response. His beard brushes against my sensitive skin. "Who do you belong to?"

"You," I say on another slow exhale.

When we get downstairs, my parent's gaze bounces between us. "You sure you don't want to stay home and rest today?" my mother asks, concern pulling at her eyes.

"I just need to be around the boys, okay?" the lie easily rolls off my tongue. It's all it takes, and they are seeing us out the door.

The ride over to Dan's is quiet.

The boys come barreling out as soon as we arrive. "Let's go shoot some shit!" Carson yells, lifting his fist in the air. He wraps his big arm around me, pulling me close, kissing me on the head. The twins may be younger than me, but they tower at least a foot over my head.

Jackson pulls up on his Harley as Dan steps outside, joining us. "Why don't you boys all go get started. Billie Rose and I are going to go into town and pick up some lunch."

Elijah's eyes narrow on me to gauge my reaction to Dan's statement and when I don't give him one, he becomes suspicious. I place my hand on his arm. "Go on. I need to talk to him. I sent him a text before we got here. This was my idea. I didn't want to hurt mom or dad's feelings, but I need him right now."

His face softens in understanding, and he kisses me on the lips before following the boys out back.

Dan nods towards his truck. He slides into the driver's side and fires up the engine. "So, where are we headed, sweetheart?"

I glance around the yard nervously, my eyes finding no good place to land. "Mom said you helped her with something after…" I let my words trail off, my gaze finally landing on his confused stare. "I-I need to go to the pharmacy to get one too."

384

His jaw clenches but he remains calm. "Okay," he says, shifting his pickup into gear.

When we get to the pharmacy, he parks and kills the engine. His gaze falls on me, picking at my nails. His big hand engulfs both of mine. "You want me to run in and get it?" he asks.

I lift my eyes to stare out the windshield, watching as a mom struggles with a car seat and a toddler, keeping him from running out in front of any cars. My hand falls to my stomach.

Dan doesn't say anything, he gets out and heads into the store. Everyone that walks by, gives him a wide berth. He comes out a few minutes later and sets a brown paper bag between us.

He then drives to the nearest coffee shop and orders me my favorite flavored coffee, drizzled with extra caramel just as I like. After that, he parks in front of a little lake at the nearby state park.

Sipping my drink, I watch a duck dip his head underwater.

"I'm going to tell you just like I told her. This is an option. Either way, I'll support you."

I set my coffee down and rip the bag open, taking the small box out. I toss it between my palms. "No one knows about this except you. Mom, um, she thinks I'm on the pill."

"But you're not?" he asks confused.

"I thought I was but the last time I got a script, I asked Lanie to pick it up. Um, Draven alluded to the fact he tampered with them." My hands nervously pick at my jeans as I speak, the skin itching underneath.

Dan places his hand on my shoulder. "I'm sorry," is all he says. He doesn't try to sugar coat it. No coddling or sweet words to make it better. That is a first.

I give him a nervous smile. "So, well, anyway, mom mentioned you saving her life, yadda yadda and here we are." Fidgeting in my seat, I fight the urge to claw the skin from my body.

He drops his hand and pulls out a cigarette, rolling down his window. After he lights it, he turns his attention back to me. "I wish you had more time to make a decision on this, but it does have a time limit, unfortunately."

"I know," I say quietly, a breeze rolls in through the windows, blowing wisps of hair into my face. Brushing them back, I decide that I can trust my uncle. He will give me good advice because he only wants what is best for me.

"What is holding you up, hun?"

My watery eyes meet his. "Draven isn't the only person I've been with."

Fear told me he would be angry, that he would bang on his chest and drive back to his house to murder Elijah.

Sometimes fear is a liar.

Dan takes a deep breath. "I can't help you make this decision, but I know someone who can. Why don't you give the kid a chance and talk to him?"

"I don't have to ask him. He will tell me to throw this away and that it doesn't matter either way." I flatten my palms on my legs. "It's not just that." My gaze roams over the lake. Tears run down my cheeks. "I can't even take care of myself, Dan. You've seen my legs."

My uncle leans over, catching my eye. "Do you feel it now?" he asks, genuinely curious and concerned.

"Yes," I blow out. "I'm barely keeping it together. There hasn't been enough time for me to process everything. I'm still so confused. My mind won't slow down."

Dan turns in his seat to face me, suddenly getting serious. "Billie Rose, you would make a fabulous mother. You can fight this and win. You will need to be honest with yourself and others, but it can be done. If you think for one second that taking that," he points to the box in my hands, "will be a mistake, then don't do it."

He sticks a big meaty finger in my chest. "You are in control here. Make a choice and I will help you get through it, either way."

"Can I sit here awhile and think about it?"

"As long as it takes." He pulls out his phone to I assume text the boys that we will be gone awhile longer. At first I wondered what excuse he would give them but then I remembered who he was, and that Big Dan didn't need an explanation.

"I'm going to go sit in the sand for a bit." Maybe my mind will slow long enough for me to make a decision. I take my coffee and the box and head down the grassy hill to the lake.

Tears fall freely down my face as I take in the beauty before me. I want to live. I do but I know it will be a constant battle to keep the blade at bay. That's not the kind of mother I want to be.

This should be a simple thing. Open the box, take out the pill and swallow. Easy but so damn hard. Fuck! I don't even know if I'm pregnant. I'm sure I'm not, so what does it matter? If I take it, no big deal. It's just a precaution.

Elijah's smiling face enters my mind. He will make beautiful babies someday, with big brown eyes just like his. Or at least that is how I see them in my mind.

What do I do?

I lie back on the ground and stare up at the clouds. But what if there is a baby and it belongs to Draven? When I picture a baby from him, I see the exact same child but always in Elijah's arms.

There is always a chance that Elijah might not stay if it…

I squeeze the box in my hand. It doesn't matter. So much has been stolen from me. I will not let Draven have this too. If I'm pregnant, this baby is mine. Mine. And that is all that matters.

My fist flies through the air, the box landing with a splash in the water. It floats there, as does my heart.

As I make my way back to the truck, I see that Dan is watching me closely.

"Ready?" he asks when I hop in.

"Yes," I whisper, my breath fogging up the glass as I look out my window. "I'm going to need you to keep this between you and I."

He starts to shake his head.

"Dan, I need time." I turn to face him. My fingers tremble as I pull my phone out and make a call to let my uncle know just how serious I am.

His brows furrow as he listens to my side of the conversation, and I watch as his big heart breaks.

"I'll be home before you know it," I say hoarsely after I hang up the phone.

He grabs the back of my head and pulls me across the seat towards him. "I'm so proud of you. You've got this, baby girl."

Elijah is pissed by the time we get back. He's pacing back and forth like a caged tiger in front of Dan's house. His gaze meets mine as we pull in.

I get out and stand in front of him.

"You never had any intention of shooting today, did you?" he asks, looking down his nose at me.

"Nope," I pop the p and turn to get in the rod, waiting for him there.

Dan says something to him, and Elijah runs his hands over his head, frustrated that I went to someone else and not to him. He storms over the gravel and jerks the door open, getting in beside me.

"Rosie, please talk to me. I'm dying inside. I see you're suffering, and you won't let me in. Please let me in," he begs.

"Elijah, I'm... I'm not okay."

He groans, gripping the steering wheel so hard I think it might break in half.

"But you can help me with something," I soothe, turning in my seat to face him.

"I'll help you with anything," he says without thought, sitting up straighter.

The corner of my mouth lifts in a smile at his eagerness to help. I almost feel bad because this is not going to end the way he wants. "I need to talk to my parents. Can you be there with me?"

His warm brown gaze pulls me in, making my toes tingle. "Absolutely," he agrees, reaching over and threading our fingers together. He pulls our hands to his mouth and places a kiss on the back of my hand.

Back at the warehouse, we find them sitting together in the kitchen, my mom's hands stained with black paint as she pulls a cup to her mouth. "Hey, you guys got a minute?"

They both look at us above the rims of their cups. I give them a big smile, and they relax. My dad goes to the coffee pot. "You guys want a cup?"

Elijah accepts and I decline, grabbing a water out of the fridge. All eyes are on me when I sit down.

"Okay, so, fuck, I'm just going to rip the band-aid off."

My dad's eyebrow bows in concern.

Roses and Skulls

"I can't do this." My hands slide under my legs so that I refrain from peeling the skin away from the edge of my nails. "Shit, I mean, I can't do this alone. I'm about to go out of my mind, I'm not going to lie."

My mom sits forward, panic settling over her features. "Baby, we are here." She starts to get up to come to me.

"No." I hold my hand up to stop her. She sits back down, her and my dad exchanging a nervous glance. "I need professional help. I called William today and he is arranging for me to enter a facility that helps people like me, who like to cut. It's a self-harm program."

Elijah tenses next to me but I continue.

"It's just north of San Diego along the coast."

The room becomes silent.

"I'm sure the therapist you had here could help," my mom suggests. I knew this would be hard for them. But I need to do this alone. I need time to think and to heal.

My dad leans forward, resting his arms on the table between us. "How long?"

"Ninety days."

Mom jumps from the table. "No, there has to be something closer."

Elijah finally says something. "It's the best in the nation. Dad went there and they helped him. He made some lifelong friends there. Said it saved his life," he says stiffly, the pain seeping out between his words. He knocks on the table. "It's nice, clean, sits right on beach. Rosie will be able to see the sun set every night."

My mother rubs her hand over her eyes, a small sigh leaving her lips.

He gives me a half smile before glancing away.

"Not to be rude but I'm not asking. I've thought about this all day. I was having a hard time before but now," I clear my throat. "Dan is driving me to the airport at six tomorrow morning."

"You sure I can't just drag you up to the cabin? The mountain air heals everything," Dad suggests gruffly.

I reach over and wrap my hand around his. "When I get back, we should definitely go the cabin. I would love that."

My heart breaks for my family. But I have to protect what's mine. My sanity, my flesh, my life, my soul, they are all on the line here.

And maybe one tiny other thing.

Chapter Thirty-Five

Billie Rose – two months later

I jump onto my bed, turning on the light in the corner of the room. My new friend, Kelsie, plops down beside me. "You are so lucky," she says, quietly rifling through the letters the receptionist just gave to me.

"You know, if you write to any of them, they will write back," I tell her.

Her cheeks turn red. "Oh, I could never initiate something like that."

"Well, I think it would be a good idea. It will be nice for you to get to know them before you get there. They are going to smother you with love," I tease.

My Uncle Dan and Aunt Lily came to visit me shortly after I got here. They fell in love with Kelsie. She's supposed to be released about the same time as me. A few days before me, actually. But anyhow, the state had been looking for her next home, she'd been terrified about where they would send her next.

Kelsie just turned sixteen a few months ago. She's a ward of the state. But she's been pretty much on her own for years. It wasn't until a mailman found her naked and crying behind a bush that the state stepped in and "helped" her. Some help they'd been.

The week following their visit, Kelsie learned that she was going to be adopted by the one and only Big Dan and his wife. I spit my drink across the table when she told me. Her green eyes shone with tears. She thought I had asked them to do it. I assured her that I didn't even know they were considering it, but I was thrilled to know Kelsie would be living a short distance from me.

A knock on our door pulls our attention away from the letters sprawled over my bed.

"Girls, you ran off before I had a chance to give you Kelsie's mail." Lou, the receptionist, lays a stack of envelopes on the dresser beside the door. "See you gals, tomorrow." She gives us a small wave and closes the door behind her.

"My letters?" Kelsie's nose wrinkles up in confusion.

I think I know where they came from. My family is the best. Hands down.

The smile on my face widens as I watch Kelsie approach them slowly as if they might disappear before her eyes.

Roses and Skulls

Kelsie is a tiny, little, bob haired blond, with huge green eyes. She's here for the same reason I am, except her story is much worse than mine. The scars littering her body are not all from her own hand.

My vision blurs as I watch her clutch them to her chest. She wipes her eyes as she joins me on the bed again. When she sets them down, I see they are indeed from my family... soon to be hers too.

She runs her finger over one that says mom and dad in the return address. "Is this real?"

I grab her hand. "It's real. Trust it, Kelsie. My aunt and uncle don't do anything half assed."

She runs her finger along the seam and begins to pull out her first letter. And I don't mean the first from Dan and Lily, I mean the first one ever.

Leaning back against the headboard, I grab my letter from Elijah, my heart beating faster as I anticipate his words.

"Billie Rose."

I glance up. Kelsie's hands are shaking. "I think that everything you went through was for me. You are the best thing that's ever happened to me." And then she shyly goes back to reading her letter, taking it over to her own bed and turning her back to me. Her shoulders shake as she reads what I'm assuming are kind and reassuring words.

My mind replays similar words said to me by mother. *"Dan is the best thing to have ever happened to me."*

I guess we never know just how much of an impact we can make on someone.

Making a new friend was something I didn't think would happen when I came here. Not after the deep betrayal I felt from Lanie. But Kelsie and I were drawn to each other. She's helped me more than she'll ever know. I know my family is going to love her as much as I do.

I focus back on the paper in my hand. It smells of him. Pulling it to my nose, I close my eyes and envision his warm brown eyes. We haven't seen each other since I left. I've only allowed Dan and Lily to visit. I knew someone from the club had to come and see me with their own two eyes, to ensure for themselves that I was well. But I needed to do this alone.

It was terrifying. My first night here, I spent crying in a little ball on my bed. Kelsie came to me, running her fingers through my long, dark hair. "It will be okay," she had whispered. "They don't hurt us here." Her words made me turn to her. The thought had never occurred to me. Again, the naïve little MC princess.

When she hugged me, my loneliness receded. I might not have my family here, but I had someone, and I had found her all on my own. A friend that no one had thrust in front of me with intentions of their own.

Elijah's letter puts a smile on my face but a nervousness in my gut. In my last letter to him, I asked if he would come pick me up. I knew my parents would be disappointed but there was no other way. I want nothing more than to ride on the back of his bike, wrap my arms around his waist and feel the wind against my skin. Even if it might be the last time.

"You okay over there?" I ask.

Kelsie sniffles and rolls over to face me. "I am fine. What about you?" she asks.

"I'm good. Really good."

She makes her way back to my bed and runs her fingers over the other letters. "How many people are in your..." I raise an eyebrow her direction and she corrects herself, "*our* family?"

I throw my head back and laugh. "Oh, Kels, this is going to take a while." I proceed to tell her who all the letters are from.

"And this one is from my cousin Jackson. His mom and my dad are brother and sister. He's adopted too."

Her green eyes are wide. "So many people. I would have been happy with one person." She takes Jackson's letter from my fingers. "Are they all kind like you?" she asks nervously.

I shake my head. "No, some of them are real assholes." I instantly regret my words at her frightened expression. "But they are all kind, kind assholes," I tease, and she relaxes. "Seriously, Kelsie, we are like any other family. Sometimes, we get angry at each other, but at the end of the day, they will always have your back." I pull her hand to my lap, running my fingers over the burn on the palm of her hand. "And you will never be alone again. They would give up everything for you."

"How do you know this?" She watches my hand run over her scars.

"Because they've done it for me."

We stare at each other for a few seconds.

Kelsie's mouth twitches and the first smile I've ever seen from her, pulls at the corner of her lips. "I am excited," she says.

I shove Jackson's letter in her hands. "Go on, enjoy your letters."

She gathers them all up and she giggles minutes later. "This Jackson, he is funny."

I've never heard her laugh before. I need to remember to give Jackson a big hug when I get home for making my friend so happy.

For the next several days, she carries those letters with her everywhere, and I notice that she's been writing back to each person. It warms my heart.

Lanie wanted a family like mine, she said so herself. Maybe I should have listened to her more. Been a better friend. I can't change the past, but I can learn from it. I'll never let Kelsie feel like my family is not her own.

I've come to terms with many things over the past eight weeks. Away from everything, I've been able to take a long hard look at myself. The Billie Rose that I used to be before grandpa died is never coming back but parts of her have. I've come to accept the new version of myself. Still a little naïve, and snippy, and sometimes revengeful. But the new version lets herself feel. All of it. Even the pain.

This place has given me the tools I'll need when I get home. There is still so much to go through. Life is rarely easy and almost never fair, but it is worth it.

It's all about family and friends and I have the best of both.

Roses and Skulls

When Dan and Lily come for Kelsie, to take her home, my uncle pulls me aside. His eyes roam over my figure and I know what he's wondering. "Are you nervous to take her home?" I ask, deflecting his attention from me.

"No," he says seriously. Dan has more confidence than anyone I've ever met. "Are you okay with it?"

My head pulls back in surprise. "Yeah, why wouldn't I be?"

"Well, for one, you're not going to be the only girl anymore." His eyebrows pull together, and I see how much this has been weighing on his mind.

I laugh. "Dan, that is a good thing not a bad one."

"I don't know, baby girl. You're awfully spoiled," he teases.

I take his hands in mine. "I'm thrilled that Kelsie is going to get to know what real love feels like. She's never had that." My gaze travels to where my aunt and her are signing release papers. A tear slips down my face as Lily gently runs her hand down Kelsie's short hair. "She's afraid of the dark and tell the boys not to scare her like they do me. You have to approach her lightly," I tell him, biting my lip to keep any other traitorous tears at bay.

Dan watches his wife and soon to be new daughter. "I already want to lock her in her room and keep all the boys away from her," he admits.

"Don't do that. Just... just be there for her if she needs you."

His eyes make their way back to me, his gaze yet again dipping to my stomach, the question he's dying to ask on the tip of his tongue. "I didn't steer you wrong that day at the lake, did I?" he asks. "Because I'm hoping I did right by you."

"You stayed by my side and let me make the decision myself. I don't regret anything. No worries."

He breathes a sigh of relief. "Good, I'm glad it all worked out."

My legs itch, but I count to ten in my head, using every skill taught to me to control my anxiety. "Yes, everything always seems to work out for the best, doesn't it?"

He nods as Lily and Kelsie make their way over to us.

Kelsie drops her eyes shyly as she approaches. I gently place my arm around her shoulders. "I'll be right behind you in a few days."

She smiles up at me brightly and I know in that moment that it's true that everything happens for a reason, and it will work out, maybe not the way we think but the way it's meant to be.

Chapter Thirty-Six

Elijah

I've been waiting for this day for three months and now it's finally here. Billie Rose and I have been sending letters to each other. Old school shit. Honestly, I think it's what we both needed. It's been nice getting to know each other on a deeper level. Sometimes, it's easier to spill your guts through pen and paper.

Her letters always smell of her and it's about killed me. I want her in my fucking arms so bad. I was thrilled when she asked me to come get her. Bring the bike she had wrote. Her old man wasn't too happy about it, and I saw the hurt in Jesse's eyes, but I didn't have it in me to care. My own selfishness won.

Billie Rose is mine.

She actually got out a few days ago, said she needed a couple of days to regroup before I came for her. She's been staying at my parent's house.

I'm as nervous as a whore in church about seeing her again.

Something hasn't been right. I can't put my finger on it. I'm assuming it's about Draven. He hurt her and I can't get it out of my mind, how will she be able to ever get it out of hers?

"Elijah," my mom calls from the kitchen when she hears me open the front door. I follow the smell of my favorite meal wafting down the hallway.

My dad is sitting at the table with a newspaper in his hand. He jumps up and rushes me, wrapping me up in a big old bear hug, my mom right behind him. "I've missed you, baby," she says, tears clinging to her lashes.

When they pull away, my eyes dart around the room. "Where is she?"

My mom guffaws, whipping her towel at me. "Not even an, *I missed you,* back?"

I rub my hands together and give her a shit eating grin. "I missed you, ma." I wrap my arms around her neck from behind, giving her a kiss on the cheek.

"She's down at the beach, told us to send you down there when you got here."

My heart does this weird dip. "You mean she's not here?" I don't know why it bothers me, but I thought she would be waiting for me, here.

Dad gives me a stern look. "Treatment did not just turn the switch off, Elijah. She's nervous about seeing you again."

"I know," I almost whine. Hearing it in my voice makes me straighten my shoulders, angry at myself for being so selfish. "I'll head down there."

He gives me a knowing smile. "Just be yourself. She doesn't want anyone to treat her differently than they did before."

My shoulders drop, air whooshing out between my lips. "Okay. But she's good, yeah?"

"She's good, son." He pats me on the back as I make my way out the back door and down to the beach.

My girl is sitting off by herself, watching the waves roll in. Wisps of her dark hair blow in the gentle breeze. I take a deep breath of the salty air, closing my eyes. When I open them, she is standing, her stormy eyes glued to me.

She looks so damn good. My mouth pulls into a full, wide smile and that is all it takes before she is running to me, jumping in my arms.

My nose buries into her neck. God, she smells good.

I carry her back down to her blanket, but she doesn't let go, so I carefully sit down and hold her and hold her and hold her.

"I've missed you, baby," I whisper into her ear, trying to push her away from me so I can see her face.

Reluctantly, she sits back, still in my lap. "I almost forgot how hot you were," she says shyly. A blush stains her rosy cheeks.

I press my lips to hers, and soon our tongues are getting reacquainted. When I pull away breathless, I look her over. "You look amazing," I tell her.

Again, her face heats from my attention. "Thank you," she says quietly, looking down between us.

She tries to climb off me, but I hold her tight around the waist. "Not yet. I just want to hold you."

Her eyes bounce between mine and I know something is not right. My gut has been telling me for a long time now, I've just been choosing to ignore it.

"God, it would be so easy to forget the rest of the world and live in the warmth of your eyes," she says, water beginning to pool in the corners of her own. She blinks twice and the tears spill down her cheeks.

"Then do it," I tell her. "Who needs the rest of the world when we have each other."

Her gaze focuses behind me, not on anything in particular. She's lost in her own thoughts. For some reason, I thought treatment would heal all her wounds. That it would be like before…

She smiles at me, tears streaming down her face. "I have something I need to talk to you about. It's why I asked for you to come. It's why I'm here and not waiting for you at your parent's."

I let her slide off my lap, and she settles next to me, pulling her legs to her chest.

We stare at the ocean, the powerful waves crashing against the beach. "You can tell me anything, Rosie. Just spill it, you're torturing me. Are you trying to call us off? Cause that's not happening…"

She cuts me off by handing me something. I stare down at it.

"I didn't lie to you. I really thought I was on the pill, but Lanie picked up my script and Draven, well, he told me he tampered with it."

My heart is beating out of control as her words sink into my thick skull, the two pink lines staring at me.

"I'm keeping it. You don't have to do anything. I don't expect…" she turns away from me. "I don't know whose it is." Her words are strangled as if she's drowning in sorrow.

No. No. This is not changing anything. I'm here to get my girl. I'm taking her home.

I'm taking them home.

"Nobody knows but my therapist and the doctor I've been seeing. You can walk away now. Well, I need a ride home but…" her voice fades.

"Rosie, why didn't you tell me before now?" I ask, turning her to face me.

She looks everywhere but at me. "I had to get stronger."

"Baby," I hush. "You shouldn't have had to go through this alone."

It's then that her watery gaze settles on me. "I've never been alone, Elijah. I know that I have many people who will stand beside me no matter what and I had your letters. I never felt alone, trust me." She turns her face towards the water. "But I needed to go slow. To think about all that had happened. You will need that too. I want you to make a decision for yourself, not for me, not for…" Her hand falls to her stomach and I feel like I've just been punched in mine. "Do what is best for you because that is what I did. I'll keep it a secret until you decide. No one has to know that we… that we've been together. It will just be mine," she finishes softly.

I stare out over the ocean as the sun begins to dip below the horizon and I let out a harsh laugh. "Did you hit your head when you were with him?"

"No, I don't think so. I don't remember," her eyes widen as my hand slowly reaches out and wraps around her throat.

"You must have, if you think for one minute that you're not mine." Placing my hand gently over her womb. "And this, this is now mine too."

"But…"

"No fucking buts, baby. You both belong to me."

She bites her lip, drawing my eyes there. God, her mouth is perfect. She is perfect.

Relief washes over her in waves as deeply born sobs wrench from her chest. I pull her back onto my lap. "Mine, Rosie. Mine," I whisper over and over until I'm sure that it will stick. "I don't need to think about it, and I don't need a fucking test to tell me it's mine either, so don't even go there." She cries harder as the sun disappears, hopefully taking any remaining doubt with it. "So, do we still get to drive fast on the way home?"

She chuckles, wiping her eyes, her forehead still pressed to my chest. "Maybe just a few miles an hour over."

"Baby, our kid is going to want to go fast. Trust me." She laughs again, finally raising her face to look at me. Her face is red and blotchy and fucking beautiful.

"I have something to give you and don't you fucking dare try to give it back. This little peanut has nothing to do with any of it. This is between me and you. Got it?" I dip my head and catch her crystal blue eyes. She's happy.

I shift my hips, almost bucking her off, making her giggle again but eventually I get it. When I open the box, her eyes widen. "Elijah," she says as her finger runs over the stone.

"Lily helped me make it. It reminds me of your eyes when you're happy."

It's a small silver band of diamonds surrounded by a sapphire, not any old sapphire but a cracked one, mended by a seam of gold.

Billie Rose stares at it and then her face drops. "Elijah, I've upended your life. It's quiet here, don't throw that all away for me. I know your parents miss you."

"Goddammit, why can't you just accept that I want this. I want you and whatever comes with that. It might be quieter here but it's boring. Have you ever known me to like the mundane?"

Her bottom lip slips between her teeth. I gently pull it out with my thumb and then I kiss her. Kiss her like I've dreamed of every night since she left. Her mouth slowly parts and she finally lets me in. My fingers wrap around her bottom, pulling her close. We are both panting by the time I pull away.

I take the box from her and slip the ring on her finger, kissing it before meeting her eyes.

"I want to believe you but how will I ever know that this is what you really want? What I just told you changes everything. I know you are an honorable man, Elijah. I knew you would say it didn't matter." Her heart and her head are at war. But I think I may know how to give her peace.

Taking her face in my hands, I try my best to reassure her. "I have a way to show you. When we get home, you'll see, and then you will have no doubt this is what I want."

My thumbs brush over her cheeks as she fights with herself. I see hope lingering in her galaxy eyes. "Okay," she whispers.

"It's a big surprise." My tongue runs over the ring in my lip and her eyes drop there, her hips rolling on their own accord.

"Bigger than this," she holds up her hand. "Or this." She rubs her hand over her stomach.

"Yes, and no." I tease.

She presses her lips to mine. "I have a surprise for you, too," she mumbles into my mouth. Her hands wrap around my shoulders.

"Give me a hint." I buck my hips and she laughs.

"Not a chance." She jumps up and starts to run. I'm up in a second, excited for the chase. I wrap my arms around her, swinging her in the air.

We continue down to the water before I set her on her feet. Walking hand in hand, she tells me how much she enjoyed seeing the sun set over the ocean every night. "I'm glad your dad recommended that place. My mind was going so fast, they really helped me."

"I think it was good for everyone, honestly. I'd bet you'd never guess that I've been having dinner with your parents a couple of times a week."

Billie Rose stops abruptly, almost yanking my arm off. "What?"

"Yep, I figured if I was going to marry you then maybe I should get to know them. Better yet, it was a chance for your dad to get to know me."

After she wraps her head around that image, we continue along.

"I even asked him permission for your hand in marriage." This time when she stops, I'm ready for it and I yank her to my chest.

"There is no way he said yes." Her hair blows around her cheeks as she shakes her head back and forth.

I flash her my best smile and a wink. "He did."

"No," she says, disbelief pulling her brows high. She grabs my shirt and shakes me. "Did he hit you?"

Laughing, I lean down and give her a kiss on the tip of her nose. "Nope. But there were some stipulations."

"So, they know about your proposal." She lays her head on my chest and sighs. "Grandpa told me that someday I would find someone who would fight for me. He said even my frightening ass parents wouldn't scare him away. I didn't believe him then, but now." She looks up at me. "Do I dare let myself believe?"

"Believe it, baby. I'm here for the long haul. We've waited a long time to be together. Remember when we were young, and we walked this same beach looking for shells. Your arm was in a sling, and I knew by the way your dad looked at me that it would be a long time before I would get to see you again. I may not have known then that we were destined to be together, but I do recall the ache that filled my chest at the thought of being away from you. I watched you meticulously pick through the shells, so concerned with finding one for everyone in your family. I wanted to be part of your family, Rosie. Not because they were bikers and cool but because I wanted you to love me like you did them."

Billie Rose pulls away from me and hits the light on her phone, kneeling in front of me, she searches the ground. She looks up and smiles. "I found the perfect one." When she stands, she places a shell in the palm of my hand. On the inside of the shell is a light pink heart. "I love you, Elijah."

I grab the back of her head and pull her into my chest. "I love you too, baby."

Chapter Thirty-Seven

Billie Rose

The drive back is nothing short of torturous. What was I thinking, asking him to bring the bike? Not because my ass can't take it but because he is close, so damn close. My hand roams over his toned abs and I can't help myself, I let it drop lower.

"Billie Rose, don't think I won't pull this bike over right here and fuck you on the side of the highway like there's no tomorrow."

I tip my head back and laugh. It's not very nice of me to tease him. His parents made us sleep in separate rooms last night. I was dog tired anyhow, so it was fine, but I don't know how much longer either of us can wait.

Am I nervous about it?

Yes.

I can't remember what Draven did to me, but I know. My therapist said that with the drugs they gave me, I will more than likely never remember. A blessing or a curse, I haven't decided. But I do know that my body is craving Elijah's.

My cheek rests over his back, right over the Skulls patch on his vest. I squeeze him tight, inhaling his scent, and enjoying his warmth. Elijah pats my hand.

"Almost home, baby."

That's what I'm really nervous about. Telling my parents and my family that I'm expecting. I have no idea how they will feel about it. Elijah's parents are driving down too, said they wouldn't miss my welcome home party for anything. They left earlier than us. I'm glad because I had a touch of morning sickness when I woke up.

Elijah was so sweet, holding my hair away from my face as I leaned over the toilet. It was embarrassing but he told me to get used to it because he was going to be seeing me in more compromising situations very soon.

We also talked more about him not wanting a DNA test. My only concern is the health of the baby. Someday, he or she might need to know... especially if it's Draven's. Anyhow, we compromised, and we will be getting a test. We're going to leave the results in the hands of someone we trust.

I told him it was okay if he decides later that he wants to know. It's his right to know. He said he wouldn't but we both agreed that if either of us need to, the option will be there.

Roses and Skulls

Tonight, we are having dinner with both sets of parents. The welcome home party isn't until this weekend. Wouldn't you know, a party. When my mom wrote to me about it, I told her to make sure she included Kelsie in the celebration. A welcome home party for both of us.

Elijah abruptly pulls off the road.

"What are we doing? We're so close," I whine. Even though I'm nervous about going home, I'm excited.

He pulls a piece of black cloth out of his pocket.

"First, I have something to prove to you," he says, his hot breath on the back of my neck as he ties it around my face.

My heart flutters wildly against his back when we take off again. What could he possibly want to show me? I come up with nothing. I just can't imagine how he's going to prove to me that he's not staying with me out of obligation. He wanted to marry me, yeah, but he wasn't banking on me being pregnant. And I'm sure he never planned on the possibility of raising another man's child.

Gravel crunches beneath the tires as we roll to a stop. Elijah helps me off the bike. "I got you," he coaxes me off. "You're not going to fall."

"I'm a little nervous," I admit, laughing lightly as he walks us a few steps, his chest to my back.

He laughs too. "Nothing to be worried about. Trust me."

"I do," I say quietly, turning my head.

413

His whiskered cheek brushes against mine. It feels nice, having his strong arms wrapped around me. He pulls one hand behind my head to untie the cloth. When it falls to the ground, he whispers in my ear, "You can open your eyes now."

I blink against the brightness until everything comes in to focus. My hand flies to my mouth. The words I try to find escape me.

"Do you like it?" he asks anxiously.

My feet move me forward and I spin around, taking everything in, the high sun reflecting a million diamonds over the lake.

"This was one of the stipulations," Elijah says, rocking back on his heals, he reaches in a pocket and pulls out a sucker, popping it in his mouth.

My head snaps back to the cabin. "How?" I shake my head in disbelief.

Elijah shrugs. "Everyone helped. Your dad said I could marry you as long as I didn't take you away. That was never my intention anyway. But this always has been."

"The first night. You said it would be a perfect place to build a home." I'm dumbfounded. Never in a million years did I expect Elijah to build us a cabin before I returned from California.

"And I was right, yeah?"

He grabs my hand and pulls me up the steps to the porch. Two hand crafted wooden rocking chairs are waiting for someone to fill them, both facing the lake. His arms come around my waist and he rubs my stomach. "Someday, we will sit here and watch our kids play in the yard."

I've been sitting in treatment, imagining the thousand ways this would go down. Me telling Elijah about the baby. Wondering where I would live with my child if he didn't want me and where we would live if he did, and nothing could have been more perfect than this. I wasted so much time worrying about things that will never come to pass.

"Say something, baby."

I turn in his arms and cup his scruffy cheeks in my hand. "It's perfect." Then I pull the sucker from his mouth and press my lips to his and kiss him, his mouth tasting like cherries.

He's the first to pull away. He takes the sucker from my hand and pushes it into my mouth. "We're not done yet." Quickly, he pulls a key out of his pocket and opens the door. He holds it open for me. When I slide by him, he smacks me on the butt lightly. A familiar pull low in my belly makes me groan out loud.

Of course, he notices. He laughs. "Sounds like you've missed me," he teases. Walking ahead of me, he spreads his arms wide. "Welcome to our casa."

My eyes roam over the beautiful wood and warm colors. "You let Lily work her magic, didn't you?"

"Yep. Wait till you see the bedroom," he wags his eyebrows.

I walk around the open living room and kitchen, running my fingers over everything. A mixture of old meets new. Elijah watches me with a smile on his face. "You really know how to treat a girl," I joke with a stupid grin on my face. One that I hope is reaching my eyes, because this is all too much.

There is a chance I have another man's baby in my womb. How can he give me all this? My eyes flit up the stairs. I don't deserve any of this. I ruined everything, all because I let my guard down.

"Come," he says seriously. A frown on his face.

Shit, I've never been very good at hiding my feelings.

We walk into our bedroom, and it's amazing. A long dresser sits at the end of the room, painted a rustic black with bright red roses covering it. It matches the headboard on the giant, king-sized bed in the center of the room. Elijah points to an attached bathroom and when I peek inside, it's just as cool as the rest of the house.

Then he swings open a door that I believe is a closet but when I step inside, I see I'm wrong. It's not a closet at all. It's... it's a nursery, painted in neutral colors. On the wall, across from the most beautiful crib I've ever seen, is a sunset. Painted with vibrant colors. Similar to the one I've looked at for nineteen years.

"Like I said, everyone pitched in," he says, leaning against the doorjamb.

My fingers dance along the edge of the crib. How did they know?

"None of us knew that you were pregnant if that's what you are thinking. This was all for the future. It's just coming faster than I anticipated but I knew we would have a family one day."

So, they didn't know. He didn't know.

Roses and Skulls

But I think someone did. I stare at the mural painted on the wall, my chest filling with a warmth I've never felt before.

"But, what if one of us couldn't have had children?" I ask quietly, turning to stare down at the pale, yellow blanket covering the small mattress.

"Then we would have adopted, Rosie. You carried a baby doll around for the first five years of your life. You were destined to be a mother and I love that. This, Rosie, this is my proof that I want this with you. I want this baby."

I take a step back, everything suddenly hitting me fast and hard.

Breathe, count to ten. Everything is fine. Just breathe.

"Baby?" Elijah takes a step towards me, confusion pulling at his brows.

Holding a hand up to him, I spin around the room. This is too perfect. Something is going to go wrong. Someone is going to take all of this away from me. Elijah deserves better than me. I'm scarred and broken.

"I'm sorry." I glance back at the crib. "I'm so sorry. He... I should have never... how can you look at me the same?"

"Look at your ring. Right now," he demands, remaining at arm's length from me.

My gaze falls on my ring. The gold glints in the light, holding two halves of the sapphire together.

"Stronger and more beautiful," he says, his voice cracking. "Yes, the baby is coming because he messed with your birth control and yes, there is a small chance it might be his, but it will never be his here." He pats his chest with two fingers over his heart. "He or she will always be mine."

I fall to the ground, and he kneels down with me. "Don't you see, Rosie? The baby is the gold to our broken bits. We are going to be stronger and more beautiful because of them."

Our eyes meet and I see nothing but sincerity in his gaze.

As I release tears that I've been holding on to for far too long, he rocks us back and forth on the floor of our baby's room.

And then I hear them, whispers from Heaven.

Elijah smiles first. "You see, even Bill approves, Rosie. Don't worry about the future, just enjoy right now. You, me, our baby, a new home. We deserve this."

I wipe my eyes and let him pull me to my feet. We make our way back through the cabin and as we step outside, I see the last chime I made, hanging from the porch. The wind has picked up and is sending the skeleton keys into each other, producing a peaceful little melody.

"My heart can't take all this happiness." I run my hand over my chest. Elijah rests his chin on my shoulder.

He takes his sucker out of my hand and puts it in his mouth as he jumps off the porch. "Well, shall we go tell our parents just how old they're getting?" Winking at me, he holds out his hand. I take it and let him pull me towards the bike.

Roses and Skulls

"Do you think they will be happy?" I ask nervously, climbing on behind him.

"Honestly, I think they will be over the moon happy." He fires up the motor and turns us around in front of our new home.

I glance over my shoulder as we pull out on the road. My eyes fall closed. A warm sensation spreads across my chest, putting a smile on my face. Happy. I'm truly happy.

My parents knock me clean over, barely giving me a chance to get off the bike as soon as we pull in.

"Never again," my dad whispers in my hair. His arms tighten around me and my mom. "I can't take you being away from us like that." Bossing me already.

The daughter I was before would have stormed away. The one I am now, squeezes him tight and whispers back, "Never again. I missed you guys so much."

He pulls away and both he and my mom check me over. "You look so good, baby," my mom coos. "You're glowing."

My dad nods in agreement. "The California sun did you good," he agrees.

Elijah and I share a knowing smile.

"I'm starving," I tell them and two seconds later we are sitting on the patio, a plate piled high of my mom's famous pasta in front of me.

They ask me a million questions about the facility and how I'm feeling, though they know the answers to most of it. The letters we have shared told them all that plus more. My dad even wrote to me. In his own handwriting. I'll treasure those letters forever.

Elijah taps his glass with his knife lightly. "As you can see, she's wearing the ring, so we have the green light to begin the wedding preparations."

Our parents nod and begin to chatter over venues, dates, all shit that I can't even wrap my head around right now. It's too much. My dad's eyes narrow on me, and he claps his hands loudly.

Everyone quiets and turns towards him.

"Billie Rose, what do you think of all this? You've been awfully quiet."

Elijah grabs my hand under the table and squeezes. I take a deep breath. "I think everything sounds lovely, but I was thinking a small ceremony. Out back. With just the club and close friends. I don't want a huge wedding."

My father leans back, his scary eyebrow crawling dangerously close to his hairline.

I feel a trickle of sweat travel down my spine. "And I think we should do it soon. Like in a few months."

And there it goes, it's as high as I've ever seen it. He knows something is not right.

"Um, I'm pregnant," I say quietly, dropping my eyes to stare at Elijah and I's intertwined hands.

Roses and Skulls

The silence that follows is like a knife through my heart. A lump begins to form in my throat and then my chair is pushed back, and my father is pulling me to stand, crushing me against his big chest.

"Baby girl," he breathes out and then he pushes me back, his tattooed hands cupping my face. "My baby is having a baby." A single tear falls down his cheek, absorbed by his greying beard. "I'm going to be a grandpa," he says, smiling wide, he shoves me back into his chest, holding me tight.

I couldn't hold back my choked sob of relief if I tried. He continues to hold me as I break down. Telling them everything they need to know about the circumstances surrounding this pregnancy.

I didn't know how much I needed this. To have his acceptance. His support.

He's always been there to catch me. I should have never doubted any of them. I was fully prepared to move out. To live on my own. Just me and the baby. I didn't know if anyone would understand my decision.

My mom's soft hair brushes over my skin as she comes up behind me and wraps her arms around us. "I'm so happy for you, baby. You will make a wonderful mother."

When they finally release me, Elijah's parents are ready to pick up where they left off. "We love you, Billie Rose. We are so happy that we are getting you as a daughter," Penny reassures me, leaning her forehead against mine.

"And the cherry on top, a new grandbaby," William adds, kissing me on the cheek.

Elijah clears his throat. "Um, hello, what about me? Don't I get any love? I mean, I know she's carrying the baby and all, but it did take my amazing little spermies to get in there."

This is his way of letting everyone know that this baby is one hundred percent his. There will be no discussion of it being any other way. He has established himself as our protector and I love him all the more for it.

My mom rushes over to him, wrapping him up and pressing kisses all over his cheeks, exaggeratedly.

He pushes her away playfully. "Ugh, okay, okay, I've had enough love."

She purses her lips, and we all laugh, everyone except the grumpy looking asshole standing next to us. My dad stomps forward, his boots thudding across the floor and then he stops directly in front of Elijah. I watch as my fiancé braces for a punch but then my dad hugs him.

Hugs him.

And then he whispers something in Elijah's ear that makes him tear up. My dad pats him on the back a little harder than normal, gives his shoulder a squeeze before walking away.

My mom and Penny chat happily about all things baby as they clear the table and William follows my dad out to the patio with two glasses and a bottle from the top shelf.

"What did he say to you?" I ask, taking his hand and pulling him down into our seats.

Elijah presses his thumbs to the corner of his eyes. Shaking his head, unable to speak.

"Please tell me," I beg, hoping that my father did not just crush the man I love.

His hand falls from his face and he stares at me with red rimmed eyes. "He told me I'm a good man and that he will be proud to be my father-in-law at home and my brother on the road. He told me he would forever be in my debt," Elijah half laughs and cries. "And then he added that he will kill me if I ever hurt either of you."

I try to stifle a giggle with a hand to my mouth, but I can't hold it in. A chuckle bursts out of my mouth. Our mother's both turn and smile. "Of course, he couldn't just leave it on the upbeat."

Elijah grabs my hand. "Don't blame him. I think I understand the man a whole lot better now." He stares at my stomach. "In fact, I feel a whole lot better knowing he'll have my back if anyone ever hurts our child."

Our child.

Never once has this man faltered.

The night remains an upbeat and happy one. After everyone retires for the evening, I ask Elijah to drive me over to Dan's.

On the way, I tell Elijah about the day I asked Dan to take me to the pharmacy.

"You should have come to me, Rosie. I would have helped you get through it."

I stare at the dashboard lights. "I was scared, Elijah. Everything happened so fast, and I was confused. Dan has always been more than an uncle to me, he's been my friend."

His gaze bounces between the road and me. He raises our entwined hands and kisses the back of my hand. "I'm glad you had him. He is one hell of man."

"And that's why I need to tell him before everyone else learns about it at the party tomorrow. I owe him that."

"Do you want me to go up with you?"

I shake my head and reach for the handle as the car rolls to a stop. "I won't be long."

He dips his head. "I'm not going anywhere."

My hand trembles as I knock on the door. There is a light on upstairs, so I know someone must be awake. Dan swings the door open and when he sees me, he scoops me off my feet and carries me into the house. "You made it home!" he says excitedly.

"Yeah," I smooth my shirt as he sets me down in the middle of the living room.

Dan's eyes bounce over me, as if he can't believe I'm really here. "Shit, I'll go wake the rest of the fam. Everyone went to bed early, excited for the party tomorrow." He makes a beeline to the stairs.

"I came here just to talk to you, uncle."

He pauses on the bottom step and when he turns, his face falls. "No."

I nod, yes.

He stares at the ceiling. Guilt pulls at the corners of his eyes as he tortures himself.

"I don't regret it. Not for one minute," I tell him.

He makes his way back to me and sits down on the couch, motioning for me to join him. "Does Elijah know?"

My bottom lip slips between my teeth and I nod, fighting that damn knot that seems to never leave me. "He says it's his." I chuckle lightly, realizing just how similar Elijah and my father are. "Actually, scratch that, he demands it's his."

Dan notices my ring and smiles. "You said yes."

"I did."

"And would that decision have been different if there was no one else to consider."

My eyes fall closed and I try to imagine it all happening any other way. When I open them, I answer with certainty, "No. I love him."

"Good." He leans over and places a kiss on my forehead.

"There is something I need you to do for me. You're the only person I trust." I fight the urge to pick at my nails.

Breathe. Count to ten. Breathe.

He tips my face with his knuckle, watching me in action as I exercise my new arsenal to fight off the demons. When I let out a long breath, he speaks. "I'll do anything for you."

"Elijah doesn't want a DNA test and neither do I, but I need to have it available for the baby's health. Especially, if there's a problem," I turn away to stare at a painting of a sunflower field in a window frame across the room.

"You have them sent to me and I'll keep them safe."

"If Elijah asks for the results, give them to him, yeah?"

He lets out a long sigh. "You have my word."

"Okay, then." I stand up. "Elijah is waiting for me in the car. I just wanted you to know before I tell everyone else."

He rises with me, pulling me into a hug. "I'm happy for you, Billie Rose."

I give him a smile in thanks. "Before I leave, how is Kelsie doing?" My eyes roam to the stairs.

He grimaces, running his hand down his face. "She's quiet and scared. I hate that for her."

Leaning my head on his shoulder, I wrap my arms around his. "Then it's a good thing she has you." I stare up at him through my lashes. "She needs someone to make her feel safe."

He pats my cheek. "I'm doing my best to be there for her."

"Honestly, Dan, that's all a daughter needs."

426

Chapter Thirty-Eight

Billie Rose

My heart beats happily as I watch Elijah and my dad play with the kids of the club. They are playing tag. When they disappear into the trees, I turn to find my mother staring at me. I slowly make my way over and sit beside her.

"Everything okay?" I ask.

Her green eyes blink a few times and I see she is fighting back tears.

"What is it, mom?"

She brushes her fingers over her forehead. "I was just wondering what it would have been like if I had been brave like you?"

I pull my head back. "Me?" I ask incredulously. "You are the strongest woman I know."

"And that is where you are wrong. I took the easy way out."

A frown pulls on my face. "Mom, your situation, and mine were so different. I don't think there is a right or wrong answer to something like this. You were so young and alone."

Her fingers trail down the side of my face. "How did you get to be so wise?" She smiles sadly. "You know, your grandfather said you were an old soul the day you were born."

I tip my head back and stare up at the sky. "You heard him, didn't you?" It's a question I've pondered over the last few months.

She drops her head. "I wanted to rip his heart out and present it to you on a silver platter when I heard what he said. But then you cut out his tongue and while I worried for your heart at doing such a gruesome thing, my inner warrior pounded on her chest. Proud of you for serving him some much-deserved justice."

Dan walks by us, pausing mid step. His eyes narrow in concern.

We both start laughing. He flips us off, continuing on once he decides we're both fine.

"When did you figure out that I knew?" she asks me.

"When I saw the mural in the baby's room, that's when I knew for sure. I had wondered before that but when I saw that sunrise, I knew it was your way of telling me it was okay. That you would be by my side."

Roses and Skulls

"I knew I couldn't be impartial on the matter. My heart was a wreck just knowing what had happened to you. I had always prayed that you would never have to make a decision like I had. But I knew Dan would be a rock for you... and that he would let you make your own decision."

"Because he was the best thing that ever happened to you," I finish for her.

We smile at each other before turning our eyes his way. Both of us jump to our feet when we see he has Jackson by the ear, dragging him away from Kelsie. I run to my new friend. "Kelsie, what happened? Are you okay?"

She shifts her weight from foot to foot, fighting the tug of a smile on her lips. "He didn't lie," she says, dipping her head.

"Who didn't lie?"

"Dan," she says quietly, staring after him. "He said he wouldn't let anyone touch me."

A full-blown smile breaks out over her face, and she hugs herself happily.

Elijah walks up behind me. "Everything okay over here?" he asks, breathless from chasing the kids out of the trees.

Kelsie holds her head up high. "You must be Elijah. I've heard a lot about you."

Elijah gives her that charming smile of his and takes her hand, kissing the back of it. "All of it good I'm sure."

She blushes and pulls her hand away shyly.

He continues charming her, "Billie Rose has done nothing but talk about her new best friend. She couldn't wait for me to meet you," he tells her.

And just when I didn't think I could fall in love with him more than I already had, my heart beats for him anew.

She beams from ear to ear. "Her best friend?" she peeks at me and brushes her short hair behind her ear.

"Yep, and thank you for that," he says. "We'll be needing a good friend to help us with the baby."

Kelsie's whole face lights up. "Of course, I would love to help."

Later that night, as the party unwinds, I find myself walking down to the trees. Elijah jogs to catch up to me.

"Whatcha doin?"

"Minding my own business, just like you should be doing."

He laughs heartily. "God, I've missed you."

I stick my tongue out and walk backwards in front of him. He stills. "Don't you even think about it, Rosie. I'll catch you."

My eyebrow cocks in challenge. "I'm pretty fast," I warn, taking a few more steps back.

He licks his lips, biting the ball of his tongue piercing. My feet stop, unable to move as I stare at the sexiest man on the planet. All dark ink, piercings, and the hottest smirk on his face. And then I run, wanting nothing more than for him to catch me.

In minutes he has me pinned to a tree; my hands trapped in his hand above my head. His nose runs along my cheek. "You want me to take you here, baby?"

My eyes dart around, stopping on the very spot Draven took his last breath.

"I-I, no."

He steps back, holding out his hands.

"Where're we going then, baby? Cause I need you, real bad. It's been way too long." He groans, his hand dipping below his belt to rearrange himself in his jeans.

"Give me five minutes and I'll meet you at the cabin."

Elijah smiles wide. "You okay?" he questions before he walks away, double checking that I'm good.

I nod. "I'm more than good. I just need a minute."

When he disappears out of sight, I walk around the place I spent most of my childhood. I sit down and run my hands over the spool table where I sat many hours making windchimes, all in hopes of hearing my grandfather.

And I breathe.

My heart is finally at peace.

It feels good to feel something other than pain. But I wouldn't change any of it.

With pain comes strength.

I stand and walk over to the spot where Draven died.

The leaves rustle gently over my head as night settles around me. I run my boot over the ground. "Thank you for the pain," I say quietly.

"I'm going to need it to protect my child from assholes like you and your father."

I'll kill any motherfucker who hurts my baby.

I tip my head back and forth as a thought enters my mind. "Maybe you were right, grandpa, I think I am a lot like my parents."

A satisfied smile flits over my face.

I pretend my grandpa is by my side. "We've slayed the dragon, my lord. What shall we do now?" I ask, straightening my imaginary MC princess crown and spitting on the ground for good measure.

The wind blows hard, the skeleton key chime whispering to me all the way from my cabin across the lake.

"You're right. It's time to return to the castle. The prince awaits."

I laugh to myself at my silliness, wiping at my eyes.

My gaze flits over the area, happy for the memories I made here. Excited for the promise of new ones.

Before I turn and walk away, I curtsey, whispering, "Goodbye, Sir Bill, until we meet again."

Epilogue

Elijah 5 years later

Tiny hands wrap around me, holding on tight to my leather cut. My daughter's little squeals of laughter make my heart happy. As I pull into Black Rose Custom Bikes, I see her mama watching us from the bay door. Billie Rose waves, a grin on her beautiful face.

I help Aurelia off my bike. She runs to her mother, wrapping her arms around her legs. "Daddy went really fast," she tattles on me.

"Oh, he did, did he?" Rosie raises her eyebrow at me.

Giving her a kiss on the cheek, I sidestep her when she tries to slap my ass. "Her mama likes to go fast too," I yell as I make my way to the office.

Aurelia skips ahead of me and heads over to the jar of suckers we keep on the desk. Her dark hair is pulled back in a French braid that bounces against her back.

"Who braided your hair?" my wife asks as we follow her.

"Kelsie," she mumbles around her candy. She brings me a cherry one and climbs up on my lap.

"Grandma and grandpa will be here soon. Don't spoil your supper by eating too much candy."

Aurelia, the gold that made us stronger, rolls her eyes. I laugh because she looks just like Billie Rose when she does it.

Rosie smacks my arm playfully and plops down behind the desk. She slides over her latest sketch of a bike we're working on for a customer. "I don't know, what do you think about the pipes? I'm thinking maybe you could go a little lower yet, but I'll leave that to you, baby," she tells me before answering the phone.

My eyes roam over the bad ass bike staring back at me. I'm telling you, there is nothing better than working alongside your soulmate, especially one as talented as her.

When she revealed her surprise to me all those years ago, I was floored. It still amazes me that she gave up her dreams of running Bill's bar for me... for us. But I couldn't be more thankful. We've turned the space into a place where our kids can come to work with us, and we both get to do what we love. Her designing the bikes and me making her visions become reality. We're making quite a name for ourselves.

"Where's my little MC princess," Dirk calls from the garage.

Roses and Skulls

"Pappa," Aurelia squeals, jumping off my lap, running out.

Rosie hangs up the phone. "That was Dan, he said he sent some ideas for his new bike over with dad."

Dirk walks in, still intimidating as fuck. He's what the ladies call a silver fox, but he only has eyes for Jesse and who the fuck blames him. Jesse is one smokin hot bitch.

My gaze falls on my wife. She still looks as young as she did the day I married her. But I'm sure she'll age just as gracefully as her parents. I'm glad my kids will get all those good genes.

Aurelia laughs when Dirk rubs his whiskered face over her cheek. "Pappa, stop." She wiggles out of his arms and runs over to the sucker jar.

Rosie scolds her, "I told you, no morè."

"I'm just getting one for brother," she says batting her big brown doe eyes at my wife.

"Fine," Billie Rose tells her, sighing loudly.

Jesse steps into the room, plopping my son onto my lap dramatically. "He's all yours." Tate looks up at me with sparkling blue eyes full of mischief.

"Were you naughty for grandma today?" I ask, bouncing him on my knee. He chuckles, grabbing for my beard so he doesn't get bucked off. He shakes his head. "No?"

His grandmother places her hands on her hips. "Don't lie to your daddy, you were a little shit today."

He rubs his eyes, clearly tired from his reign of terror.

"Tate escaped out the back door and it took your dad and I a full thirty minutes to find him. I just about called the police," Jesse says, throwing her hands in the air.

My wife stands up and walks over to us. She pulls Tate from my arms and starts tickling him. "Where did you hide this time?" she asks.

"Billie Rose, don't encourage him," her mother scolds.

Tate stares at his mother like she is the brightest star in the sky. "I hide in the trees, mama." He rubs his little nose over her chest, snuggling against her, his eyes getting droopy now that he's in his safe space.

"Your father had to climb up and get him." Jesse kisses him gently on the cheek, she may grumble about his antics, but that woman loves him with a fierceness second only to his mother.

My wife looks at her father. He reaches out and cups her cheek, pulling her and my son into his arms. He whispers something and she smiles. I'm sure it has something to do with the time he had to climb up a tree to retrieve her.

"We'll see you guys back at the warehouse," Jesse says. "Don't be late, the party starts at seven." She takes my daughter's hand. "Ready to help grandma bake some goodies for the party?"

Aurelia nods, her sucker stick hanging from her mouth. They walk out and Billie Rose goes back behind the desk, settling in her chair, our son draped over her big belly.

Roses and Skulls

"You know, you can lay that kid down, yeah?" I nod over to the leather couch in the sitting area.

She runs her cheek over his head. "I know but he isn't going to be the baby much longer."

Dirk bops back in. "Shit, I almost forgot to give you this. Dan said it's something for the new bike." He pulls a curled up, manilla envelope out of his pocket, tossing it on the desk.

"Thanks, dad. See ya tonight," Rosie says.

He waves, lighting up a cigarette on the way out.

Tate sits up, looking around with sleepy eyes. When he sees where he is, a dopy smile pulls on his mouth as his eyes fall closed again, his head drops back to my wife's chest.

She giggles, her face lighting up as she stares at him. She's right, the newest member of the Skulls will be here in three short weeks. It's the reason for the party. Last one before the big event. Honestly, I think Jesse throws a party for everything just because she loves to have her family around. Period. She was alone for so many years it makes sense. I don't mind because I love it. Party on, hell yeah.

My wife opens the envelope from Dan, awkwardly reaching around our son to do so. "I'm anxious to see what Big Dan has in mind for his bike.

"Yeah, that dyna wide glide was a good call for this custom. It will fit his fucking tall ass perfectly. I'm excited to get started on it."

I run my finger over my wife's latest sketch, looking it over again when her sniffle draws my attention upward. Jumping to my feet, I rush over to her. "What's wrong? Is it time?" I ask, snatching my sleeping son off his mother and laying him on the couch before heading back over to her.

Her eyes are glued to a piece of paper in her hand. It's shaking in her grip.

"Baby?" I drop to my knees in front of her.

She hands the paper to me, one hand covering her mouth to keep her sobs silent. I take it, sitting back on my haunches to see what made her so upset. I fall back on my ass when I see what it is.

It's the paternity test we had done on Aurelia.

I can't stop my eyes from reading on, even though I've always said I didn't need to know, and I don't. She's mine. And I'll kill any motherfucker who says differently. But now that the answer is here for the taking I... shit... I want to know.

Billie Rose slides down to the floor with me, wrapping her arms around my neck. "She's yours, baby," she whispers in my ear, burying her face in the crook of my neck.

Mine. I always knew it. From the moment Billie Rose told me she was pregnant, I knew.

My mind wanders back to the day she was born.

Her little chin wobbled as she wailed while the nurse checked her out and cleaned her. My heart exploded when I placed my finger against her tiny palm, and she grabbed on for dear life.

Mine.

Roses and Skulls

We blinked at each other, and she quieted. I thought about my family and Rosie's as I stared into her soulful eyes. I thought of all the blood, sweat, tears and pain that lead to this very moment. I'm sure everyone who suffered would agree with me that it was all worth it. For this one moment in time, it was worth it.

I glanced up to see both set of parents watching us through the glass. Choking on a sob, I gave them a thumbs up with my free hand. They all visibly breathed a sigh of relief. Aurelia was healthy and that was all that mattered. I didn't waste time beating myself up, looking for similarities to myself. She was mine. I was sure of it because she had just filled my entire heart with love.

I bent down and kissed her dark fuzzy head. "I love you, baby girl."

Billie Rose crawls on my lap, her belly the only thing separating us. "I love you," she whispers as she presses her lips to mine.

My arms wrap around her, holding her close. "I love you too, Rosie."

Later that night, I pull Dan aside and thank him for his unexpected gift.

He shrugs his shoulders. "You've proved yourself over and over, kid. Just thought it was time that you knew."

Billie Rose walks towards us, a pained expression on her face. Dan and I both stand. She stops as a loud splash hits the tile. All three of us look down at the floor, our mouths falling open. Billie Rose and I slowly raise our heads, our eyes wide.

"Well, don't just stand there, kid, get the truck," Dan bellows.

That jump starts me into action, frantically grabbing the keys out of my pocket.

Billie Rose lets out a loud cry, halting me in my tracks, I turn back.

I place my hand under her belly as she bends over, bracing herself on Dan's arm.

"Argh, it's, shit, it's too late. He's coming," she grits through clenched teeth.

Dan and I help her over to the rug, helping her to lie down. "Jesse!" I yell, hoping to god my mother-in-law hears me. Dan is shoving pillows under her head as I run down the hall, sliding into the bathroom to get some towels. Towels and water. We need water.

Just as I'm getting back. Dirk and Jesse are kneeling down beside their daughter.

"Ahhhhh," Billie Rose screams.

"Oh my god, another little shit," her mother announces, wiping my wife's hair out of her eyes. "This one's going to be worse than the last. He's coming fast."

My wife pants as I kneel between her legs and start peeling her wet pants off of her. Dirk and Jesse, work together to cradle my wife's head and hold her upright, reminding her to breathe.

"I'm out," Dan says, throwing his hands up in the air.

"Uncle Dan," my wife cries, halting the big guy in his tracks. "Please stay."

He runs his big hand over his head, but stays, dropping down beside me. I don't know if this man knows how to tell my wife no.

Lily comes hauling ass around the couch, covering her mouth at the scene before her.

"Call 911," Dan tells her.

My hands shake as I gently shove my wife's knees apart. "Oh, shit, Rosie. I can see his head. Fuck this is so cool." She lets out another loud wail. "Push baby, you need to push."

And like the fucking queen she is, she pushes. It doesn't take long and suddenly the baby is out and the slippery little guy is wailing loudly in my arms. Dan helps me wrap him in a towel as he tries out his new lungs.

I smile up at Billie Rose, her head resting against her father's chest. "He's perfect, baby," I gently lay him against her breasts. The baby settles when her arms wrap around him.

Jesse leans down and presses a kiss to his little head. "So, precious," she whispers.

Tears stream down my wife's face as she turns her eyes to each one of us. I know what she's thinking. We've spoke of it often. The guilt she feels for trying to push everyone away all those years ago. Time may heal but some kinds of pain always remain. "What would I do without all of you?" she asks, her voice broken and hoarse.

"What's his name?" Lily asks, crouching down beside her husband.

Billie Rose looks at me and I nod my head.

"His name is Daniel."

Jesse and Lily both let out little noises that tell me they are happy with our choice. The big guy stills beside me. "You guys shouldn't give your kid such a fucked-up name," he grumbles.

Dirk's eyebrow shoots up, warning his brother, his VP, that he better switch gears, and fast.

Dan drops his head. "I love you so much, Billie Rose. Your grandpa would be real proud of you. I'm honored to share a name with the little guy," he says humbly.

He pats me on the back and kisses the top of my head.

Yeah, the big guy is an old softie.

Jesse brings the kids in before we head to the hospital to get both mom and baby checked out. Tate wraps his arm around his baby brothers head, bringing him close. "My brother," he says quietly, staring into little Dan's eyes. Aurelia is busy studying his tiny feet, asking my wife a million questions.

The club is gathered round as the EMTs haul Billie Rose and the baby out of the warehouse.

As we're riding to the hospital, I lean down and gently place a kiss to her lips. "Always have to be the life of the party, yeah?" I tease.

She smiles up at me, our baby suckling at her breast as the ambulance ride jostles us around. "Just trying to keep it interesting," she jokes back.

Her thumb brushes over our little dude's dark wet hair.

442

Roses and Skulls

"I hate seeing you in that much pain," I tell her honestly, the EMT smiles at me as he leans over to wrap a cuff around her arm.

Billie Rose tips her ring finger, staring at it. "Every time your heart cracks for me, I imagine it sealed with gold," she says wistfully, tipping her head like she's listening for something.

Then I hear it too.

As I find the source of the noise, a miniature windchime hanging from the rearview mirror, she rubs her face against my hand. Murmuring sleepily with a beautiful smile on her face, she whispers, "You are the knight in shining armor that Sir Bill told me would come."

Her eyes fall closed, our baby's tiny fist rests over her breast as he sleeps too. My heart damn near explodes. I turn back to the windchime, happy that I can finally hear him too.

The Skull creed rolls in my head, and I make a vow to Bill. "I will always protect what's mine. Thank you for telling her that I was coming. I was always on my way," I say quietly over my girl.

Her tired eyes open a fraction, and she smiles at me. "I'm glad I'm not the only crazy one."

I laugh lightly and press my forehead to hers. "Crazy in love," I say against her lips.

About the Author

LM Terry is an upcoming romance novelist. She has spent her life in the Midwest, growing up near a public library which helped fuel her love of books. With most of her eight children grown and with the support of her husband, she decided to follow her heart and begin her writing journey. In searching for that happily ever after, her characters have been enticing her to share their sinfully dark, delectable tales. She knows the world is filled with shadows and dark truths and is happy to give these characters the platform they have been begging for. This is her eight novel.

Facebook: https://www.facebook.com/lmterryauthor/

Website: https://www.lmterryauthor

Made in the USA
Las Vegas, NV
30 May 2022

49547147R00267